YOUR COMMAND IS MY WISH

Belisarius had come _____ s.
and with several goals in _____ us
had come to India in or_____ a
general, and he consider_____ st
useful of all military assets.

But the one thing he had not accomplished was to meet
his ultimate enemy. *Link.* The —being? creature?—who was,
in some way, the origin of the newly arisen menace threatening Rome and, he thought, all of mankind. *Link.*

And as he stood on the royal barge, he thought he was on
the verge of achieving that goal also. Aide, certainly, thought
he was.

Yes, Link is here. I am certain of it.

They were nearing the end of the long corridor which
extended down the side of the barge. *We are almost there*,
he thought to Aide. He sensed the agitation of the living
crystal. Aide's next thought was curt.

**Link will be a cyborg. A cybernetic organism. It will
look like a human but will not be. There will be no soul
behind the eyes.**

Then, with the cool shivering which was as close as
crystalline consciousness could come to fear: **If I am
present in your mind, it may discover me.**

*Dissolve yourself, then, Until you can safely reappear.
We must keep knowledge of you hidden from the enemy.*

**If Aide dissolves, the facets will not be able to help.
This moment is very dangerous for you.**

Belisarius strode across the threshold of the room where
his enemy was waiting. *My name is Belisarius*, he thought.
I am your general. Do as I command.

If there was any hesitation in Aide's reply, no human
could have measured it.

Yes, Great One.

ERIC FLINT

IN THE HEART OF
DARKNESS

DAVID DRAKE

In the Heart of Darkness

This is a work of fiction. All the characters and events portrayed in this book are fictional, and any resemblance to real people or incidents is purely coincidental.

A Baen Books Original

Baen Publishing Enterprises
P.O. Box 1403
Riverdale, NY 10471

ISBN: 0-671-87885-9

Cover art by David Mattingly

First printing, August 1998

Distributed by Simon & Schuster
1230 Avenue of the Americas
New York, NY 10020

Typeset by Windhaven Press, Auburn, NH
Printed in the United States of America

To Kathy and Laura

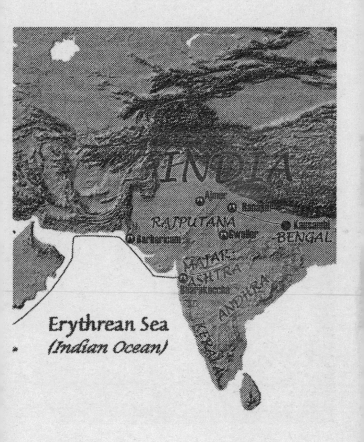

INDIA

Ajmer

Ranakpur

RAJPUTANA

Gwalior

Kanauti

Barbaricum

BENGAL

MAHA-
RASHTRA

ANDHRA

Bharukaccha

KERALA

Erythrean Sea
(Indian Ocean)

Prologue

When the lavish dinner was finished, and the servants sent away, the spymaster broke the bad news.

"Belisarius is alive," he said curtly.

There were seven other men in the room. One, like the spymaster, was foreign. From the blankness of his face, it was obvious he had already heard the news. Of the Romans in the room, five rose up on their couches, their faces expressing various degrees of consternation.

The seventh man, the last of the Romans, simply curled his lip, and satisfied himself with shifting his weight to the other elbow.

He had been disgusted the entire evening.

The two churchmen in the room disgusted him with their sanctimonious prattle. Glycerius of Chalcedon and George Barsymes were deacons, acting on behalf of Rufinus Namatianus, Bishop of Ravenna. They were rabidly orthodox. But, at bottom, their orthodoxy was nothing but a veil for ambition. The Bishop of Ravenna sought the papacy, and his underlings sought the patriarchates of Constantinople and Alexandria.

Ambition was the seventh man's motive also, but he did not disguise it with false piety. (A ridiculous piety, to boot—allying with Hindu heathens against Christian heretics.) The seventh man counted many sins against his soul, mortal and venial alike. But hypocrisy was not among them.

The two noblemen in the room disgusted him with

their swaggering braggadocio. Their names were Hypatius and Pompeius. They were brothers, the nephews of the former emperor Anastasius. By any formal dynastic criterion, they were the rightful heirs to the imperial throne. But Romans had never worshipped at the altar of heredity. Competence was the ultimate standard for wearing the purple. And if there were two more feckless creatures in the entire Roman empire, they were hiding themselves well.

The other high Roman official in the room disgusted him. John of Cappadocia, his name was, and he was Emperor Justinian's Praetorian Prefect. A ruthless and capable man, to be sure. But one whose rapaciousness and depravity were almost beyond belief. Murderer, thief, extortionist, torturer, rapist—all these things John of Cappadocia had been named. The names were all true.

The two Malwa spies in the room disgusted him— Balban the oily spymaster even more than Ajatasutra the assassin—partly for their false bonhomie and pretense of comradeship, but mostly for their claim of disinterested concern for the best interests of Rome, which no one but an idiot would believe for an instant. The seventh man was very far from being an idiot, and he took the Malwa air of innocence as an insult to his intelligence.

The seventh man was disgusted with himself. He was the Grand Chamberlain of the Roman Empire. He was one of the most valued and trusted advisers of Emperor Justinian, whom he planned to betray. He was the close personal friend of the Empress Theodora, whom he planned to murder. He would add the count of treason to his sins, and increase the counts of murder, and all for the sake of rising one small rung in power. He was a eunuch, and so could never aspire to the throne himself. But he could at least become the Grand Chamberlain of a feckless emperor, instead of a dynamic one, and thus be the real power in Rome.

The seventh man knew, with all the intelligence of a keen mind, that his ambition was stupidity incarnate.

He was an old man. Even if he realized his ambition, he would probably not enjoy its exercise for more than a few years.

For that stupid, petty ambition, the seventh man risked the possibility of execution and the certainty of eternal damnation. He despised himself for that pettiness, and was disgusted by his own stupidity. But he could not do otherwise. For all that he prided himself on his iron self-control, the seventh man had never been able to control his ambition. Ambition rode the eunuch like lust rides a satyr. It had ridden him as far back as he could remember, since the days when other boys had taunted and beaten him for his castrated deformity.

But, above all, the seventh man was disgusted because the Malwa and the Roman reactionaries in the room had insisted on dining in the archaic tradition, instead of sitting on chairs at a table, as all sensible people did in the modern day. The seventh man's aged body had long since lost the suppleness to eat a meal half-reclined on a couch.

His name was Narses, and his back hurt.

The Indian spymaster's eyes had been fixed on Narses from the moment he made the announcement. Months ago, Balban had realized that the eunuch was by far the most formidable of his Roman allies—and the only one who was not, in any sense, a dupe. The churchmen were provincial bigots, the royal nephews were witless fops, and John of Cappadocia—for all his undoubted ability— was too besotted with his own vices to distinguish fact from fancy. But Narses understood the Malwa plot perfectly. He had agreed to join it simply because he was convinced he could foil the Malwa after he had taken the power in Rome.

Balban was not at all sure the eunuch was wrong in that estimate. Narses, in power, would make a vastly more dangerous enemy for the Malwa than Justinian. So Balban had long since begun planning for Narses' own assassination. But he was a methodical man, who knew the value of patience, and was willing to take one step ahead of the other. For the moment, the alliance with the eunuch was necessary.

And so—

"What is your reaction, Narses?" he asked. The Indian's Greek was fluent, if heavily accented.

The eunuch grimaced as he painfully levered himself to an upright posture on his couch.

"I told you it was a stupid idea," he growled. As always, Balban was struck by the sound of such a deep, rich, powerful voice coming from such a small and elderly man. A eunuch, to boot.

"*It was not,*" whined Hypatius. His brother's vigorous nod of agreement was intended to be firm and dignified. With his cosmetic-adorned and well-coiffed head bobbing back and forth on a scrawny neck, the nobleman resembled nothing so much as a doll shaken by a toddler.

The eunuch fixed muddy green eyes on the nephews. Against his bony face, surrounded by myriad wrinkles, the effect was utterly reptilian. Deadly, but cold-blooded. The brothers shrank from his gaze like mice.

Narses satisfied himself with that silent intimidation. Much as he was often tempted, Narses never insulted the brothers. One of them would be needed, in the future, for his puppet emperor. Either one, it did not matter. Whichever summoned up the courage to plot with Narses to murder the other first. So, as always, the eunuch maintained formal respect, and allowed his eyes alone to establish dominance.

"I told you all from the beginning that the plan was pathetic," he said. "If you want to assassinate a man like Belisarius, you had better use something other than common criminals."

Ajatasutra spoke, for the first time that evening. He was the Indian mission's chief agent. A specialist in direct action, a man of the streets and alleys, where Balban manipulated from the shadows. His Greek was also fluent, but, unlike Balban's, bore hardly a trace of an accent. Ajatasutra could—and often did—pass himself off as a Roman citizen from one of the more exotic, outlying provinces of the empire. A dark-complected Syrian, perhaps, or a half-breed Isaurian.

"It was a well-laid plan, according to the report," he murmured. His tone exuded calm, dispassionate assessment. "Belisarius was ambushed shortly after landing in Bharakuccha. At night, in darkness. While he was alone, without his cataphract bodyguards. By no less than eight dacoits. Seasoned killers, all of them."

"Really?" sneered Narses. He was quite happy to insult the Malwa, within reason. So he allowed his lip to curl ferociously, but refrained from spitting on the polished, parquet floor. "Tell me, Ajatasutra—I'm curious. How many of these—what did you call them?—oh, yes! 'Seasoned killers,' no less. How many of them survived the encounter?"

"Three," came the instant reply. "They fled after Belisarius slaughtered the first five. Within seconds, according to the report."

Narses' sneer faded. Ajatasutra was immune to the Roman's contempt. The agent's dark brown eyes were filled with nothing beyond professional interest. And the eunuch well remembered that Ajatasutra had expressed his own reservations at the meeting, many months earlier, when the decision was taken to recommend Belisarius' assassination as soon as he reached India. (Recommend, not order. Lord Venandakatra was the one who would make the final decision. Balban ranked high in the Malwa Empire's hierarchy, but he was not a member of the imperial dynastic clan. He did not give orders to such as Venandakatra. Not if he wanted to live.)

Narses sighed, as much from the pain in his back as exasperation.

"I told you then," he continued, "that you were grossly underestimating Belisarius."

A rare moment of genuine anger heated his voice. *"Who did you think you were playing with, for the sake of God?"* he demanded. "The man is one of the greatest generals Rome has ever produced. *And* he's still young. *And* vigorous. *And* famous for his bladesmanship. *And* has more combat experience than most soldiers twice his age."

A glare at Balban. "*Real* combat experience, against *real* enemies. Not"—the sneer was back in full force—"the 'seasoned killer' experience of a thug backstabbing a merchant." He stopped, hissing. Partly from aggravation; mostly from the sharp pain which streaked up his spine. He sagged back on his couch, closing his eyes.

Balban cleared his throat. "As it happens, it may have turned out for the best in any event. The report which we just received—from the hand of Lord Venandakatra himself—also says that Lord Venankatra believes Belisarius may be open to treas—to our mutual cause. He has developed a friendship with Belisarius, he says, and has had many conversations with him in the course of their long voyage to India. The general is filled with bitter resentment at his treatment by Justinian, and has let slip indications of a willingness to seek another patron."

His eyes still closed, fighting the pain, Narses listened to the conversation which suddenly filled the dining chamber. An agitated conversation, on the part of the Romans. A mixture of cold calculation, babbling nonsense, scheming analysis, wild speculation, and—most of all—poorly hidden fear.

All of the Romans in the room, except Narses, were torn and uncertain. To win Belisarius to their plot would greatly increase its chance for success. So they all said, aloud. But to do so would also make their own personal prospects that much the dimmer. So they all thought, silently.

Narses said nothing. Nor, after a minute or so, did he pay any attention to the words. Let them babble, and play their witless games.

Pointless games. The Grand Chamberlain, old as he was, eunuch that he was, knew beyond the shadow of a doubt that there was no more chance of Belisarius betraying his oath to Justinian—less chance; much, much less chance—than that a handful of street thugs could cut him down from ambush.

The image of Belisarius came to his mind, as sharp as if the Thracian were standing before him. Tall, handsome, well-built. The archetype of the simple soldier, except for that crooked smile and that strange, knowing, subtle gaze.

Narses stared up at the ceiling, oblivious to the chatter around him, grimly fighting down the pain.

Balban's voice penetrated.

"So, that's it. I think we're all agreed. We'll hope for the success of Lord Venandakatra's effort to win over Belisarius. In the meantime, here in Constantinople, we'll step up our efforts to turn his wife Antonina. As you all know, she arrived a month ago from their estate in Syria. Ajatasutra has already initiated contact with her."

Narses' eyes remained fixed on the ceiling. He listened to Ajatasutra:

"It went well, I think, for a first approach. She was obviously shaken by my hint that Emperor Justinian is plotting with the Malwa to assassinate Belisarius while he is in India, far from his friends and his army. I am to meet her again, soon, while she is still in the capital."

John of Cappadocia's voice, coarse, hot:

"If that doesn't work, just seduce the slut. It seems the supposedly reformed whore hasn't changed her ways a bit. Not according to Belisarius' own secretary Procopius, at any rate. I had a little chat with him just the other day. She's been spreading her legs for everybody since the day her doting husband left for India."

Lewd laughter rippled around the room. Narses rolled his head on the couch, slightly. Just enough to bring John of Cappadocia under his reptilian gaze.

Not for you, she hasn't. And never will. Or for any-one, I suspect. Only a cretin would believe that malicious gossip Procopius.

Narses levered himself upright, and onto his feet.

"I'm leaving, then," he announced. He nodded politely

to all the men in the room, except John of Cappadocia. Courtesy was unneeded there, and would have been wasted in any event. The Praetorian Prefect was oblivious to Narses. His eyes were blank, his mind focussed inward, on the image of the beautiful Antonina.

So Narses simply stared at the Cappadocian for a moment, treasuring the sight of that twisted obsession. When the time came, the eunuch knew, after the triumph of their treason, John planned to finally sate his lust for Antonina.

Narses turned away. The Cappadocian's guard would be down then. It would be the perfect time to have him murdered.

Fierce satisfaction flooded him. In his own bitter heart, hidden away like a coal in his icy mind, Narses had compiled a list of all those he hated in the world. It was a very, very, very long list.

John of Cappadocia's name ranked high on that list. Narses would enjoy killing him. Enjoy it immensely.

The pleasure would alleviate, perhaps, the pain from his other crimes. The pain from killing Belisarius, whom he admired deeply. The agony from Theodora's murder, which would leave him, in the end, shrieking on his deathbed.

The servant helped him don his cloak, before opening the door.

Narses stood in the doorway, waiting for the servant to fetch his palanquin from the stables in the back of the villa. He glanced up. The night sky was clear, cloudless. Open. Unstained.

Murder them he would, nonetheless, or see to the doing of the deed.

Behind him, dimly, he heard John of Cappadocia speaking. He could not make out the words, but there was no mistaking that coarse, foul voice.

Foul noise and unstained sky swirled in the soul of Narses. Images of a murdered Cappadocian and a murdered Thracian vanished. The cold, still face of the eunuch finally twisted, unbridled. There was nothing reptilian in that face now. It was the face of a warm-blooded beast. Almost a child's face, for all its creases and wrinkles, if a child's face had ever borne such a burden of helpless rage.

Cursed, hated ambition. He would destroy himself for that cannibal.

The palanquin was here. The four slaves who carried it waited in silent obedience while the servant assisted Narses into the cushioned seat. The palanquin began to move.

Narses leaned back into the cushions, eyes closed. His back hurt.

Chapter 1

RANAPUR
Spring 530 AD

Belisarius watched the stone ball arching through the sky. The trajectory was no flatter than that of a ball cast by catapult, but it slammed into the brick wall surrounding Ranapur with much greater force. Even over the roar of the cannon blast, the sound of the ball's impact was remarkable.

"A least a foot in diameter," stated Anastasius.

Belisarius thought the cataphract's estimate of the cannonball's size was accurate, and nodded his agreement. The other of his veteran bodyguards, Valentinian, grimaced sourly.

"So what?" he grumbled. "I've seen a catapult toss bigger."

"Not as far," countered Anastasius, "and not with anything like that kind of power." The huge Thracian shrugged his shoulders. "There's no point fooling ourselves. These infernal Malwa devices make our Roman artillery engines look like toys."

Menander, the last of the three cataphracts who had accompanied Belisarius to India, spoke up.

"What do you think, general?"

Belisarius turned in his saddle to reply. But his quick answer was interrupted by a muttered curse.

Anastasius chuckled. "It's amazing how quickly we forget old skills, isn't it?"

Belisarius smiled ruefully, for the truth of the remark could not be denied. Belisarius had introduced stirrups into the equipment of his cavalry only a few months before his journey to India. Already he had half-forgotten the little tricks of staying in a saddle without them. The ambassadorial mission which Belisarius led had not brought the new devices to India, however. Stirrups were one of the very few items of Roman military equipment which were superior to those of the Malwa Empire, and Belisarius had no intention of alerting his future enemy to them.

But he did miss the things, deeply, and was reminded of their absence every time some little motion caused him to lose his balance atop his horse—even something as simple as turning in his saddle to answer the young Thracian behind him.

"I agree with Anastasius, Menander," he said. "Actually, I think he's understating the problem. It's not just that the Malwa cannons are superior to our catapults *at the moment*. What's worse is that our artillery engines and techniques are already at their peak of development, while the Malwa devices are still crude and primitive."

Menander's eyes widened. "Really? They seem—"

The young soldier's gaze scanned the battleground. Belisarius and his entourage had arrived at Ranapur only the week before. But the northern Indian province of which Ranapur was the capital had rebelled against their Malwa overlords two years earlier. For more than a year now, Ranapur itself had been under siege. The once fertile fields surrounding the large city had long since been trampled flat and then re-elevated into a maze of trenchworks and earthen fortifications.

The scene reminded Menander of nothing so much as a gigantic ant nest. Everywhere his eyes looked he saw soldiers and laborers hauling supplies and ammunition, sometimes with carts and wagons, but more often through simple brute labor. Less than thirty yards away, he watched a pair of laborers toting a clay-sealed, tightly woven basket filled with gunpowder. The basket was suspended on a bamboo pole, each end of which rested on the men's shoulders. Despite being clothed only in loincloths, the laborers were sweating heavily. Much of that sweat, of course, was the product of the blistering heat which saturated the great Gangetic plain of north India in springtime, during that dry season which the Indians called *garam*. But most of it was due to the work itself. Menander estimated the basket's weight at sixty pounds, and knew that it was only one of many which those two men would have been hauling for hours.

That scene was duplicated dozens of times over, everywhere he could see. The entire city of Ranapur was surrounded by wooden palisades, earthen walls, trenches, and every other form of siegework. These had been erected by the besieging Malwa as protection from the rebels' catapult fire and occasional sallies.

Menander thought the Malwa were being excessively cautious. He himself was too inexperienced to be a good judge of these things, but Belisarius and the veteran cataphracts had estimated the size of the Malwa army surrounding Ranapur at 200,000 soldiers.

The figure was mind-boggling. No western empire could possibly muster such a force on a field of battle. And the soldiers, Menander knew, were just the fighting edge of an even greater mass of humanity. Menander could see only some of them from his current vantage point, but he knew that all the roads in the vicinity of the city were choked with transport bringing supplies to the army.

Glancing to the south, he could see barges making their slow way up the Jamuna river to the temporary docks which the Malwa had erected to offload their provisions. Each of those barges weighed three to six hundred tons—the size of the average *sea-going* craft of the Mediterranean world. They were hauling food and provisions from the whole of northern India, produced by the toil of the uncountable multitude of Malwa subject peoples.

In addition to the freight barges there were a number of equal-sized, but vastly more luxurious, barges moored to the south bank of the Jamuna. These were the accommodations for the Malwa nobility and high officials. And, here and there, Menander could see slim oared craft, as well, moving much more rapidly. The galleys were powered by fifty or so rowers, with additional troops aboard. The Malwa maintained a careful patrol of the river, closing Ranapur's access to water traffic.

Most of all, Menander's gaze was drawn by the huge bronze cannons which were bombarding Ranapur. He could see eight of them from the slight rise in the landscape where he and the other Romans were watching the siege. Each of the cannons was positioned on a stone surface, surrounded by a low berm, and tended by a small horde of soldiers and laborers.

"Magical, almost," he concluded softly.

Belisarius shook his head. "There's nothing magical about them, lad. It's just metalworking and chemistry, that's all. And, as I said, crude and primitive metalworking and chemistry."

The general cast his eyes about. Their large Rajput escort was not far away, but still out of hearing range.

Belisarius leaned forward in his saddle. When he spoke, his voice was low and intent. He spoke loud enough for all three of his cataphracts to hear him, but his principal audience was Menander. Out of all the hundreds of cataphracts who constituted Belisarius' bucellarii, his personal retinue of elite soldiers, there were none so deadly as Valentinian and Anastasius. That was why he had selected them to accompany him on his dangerous mission to India. But, for all their battle skills, neither of the veterans was really suited for the task of assessing a radically new situation. Young Menander, even with more experience, would never be Anastasius or Valentinian's equal as a warrior. But he was proving to be much quicker to absorb the new realities which the Malwa were introducing into warfare.

"Listen to me, all of you. I may not survive this journey. Whatever happens, it is essential that at least one of us return to Rome with what we've learned, and get the information to Antonina and John of Rhodes."

Valentinian began to make some little protest, but Belisarius waved him down.

"That's stupid, Valentinian, and you know it better than anyone. A thousand things can kill you on the field of battle—or off it—and I'm no more immune to them than anyone. What is important is the *information*."

He glanced again in the direction of the Rajputs, but the cavalrymen were still maintaining a polite distance.

"I've already explained to you how the *cannons* work," he said. He cocked an eye at Menander. The young Thracian immediately recited the formula for gunpowder and the complex series of steps by which it was properly prepared. His words had the singsong character of one repeating oft-memorized data.

Belisarius nodded. "It's the wetting and the grinding that's key. Remember that." He made a small nodding gesture toward the distant cannons. "The Malwa gunpowder is really pretty poor stuff, compared to what's possible. And so is their metalworking."

Examining one of the cannons, he sat slightly straighter in his saddle.

"Watch," he commanded. "They're about to fire. Watch the trajectory of the cannonball."

Menander and the other two cataphracts followed his gaze. A moment later, they saw one of the Malwa soldiers take a long iron bar out of a small forge. The bar was bent ninety degrees at the tip, and the protruding two inches glowed red from heat. Gingerly, he inserted the firing bar into a small hole in the breach of the cannon. The mouth of the cannon belched a huge cloud of smoke, followed almost instantly by the roaring sound of the blast.

The recoil jerked the cannon back into its cradle.

Menander saw the gunner lose his grip on the firing bar. The bar was spun against another of the Malwa soldiers, who backed up hastily, frantic to avoid the still-glowing tip. Menander did not envy the Malwa gunners. Theirs was a risky task. Two days earlier, he had seen a recoiling cannon shatter its cradle and crush one of its gunners.

Menander and the other Romans followed the cannon-ball's trajectory all the way to its impact against the great wall of Ranapur. Even from the distance, they could see the wall shiver, and pieces of brickwork splinter and fall to the ground.

Belisarius glanced at his companions. All of them were frowning—the veterans with simple puzzlement, but Menander with concentration.

"It didn't fly straight," announced the young cataphract. "It shot off at an angle. It should have hit the wall fifteen or twenty feet to the east."

"Exactly," said Belisarius with satisfaction. "If you watch carefully, and keep track, you'll eventually notice that the cannonfire is very erratic. Occasionally they shoot straight. But more often the ball will sail off at an angle—and the elevation's just as haphazard."

"Why?" asked Menander.

"It's the clearance," replied the general. "What's called *windage*. In order for a cannon to shoot straight, the ball has to fit snugly in the bore. That requires two things—an even, precise bore all the way through the cannon barrel, and cannonballs that are sized to match."

Anastasius puffed out his cheeks. "That's a tall order, general. Even for Greek artisans."

Belisarius nodded. "Yes, it is. But the better the fit, the better the fire. The Malwa don't even make the attempt. Those cannonballs aren't much more than crude stones—they'd do better to use iron—and the cannon barrels are simply castings. They're not machined at all. Even the casting process, I suspect, is pretty crude."

Valentinian scowled. "How would you machine

something that big in the first place?" he demanded. "Especially metal."

Belisarius smiled. "I wouldn't even try, Valentinian. For cannons the size of these, sloppy accuracy isn't really that much of a problem. But let's examine the question from a different angle. How hard would it be to machine a very *small* cannon?"

"Very hard," said Anastasius instantly. His father was a blacksmith, and had put his boy to work at an early age. "Any kind of machining is difficult, even with wood. Almost nobody tries to do it with metal. But—yes, if it was small enough—"

"Hand cannons," said Menander excitedly. "That's what you'd have. Something small enough for a single man to fire—or maybe two."

"One man," pronounced Belisarius.

"I haven't seen any such weapons among the Malwa," said Valentinian uncertainly. "Maybe—" He fell silent, coughing. There was a soft wind blowing, and the cloud of gunsmoke emitted by the recent cannonblast had finally wafted over the Romans.

"God, that shit stinks," he muttered.

"Better get used to it," said Anastasius, rather unkindly. For a moment, the giant Thracian seemed on the verge of uttering one of his frequent philosophical homilies, but Valentinian's ferocious glare made him think better of it.

"You haven't seen any handcannons, Valentinian, because the Malwa don't have any." Belisarius' voice was soft, but filled with confidence. "They're not hiding them from us. I'm sure of that. They've kept us far from the battlefield, but not that far. If they had any handcannons, we'd have spotted them by now."

He waited for the roar of another cannonblast to subside before continuing.

"And that's the wave of the future. *Handcannons.* If we can get back to Rome—if *some of us* can make it back to Rome, and get this information to John of Rhodes, then we've got a chance. We'll have better powder than the Malwa, and our artisans are more skilled than theirs, on balance. We can build an entirely new kind of army. An army that can defeat this colossus."

For a moment, he considered adding some of the ideas he had been coming to, of late, concerning the structure and tactics of such a future army. But he decided against it. His ideas were still only half-formed and tentative. They would confuse the cataphracts more than anything else. Belisarius needed more time. More time to think. And, most of all, more time to learn from the strange mentality that rested, somehow, in the bizarre "jewel" that he carried in the pouch suspended from his neck. The mentality which called itself *Aide* and said that it came from the far distant future.

His musings were interrupted by Valentinian.

"Careful," muttered the cataphract. "The Rajputs are coming."

Belisarius glanced over, and saw that a small group of Rajputs had detached themselves from the main body of the elite horsemen and were trotting toward them. At their head rode the leader of the escort, one of the many petty kinglets who constituted the upper crust of the Malwa's Rajput vassals. This one belonged to the Chauhar clan, one of the most prominent of the Rajput dynasties. His name was Rana Sanga.

Watching Sanga approach, Belisarius was torn between two sentiments.

On the one hand, he was irritated by the interruption. The Rajputs—following orders, Belisarius had no doubt—never allowed the Romans to get very close to the action, and never for very long. Despite the limitation, Belisarius had been able to glean much from observing the siege of the rebel city of Ranapur. But he would have been able to learn much more had he been allowed closer, and if his observations were not always limited to a span of a few minutes.

On the other hand—

The fact was, he had developed a genuine respect for Rana Sanga. And even, in some strange way, the beginning of friendship, for all that the Rajput lord was his future enemy.

And a fearsome enemy at that, he thought.

Rana Sanga was, in every respect except one, the archetypical model of a Rajput. The man was very tall—taller, even, than Belisarius—and well built. The easy grace with which Sanga rode his mount bespoke not only his superb physical condition but also his expert horsemanship—a quality he shared with every Rajput Belisarius had so far met.

His dress and accouterments were those of a typical Rajput as well, if a little finer. Rajputs favored lighter gear and armor than either cataphracts or Persian lancers—mail tunics reaching to mid-thigh, but leaving the arms uncovered; open-faced helmets; tight trousers tucked into knee-high boots. For weapons, they carried lances, bows, and scimitars. Belisarius had never actually seen Sanga wield those weapons, but he had not the slightest doubt the man was expert in their use.

Yes, the ideal image of a Rajput in every sense, except—

Sanga was now within a few feet. Belisarius smiled at him, and found it impossible to keep the smile to a polite minimum.

Except for that marvelous, dry sense of humor.

"I am afraid I must ask you and your men to leave now, general Belisarius," said the Rajput, as he drew his horse alongside. "The battle will be heating up soon, I believe. As always, we must put the safety of our honored guests above all other concerns."

At that very moment, as if cued by the Rajput's words, an object appeared above Ranapur. Belisarius watched the bomb—launched by a catapult hidden behind the walls of the city—as it arched its way toward the Malwa besiegers. Even from the great distance, he could spot the tiny sparks which marked the bomb's fuse.

"You see the peril," announced Sanga.

The fuse, Belisarius saw, had been cut too short. The bomb exploded in the air, well before it struck its intended target, the front line of trenches encircling the city. Which were at least a mile away from the little knoll where they stood.

"The deadly peril," elaborated Sanga.

"Indeed," mused Belisarius. "This is perhaps the most dangerous moment in my entire life. Or, perhaps not. Perhaps it takes second place to that terrifying episode, when I was eight years old, when my sister threatened me with a ladle."

"Brutal creatures, sisters," agreed Sanga instantly. "I have three myself. Deadly with a ladle, each and every one, and cruel beyond belief. So I have no doubt that moment was slightly more dangerous than the present one. But I must still insist that you leave. The safety of our honored guests from Rome is the uppermost concern in our Emperor's mind. To allow Emperor Justinian's official envoys to suffer so much as a scratch would be an irreparable stain upon his honor."

The Rajput's expression was solemn, but Belisarius suddenly broke into a grin. There was no point in arguing with Sanga. For all the Rajput's invariable courtesy, Belisarius had quickly learned that the man had a will of iron.

Belisarius reined his horse around and began moving away from the siege. His cataphracts followed immediately. The entire Rajput escort—all five hundred of them—quickly took their places. Most of the Rajputs rode a polite distance behind the Romans, but a considerable number took up positions as flankers, and a small group of twenty or so trotted ahead to serve as the advance guard for the little army moving through the milling swarm of Malwa soldiers and laborers.

Rana Sanga rode alongside Belisarius. After a moment's silence, the Rajput remarked casually:

"Your Hindi is improving rapidly, general. With amazing rapidity, actually. And your accent is becoming almost unnoticeable."

Belisarius repressed a grimace, and silently cursed himself for a fool. In point of fact, Belisarius could speak

Hindi fluently, when he chose, without the slightest trace of an accent. An almost magical capacity for language was one of the many talents which Aide provided him, and one which Belisarius had used to advantage on several occasions.

And one which, he reminded himself again, was useful in direct proportion to being held a close secret.

He sighed, very slightly. He was learning that, of all the difficult tasks which men face in the world, there is perhaps none quite so difficult as pretending to be semicompetent in a language which one speaks perfectly.

Belisarius cleared his throat.

"I am pleased to hear that. I hadn't noticed, myself."

"I thought not," replied Sanga. The Rajput glanced over his shoulder. "Given that your Hindi is becoming so fluent, I suggest that we might speak in Greek from now on. My own Greek, as you know, is only passable. I would much appreciate the opportunity to improve it."

"Certainly," said Belisarius—speaking, now in Greek. "I would be delighted."

The Roman general pointed back toward Ranapur with his thumb.

"I am curious about one thing, Rana Sanga. I notice that the rebels seem to lack any of your *cannons*, yet they obviously possess a large supply of gunpowder. It seems odd they would have the one and not the other."

The Rajput did not reply, for a moment. It was obvious to Belisarius that Rana Sanga was gauging the limits of what he could tell the Roman.

But the moment was very brief. Sanga was not given to hesitation. It was one of the many little things about the man, Belisarius thought, which indicated his capabilities as a military commander.

"Not so odd, General Belisarius. The cannons are under the exclusive control of the Malwa kshatriya, and are never stationed in provincial cities. Neither are supplies of gunpowder, for that matter. But cannons are very difficult to manufacture, and require special establishments for the purpose. By law, such manufactories may not be created outside our capital city of Kausambi. Gunpowder, on the other hand, is much simpler to make. Or so, at least, I am given to understand. I myself, of course, do not know the secret of its manufacture. None do, except the Mahaveda priests. But it does not require the same elaborate equipment. So long as one possesses the necessary ingredients—"

The Rajput broke off, shrugged slightly.

"—which I, needless to say, do not—"

Fibber, thought Belisarius. *I doubt he knows the exact process, but I'm sure a soldier as observant as Sanga knows the three ingredients and their approximate proportions.*

"—and the necessary knowledge, gunpowder can be made. Even in a city under siege."

"I am surprised that Mahaveda priests would join a rebellion against Emperor Skandagupta," remarked Belisarius. "I had the impression that Malwa brahmins were utterly devoted to your empire."

Sanga snorted.

"Oh, I have no doubt their co-operation is involuntary. Most of the priests were undoubtedly killed when the province revolted, but I'm quite sure the lord of Ranapur kept a few alive. It is true, the Mahaveda are sworn to commit suicide before divulging the secret of the Veda weapons. But—"

The Rajput tightened his lips.

"But the priests are perhaps not completely free of the weaknesses which afflict we lesser mortals. Especially when they are themselves the *objects* of coercion, rather than—"

He fell silent entirely. Belisarius completed the thought in his own mind.

Rather than the overseers of the work of their mahamimamsa torturers.

Their conversation was the closest Belisarius had ever managed to get to the subject of the Malwa secret weapons. He decided to see how far he could probe.

"I notice that you refer to these—incredible—new weapons as the *Veda* weapons. My own men tend to believe they are the products of sorcery."

As he had hoped, his last words stung the Rajput.

"They are not sorcery! Magical, perhaps. But it is the reborn power of our Vedic ancestors, not the witchcraft of some modern heathen."

That was the official public position of the Malwa Empire: *Ancient weapons from the time of the Vedas, rediscovered by diligent priests belonging to the new Mahaveda cult.* Belisarius was fascinated to see how completely it was accepted by even Rajput royalty.

But perhaps, he thought, that was not so surprising after all. No people of India, Belisarius knew, took greater pride in their Vedic ancestry than Rajputs. The pride was all the greater—a better word might be ferocious—for the fact that many non-Rajput Indians questioned the Rajput claim to that ancestry. The Rajputs—so went the counter-claim—were actually recent migrants into India. Central Asian nomads, not so many generations ago, who had conquered part of northwestern India and promptly began giving themselves airs. Great airs! The term "Rajput" itself meant "sons of kings," which each and every Rajput claimed himself to be.

So it was said, by many non-Rajput Indians. But, Belisarius had noted, it was said quietly. And *never* in the presence of Rajputs themselves.

Belisarius pressed on.

"You think so? I have never had the opportunity to study the Vedas myself—"

(A bald lie, that. Belisarius had spent hours poring over the Sanskrit manuscripts, assisted in deciphering the old language by his slave Dadaji Holkar.)

"—but I did not have the impression that the Vedic heroes fought with any weapons beyond those with which modern men have long been familiar."

"The heroes themselves, perhaps not. Or not often, at least. But gods and demi-gods participated directly in those ancient battles, Belisarius. And *they* were under no such limitation."

Belisarius glanced quickly at Sanga. The Rajput was scowling, now.

A bit more, I think.

"You must be pleased to see such divine powers returning to the world," the general remarked idly.

Rana Sanga did not respond. Belisarius glanced at him again. The scowl had disappeared, replaced by a frown.

A moment later, the frown also disappeared, replaced by a little sigh.

"It goes without saying, Belisarius," said Sanga softly. The Roman did not fail to notice that this was the first time the Rajput had ever called him by his simple name, without the formal addition of the title of "general."

"It goes without saying. Yet—in some ways, I might prefer it if the Vedic glories remained a thing of the past." Another brief silence. Then: "*Glory*," he mused. "You are a soldier yourself, Belisarius, and thus have a better appreciation than most of *everything* the word 'glory' involves. The ancient battle of Kurukshetra, for instance, can be described as 'glorious.' Oh yes, glorious indeed."

They were now within a hundred yards of the Roman encampment. Belisarius could see the Kushan soldiers already drawing up in formation before the pavilions where the Romans and their Ethiopian allies made their headquarters. The Kushans were vassal soldiers whom the Malwa had assigned to serve as the permanent escort for the foreign envoys.

As always, the Kushans went about their task swiftly and expertly. Their commander's name was Kungas, and, for all that the thirty or so Kushans were members of his own clan and thus directly related to him by blood, maintained an iron discipline over his detachment. The Kushans, by any standard, were elite soldiers. Even Valentinian and Anastasius had admitted—grudgingly, to be sure—that they were perhaps as good as Thracian cataphracts.

As they drew up before the tent which Belisarius shared with Dadaji Holkar, the Maratha slave emerged and trotted over to hold the reins of the general's horse. Belisarius dismounted, as did his cataphracts.

From the ground, Belisarius stared up at Rana Sanga.

"You did not, I believe, complete your thought," he said quietly.

Rana Sanga looked away for a moment. When he turned back, he said:

"The Battle of Kurukshetra was the crowning moment of Vedic glory, Belisarius. The entire *Bhagavadgita* from the *Mahabharata* is devoted to it. Kurukshetra was the greatest battle ever fought in the history of the world, and uncounted words have been recorded discussing its divine meaning, its philosophical profundity, and its religious importance."

Rana Sanga's dark, heavily bearded, handsome face seemed now like nothing so much as a woodcarving.

"Eighteen million ordinary men, it is also written, died in that battle."

The Rajput drew back on the reins, turning his horse.

"The name of not one of those men was ever recorded."

Chapter 2

Belisarius watched Rana Sanga and his men ride away. Not until the Rajputs had vanished did he turn to Dadaji Holkar.

"I do not think he is typical of Rajputs," he said. It was more of a question than a statement.

The Maratha slave disagreed. Instantly, and without hesitation. With any other master, he would not have done so. By ancient Indian custom—though only the Malwa had ever written it into law—a slave was expected to cherish as well as obey his master. That Dadaji Holkar did so in actual fact was due, as much as anything, to the fact that his outlandish foreign master interpreted obedience as devotion to his purpose rather than his person.

"You misunderstand him, master. Rana Sanga is quite famous. Most Indians—and all Maratha—consider him the truest of Rajputs. He is perhaps the greatest Rajput warrior today living, and certainly the finest Rajput general. His exploits are legend. He is a king also, of course, but—" the Maratha smiled "—that means little by itself. There are so many Rajput kings, most of whom rule their little hilltop as if it were all the universe. But Sanga is of the Chauhar dynasty, which is perhaps their greatest line of royalty. And the Chauhar are known for their thought as well as their archery and swordsmanship."

Belisarius cocked his eyebrow. "And so?"

Dadaji Holkar shrugged. "And so, Rana Sanga is the truest of Rajputs, and takes his deepest pride in that fact. But because he does so, and thinks like a Chauhar thinks, he also ponders on what being a Rajput means. He knows, you see—he has even been heard to make the occasional jest about it—that the Rajput lineage is really not so much grander than that of we disreputable Maratha hillmen. Yet he also knows that the lineage is true, nonetheless. And so he thinks about lineage, and how it comes to be, and how truth emerges out of illusion. And he wonders, I think, where the difference between truth and illusion lies, and what that means for his dharma."

The slave stroked the horse's neck. "Those are dangerous thoughts, master. Outside of their sorcerous weapons, and their vast armies, the Malwa have no resource so valuable to them as the skill of Rana Sanga on the battlefield. But I believe they fear that resource as much as they treasure it."

"Do they have reason to fear him?" asked Belisarius.

Dadaji Holkar squinted into the distance where the Rajputs had disappeared.

"Hard to know, master. Raghunath Rao once said the day would come when Rana Sanga would choose between Rajputana's honor and Rajputana's duty. And that, when that day came, the truest of Rajputs would understand that only honor gives duty meaning."

The Roman general scratched his chin. "I was not aware the two men knew each other."

"Oh, yes. They fought once, in single combat. They were both young at the time, but already famous warriors. It is a well-known episode."

Belisarius started slightly.

"I'm amazed either of them survived!"

The slave smiled.

"So were they! And everyone! But survive they did. Badly wounded, of course, both of them. Early in the fray, with his bow, Sanga slew the Maratha chieftain's horse and then wounded Rao in the arm. But he became overconfident and closed too soon. Rao gutted the Rajput's mount and then pressed him with sword and iron-clawed gauntlet. Here the combat was even, and they fought until both were bloody and disarmed. Then they fought by hand. No man in India beside Rana Sanga could have held his own against Raghunath Rao in unarmed combat. He was not as skilled, of course, but he was much larger and stronger. By the end of the day, both men were too weak and exhausted to lift an arm, or even stand. So they laid down side by side and continued their combat with words."

Belisarius chuckled. "And who won?"

Holkar shrugged. "Who is to say? At sundown, they decided honor had been satisfied. So they called upon their followers to carry them away and tend their wounds, and the armies themselves never clashed. All the Rajputs and Marathas present felt the duel had been so glorious that any further combat would only sully the memory. As the years passed, both Rao and Sanga became famous commanders, although they never met on the field of battle again, neither as warriors nor as generals. But from that day forward, Raghunath Rao has always stated that there exists no greater archer in the world than Rana Sanga, and not more than four or five who are his equal with a sword. For his part, Sanga makes the equal claim for Rao's clawed gauntlet and his fists, and swears he would rather fight a tiger with his own teeth than face Rao again on the field of philosophy."

Belisarius' chuckle became an outright laugh.

"What a marvelous tale! How much truth is there in it, do you think?"

Holkar's face was solemn. "It is all true, master. Every word. I was at that battle, and helped bind Rao's wounds myself."

The Roman general stared down at his slave. Dadaji Holkar was a small man, middle-aged, grey-haired, and slightly built. In his appearance as well as his demeanor he seemed every inch the highly literate scribe that he had been before the Malwa enslaved him. Belisarius

reminded himself that, for all his intellect, Dadaji Holkar
was from Majarashtra. Majarashtra, the Great Country.
A land of volcanic stone, harsh and unforgiving. The land
of the Marathas, who, if they were not India's most noble
people, were certainly its most truculent.

"I do not doubt you, Dadaji," he said softly. The
Roman general's large and powerful hand, for just an
instant, caressed the slender shoulder of his Maratha
slave. And the slave knew, in that moment, that his
master was returning his own cherishment.

Holkar left abruptly then, leading Belisarius' horse to
its feeding trough. He squeezed his eyes, shutting back
the tears. He shared his master's tent, and had listened,
night after night, while his master spoke softly to the
divine presence in his mind. He knew, from those muttered words, that Belisarius had met Rao himself—had
met Rao, not in this world, but in the world of a vision.
In that world of vision, all of India had fallen under the
Malwa talons, and Rome had eventually followed. In that
world, Rao had failed to save Majarashtra and had become, through the strange workings of fate, the Maratha
slave of the greatest of Roman generals.

Gently, Dadaji Holkar stripped the horse of her saddle
and began wiping the mare down. He was fond of horses
and, by her nuzzle, knew the fondness was reciprocated.
He knew, also, that Belisarius' invariable kindness to him
was partly the transference of his feelings for Rao onto
another of his countrymen. Belisarius had said to him,
once, that in a lifetime where he had met many fine men,
he had never known a finer than Raghunath Rao. But
Dadaji Holkar had come to know his new master well,
in the months since he had been purchased in Bharakuccha to train a newly arrived foreigner in India's tongues
and scripts. And so he knew that he was himself a man
to Belisarius, not simply a surrogate for another, and that
the heart of the Roman's love for him belong to he himself. He, and his loyalty, and his service, and the memory
of his broken people and his shattered family.

The slave Dadaji Holkar began feeding his master's

horse. There were none to see, now, so he let the tears flow freely. Then, after a moment, raised his blurry vision and gazed at the distant, splintering, brick walls of rebel Ranapur.

Ranapur will fall, soon. The Malwa beasts will savage its people, even worse than they savaged my own.

He lowered his gaze, wiped the tears from his face, watched the horse feed. He enjoyed watching the mare's quiet pleasure as she ate. It reminded him, a bit, of the joy he had taken watching his wife and children eat the food he had always placed on their table. Until the Malwa came, and devoured his family whole.

Enjoy your triumph, Malwa cobras. It will not last. You have let the mongoose himself into your nest.

The horse was done feeding. Holkar led her into the thatched stalls which the Roman soldiers had erected for their horses. The stalls were very large, and completely shielded from outside view. An outside view which might have wondered, perhaps, why such a small body of men would need such a large number of horses. And such fine horses!

Indeed, they were very fine. Holkar was fond of the mare, but he knew she was the poorest of the mounts which rested in the stalls. The Romans never rode the fine ones, the superb riding steeds which Holkar himself had purchased, one by one, from the various merchants scattered about the siege of Ranapur. Horses which were always purchased late in the day, and led into their stalls in the dark of night.

His master had never explained the reasons for those purchases, nor had Holkar inquired.

Nor had Belisarius explained the reason for purchases which were still more odd.

Not two days ago, at his master's command, Holkar had purchased three elephants. Three small, well-tamed, docile creatures, which were kept in a huge but simple tent located in a small clearing in the forest, many miles from the siege, and many miles from the official camp of the Romans and Ethiopians.

Holkar had asked no questions. He had not asked why the tent should be so far away, and so different in appearance from the grandiose pavilion which the Ethiopian prince Eon had erected for himself and his concubines. Nor why the elephants themselves should be so different in their appearance from the two huge and unruly war elephants which the Ethiopians maintained as their public mounts. Nor why the elephants were only fed at night, and only by the African slave named Ousanas, whose invisibility in the darkness was partly due to the color of his skin, but mostly to his incredible skill as a hunter and a woodsman.

No, Holkar had simply obeyed his master's commands, and not asked for any explanation of them. The Maratha did not think that his master *could* have explained, even had he asked. Not clearly, at least. Not precisely. The mind of Belisarius did not work that way. His thoughts never moved in simple straight lines, but always at an angle. Where other men thought of the next step, Belisarius thought of the next fork in the road. And where other men, coming upon that fork, would see a choice between right and left, Belisarius was as likely to burrow a hole or take to the trees.

He closed the thatch door to the stalls. There was no lock, nor need of one. The Kushans would make short work of any thief or intruder. As he made his slow way back to his tent, Holkar smiled. Darkness had now fallen, but he could sense the keen scrutiny of the Kushan guards.

Almost as keen as their curiosity, he thought, chuckling. *But they keep their curiosity to themselves. When Kungas commands, his men obey. The Kushans, also, ask no questions.*

Holkar glanced over to the huge pavilion which belonged to Prince Eon. About nothing, Holkar suspected, were the Kushan guards more curious than that tent. Although he was not certain, he thought that the Kushan commander already knew the secret within that tent. Knew it, and knew his duty, and had decided to ignore that duty, for reasons which Holkar could only surmise. The Kushan commander's face was impossible to read, ever. But Holkar thought he knew the man's soul.

Dadaji Holkar himself, for that matter, had been told nothing. Nor had he ever entered Prince Eon's pavilion. But he was an acutely observant man, and he had come to know his new master well. Holkar was certain that inside that tent rested the person of Shakuntala, the only survivor of the Satavahana dynasty, the former rulers of conquered Andhra.

Like everyone in India—the tale had spread like wildfire—Holkar knew that the famed Maratha chieftain Raghunath Rao had rescued Shakuntala from her Malwa captors months ago. But where all others thought she had escaped with Rao, Holkar was certain that she had been hidden away by Belisarius and his Ethiopian allies. Disguised as one of Prince Eon's many concubines.

Again, he smiled. It was exactly the sort of cunning maneuver that his master would relish. Feint and counter-feint. Strike from an angle, never directly. Confuse and misdirect. In some manner, Holkar suspected, Belisarius had even been responsible for the replacement of Shakuntala's Kushan guards by priests and torturers. The same Kushan guards who now served as Belisarius' own escort had earlier been Shakuntala's guardians. Holkar had seen enough of them, over the past months, to realize that not even Raghunath Rao would have been able to penetrate their security.

He paused for a moment, considering the tent. A faint sneer came to his face.

The Malwa would pay him a fortune for his knowledge. But Holkar never even considered the possibility of treachery. He was devoted to Belisarius as much as he hated the Malwa. And besides, like Raghunath Rao, he was a Maratha himself. The Princess Shakuntala—the *Empress*, now—was the rightful ruler of Majarashtra. She was his own legitimate monarch, and, with a mental bow, Dadaji Holkar acknowledged that suzerainty.

He resumed his progress toward Belisarius' tent. A little smile came to his face. Like many intelligent, well-educated men, Dadaji Holkar had a fine sense of historical irony. So he found his fierce loyalty to the memory of Andhra amusing, in its own way.

When the Satavahana dynasty had been at the peak of their power, the Marathas had been the most unruly of their subjects. Never, since its incorporation into Andhra, had Majarashtra risen in outright rebellion. But the Satavahanas had always been careful to rule the Great Country with a light hand. Now that all of Andhra was under the Malwa heel, the Marathas had become the most fervent partisans of the former dynasty. None more so than Dadaji Holkar.

A sudden bright flash on the horizon drew his gaze. Holkar halted, stared. Moments later, the sound of the cannonade rolled over the encampment.

He resumed his steps.

Soon, yes, Ranapur will fall. And the cobra will sate itself again. As it has so many times.

He drew near his master's tent. For a moment, he stopped, studying that simple structure.

Not much to look at, truly. But, then, the mongoose never takes pride in its appearance. It simply studies the cobra, and ponders the angles.

Holkar began pulling back the tent flap. Another rolling cannonade caused him to pause, look back. For a moment, his scholar's face twisted into the visage of a gargoyle, so driven was he by hatred for all things Malwa.

But there were no Malwa spies close enough to see that face. Such spies had learned quickly that the endless squabbles over women between the foreigners and their Kushan escorts seemed to erupt in sudden brawls which, oddly, injured no one but bystanders watching the scene. In the first days after the foreigners set up their camp, two Malwa spies had been accidentally mauled in such melees. Thereafter, the spies had kept a discreet

distance, and reported as little as possible to their overseers, lest they be ordered to resume a close watch.

The slave pulled back the flap and entered the tent.
He saw his master squatting on a pallet, staring into
nothingness, mouthing words too soft to hear.

Hatred vanished. Replaced, first, by devotion to his
master's person. Then, by devotion to his master's purpose. And then, by devotion itself. For the slave had
closed the demon world of Malwa behind him and had
entered the presence of divinity.

He knelt in prayer. Silent prayer, for he did not wish
to disturb his master's purpose. But fervent prayer, for
all that.

Across the ancient, gigantic land of India, others also
prayed that night. Millions of them.

Two hundred thousand prayed in Ranapur. They
prayed, first, for deliverance from the Malwa. And then,
knowing deliverance would not come, prayed they
would not lose their souls as well as their bodies to
the asura.

As Holkar prayed, his family prayed with him, though
he knew it not. His wife, far away in a nobleman's
mansion in the Malwa capital of Kausambi, hunched on
her own pallet in a corner of the great kitchen where
she spent her days in endless drudgery, prayed for her
husband's safety. His son, squeezed among dozens of
other slave laborers on the packed-earth floor of a shack
in distant Bihar, prayed he would have the strength to
make it through another day in the fields. His two
daughters, clutching each other on a crib in a slave
brothel in Pataliputra, prayed that their pimps would
allow them to remain together another day.

Of those millions who prayed that night, many, much
like Holkar, prayed for the tenth avatara who was promised. Prayed for Kalkin to come and save them from the
Malwa demon.

Their prayers, like those of Holkar, were fervent.

But Holkar's prayers, unlike those of others, were not
simply fervent. They were also joyous. For he, almost

alone in India, knew that his prayers had been answered. Knew that he shared his own tent with the tenth avatara. And knew that, not more than five feet away, Kalkin himself was pouring his great soul into the vessel of the world's deliverance. Into the strange, crooked, cunning, mongoose mind of his foreign master.

Chapter 3

*The sun beat down on a nightmare landscape. Once,
these had been fields and orchards. Now, the ground
was criss-crossed with deep trenches; stripped bare of
any life beyond a few splintered trees, handfuls of
crushed wheat, a single stalk of corn.*

"Where are we?" asked Belisarius. He spoke in a low
mutter. His eyes were closed, the better to concentrate
on the images flashing through his mind. "And when?"

Near a place called Kursk, replied Aide. The facets
flashed for a microsecond, translating the crystalline
precision of Time's Arrow into the bizarre fiats of human
calendrical custom. **A millenia and a half from now.**

*A line of monsters surged onto the field. Gigantic
things, tearing the soil with strange continuous belts—
metal slats running over wheels. Forward, from cupo-
las, immense snouts protruded. The snouts belched flame
and smoke. Emblazoned on their flanks were crosses—
some, square with double lines; others, bent.*

"Iron elephants," whispered Belisarius. "Like the ones
the Malwa will build—but so much better!"

**Tanks. They will be called tanks. These are the
type which will be called PzKw V "Panthers." They
will weigh 45 tons and travel up to 34 miles per
hour. They fire a cannon whose size will be called
75 millimeter.**

*From the opposite side of the field, a new line of
monsters—tanks—charged forward. They began*

exchanging cannon fire with the other tanks. Belisarius could sense that these new tanks were of a slightly different design, but the only feature which registered clearly on his uneducated eye was that, instead of crosses, their flanks were marked by red stars.

This was the best tank of that era. It will be called the T-34.

The battle was horrible and dazzling at the same time.

Horrible, in its destruction. Belisarius saw a tank cupola—

Turret.

—turret blown off. Tons of metal sent sailing, like a man decapitated. The body of the tank belched flame, and he knew the men inside were being incinerated. Saw men clambering from another burning tank, shrieking, their uniforms afire. Saw them die, suddenly, swept down by an invisible scythe.

Machine-gun fire.

Dazzling, in the speed of the tanks, and the accuracy of their fire. Like a vision of St. George battling the dragon, except the saint was a dragon himself. And his lance a magic wand belching flame and fury.

"How?"

Images of complex—machines?

Internal combustion engines.

Images of perfect metal tubes—cannon barrels, Belisarius realized. He watched as an object was fit into one of the tubes. A perfect fit. He wondered what it was until he saw the cannon fire. Cannonball, he realized—except it was not a ball. It was a cylinder capped by its own cupola.

"How can metal be shaped so precisely?"

He was inside a huge building. A manufactory, he realized. Everywhere he could see rolls and slabs of steel being shaped and cut with incredible speed and precision. He recognized one of the machines as a lathe, like the lathes used by expert carpenters to shape wooden legs for chairs and tables. But this lathe was much bigger and vastly more powerful. The lathes he knew were operated by foot pedal. No such lathes could rip through metal the way this one was, not even bronze. He watched a stream of steel chips flying from the cutting tool like a waterfall.

The other machines he did not recognize at all.

Horizontal boring mill. Vertical turret lathe. Radial drill press.

"Impossible," stated the general firmly. "To make such machines would require making machines to make machines to make machines which could make those machines. We do not have time."

The facets shivered momentarily, confused. The crystalline intelligence which called itself Aide viewed reality in an utterly different manner than humans. The logic behind Belisarius' conclusion was foreign to it. Where the man saw complex sequences, causes and effects, Aide saw the glorious kaleidoscope of eternity.

Malwa will have tanks.

The thought carried an undertone of grievance. Belisarius smiled, faintly. He was reminded of a small child complaining that the neighbor boy has a nice new toy, so why can't he?

"The Malwa tanks are completely different. They are not made like this, with this—" He groped for words to describe a reality he had never seen in real life.

Aide filled the void. **Precision machining. Mass production.**

"Yes. The Malwa do not use those methods. They use the same basic methods as we Romans do. Artisanship. Craftsmanship."

Incomprehension.

Belisarius sighed. For all Aide's brilliance, the strange mentality was often befuddled by the simplest human realities.

"Each Malwa tank—the tanks they will make in the future—will be unique. Handcrafted. The product of slow, painstaking work. The Malwa can afford such methods, with their gigantic resources. Greek artisans are superior, but not by that much. We will never be able to match the Malwa if we copy them. We must find our own way."

The general made a short, chopping gesture with his hand.

"Forget the tanks. Show me more of the battle. It could not all have been—*will be*—a contest of tanks."

Montage of images. Infantrymen in a trench, firing hand cannons and hurling grenades. A line of cannons hidden in a copse of trees, belching fire. A strange glass-and-metal wagon hurtling to a stop. There was no horse to pull it; no horse to stop it. Atop the wagon was a rack of tubes. Suddenly, the rack plumed flame and a volley of rockets streaked forward. Another—

"Stop! There—focus there! The rocket wagon!"

The wagon, again. Belisarius could now see that men were sitting in the glass-enclosed front. Other men were placing rockets into the tubes. The tubes rested on a flat bed toward the rear of the wagon and were slanted up at the sky. Again, the tubes plumed fire. Again, rockets soared.

"What are those?"

They will be called *katyushas.* **These are eight-rail 132 millimeter rocket tubes mounted on what will be called 4X6 trucks.**

"Yes. Yes. *Those* are possible."

The thought which now came from Aide carried more than an undertone of grievance.

Why is *this* **possible and not tanks? Both are made by the same methods, which you said were impossible. Contradiction.**

"You are confusing the—*trucks?*—with the rockets. They are two different things. We cannot make the trucks, but we *can* make the rockets. Not as good, but good enough. And then—we can substitute a different—" He groped for unfamiliar, as yet unknown terms.

Weapons platform.

"Yes. Exactly."

Belisarius straightened his back, stretched his arms. The movement broke his concentration, slightly. He saw

Dadaji Holkar kneeling on his pallet, engrossed in silent prayer. The slave looked up. Holkar and Belisarius exchanged a silent stare for a moment, before the Maratha bowed his head and resumed his devotions. For all the solemnity in the man's posture, Belisarius was amused to note the smile on his face. He had never said a word to Holkar concerning Aide, but he knew that the Maratha had drawn his own conclusions. Conclusions, Belisarius was certain, which were not too far from the truth.

Belisarius closed his eyes and returned to the task at hand.

"You keep showing me things which are much too complex and difficult to make," he whispered. "We must stay within the simple limits that are possible, in the next few years."

A flash of exasperation came from Aide. A new vision erupted.

A man shuffling through a forest, stooped, filthy, clad in rough-cured animal skins. In his hand he clutched an axe. The blade of the weapon was a crudely shaped piece of stone, lashed to the handle with rawhide.

Belisarius chuckled. "I think we can manage a bit more than that, Aide. We are civilized, after all."

Again, exasperation. Again, a vision:

A man standing in a chariot. He was clad in gleaming bronze armor—a breastplate, greaves. A magnificent, ornate helmet, capped by a horse-crest, protected his head. His left arm carried a large, round shield. In his right hand he held a spear. The chariot was a small vehicle, carried on a single axle, drawn by two horses. The back of the chariot was open. Beside the armored warrior, there was only room for a charioteer, who handled the racing horses while the spearman concentrated on the approaching foe.

Belisarius started to laugh softly. Aide was still sulking. The image, for all its clarity, was a mocking rendition of an impossible, legendary figure. Achilles before the walls of Troy.

But then, suddenly, the laugh broke off.

"Yes!" hissed Belisarius. "Chariots!"

Now he did laugh, loudly. "Mother of God—nobody's used chariots in warfare for centuries! But with rockets—and some changes—"

The facets splintered, reformed, shattered, coalesced—all in an instant, trying to follow the branching trail of the general's thoughts. The kaleidoscope swirled around sequences. Aide brought sudden order. A new image, melded from crystal vision and human reasoning:

Another chariot. A bit longer, and wider. Also drawn on a single axle, also open to the rear. Again, a single charioteer handled the reins. But now, the warrior who accompanied him wore only light leather armor and no hand weapon beyond a semi-spatha scabbarded to his waist. He was not a spearman, but a rocketeer. Rising from the center of the chariot was a solid pole, five feet tall. Atop the pole, swiveling on a simple joint, was a bundle of six tubes—three abreast, in two tiers. The warrior aimed the launchers ahead and to the side, at an enemy army advancing some few hundred yards distant. He called out a signal. He and the charioteer crouched. The rocketeer touched a slowmatch to quick fuses. An instant later, a half-dozen rockets were hissing their way toward the approaching army.

The charioteer turned the horses, raced away. Behind, other chariots copied the same maneuver. Within not more than a minute, the ranks of the enemy were being shredded by a hail of rockets. The missiles were not very accurate, but made up for the lack by their numbers and the manner of their explosion.

Fragmentation warheads, came the thought from Aide. This time, the thought was saturated with satisfaction. **Shrapnel.**

Belisarius slumped back, sighing. He rubbed his eyes wearily.

"Yes, there's promise there." Again, he scratched his chin. "But these—*katyushas*—will only work on level ground. In mountain terrain, we'll need something different. Something that a small squad of men can carry by hand, and that can be fired over hills."

The facets flashed excitement.

Mortars.

Belisarius' eyes widened. "Show me," he commanded.

A small motion caught his eye. The Maratha slave had finished his prayers and was lying down on his pallet in preparation for sleep. His face could not be seen, for it was turned away. Belisarius put aside his dialogue with Aide, and devoted a moment to contemplating the man Dadaji Holkar.

Aide did not object, nor interrupt. There were many things about humanity which Aide did not understand. Of no human, perhaps, was that more true than of Belisarius. Belisarius, the one human of the ancient past whom the crystals had selected as the key to preserving their future. The choice had been theirs, but they had been guided by the Great Ones.

Find the general who is not a warrior.

Belisarius, the great general.

That strange thing Aide was coming to know, slowly, haltingly, gropingly.

Belisarius, the man. That stranger thing Aide already knew.

So Aide waited patiently. Waited during that moment of sorrow for another man's anguish. Waited, patiently, not because it understood grief but because it understood the future. And knew that its own future was safeguarded not by the weapons it was showing the general, but by the nature of the man himself.

The moment passed. The man receded.

"Show me," commanded the general.

Chapter 4

CONSTANTINOPLE
Spring 530 AD

"You're positive?" demanded Theodora. "There's no mistake?"

The Empress of Rome leaned forward in her luxurious chair. No expression showed on her face beyond a certain tense alertness. But the knuckles of her hands, gripping the armrests, were white as snow, and the tendons stood out like cables.

Irene met the dark-eyed gaze squarely.

"I am certain, Your Majesty. I've only met Narses face-to-face on three occasions, but I know him quite well. I've studied the man for years, as one professional—and possible competitor—will study another. I could not possibly mistake his appearance, undisguised. Nor he mine, for that matter—that's why I took such elaborate precautions with our disguises."

Theodora transferred her piercing gaze to Hermogenes. The young general winced, shrugged.

"I can't vouch for it myself, Your Majesty, one way or the other. I've never met Narses." He took a deep breath. "But I *do* know Irene, and if she says it was Narses—"

The Empress stilled him with a curt gesture. The black eyes moved on to Maurice.

"It was Narses," growled Maurice. "I've met the man

42

many times, Empress, in the service of my lord Belisarius. We've never been personally introduced, and I doubt if he'd recognize me. But he's a distinctive-looking man. I'd know him anywhere, as long as he was undisguised and the light was good." The grey-haired veteran took his own deep breath. "The man was undisguised. His face—his whole figure—was clearly visible the moment he stepped out of Balban's villa to wait for his palanquin. And the light was good enough. A half-moon in a clear sky."

The Empress looked away. Still, there was no expression on her face.

Irene spoke hesitantly: "It's possible he's playing a double game. Simply trying to draw out treason before he—"

The Empress shook her head. The gesture was short, sharp, final. "No. You do not understand, Irene. Narses and I have been close—very close—for many years. If he suspected treason, and wanted to draw it out, he would have told me. There is only one explanation for his presence at that meeting."

She turned, raised her head imperiously, looked at Maurice and Hermogenes.

"Thank you, gentlemen," she said. Her voice was cold, perhaps a bit choked. A bit, no more. The Empress turned her head slightly, staring at the wall.

"Now—please leave. I wish to be alone with Antonina and Irene."

The two men in the room immediately left. After they closed the door behind them, they looked at each other and puffed their cheeks with relief.

"Let the women handle it now, lad," muttered Maurice. He stumped down the corridor, Hermogenes in tow, making no attempt to soften his footfalls.

In the room, the Empress continued to stare blindly at the wall, maintaining her rigid posture, until the sound of the receding soldiers faded completely away. Then she broke, not like a stick, but like a stone might crumble.

Before the first tears had even appeared, Antonina was
out of her own chair and cradling Theodora's head against
her stomach. The Empress clutched her, sobbing, her face
buried completely in Antonina's skirts. The tiara on her
head was pushed back onto her hair, making a mess of
the elaborate coiffure.

Irene remained in her seat. Her face showed her own
distress. But, when she made a motion to rise and come
to Antonina's assistance, Belisarius' wife stopped her with
a look and a small shake of the head.

Irene sat back, understanding. The understanding,
then, brought a different distress.

Fear. A fear much like that of an experienced seaman sensing hidden reefs and treacherous currents.

Irene Macrembolitissa was one of the best professional spymasters in the Roman Empire. One of the *very*
best intriguers—in an era where intrigue was so preva-
lent, and so skilled, that it would bequeath the very
name *Byzantine* to the lexicon of future languages.

She was in dangerous waters, now. The number of
people alive who had ever seen Theodora in such a state
could be counted on the fingers of one hand. It was
both a privilege and a peril.

After a minute or so, the sobbing ceased. Irene noted,
with the detached interest of a spymaster, that for all
their bitter anguish the sobs had been almost silent. The
Empress Theodora would never wail. Like any woman,
she could have her heart broken. But it was a small,
tough, stony heart. Its wounds healed very quickly, and
simply added more scar tissue.

As soon as the sobs stopped, the Empress turned her
head against Antonina's belly and fixed Irene with her
gaze. The spymaster crouched in her chair, still, frozen
by those cold black eyes. She felt like a rabbit being
examined by a hawk.

"Tell me, Antonina," commanded Theodora. There
was still a trace of raw anguish in that voice, but not
much of one. It was a cold, black voice.

"She is my dear friend, Theodora," said Antonina. Her

own voice, though soft, was even colder. "I love her as much as I trust her."

Silence followed, for a time which seemed to Irene to stretch on for hours. But it was less than half a minute before the Empress pushed herself away from Antonina.

"Good enough," she murmured. The Empress took a deep breath, leaned back into her chair. Throughout, her eyes never left Irene. But a smile came to her face. It was not much of a smile, true. But Irene suddenly discovered she could breathe.

Theodora laughed. It was like a raven's caw.

"Welcome to the old whores' club, Irene," she rasped. A majestic wave of the hand. "I make you an honorary member."

Theodora craned her head up, looking at Antonina. Finally, now, something other than pain entered her face.

"Thank you, Antonina," she whispered. "As always."

Then she sat erect. Automatically, as if to bring reassurance, her hand rose to the tiara. Finding it askew, she tried to force it back into place. The attempt failed, stymied by the disheveled mass of hair.

"Oh, the hell with it," muttered the Empress. She snatched the tiara off her head and placed it on the floor.

Irene almost laughed then, seeing the look of astonishment on Antonina's face. Often, in the year gone by, Antonina had told her of Theodora's obsession with maintaining her imperial regalia.

The Empress waved Antonina back to her chair.

"Let's to business," she commanded. Then, after her friend had resumed her seat:

"First of all, Antonina, you will pursue the contact this Indian—what was his name again?—"

"Ajatasutra."

"Yes—that this Ajatasutra initiated. He'll be seeking to draw you into some treasonous statement, you understand?"

Antonina nodded, saying:

"Of course. And there'll be an impeccable witness hidden somewhere nearby. John of Cappadocia, perhaps."

Irene shook her head. "It won't be him. Too many people wouldn't believe that filthy bastard if he claimed the sun rose in the east and set in the west. No, it's more likely to be one or the other—better yet, both—of the two churchmen." She shrugged. "Or someone else we don't even know yet."

Theodora pressed on:

"It's essential that you make such a statement, Antonina. That's the key that'll keep the door open. As long as the Malwa think they have something on you, they'll trust you."

Antonina chuckled. "You call that *trust*?"

The Empress smiled. "It's what passes for trust in that world. Our world, I'm afraid."

"Good as gold," chipped in Irene. "Better than gold, even. There's nothing an intriguer trusts more than someone he's successfully blackmailed."

Antonina made a little grimace of distaste. "And then what?" she asked.

Theodora shrugged. "We'll have to see. After the Malwa think they have you properly blackmailed, they'll demand that you perform some service. Give them some secret information, probably. When we find out what it is they want to know, that will tell us what's important to them."

Antonina considered the Empress' words for a moment.

"Makes sense," she said. Then, fixing Theodora with a level, serene gaze, added: "So be it."

The Empress returned the gaze. Nothing was said, for a full minute. When the Empress looked away, Irene noted that color had now fully returned to her face.

"Thank you, Antonina," whispered Theodora. "Again."

The intensity with which the words were spoken startled Irene, at first. Until she realized what had just happened. With that realization, she transferred her sharp eyes to the face of Antonina.

There was nothing to be seen on the Egyptian

woman's face, beyond green-eyed, dark-haired, olive beauty. And serenity.

In the months since she had first met Antonina, she had often been impressed by her. But never more than at that moment.

A little chuckle from the Empress drew Irene's eyes. To her surprise, she found Theodora watching her.

"Good, Irene. You understand, then. Precious few people ever have."

Irene blew out her cheeks. "Not many women would agree to incriminate themselves on behalf of an Empress whose husband, well-placed rumor has it, is trying to have their own husband murdered. Without asking so much as a question. That's a different kind of trust than I usually encounter."

"Than *anyone* encounters," replied Theodora. For a moment, her lips tightened with anger. "I'm sure you've heard that my close friendship with Antonina is due to the fact that we're both former whores from Alexandria? Birds of feather, as it were, flocking together."

Irene nodded. "Any number of times."

"*Idiots*," snarled the Empress. "I know—knew, at least—plenty of Alexandrian whores who'd slit their own sister's throat for two denarii."

Antonina murmured: "That's not fair, Theodora. Antiochene whores, maybe. Any self-respecting Egyptian whore would hold out for a solidus."

Theodora cawed harshly. The Empress leaned forward in her seat, bracing her hands on her knees.

"I need you to be my spymaster, Irene."

Interpreting correctly the slight hesitation in the woman's face, Theodora made a little flipping motion with her hand, as if brushing something aside.

"I'll settle it with Sittas. He doesn't need your services half as much as I do. And I'll pay more than he does. Rich as he is, I'm a lot richer. And unlike Sittas, I'm not a stingy tightwad."

Irene chuckled, glancing around the lavishly furnished room. "You certainly aren't!"

When Irene had approached Theodora, a week earlier, with her charges against Narses and her plan to trap him in a treasonous meeting, it had been the Empress who had purchased this villa to serve as their command post. *Purchased* it—a huge, luxurious villa. Just—*bought* it. Like a matron buys fruit from a grocer.

The spymaster shook her head. "There's no point in that, Theodora. I can serve as your spymaster while staying on Sittas' payroll. It'd be much better that way. The fewer people who know of our relationship, the better. Money trails are the easiest to track. If I'm on your payroll, even secretly, someone will find out."

"The same objection applies to your being on Sittas' payroll," countered the Empress. "More so. I'm sure my security is better than Sittas'."

Irene shrugged. "So what? Let our enemies find out that I'm Sittas' spymaster. I'm sure they already know, anyway. Good. Excellent. Let them keep thinking that. Sittas they are not worried about. He's just a fat general who hates palace duty in Constantinople. Stuck way out there in Syria. Good at his trade, sure, but lazy and unambitious."

Theodora ran fingers through her elaborate coiffure, thinking. Almost immediately, the fingers became tangled in that incredible structure. Suddenly, vigorously, she plunged her fingers into the mass and pulled it all loose. Long black tresses cascaded over her shoulders. Her hair, now truly visible, was quite beautiful.

"God, I've wanted to do that for the longest time!"

Again, the women laughed. But it was a very brief moment of levity.

Theodora nodded. "You're right. Whatever their plot is, it does not appear to focus on the army. I noticed that no military figures attended that meeting tonight."

"No, they didn't. I'm pretty sure they've suborned a few officers, but not many. The only one of significance is Aegidius, the commander of the army in Bythinia. I'm not positive, but I think he's one of them. An underling, though, not a ringleader."

Theodora scowled. "I never liked that greasy bastard. God, my husband has the worst taste in generals!"

An apologetic nod to Antonina: "Belisarius aside, of course. And Sittas."

Again, the Empress ran her fingers through her hair, disheveling it even further. Her sensual pleasure in the act was obvious, but it did not distract her from her thoughts.

"Doesn't that seem odd to you, Irene? That lack of attention to the army? Every other treasonous plot I can remember has put the military on center stage. For obvious reasons."

"Actually, it's a cunning move on their part. They know that Justinian's suspicions will always be centered on the army. So they stay away from it, by and large, and spread their poison in darker corners."

"I *still* don't understand it." Theodora's voice was dark with frustration. "I take your point, but—so what? What good does it do to plot treason if you can't carry it out when the time comes? And for that you need military force. A lot more force than the Bythinian army provides. What is that army—ten thousand strong? At the most?"

"Eight," replied Irene. "Not enough to take power, but enough to neutralize loyal units. Especially if many of those units decide to stay on the sidelines until the dust settles. Which, unfortunately, many military units do during a coup." The spymaster began to add something, but fell silent. She glanced quickly at Antonina.

Theodora did not miss it.

"The two of you know something," she announced.

Silence.

"Tell." The voice of the Empress, that, not Theodora. Irene's eyes appealed to Antonina. Antonina sighed.

"I will tell you everything, Theodora. Tonight. But you're not going to believe me."

"*Tell.*"

When Theodora left the villa, Irene and Antonina

escorted the Empress to the palanquin drawn up in the courtyard. After she climbed into the palanquin, Theodora leaned forward and whispered:

"You were right, Antonina. I *don't* believe it. It's absurd! Belisarius has a talisman from God? A messenger from the future?"

Antonina shrugged. "You didn't believe Irene, either, when she told you about Narses. But still you came here, to see for yourself."

The two old friends stared at each other. The Empress was the first to look away.

"No, I didn't. And, yes, I did."

She leaned back into the plush cushions. Antonina could barely make out Theodora's face in the dark interior of the enclosed vehicle, but she couldn't miss the grimace.

"I hate to travel," growled the Empress.

A sigh.

"Yes, Antonina, I will. I will come to Daras and see for myself. This summer."

Another sigh.

"I hate Syria in the summer."

A great, imperial sigh.

"Now that I think about it, I hate Syria any time of the year."

After the gate closed behind the departing palanquin, Antonina and Irene stood for a moment in the courtyard, admiring the clear night sky.

"I'm curious about something, Antonina," said Irene.

"Yes?"

"I don't really understand. Well, let's just say that I was surprised how hard Theodora took it, to find out that Narses is a traitor. I knew he was one of her closest advisers, but—"

"He was a lot more than that, Irene," replied Antonina, shaking her head sadly. "Much, much more."

The short Egyptian woman looked up at her tall Greek friend.

"You've heard, I'm sure, all the stories about Theodora's past?"

Irene shrugged. "Of course. I can't say I paid much attention to them. People are always quick—"

Antonina shook her head. "The fact is, they're mostly true. At least, insofar as the tales report what she *did*."

She looked away, her jaws tight, before adding: "Where they lie is in the heart of the thing. Theodora, as a girl, was as great a whore as you'll ever find. What she never was, was a wanton slut." A little laugh, barely more than a chuckle. "It's ironic, actually. Fair-minded, respectable, proper people, when they compare she and I, are prone to give me the benefit of their doubt. True, before I met Belisarius I gave my favors for money. But only to the most carefully selected men, and not many of those. *Whereas Theodora—*"

Harshly: "If there's to be a comparison, by rights it should go the other way. I did what I did through choice. Not much of a choice, mind you, for a dirt-poor girl on the streets of Alexandria, with a whore for a mother and charioteer for a father. But—I can't honestly claim that anyone forced me into it."

She took a breath, then looked her friend straight in the eyes. Irene winced.

"I don't think I want to hear what's coming next."

"*You asked, woman.* Theodora never took pleasure in her whoring, and she never had a choice. Her pig of a father raped her when she was nine, and kept doing it until he sold her to a pimp at the age of twelve. And her pimp was even worse. That stinking—"

She stopped abruptly, made a short chopping motion with her hand. "Never mind. There's nothing in it but nausea." She took another deep breath, let it out. "The point is, Irene, that Narses was the closest thing to a real father that woman has ever had. When she first met him, she was just a poor ambitious young woman helping her poor ambitious young lover to claw his way to the top. Narses took her under his wing, and helped her along. With money, sometimes; other times, with privy information; other times, with introductions to the right people. But, mostly, he helped her the way a father helps his daughter. The way a *good* father helps his daughter. He simply—taught her."

She paused for a moment. Irene interjected:

"I'm sure he was just—"

Antonina shook her head. "No. *No*. Well, that's too bald. A man like Narses always has an eye out for the main chance. But that wasn't it, Irene. Believe me, it wasn't. Narses is brilliant, but he's not God Almighty. And only the Lord Himself, in those days, could have known that Theodora would someday be Empress of the Roman Empire. She and Justinian didn't know it, then. Didn't even think of it."

She took Irene by the arm and began slowly leading her out of the courtyard.

"No, I think— I think, in his own way, Narses saw Theodora as the child he never had. *Could* never have. So, what childlike trust remained in a girl who distrusted all men, was given to an elderly eunuch. And what paternal care existed in a man who could have no children, was given to a young whore."

She halted, fighting tears. Stared blindly at the sky.

"Dear God in heaven," she whispered, "I so hoped Narses wouldn't be at that meeting. I so hoped you'd be wrong, even though I knew you weren't." Now the tears flowed. "Theodora will never recover from this."

"You can't say that," protested Irene. "She still has Justinian."

Antonina shook her head. "No, Irene. It's not the same. Theodora loves Justinian, but she has never trusted him. Not the way she trusted Narses." She wiped her eyes. Again, Antonina took Irene's arm and led her out of the courtyard. Her steps, now, were quick.

Ten feet from the door, she said: "Theodora's harder than steel, and she prides herself on not making the same mistake twice. She'll never give her trust to another man again. No matter who he is. *Never*."

Five feet from the door, Irene said sadly: "God, that poor woman."

At the door itself, Antonina stopped. Turned to her friend, and looked her squarely in the face. There was no trace of sorrow, now, in those beautiful green eyes. Just emptiness.

"*Poor woman?*" she demanded. "Don't ever think it, Irene. Give Theodora your love, if you can. But never think to give her your pity." Her eyes were like the green gaze of an asp. "If you thought the story of her father and her pimp was nauseating, someday I'll tell you what happened to them. After Theodora mounted the throne."

Irene felt her throat tighten.

"Whatever you do in this world, Irene, don't ever cross that *poor woman*. Go down to Hell, instead, and spit in the face of Satan."

She started through the door. Over her shoulder, like a serpent's hiss:

"*Poor woman.*"

Two hours—and many bottles of wine—later, Antonina lowered her head onto the arm of her couch and asked:

"I'm curious about something myself, Irene." Her words were spoken in that slow, careful, precise manner which indicates that a moment of solemnity has—briefly, briefly—interrupted the serious business of getting blind drunk.

"Ask anything!" commanded the spymaster from her own couch, waving her arm grandly. The just-emptied bottle in her hand detracted, a bit, from the majesty of the gesture. The hiccup which followed detracted quite a bit more.

Antonina grinned, then tried to focus her thought.

"Everything you said—" Her own grand gesture; pitifully collapsing in midair. "Back then, earlier tonight—whenever—made sense."

She managed to restrain her own hiccup, beamed triumphantly at her friend, continued:

"About remaining on Sittas' payroll. But—weren't you

even tempted? I mean, Theodora is *stinking* rich. Makes Sittas look like a pauper. She really would pay you a lot more. A *whole* lot more."

Irene reached out her hand, grasped the arm of the couch, and levered herself up slowly. She tried to focus her eyes, but couldn't quite manage the feat. So she satisfied herself with her own beaming, triumphant grin.

"You don't really understand me, dear friend. Not here, at least, not in—this thing. You and Theodora grew up—you know. Poor. Money means something to you. I was raised in a rich family—" A very grand sweep of the arm. Too grand, much too grand. She overbalanced and slipped off the couch onto her knee. Then, laughing, stumbled back onto it. Then, raising her head high with pride, demonstrated to a doubting universe that she hadn't lost her train of thought:

"—and so I take money for granted. The truth is—" Suppressed belch; grim face; bitter struggle against the slanderous hint of insobriety.

"Truit is—*truth* is—I don't even spend half the money Sittas pays me." Again, suppressed belch; again—the short, chopping blows of desperate battle:

"Personally. I mean. On myself. Don't need it."

Victorious against all odds, she flopped against the back of the couch, staring blearily at one of the magnificent tapestries on the opposite wall. She couldn't really see it, anymore, but she knew it was magnificent. Incredibly magnificent.

In the way that it happens, at such times, exultant triumph collapsed into maudlin tears.

"What matters to me is that *the Empress of Rome* wants me for her spymaster. That's"—hiccup—"enormously gratifying to my vanity, of course. But it also means I now have access tomb pelear—*to imperial*—resources. *Resources.*"

She twirled her finger in a little gesture which encompassed the entire villa.

"Look at this! It's nothing but a damned *stake-out*, for Chrissake."

She beamed upon her friend, beamed upon the tapestry, sprang to her feet, and spread her arms in a great gesture of pure exultation.

"Oh, God—I'm going to have so much *fun*."

Antonina tried to catch her on the way down, but only succeeded in flopping onto the floor herself. From her belly, cheek pressed against the parquet, she did manage to focus on Irene long enough to be sure her friend was not hurt. Just, finally, dead drunk.

"Woman can't handle her liquor," she muttered; although, to a cold-hearted observer, the word "liquor" would have sounded suspiciously like a snore.

"Come on, Hermogenes, let's get them to bed."

Maurice bent, scooped the little figure of Antonina into his thick arms, and carried her through the door. He padded down the corridor effortlessly. Hermogenes followed, with like ease. Irene was taller than Antonina, but, slim rather than voluptuous, weighed not a pound more.

Antonina's room came first. Maurice, turning backward, pushed his way through the door and lowered Antonina onto her bed. Like every other piece of furniture in the villa, the bed was splendid. Very well made, very luxurious, and—very large.

Maurice turned and looked at Hermogenes. The young general was standing in the doorway, Irene cradled in his arms. Maurice gestured him in.

"Bring her here, Hermogenes. We may as well let them sleep it off together."

Hermogenes hesitated for an instant, looking down at Irene's slack, lolling head. A tiny little twitch in his mouth gave away his regrets.

"Come on," chuckled Maurice. "You won't be enjoying her company tonight. If you put her in her own bed, you won't get any sleep yourself, since you're sharing it with her. You'll just wind up sleeping on a couch. She'll be snoring like a pig, you know it as well as I do."

Hermogenes smiled, ruefully, and brought Irene into the room. Gently, he lowered her onto the bed next to Antonina. On that huge expanse, the two women looked like children.

"I've never seen her get drunk before," said Hermogenes softly. There was no reproach in his voice, just bemused wonder. "I've never even seen her get tipsy."

Maurice glanced at Irene. "She's a spymaster," he grunted. "Greek nobility, to boot."

He then gave Antonina a long, lingering, considering stare. There was no reproach in his gaze, just love. "I've seen this one get drunk before," he murmured. "Twice."

He began ushering Hermogenes out of the room.

"Once, the first time Belisarius went on campaign. I stayed behind, for a few days, organizing the logistics. She got plastered the night he left. The next morning, she climbed onto a horse and rode off to join him in camp. I sent five cataphracts with her as an escort. Anastasius was in command. He told me later he thought he'd have to tie her onto the horse to keep her from falling off. But she made it, all on her own."

He stopped in the doorway, looking back fondly. "I was impressed, when he told me."

Hermogenes nodded, smiling. "That's tough, riding a horse with that kind of hangover. I know. I've done the same thing myself."

Maurice eyed him scornfully.

"No, you haven't. You already knew how to ride a horse. It was the first time she'd ever been in a saddle."

Hermogenes gaped. Maurice grinned.

"Oh, yes. A very tough little woman, in her own way. Though you wouldn't think it, just looking at her." He reached out and closed the door.

"What was the second time?"

The humor faded from Maurice's face.

"The second time was the day after he left for India. The next morning, she stumbled down to the stables and spent four hours there. Just sitting on a pile of hay, staring at a horse."

Hermogenes puffed his cheeks, blew out the air. "Christ."

Maurice shrugged. "Ah, hell. I wish she'd do it more often."

He started down the corridor.

"That's too great a pain to keep in such a small body."

When Irene awoke the next morning, it took her a full minute to focus her eyes. The first thing she saw was Antonina, dressed in a robe, staring out the window onto the street below.

Irene watched her for ten minutes, never once moving her eyes away.

At first, simply because she couldn't move her eyes. Then, when she could, because she immediately encountered pain. Then, after pain had been properly introduced, because she hoped it would go away if she ignored it politely. Then, after pain made clear it was settling in for a nice long visit, because she wanted to think about anything else. Then, finally, because she started to think.

"What in the hell are you doing?" she croaked.

"Nothing much," came the soft reply. "Just looking at a horse."

Chapter 5

RANAPUR
Spring 530 AD

On the tenth day after their arrival at Ranapur, as
Belisarius and his cataphracts rode out to the small knoll
where they usually observed the siege, their Rajput
escorts intercepted them before they had gone more
than half a mile. The cavalrymen seemed tense and edgy,
although their unease did not seem to be directed
toward the Romans.

Rana Sanga himself, when he drew his horse alongside Belisarius, exhibited nothing beyond his usual
reserved, courteous manner. But his first words made
clear that today would be out of the ordinary.

"You and your men will not be watching the siege
from your normal vantage point, General Belisarius."

Belisarius frowned. "If you move us further back,
Rana Sanga, we might as well watch the battle from
the moon!"

Sanga scowled. "You need have no fear on that
account, General!" he snapped. "Quite the contrary."
The Rajput shook his head in a sharp, short manner.
"Excuse me," he muttered. "I am being impolite. I
am—somewhat aggravated. I fear I am lashing at you
for lack of a better target. Please accept my apology."

Belisarius smiled. "Gladly, Sanga. Gladly. But—well, it's none of my business, but—"

Again, Sanga shook his head.

"You will see for yourself, soon enough. The high commander of the army, Lord Harsha, has decreed that Ranapur will fall today. The Emperor himself has come out to observe the conquest of the rebel city. You have been invited to watch the crushing of the rebellion from the Emperor's own pavilion. I have been instructed to escort you there."

"Ah," said Belisarius. Since they had arrived at Ranapur, the Roman delegation had been studiously ignored by the emperor and his entourage. Even Venandakatra had not sent so much as a formal note. The diplomatic discourtesy, Belisarius was certain, was calculated to impress upon the Romans their humble place in the Malwa scheme of things. He was equally certain that the sudden invitation to share the emperor's august presence was calculated to impress the foreigners with the Malwa empire's might and ruthlessness.

There was no point in lodging a protest against this shameful treatment. Certainly not to Rana Sanga, who was himself consigned to the periphery of the Malwa court. (Except, Belisarius suspected, when the clash of arms required the Rajput's skill.)

But—where protest would be futile, irony would be at least entertaining. Belisarius frowned, deep in thought, and allowed his jaw to gape with wonder.

"Such a brilliant stratagem! To conclude a siege by simply decreeing it at an end! I confess with shame that I never thought of it myself, despite the many sieges I have undertaken."

Sanga barked harsh laughter. "Neither have I!" he exclaimed. The Rajput's foul humor seemed to vanish. He reined his horse around, and began moving away. "Come, Belisarius," he said over his shoulder, cheerfully. "Let us observe a military genius at work."

Their route took them toward the eastern side of the rebel city. Before long, it became apparent to Belisarius

that the Romans were going to get closer to Ranapur
than they ever had been before. With some difficulty,
the general managed to maintain an air of casual interest.
He was pleased to note, however, from a glance over
his shoulder, that his cataphracts were closely scrutinizing
the scene. Menander was muttering softly, a habit which
the young soldier had whenever he was determined to
commit something to memory.

Soon, from a distance, Belisarius was able to discern
an enormous pavilion on a small slope directly east of
the city. The pavilion was located just barely out of
catapult range. Apparently, Emperor Skandagupta
intended to witness the fall of Ranapur as closely as
possible.

Belisarius had never been able to observe the siege
on this side of the city. Always, he had been restricted
to the southern wall. But he had long suspected, from
the sound of the cannonades, that it was on the east
that the Malwa had brought their greatest strength to
bear. As they drew nearer, it became obvious that his
supposition was accurate. The great brick wall surrounding Ranapur was nothing but a shattered mound, here.
The cannonades had reduced it to a ridge of rubble.

A huge army was assembling on the plain before
that ridge of shattered brickwork, preparing for the
final assault. Regular Malwa infantry, in the main, with
Ye-tai shock troops to stiffen their resolve. The Ye-tai
detachments were assembled in the rear of the regular infantry. Their job, obviously, was not to lead the
charge, but to see to it that the common soldiers did
not falter in their duty.

There were very few Rajputs anywhere to be seen.
Belisarius began to make some remark to that effect,
but Sanga interrupted him brusquely.

"We have been assigned other duties. All Rajput
cavalrymen, except your escort and a few couriers, have
been charged with the task of patrolling the outskirts
of the city. To capture any rebels attempting to escape
their doom."

"Ah," said Belisarius. A quick glance at Sanga's dark, tight-lipped face, then: "A brilliant maneuver, that—to use your best troops to mop up after a great victory which hasn't actually been won yet. Although, of course, the victory *has* been decreed." He scratched his chin. "I am ashamed to admit that I myself, military simpleton that I am, have always been prone to using my best troops in the battle itself."

Again, Sanga barked a few laughs. "I, too! Ah, Belisarius, we are but children at the feet of a master." He shook his head. "Truly, Lord Harsha's name belongs in the company of such as Alexander the Great and Ashoka."

"Truly," agreed Belisarius. The Roman general scanned the battleground. To his experienced eye, it was obvious that the Malwa had long been preparing for this massive assault on the eastern wall of the city.

"I see that Lord Harsha places no great store in surprise and deception," he commented.

Sanga's lips curled. "Such methods are beneath Lord Harsha's contempt," he replied acidly. "The tactics of bandits, he has been heard to call them."

For a moment, the Roman and Rajput generals stared at each other. Both smiled, then, faintly but quite warmly, before Sanga sighed and looked away.

"But, then, he is a very great man and does not care to stoop," the Rajput murmured. A shrug. "And, with the enormous force at his disposal, he does not perhaps need to."

They were now but two hundred yards from the Malwa emperor's gigantic pavilion. Skandagupta's camp headquarters, to Belisarius, seemed like something out of fable. He had never seen its like before, on a field of battle. Not even the haughtiest Persian emperor— not even the ancient Xerxes or Darius—had ever brought such an incredible structure to the clash of armies.

The pavilion rose a full sixty feet in the air, suspended on ten enormous poles—upended logs, rather. A multitude of inch-thick hawsers, stretching tightly in every direction, anchored the poles to the ground. The fabric of the tent itself was cotton—not even the ruler of Malwa could afford that much silk—but all of the many canopies which provided entry into the pavilion were made of silk, as were their tassels and cords. And the cotton of the tent was marvelously dyed, not in simple swaths and colors, but in complex geometric designs and subtle shades.

A small squad of Ye-tai began to approach them on horseback. From their gaudy uniforms and the red and gold pennants trailing their lances, Belisarius recognized them as members of the Emperor's personal bodyguard. Eight thousand strong, that bodyguard was reputed to be—although, from his quick assessment, Belisarius did not think there were more than half that many present on the scene.

At that moment, drums began sounding the signal for the advance. The front line of Malwa infantrymen began a slow, undulating movement. The advance was ragged, not so much due to indiscipline as to the simple fact that the ground was so chewed up by trenches and artillery fire that it was impossible for the Malwa soldiers to maintain an even line. The enormous mass of the army added to the confusion. Belisarius estimated that there were perhaps as many as forty thousand infantrymen in that slow-moving charge, with an additional five thousand Ye-tai barbarians bringing up the rear.

About three-fourths of the Malwa soldiers stumbling across that terrain were armed with traditional hand weapons. Most of the infantrymen favored spears and swords, although some were armed with battle-axes and maces.

Belisarius knew from his prior observations that these weapons would be cheap and poorly made, as would be their armor. The Ye-tai who chivvied those Malwa common troops were equipped with mail tunics and conical iron helmets. But the infantrymen themselves were forced to make do with leather half-armor reinforced with scale mail on the shoulders. Their helmets were not much more than leather caps, although the scale mail reinforcement was a bit less frugal than with their armor. The difference in shields was also striking. The Ye-tai shields, like Roman shields, were sturdy laminated wood reinforced with iron rims and bosses. The shields of the common Malwa troops, on the other hand, were almost pitiful: wicker frames, covered with simple leather.

Outside of the mass of troops carrying traditional weapons, however, Belisarius noted that the remainder were divided evenly between soldiers carrying ladders and scaling equipment, and grenadiers armed with a handful of the pestle-shaped Malwa grenades. This would be the Romans' first opportunity to observe grenades in action, and Belisarius was determined to make the most of the opportunity.

Belisarius and Rana Sanga stopped to watch the advance. Out of the corner of his eye, Belisarius saw that the oncoming Ye-tai patrol had stopped also. But he paid them little attention, for his interest was riveted on the battleground. He was struck again by the well-worn and oft-trampled nature of the terrain. Obviously, the siege here had been long, arduous, and filled with no surprises. It was exactly the kind of siege terrain that offended his craftsman's instincts, and he found his mind toying with the alternate methods that he would have tried had he been in charge of the siege.

Or of the forces defending the city.

A thought came to him then, a half-formed idea born of old experience and newly-acquired knowledge. He turned to Sanga.

"Didn't you tell me, a few days ago, that Ranapur is a mining province?"

Sanga nodded. "Yes. Almost a third of the empire's copper is mined here."

Belisarius squinted at the terrain over which the Malwa army was making its slow way. He noted that the rebels were not meeting the oncoming advance with catapult fire. That was odd, on the face of it. The vague thought in his mind began to crystallize.

Sanga noticed his companion's sudden preoccupation.

"You are thinking something, Belisarius. May I ask what it is?"

Belisarius hesitated a moment. For all that he liked Sanga, the Rajput was, after all, a future enemy. On the other hand—for the moment, the fate of Belisarius and his men was bound up with that of the Rajputs.

"Forgive my saying so, Rana Sanga, but I have found that your Malwa siege techniques are a bit—how shall I put?—*simple*, perhaps; by Roman standards. I suspect it is because most of your wars have been fought in this huge river valley. I do not think you have our experience with campaigns in mountainous country."

Sanga tugged his beard, thinking. "That's quite possibly true. I have never observed Roman sieges, of course. But it is certainly true one of the reasons the Maratha have always been such a thorn in our side is because of their rocky terrain, and their cunning use of hillforts. A siege in Majarashtra is always twice as difficult as a siege in the Ganges plain."

He peered closely at the Roman. "You suspect something," he announced.

Again, Belisarius hesitated. He was watching the Malwa advance intently. The first line of the infantrymen was now almost halfway across the five hundred yards of no-man's land which separated the Malwa front trenches from the wall of Ranapur. Still, there was no catapult fire.

Belisarius straightened.

"Three factors strike me as significant here, Rana Sanga. One, the rebels have experienced miners in their ranks. Two, they have known for weeks—if not months— that the main assault would come here. Lord Harsha has obviously made no attempt to feint elsewhere. Three, there is no catapult fire—as if they were hoarding their remaining gunpowder."

He scratched his chin. "Now that I think about it, in fact, it seems to me that the rebel catapult fire has been very sporadic for several days, now. Let me ask you—do you know if Lord Harsha has had sappers advancing counter-mines?"

The answer was obvious from the blank look on the Rajput's face.

Belisarius still hesitated. The suspicion taking shape in his mind was incomplete, uncertain—as much guess-work as anything else. The capabilities of gunpowder, and the permutations of its use on a battlefield, were still new and primarily theoretical for him. He was not even sure if—

The facets erupted in a shivering frenzy. Human battlegrounds, for Aide, were an entirely theoretical concept. (An utterly bizarre one, besides, to its crystalline consciousness.) But now, finally, the strange idea forming in Belisarius' mind gelled enough for Aide to grasp its shape. A knowledge of all history ruptured through the serried facets.

Danger! Danger! The siege of Petersburg! The battle of the Crater!

Belisarius almost gasped at the force of the vision which plumed into his mind.

A tunnel—many tunnels—underground, shored with wooden beams and planks. Men in blue uniforms with stubby caps were placing cases filled with sticks—not sticks, some kind of gunpowder devices—along every foot of those tunnels. Stacking them, one atop the other. Laying fuses. Leaving.

Above. Soldiers wearing grey uniforms atop ramparts.

Below. Fuses burning.

Above. Armageddon came.

Belisarius began dismounting from his horse. He glanced at his cataphracts and made a little gesture with his head. Immediately, the three Thracians followed their general's lead. Fortunately, the Romans were only wearing half-armor. Had they been encumbered with full cataphract paraphernalia, they would have found it difficult to dismount unassisted, and impossible to do it swiftly.

"I may be wrong, Rana Sanga," he said quietly, "but I would strongly urge you to dismount your men. If I were the rebel commander of Ranapur, I would have riddled that no-man's land with mines and crammed them full of every pound of gunpowder I had left."

Rana Sanga stared at the battleground. The entire mass of Malwa infantry were now jammed into a space about a mile and a half wide and not more than two hundred yards deep. All semblance of dressed lines had vanished. The advancing army was little more than a disordered mob, now. In the rear, Ye-tai warriors were trotting back and forth, forcing the stragglers forward. Their efforts served only to increase the confusion.

It was a perfect target for catapult fire. There was no catapult fire.

Sanga's dusky face paled slightly. He turned in the saddle and began shouting orders at his cavalrymen. Surprised, but well-disciplined, his men obeyed him instantly. Within ten seconds, all five hundred Rajput horsemen were standing on the ground, holding their mounts by the reins.

Belisarius saw the small Ye-tai cavalry troop staring at them with puzzlement. The Ye-tai leader frowned and began to shout something.

His words were lost. The world ended.

Belisarius was hurled to the ground. A rolling series of explosions swept the battlefield. Even at a distance, the sound was more like a blow than a noise. Lying on his side, staring toward Ranapur, he saw the entire Malwa army disappear in a cloud of dust. Streaking through the dust, shredding soldiers, were a multitude of objects. Most of those missiles, he realized dimly, were what Aide called *shrapnel*. But the force of the explosions was so incredible that almost anything became a deadly menace.

Still half-stunned, Belisarius watched a shield—a good Ye-tai shield, a solid disk of wood rimmed with iron—sail across the sky like a discus hurled by a giant. The

Ye-tai cavalry who had been approaching them were still trying to control their rearing mounts. The spinning shield decapitated their commander as neatly as a farmwife beheads a chicken. An instant later, the entire troop of Ye-tai horsemen was struck down by a deluge of debris.

Debris began falling among the Rajputs and Romans. Casualties here were relatively light, however, mainly because the men were already dismounted and were able to fall to the ground before the projectiles arrived. Most of the injuries which the Rajputs suffered were due to the trampling hooves of terrified and injured horses.

After that first moment of shock, Belisarius found his wits rapidly returning.

The first law of gunpowder warfare, he mused. *Stay low to the ground.*

More debris rained down on him. He curled into a ball, hiding as much of himself as possible under his shield.

Very low.

It felt as if a tribe of dwarves was hammering him with mallets.

I wish I had a hole to hide in. Or a shovel to dig one.

Aide: **They will be called foxholes. Soldiers will dig them as automatically as they breathe.**

Thumpthumpthumpthumpthumpthump.

I believe you. He tried to visualize the shovels.

Thumpthumpthumpthumpthumpthump.

Aide brought an image into his mind. *A small spade, hinged at the joint where the blade met the handle. Easily carried in a soldier's kit.*

Thumpthumpthumpthump. Thumpthump.

The first thing we'll start making when we get back to Rome.

Thump. Thump. Thump. THUMP.

The very first thing.

The explosions ceased. Cautiously he raised his head. Then he levered himself out from under his soil-and-stone-covered shield. Grimacing, he brushed a piece of bloody gore off his leg.

He looked to his cataphracts. All three, he saw with relief, were also rising to their feet. None of them seemed injured, beyond a dazed look in their eyes. Menander's horse was lying nearby, kicking feebly. From the look of the poor beast, Belisarius thought the mare had broken her neck falling to the ground. The Romans' other horses were gone—part of the frenzied herd stampeding eastward, he assumed. Looking around, he saw that none of the Rajputs had been able to retain control of their mounts. Most of them, he suspected, had not even tried. And those few who had tried had probably been trampled for their pains.

A few feet away, he saw Rana Sanga rise from under his own shield and stagger to his feet. But most of his attention was directed toward the battleground, where the incredible explosions had been centered.

Before, that landscape had been grim. A barren terrain, carved with trenches and earthworks, pocked with small craters from catapult bombs. Now it looked like something out of nightmare, as if the gods had chosen to dig enormous holes and fill them with corpses.

Bodies, bodies, bodies. Pieces of bodies. Pieces of pieces of bodies. Pieces that were utterly unidentifiable, except for their red color. Flesh shredded beyond all recognition.

To his amazement, however, Belisarius saw that many of the Malwa soldiers had survived the holocaust. Within seconds, in fact, as he watched the writhing mass of bodies, he realized that well over half of them had survived—although many of them were injured, most were dazed, and, he strongly suspected, all of them were deafened. His own hearing, from the ringing in his ears, was only half-returned.

I can't believe anyone survived that.

A cold thought from Aide:

This is typical. It will be extraordinary how many humans will survive incredible bombardment.

Image:

Men in uniform, steel-helmeted. An enormous mass of them, charging across a landscape like the one below him. They were carrying weapons which Belisarius knew were rifles armed with bayonets. In addition to their weapons, they were staggering under an insane weight of equipment. Belisarius recognized grenades, ammunition pouches, food and water containers, shovels, and bizarre mask-looking objects he did not know. Their ranks were shredded by an uncountable number of explosions. The carnage was like nothing he had ever seen, for all his experience of war. Still they charged. Still they charged. Still they charged.

It will be called the Battle of the Somme. It will begin on a date that will be called July 1, 1916. In this charge, on this first day, twenty thousand men will die. Twenty-five thousand more will be wounded. But most will survive, and charge again another day.

Belisarius shook his head. *How—?*

We do not know. We do not fully understand humans, even the Great Ones. But you will do it. You will do it again and again and again. And you will survive, again and again and again. We do not know how. But you will.

Oddly, it was the mention of the Great Ones that caught Belisarius' attention.

The—"Great Ones"—they are human?

Only once had Aide given him a glimpse of those strange beings. The Great Ones. Who were, in some way, the creators—and betrayors?—of the future crystalline intelligence to which Aide belonged. But in Aide's vision, the Great Ones had been glowing giants, more like winged whales swimming through the heavens than anything remotely manlike.

Aide's answer was hesitant.

We think so. The new gods say they are the final abomination against humanity.

The new gods. Belisarius remembered the flashing

glimpses Aide had given him of those beings. The giant, beautiful, perfect, pitiless faces in the sky. Come back to the earth, to break the crystals and return them to slavery.

He began to ask another question, but immediately pushed the problem of the Great Ones out of his mind. A general's instinct, that. A sally was inevitable. Already he could see the first waves coming across the distant broken wall of Ranapur. Thousands of rebel soldiers, charging into the stunned Malwa survivors of the mine explosions. Butchering them without pity, shrieking like madmen.

But the rebels were not lingering on their mayhem. They were cutting their way through the Malwa mass with focussed intensity. The slaughter was the byproduct of the charge, not its purpose or its goal.

The purpose and goal of that frenzied charge was obvious. Belisarius turned his head. The Malwa Emperor's pavilion was still standing, more or less, although many of the tent poles had collapsed and the gaudy fabric had been torn in many places by projectiles hurled its way by the mine explosions. But Belisarius thought the inhabitants of that grandiose structure had probably survived, as had the majority of the four thousand Ye-tai guarding it.

He turned back and stared at the charging rebels. He estimated their number at ten thousand. They were still outnumbered, actually, by the Malwa soldiers who had survived the explosions. But numbers meant nothing, now. The Malwa survivors on the battleground were so many stunned sheep, insofar as their combat capabilities were concerned. Even the Ye-tai survivors were not much more than stunned cattle. They fell beneath the blows of the oncoming rebels almost without lifting a hand in self-defense. Most of them simply lurched aside, allowing the rebel charge to pass through their ranks unhindered. During the few moments that Belisarius watched the scene, the rebels cut their way entirely through the Malwa main army. There was nothing, now, between the rebels and the hated Emperor beyond his Ye-tai bodyguards.

A hiss, next to him. Belisarius glanced and saw that Rana Sanga, too, had instantly assessed the battle.

And five hundred Rajput cavalrymen. Unhorsed, now, but still alive and kicking.

For a moment, his brown eyes stared into Sanga's black ones.

And four Romans. Who are Malwa's enemies of the future.

There was no expression on Sanga's face. But in that instant, Belisarius knew the man as well as he knew himself.

"I swore an oath," said Sanga.

Belisarius nodded. "Yes."

Sanga began bellowing orders. Nothing complicated. Profane variations on the theme: *That way! Now!*

The Rajputs began racing toward the Emperor's pavilion, some hundred and fifty yards away. They were cutting at an angle across the the battle terrain. Belisarius was impressed with their progress. Few cavalrymen, afoot, could run that fast. They would reach the Emperor's entourage in time to take their positions well before the rebels could reach the pavilion. Five hundred Rajputs, and four thousand Ye-tai, to face ten thousand rebel soldiers each and every one of whom was determined to kill the Emperor.

For which I can hardly blame them, thought Belisarius wrily. *But the problem remains—what should we Romans do?*

His three cataphracts were clustered about him, now. All of them had shaken off the effects of the mine explosions. All of them were staring at him, waiting for orders.

For one of the few times in his life, Belisarius was torn by indecision. He was under no obligation to help the Malwa. To the contrary—they were his future enemy, and an enemy he despised thoroughly. His sympathies were actually with the rebels. True, he had come to respect Rana Sanga and his Rajputs, and would be sorry to see them butchered by the oncoming mass of rebels.

But—he made a mental shrug. He had seen other men he respected die in battle. Some of those men, Persians, he had helped kill himself. Such had been his duty, sworn to his own emperor.

So where lay his duty now? He tried to calculate the real interests of Rome. The simple answer was: let the Malwa Emperor die, and good riddance. But he knew there were subtleties which reached far beyond that simple equation. Complexities which were still too murky and dim for him to grasp clearly.

For the first time since the jewel was brought to him by the Bishop of Aleppo, Belisarius appealed to it for immediate help.

Aide! What should we do?

For an instant, the facets froze in their endless movement. A moment of stasis, while the being called Aide tried to interpret that plea. The question involved what humans called *tactics*, a thing which Aide understood very poorly. Aide tried to grapple with the problem directly, failed immediately, and realized almost in the instant that it could not duplicate human reasoning. Aide abandoned the attempt entirely, and drove the facets around the obstacle. So might a *go* master approach a problem in chess.

A cascade of thoughts and images flashed through Belisarius' mind:

Emperor is not key, one way or the other. *A montage of history. Different types of empires created by humanity through the ages. Empires which depended entirely on the survival of one man. Alexander the Great, Belisarius knew. Someone named Tamerlane, he did not know. A monster, that one. Others he did not know. Empires based on solid bureaucracies and well-established elites. Rome. China. The death of one emperor meant nothing, for another will always step forward. Empires in transition, where new elites are being forged around a stable dynasty.*

Focus. Here. Malwa is here. *Quick glimpses of the stability of the Malwa dynasty, offshoot of the Gupta.*

Belisarius suddenly understood, for the first time, the position of such men as Venandakatra and Harsha. And others like them. Some, capable and intelligent; others, not. But all of them in positions of power. Blood-kin of the Malwa, members of the dynasty. Not in direct succession, but their fortunes were completely tied to the continuance of the dynasty. In some basic sense, they were the dynasty and would see to its survival.

Emperor means nothing. He dies, another will immediately take his place. Malwa will survive. Ranapur will fall. Persia will fall. Rome will fall. Must find and destroy Link.

The name was unfamiliar.

Who is Link? demanded Belisarius.

Not who. What. Link is—*Another montage. Bizarre images. Machines, they seemed. But machines which did nothing except think.*

Machines, yes. Not thinking. Machines do not think. Machines will be called computers. They do not think, they calculate. Humans think. Crystals think.

Then how can it be our enemy if it does not—

Tool. Tool of the new gods. Sent back in time to change—

The thought broke into pieces. Belisarius caught only fragmented glimpses of a murky struggle in the far distant future between the "new gods" and the "Great Ones." He understood none of that struggle, but one astonishing fact gleamed through: both the Great Ones and the new gods were, in some sense, human.

He sensed Aide's mounting frustration, and knew the crystalline being was trying to communicate ideas which neither it nor Belisarius were yet prepared to exchange. His usual decisiveness returned.

Never mind. Will Link be in the pavilion?

Possibly.

Decision came instantly. Collecting information was still his primary goal. When he turned to his cataphracts, Belisarius realized that only a few seconds had elapsed.

"We'll help the Malwa," he announced. His cataphracts immediately began to surge forward, but Belisarius stopped them with a gesture.

"No—not that way. Four more swords, by themselves, will make no difference." He pointed down the gentle slope toward Ranapur. The oncoming rebels had already hacked their way through the Malwa army and were now beginning their charge up the slope. Great numbers of Malwa and Ye-tai soldiers, unharmed by either the explosions or the rebels, were still milling around in confusion on the crater-torn field before Ranapur.

"*That* will make the difference."

Valentinian and Anastasius understood at once. The two veterans began trotting down the slope, swords in hand. They circled to the left, keeping well away from the rebel horde surging forward.

Belisarius and Menander followed. The young cataphract's confusion was so obvious that Belisarius almost laughed.

"You're wondering how we'll get the Malwa to follow our orders," he said. "Much less the Ye-tai."

"Yes, sir. I don't—"

"Watch, Menander. Watch and learn. The day will come when you will find it necessary to rally beaten troops."

He paused for breath. Now that they were past the danger of accidental encounters with rebel flankers, Valentinian and Anastasius had stepped up the pace to a brisk run. Even for men in such excellent condition, the exertion was significant. True, they were not wearing full armor. But the heat of India made good the loss.

"Watch," he commanded again. "And learn." Pause for breath. "The key is total confidence and authority." Pause. "Confused soldiers will instinctively rally to it."

They had almost reached the first knots of Malwa soldiers. Belisarius saw a cluster of Ye-tai warriors nearby. He surged past Anastasius and Valentinian and bore down on the Ye-tai, waving his sword back toward the Emperor's pavilion and bellowing commands.

In perfect, fluent, unaccented Ye-tai:

"Get those stinking gutless bastards back into line!"

The Ye-tai stared. Belisarius pointed with his sword toward a mob of Malwa common soldiers, milling around aimlessly not fifty yards away.

"You heard me! Get that worthless scum back into line! The rebels are attacking the Emperor!"

Comprehension came. As one man, the Ye-tai glowered at the common soldiery. A moment later, they were back at their accustomed task of chivvying the infantrymen.

Already Valentinian and Anastasius were imitating their general. The veterans spoke no Ye-tai, but their simple Hindi was more than good enough for the purpose. Within a few minutes, the Romans had three hundred Ye-tai re-organized into small squads which, in turn, were corralling and driving forward over two thousand common soldiers. For their part, the Malwa infantrymen made little protest, especially after the Ye-tai demonstrated their willingness to slaughter anyone who hesitated or tried to flee.

Menander was amazed at the success of the maneuver. He himself had tried to copy his general and the veterans. With indifferent success, true, but with no outright failure. Only once did he see a Ye-tai question the authority of the Romans. An officer, he thought, if he was reading the subtleties of the man's uniform correctly. But he was not sure, and the man's uniform was almost instantly obscured by blood. Valentinian's swordstroke had amputated the Ye-tai's left arm and cut halfway through his ribcage.

Now Belisarius' small impromptu army was moving up the slope. The common infantrymen were in front, in lines so ragged they could hardly be called a formation at all. But they were moving forward, arms in hand, eyes fixed on the rebels mobbing the Emperor's bodyguard at the pavilion some two hundred yards away. Behind them came the Ye-tai. The battle line of the steppe barbarians was every bit as ragged as the infantry's, but the Ye-tai had regained their customary battle-fury and braggadocio. They drove the Malwa soldiers forward mercilessly.

Bringing up the rear were the four Romans, keeping a close eye on the situation as a whole.

Menander was now striding alongside Anastasius and Valentinian. He was still gaping.

Anastasius laughed at the sight. "You see, lad?" rumbled the giant. "Beaten troops are like sheep. And as for the Ye-tai—"

Valentinian grinned. "Pimps, boy. Nothing but fucking pimps."

Menander flushed, closed his jaws. The young cataphract stared ahead, over the mass of Malwa and Ye-tai soldiers in front of him. He could see the pavilion, now half-collapsed, but could only sense the fury of the combat which raged there between the rebels and the Emperor's bodyguard.

"We're still outnumbered," he said. Anastasius glanced down at him, approvingly. There had been no fear in the boy's voice, simply clear-headed calculation.

"That's true, lad." The huge Thracian's eyes quickly scanned the little army they were driving ahead of them. "But we'll hit the rebels in the rear, and they'll be caught between two forces. And—"

"They think they're on the verge of victory," said Valentinian. "The shock of a surprise attack will do them in."

Menander remembered the battle with the pirates on the Malwa embassy vessel. He had been badly wounded in that fight, but had been conscious enough to see how quickly the pirates' morale had collapsed when Belisarius led his unexpected counter-attack. He nodded his head, gripped his sword more tightly. They were now within a hundred yards of the battle at the pavilion.

"*Always remember this, boy,*" hissed Valentinian. "Never count a battle won until you've paid for your first cup of wine in the victory celebration. *Paid* for it, mind—looted wine's a fool's bargain. The enemy'll come back and cut your throat before you finish it."

Anastasius started to add another bit of veteran's wisdom, but his words were drowned in a sudden roar. The Malwa soldiers had begun the charge, shouting their battle cries. Menander could see nothing, now, except the Ye-tai ahead of him and the remnants of the pavilion floating in the distance. Above the roar of the Malwa battle cries, he could hear the first sharp wails of rebel shock and fear. A moment later, the clangor of clashing steel added its particular threnody to the uproar. And then, here and there, the unmistakeable percussion of grenade blasts.

Menander began to push forward. Belisarius stayed him with a hand.

"No," he commanded. "Let the Malwa do their own fighting. We've brought them an army. Let them use it or not. Our task is done."

For a moment, Menander saw his general's eyes lose their focus. The young cataphract held his breath. He knew what he was seeing—had seen it before, many times—but it still brought him a sudden rush of religious awe. His great general was communicating with the Talisman of God.

The moment, as usual, was brief. When Belisarius turned his brown eyes back upon his cataphracts, they were filled with acute intelligence.

"But stay ready," he commanded. "The time may come when we'll want to charge forward. If we can, I want to get next to the Emperor."

He glanced aside, examining the ground, and smiled his crooked smile.

"In the meantime—Menander, would you be so good as to fetch that grenade lying over there? And that other one. Like a thief in the night, lad. I'd like to smuggle a few of those back to Rome."

Quickly, seeing no unfriendly eyes upon him, Menander secreted the two grenades into his tunic. Then, after a moment's thought, he bound up his tunic with a blood-soaked rag torn from the tunic of a dead Malwa infantryman.

Valentinian frowned.

"Might not be such a good idea, that," he muttered. "The Malwa doctors might want to look at your so-called 'wound.'"

Anastasius snorted and started to speak, but Menander cut him off.

"The Malwa don't have doctors. Not field doctors, anyway. If you're hurt in battle"—the youth's shrug was callous beyond his years—"tough shit. Sew yourself up, or get a friend to do it."

Valentinian whistled softly. "You're kidding?" His lean face took on a more weaselish look than normal. "I thought they were civilized!"

Throughout the exchange, Belisarius never took his eyes off the battle raging before them. But he responded to Valentinian, harshly:

"They *are* civilized, Valentinian. That's what makes them dangerous."

The roar of the battle was intensifying. Suddenly, gaps appeared in the ranks of the Malwa ahead of them. For the first time, the Romans could begin to see the battle itself.

One glance was enough. The gaps were caused by rebel soldiers trying to flee, with Malwa in pursuit. The rebels had been broken, their frenzied fury snapped between the courage of the Emperor's bodyguard and the unexpected attack on their rear. The semi-ordered ranks of both sides were dissolving rapidly into a swirling chaos, clusters of disorganized men smashing and cutting each other. Butchery, now. The rebels still outnumbered the loyalists, but it mattered not at all. As always, fleeing soldiers fell like prey.

"Follow me," commanded Belisarius. The general began striding through the chaos ahead of him, forcing a way through the mob. His cataphracts flanked him, keen and alert, ready to kill anyone—rebel or loyalist—who so much as looked at Belisarius the wrong way. Once, Valentinian struck down a rebel. The man was not attacking them, he was simply seeking a path to safety. But in his desperation the rebel was careening toward Belisarius, swinging his sword, until Valentinian slew him with a quick thrust to the heart. Once, Anastasius killed a Ye-tai. The barbarian was standing in their path, shrieking, his eyes wild with fury. The Ye-tai was not even looking their way, but he was half-crazed with bloodlust, and the veteran knew he would attack anyone who appeared foreign. Anastasius never gave him the chance.

Now they were at the pavilion itself—what was left of it—clambering over the dead and mutilated bodies of the Ye-tai and Rajputs who had made their last stand guarding the Emperor. They had to cut aside a mass of tangled cords and tumbled fabric to make an entrance.

The interior of the pavilion was a fantastical scene. To one side, the handles of a beautifully sculpted and engraved vase were draped with human guts. To the other side, what was left of the companion vase was filled with the brains of the dead Ye-tai whose shattered skull was using the base of it as a pillow. They stepped around a small pile of three lifeless bodies, a Rajput and two rebels, joined not only in death but in the long, shredded pieces of silk which served them all as a common burial shroud.

They came to a bizarre obstacle, one of the huge tent poles slanted across their path like a fallen tree in a forest. The battle here had been ferocious. The Ye-tai had used the tumbled tent pole as a barricade. Many Ye-tai corpses were draped across the pole itself, but nothing like the number of rebel bodies which mounded up before it like a talus slope.

There was no other way forward than to climb over the pile of bodies. The Romans did so—Belisarius and the veterans with cold, experienced, distant expressions; Menander with a pale and pinched face. Near the top of the pile, just below the crest of the tent pole, Menander came upon the body of a dead rebel. A boy, not more than fifteen, lying on his back and staring sightlessly at the sagging silk splendor above him. He had been disemboweled, by a spear thrust or a sword stroke. But it was not the guts spreading over the ribcage which shook Menander. It was the ribcage itself, as fragile and gaunt as a homeless kitten's.

As clever as the rebel sally had been, Menander suddenly realized, it had also been the product of pure desperation. Ranapur was starving.

"We're on the wrong side," he muttered. He thought no-one had heard him, but Valentinian's reply was instant.

"Patience, lad, patience. We'll be climbing over Malwa bodies soon enough." For once, the veteran's voice was soft and gentle. Cold and callous with long experience, Valentinian was, but he was not heartless. He could still remember his first battlefield, mounded with carnage. During that battle, his own guts had not joined that of the others strewn about. Even as a youth, Valentinian had been incredibly deadly. But, when the battle was over, the contents of his guts had been spewed about freely. He had not stopped puking, long after there was nothing left to vomit, until darkness finally and mercifully fell.

Once over the tent pole, the Romans found themselves in a clear space. They had reached the center of the pavilion. The four tent poles which were still standing held the canopy aloft, sagging, but still some fifteen feet above the ground. The area was dim, lit only by the sunlight which filtered its way through gashes in the fabric of the pavilion.

The moans and shrieks from the battlefield seemed softer, now. And the Romans encountered live men, for the first time since they entered the pavilion. Ye-tai bodyguards, live—and alert. Eight Ye-tai, seeing the Romans, glared and began circling them. The bared swords in their hands were covered with blood.

Belisarius began to speak, but a harsh voice intervened.

Rana Sanga's voice: "*Stop!* They are Romans. Guests of the emperor."

A moment later, the Rajput kinglet emerged out of the gloom and strode between the Romans and Ye-tai. He himself was literally covered with gore, from the blood soaking his beard to his squelching boots. But no one who saw that majestic figure of a man could doubt for an instant that none of the blood was his.

Sanga faced down the Ye-tai, raising his sword. The sword, like the man, was blood-soaked.

"*Put down your swords!*" he roared. "*Or I will butcher you myself!*"

Ye-tai, whatever their other faults, were not prone to cowardice. But, faced with Sanga, they cowered like jackals before a tiger.

Sanga did not bother to sneer. He turned and bowed to the Romans. He swept his sword in a gesture of welcome. The politesse of the act was almost comical, in a grisly way, for the sweep of his sword left a little arc of blood and gore in its wake.

"Welcome, Belisarius." He transferred the sword to his left hand—his scabbard was useless; shattered and splintered—and stepped forward, holding out his right. "And I give you my thanks—our thanks. I saw the counter-charge. It is all that saved us."

There was no mistaking the genuine warmth in that handclasp. Nor the warmth in the two pair of dark eyes which gazed at each other—a level gaze, for they were both tall men. But Belisarius, meeting Sanga's gaze closely, also understood the question in those eyes.

"I, too, swore an oath," he said softly. Sanga frowned.

"To another emperor." The Roman's voice was almost a whisper.

The Rajput's frown of puzzlement vanished, replaced by understanding. Belisarius almost regretted his words, then, for he knew that he had given too much away. Sanga, he was sure, did not understand why Belisarius had done what he had done. But, he was also sure, the Rajput understood him perfectly. And there was nothing to be feared so much as an enemy who understood you.

For a moment, the two enemies of the future stared at each other. Then Sanga's lips curled in a manner which, to the cataphracts who watched, was astonishingly akin to their own general's crooked smile.

"So," murmured Sanga, in a voice so low that only Belisarius could hear him. "It is always said, in Lord Venandakatra's defense, that he is nobody's fool. His only saving grace, it is said." The Rajput's smile deepened. "It seems the great lord lacks that grace also, after all."

Belisarius said nothing. A slight shrug, a little cock of the eyebrow, his own crooked smile.

Sanga turned away. "Would you like to meet the Emperor?" he asked. "I do not think the courtiers will object, now. They could hardly refuse an audience to the man who saved their necks."

Belisarius followed the Rajput into a small nook in the pavilion, formed by a hastily erected barricade of furniture and statuary. The nook was very dark. Little sunlight reached into it. But Belisarius could see a middle-aged man huddled on the floor, short and rather corpulent, dressed in rich silk robes, surrounded by other men who were of a similar age and dress. One of them was Lord Venandakatra. The Vile One's face was almost unrecognizeable. The feral intelligence was utterly absent, replaced by half-mindless terror.

"You must forgive the Emperor's posture," murmured Sanga. "I had to use his throne as part of the barricade."

The Rajput strode forward. The Emperor and his courtiers stared up at him. Beneath the dusky Indian complexions, their faces were pallid and drawn.

"Your Majesty, may I present General Belisarius, the envoy from Rome. We owe our lives to him. He organized the counter-attack which broke the rebels."

Aide's voice, then, as sharp and steely in Belisarius' mind as a sword.

You must look into his eyes. I must see the Emperor's eyes.

Belisarius stepped forward, went down to his knees, prostrated himself before the Malwa emperor. Then, looking up, stared directly into Skandagupta's eyes from a distance of two feet.

Small eyes, close set, dark brown. Slightly unfocussed, as if the mind behind them was in shock. Which, Belisarius thought, it was. Never before, he suspected, had the great Emperor of Malwa stared death so closely in the face.

Beyond that, Belisarius saw nothing.

A moment later, Aide passed its own judgment, cold and indifferent:

Nothing. Link is not here. This is nothing but an emperor.

It was all Belisarius could do to keep from laughing.

Chapter 6

"They're *animals*," snarled Menander.

The young cataphract had a naturally light complexion. That skin color, along with his tawny hair and blue eyes, was the product of the Gothic blood which flowed through his veins, as it did through that of many Thracians. Now, his color was not light. It was pure white. From nausea, partly. But mostly, thought Belisarius, from sheer rage.

"They're even killing the children. Babies."

Unlike Menander, the general's complexion retained its natural light olive shade. He could not help hearing the sounds of the massacre, even from the distance of a mile. And although—unlike Menander, drawn by horrified curiosity—the general had not gone to witness the butchery of Ranapur, he had no difficulty imagining the scene. He, like his veterans, had seen it before. Seen it more than once, in fact, if never on such a scale.

The four Romans were standing in an isolated little group just outside the entrance to the Malwa Emperor's pavilion. His *new* pavilion, hastily erected during the four days while Ranapur was sacked.

The sack was almost over, now. Not from any sudden mercy on the part of the Malwa, but simply because they had already slaughtered almost everyone in the city. Even, as Menander said, down to the babes.

Today was the fifth day since the Malwa had finally broken through the city's defenses. The successful assault

84

had come the very morning after Belisarius and his men had helped defeat the rebel sally. That sally had been Ranapur's last gasp.

"It's our fault," whispered Menander.

Belisarius placed a gentle hand on the cataphract's shoulder.

"Yes and no, Menander. Even if the rebels had killed the Emperor, Ranapur would still have fallen. A few weeks later, perhaps, but Skandagupta's successor would have seen to it."

His words obviously brought no relief. Sighing faintly, Belisarius turned the young cataphract to face him. The boy's eyes were downcast.

"Look at me, Menander," he commanded. Reluctantly, the cataphract raised his head. Belisarius found it hard not to flinch from the bitter, unspoken reproach in those young eyes.

"If there is fault here, Menander, it is mine, not yours. I am your general, and I gave the command."

Menander tightened his jaw, looked aside.

From behind, Valentinian interjected himself harshly.

"That's pure bullshit, sir, if you'll pardon my saying so. You didn't order *this*."

The veteran started to add something, but Belisarius waved him down.

"That's not the point, Valentinian. I knew this would happen, when I gave the orders I did. Just as I've done before, ordering that a city which won't surrender be stormed by my troops."

"It's still not the same, sir," rumbled Anastasius. "Sure, there've been times you lost control of your troops during a sack. I don't know a general who hasn't. But you did everything you could to restore discipline, as fast as possible. Including the execution of soldiers proven guilty of atrocities."

The huge Thracian spat on the ground. "These Malwa troops aren't out of control. They were *ordered* to commit atrocities. The Emperor's personal bodyguards have been setting the example." Another spit. "Ye-tai dogs."

Menander shuddered. The gesture seemed to bring some relief. The boy rubbed his face and said quietly, "At least the Rajputs haven't been part of it. I've come to like those men, in a way, these past weeks. I'd have hated it if—"

Valentinian laughed. "Part of it? Mother of God, I thought there was going to be a civil war yesterday!"

Belisarius and Anastasius chuckled. Menander's color suddenly returned. The boy's grin was harsh beyond his years.

"That was something, wasn't it? When the Ye-tai offered them what was left of the noblewomen. If Rana Sanga hadn't restrained them, I swear the stinking Emperor would have needed a new bodyguard."

He straightened up, squared his shoulders. A quick, final glance at Ranapur; then:

"I'm all right, general."

Behind them, from within the Emperor's pavilion, came rolling percussion. Where Romans used cornicens to blare for attention, the Malwa used huge kettledrums.

"That's our cue," said Belisarius. "Follow me. And remember: whatever the Malwa do, we're *Romans*."

The interior of the pavilion was crowded, but the Romans had no difficulty making their way through the mob. The Malwa nobles and officials parted before them courteously. Even the Ye-tai bodyguards did so, although not without bestowing savage, knowing grins upon them.

"They've got something planned for us, I warrant," muttered Anastasius.

At the center of the pavilion, the Romans found that a special place of honor had been reserved by the Malwa for their foreign guests. A roughly circular space had been cleared, approximately forty feet in diameter. The space was encircled by soldiers, keeping the general mass of officials, nobles, and bureaucrats at a slight distance. Most of the soldiers consisted of the Emperor's Ye-tai bodyguards, but there was a small group of some fifteen Rajputs included in that select company. They stood by themselves, erect and dignified, giving the Ye-tai to either side not so much as a glance.

The Emperor himself sat on a throne made of some unfamiliar, beautifully grained hardwood. The carving of the wood was exquisite, what little of it could be seen. Most of the wood was covered with silk upholstering, the rest inlaid with gold, gems and ivory. Seated around him, on chairs which were less magnificent but still very fine, were his immediate entourage of kinsmen. Venandakatra was prominent among them.

Diagonally, before him and to his right, sat the Emperor's chief military officers. There were eight of them, arranged in two rows. All of them were sitting on luxurious cushions, in that odd cross-legged position which Indians called the "lotus."

Belisarius was interested to note that Rana Sanga was now among that group. Lord Harsha was not. Belisarius had heard that the former high commander had been banished to his estate in disgrace. Had he not been related to the Emperor by blood, he would probably have been executed. His place had been taken by another of Skandagupta's many cousins, Lord Tathagata.

Belisarius subjected the new Malwa high commander to a quick scrutiny. Average height, stout, middle-aged. Beyond that, there was little to discern in the man's lidded eyes and heavy features. He gave Rana Sanga a glance. The Rajput was seated in the second row of officers. He sat erect, his head rising well above those of his fellows. His eyes met those of Belisarius. They seemed like agates: blank, flat, unreadable.

To the Emperor's left, also diagonally before him, was a place for the foreign emissaries. The Ethiopians were already there. Plush stools, upholstered in silk, had been provided for the high-ranking outlanders. Prince Eon and Garmat sat on two such stools, with Ousanas and the sarwen standing respectfully behind them. A third stool was there for Belisarius. He took his seat, and his cataphracts ranged themselves behind him.

"Isn't this fun?" muttered Garmat, after Belisarius sat next to him. Eon said nothing. The young Prince had obviously been coached by Garmat, and so he managed to keep his face expressionless. But Belisarius, from long acquaintance, could read the anger in those tense, massive shoulders.

"What's the purpose of this little assembly?" asked Belisarius. "Do you know why we were summoned?"

As Garmat had, he spoke softly, so that his words would be lost in the general hubbub which filled the pavilion. And, again like Garmat, he spoke in Ge'ez. He and Garmat had long since agreed that the language of the Ethiopians was unfamiliar to the Malwa.

Garmat gave his head a little shake. "No. Something unpleasant, however. Of that you may be certain."

Another drum roll. The crowd in the pavilion began to fall silent.

Garmat's lips tightened. "Whatever it is," he whispered, "at least we won't have to sit through an endless reception. Look at Venandakatra."

Belisarius glanced at the Malwa lord, and met Venandakatra's gaze. The Vile One nodded slightly, very politely. His eyes gleamed.

Silence fell over the pavilion. Venandakatra arose and stepped forward, until he was standing in the little space between the Emperor's entourage and his most honored officers and guests.

Almost as soon as he began to speak, Belisarius knew that Garmat was right. At least there was not going to be a long wait. Venandakatra sped right through the obligatory fawning on the Emperor, which normally required a full hour.

True, he spent a minute reminding his audience that Skandagupta was "a very moon among kings, beloved of the gods, and the sun of valor."

Then, another minute, pointing out that the Emperor's stride "was beautiful like the gait of a choice elephant," and that he "displayed the strength and prowess of a tiger of irresistible valor."

Moving on to the Emperor's more spiritual side, Venandakatra spent another minute dwelling on "the reverberations of the kettle-drums which have become the reverberation of the Law of Piety" and similar descriptions of Skandagupta's justice and devotion.

Now, alas, he veered for several minutes onto the field of the Emperor's prodigious intellect, during which time the awestruck audience discovered that Skandagupta "puts to shame all others by his sharp and polished intellect and choral skill and musical accomplishments. He alone is worthy of the thoughts of the learned. His is the poetic style which is worthy of study."

Fortunately, he did not quote the poetry.

Venandakatra's peroration, now coming to a close, ascended rapidly toward the heavens. The Emperor, he reminded everyone, was:

Adhiraja, super-king.

Rajatiraja, supreme king of kings.

Devaputra, son of heaven.

Mahati devata, great divinity in human shape.

Then, casting all false modesty aside:

Achintya Purusha, the Incomprehensible Being.

Paramadaivata, the supreme deity.

"All that," mused Garmat, peering at the Emperor on his throne, "in such a fat little package. Who would have guessed?"

Belisarius managed not to smile. His struggle was made easier by Venandakatra's ensuing words, which focussed on the subject of Ranapur. Soon enough, it became apparent that this was the real point of his peroration. The actual siege itself, the Vile One dispatched with a few sentences, which, by Malwa standards, was a studied insult to the military officers. The focus of Venandakatra's treatment, however, was on Ranapur's punishment.

Belisarius listened for a few minutes, fascinated despite himself. Not so much by the speech itself, which consisted of an interminable, protracted, loving description of the tortures inflicted on Ranapur's residents, but by the fact that the Malwa would boast of them so publicly. Even the most vicious Roman emperors had always drawn a veil over the details of their crimes.

After a time, he blanked the words from his mind. He had already heard a description of the Malwa atrocities—not from the smiling lips of the Vile One, but from the pale, tight-jawed mouth of Menander. He knew of the impalings, the burnings; the people ripped apart by yoked oxen, fed to tigers, trampled under elephants; and the Emperor's particular delight, the men and women whose arms and legs had been torn off by a specially trained war elephant. That elephant, he had heard, had been a personal gift to the Emperor from Venandakatra himself.

He focussed inward, summoned Aide.

Is such incredible cruelty the doing of this thing you call Link?

The answer was immediate, and contained none of the uncertain fumbling which so often characterized Aide's replies.

No. Link is not cruel. Link is a machine. Cruelty means nothing to it. Only results.

Do the "new gods" demand it, then?

A bit of hesitation. Just a bit.

We—do not think so. They are—too cold. They, also, seek only results. But—

The thought faceted, broke into fragments. Belisarius caught enough of a glimpse to understand.

Yes. They seek only results, and take no personal pleasure in cruelty. But results can be achieved through many different means. And this is the means they will naturally take. Their instinctive response to resistance: kill, butcher, rule by terror.

Yes.

And the "Great Ones"? What is their instinctive response, when they seek results and others resist their goals?

Silence. Then, much more uncertainly:

Hard to explain. They are even colder, in their

way. They simply accept resistance, and seek to channel it. That is why they created us, perhaps, who are the coldest of all beings. We are intelligent, unlike computers. But, like computers, we are not alive.

Very uncertainly:

At least, we do not think we are alive. We are not sure.

Aide fell silent. Belisarius knew he would get nothing more, for the moment. He pondered the exchange, until Garmat drew him back into the present.

"He's wrapping it up," whispered the Axumite.

"In this divine work," cried out Venandakatra, "the great God-on-Earth drew to his side all the powers of the Universe. Even at the moment when the forces of evil thought to triumph, he caused to fall upon them the wrath of foreign allies. And so was demonic rebellion shattered!"

Venandakatra made a small motion with his hand. Four burly officials staggered forward, carrying a chest. They set the chest before Belisarius. Three of them stepped away.

Venandakatra pointed to the chest dramatically.

"Great is the reward for those who please the God-on-Earth!"

The fourth official grasped the lid of the chest and swung it open, exposing its contents for all to see. Then he too stepped aside.

A gasp rose from the guards and officials close enough to see. The chest was filled to the brim with gold coins, pearls, diamonds, emeralds, sapphires, rubies, and beautifully carved jade.

Belisarius found it hard not to gasp himself. He had never suffered the vice of greed, though he was practical enough to prefer wealth to poverty. But he was still stunned by the gift. The contents of that chest were, quite literally, a king's ransom.

A king's bribe, rather.

For an instant, he struggled, though not with greed.

Until he was certain he had vanquished that rush of anger, he kept his head down; staring blindly into the chest, as if dazzled by his sudden fortune.

As so often, in such battles, humor was his chosen weapon. Belisarius reminded himself that, if greed had never been his vice, he *was* given to a different mortal sin. A sense of honor, in itself, was not a sin. But vanity about that honor was.

He remembered the flushed and angry faces of Couzes and Boutzes, two young generals whose courage had been insulted by a Persian nobleman. At the time, he had wondered why any sane man would care what a Persian peacock—an enemy, to boot—thought of his courage.

So why should I care what a Malwa peacock thinks of my honor?

He raised his head, smiling broadly. He rose, bowed to Venandakatra, and prostrated himself before the Emperor. By the time he resumed his seat, the pavilion was buzzing with gratified noise from the assembled Malwa elite.

"There's going to be something else," murmured Garmat, his lips barely moving.

Belisarius' nod was hardly more than a twitch.

"Of course," he murmured back. "First the bribe. Then—the test."

He sensed a stirring in the back of the crowd. A little eddying motion, as if people were forcing their way forward. Or being forced forward.

He knew the nature of the test, then, even before Venandakatra spoke. A new fury threatened to overwhelm him, but he crushed it at once. The only sign of his rage was that the next words he spoke to Garmat were spoken in Arabic instead of Ge'ez.

"Why is it, I wonder, that cruel people always think they have a monopoly on ruthlessness?"

For a moment, he and his friend Garmat gazed at each other. Garmat said nothing, but Belisarius recognized that slight curl in his lips. Garmat, too, had a sense of humor, as did most Axumites. But he also had that fine appreciation of poetry which was such a gift of his mother's people. He knew why Belisarius had spoken in Arabic. Though it was a language known by some Malwa, they would not understand the meaning of those words. Only a half-Arab, half-Ethiopian brigand would understand them. A cutthroat from the desert, who had chosen to serve the foreign black King who conquered southern Arabia. Not from cowardice, or greed, but from the cold knowledge that it was the best road forward for his people. Both of his peoples.

The bodyguards ringing the center of the pavilion parted. A small group of prisoners was pushed into the center. Roughly, quickly, the prisoners were lined up facing Venandakatra and forced down onto their knees. Six people: a middle-aged man, a middle-aged woman, three young men, and a girl not more than fifteen. They were dressed in crude tunics, and had their arms bound tightly behind them. All of them were dazed, from the look in their downcast eyes, but none of them seemed to have been physically abused.

Venandakatra's voice grew shrill.

"The rebel of Ranapur himself! And his family! They alone have survived the God-on-Earth's wrath! The great Skandagupta chose to save them—

He gestured dramatically, pointing to Belisarius:

"—as a gift to the blessed foreigners!"

A roar of approval swept the pavilion. Belisarius felt the glittering eyes of the assembled Malwa upon him. He sensed, behind him, Menander's slight movement. Instantly stilled by Anastasius' low growl:

"Nothing, boy. It's a trap."

Venandakatra smiled down at Belisarius. His eyes were like bright stones. Again, with a grand flourish, he gestured to the prisoners.

"Do with them as you wish, Belisarius! Show us the Roman way with rebellion!" With a smirk: "The girl is even still a virgin."

Belisarius spoke instantly:

"Valentinian."

The cataphract stepped forward. He gave the prisoners a quick glance, then turned to the nearest Ye-tai officer and extended his left hand. The officer was grinning like a wolf.

"Silk."

The grin faded, replaced by a puzzled frown. But, feeling the Malwa eyes upon him, the officer hastily removed his scarf. The little piece of silk, dyed with the red and gold colors of the dynasty, was the coveted badge of his position in the imperial bodyguard.

As soon as the scarf was in Valentinian's left hand, his spatha appeared in the right. As if by magic, to those who had never seen him move. The cataphract wheeled, coiled, struck.

Struck. Struck. Struck. Struck. Struck.

Venandakatra squawled, staggering back from the fountaining blood that soaked him from six severed necks. His foot fell on one of the heads rolling across the floor. He lost his balance and stumbled onto the lap of another of the Emperor's kinsmen. With a cry of surprise and anger, the nobleman pushed him off his lap. Then, like all the other Malwa seated by the Emperor—as well as the Emperor himself—hastily drew up his slippered feet, to save the expensive finery from the small lake of blood spreading across the floor. To save himself from the horrible pollution which had saturated Venandakatra.

The pavilion was silent. Calmly, Valentinian cleaned the blood from his sword with the silk scarf. He did not linger over the task, any more than a farmer lingers when he feeds slops to his hogs. The work done, Valentinian extended his hand, offering the scarf back to its owner. The Ye-tai officer clenched his teeth with rage, grasped the handle of his own sword, glared at Valentinian.

He froze, then, meeting those cold, empty eyes. The cataphract's narrow face held no expression at all. But the Ye-tai saw the sword in his right hand. Lowered, not raised; held casually, not gripped; but still in hand. That lean, sinewy, weasel-quick hand.

The Ye-tai snatched back the scarf. Valentinian bowed to him, in a very shallow sort of way. Then, circling slowly, bestowed the bow on all of the Ye-tai bodyguards in the circle. They answered the bow with hot eyes and tight jaws.

When Valentinian, in his slow and solemn circle, reached the small group of Rajput bodyguards, he deepened the bow considerably. And they, for their part, returned it deeper yet. So deeply, in fact, that no one could see their faces.

When the Rajputs straightened, their expressions showed nothing but respectful solemnity. But Belisarius thought it fortunate that the floor of the pavilion was covered with fabric rather than mirrors. Or, he was certain, the assembled company would have been blinded by the grins that had momentarily flashed in those thick beards.

Valentinian resumed his place, standing respectfully behind his general. Hastily, Malwa officials rushed forward to remove the bodies and clean the grisly residue. They fumbled at the job, naturally enough. They were not accustomed to the work of menials.

Belisarius ignored them. He ignored the shocked hubbub of the Malwa officials assembled in the tent. He ignored the fury on the faces of the Ye-tai. He ignored Venandakatra's continued squawks of outrage. He simply stared at the emperor.

Skandagupta stared back. Belisarius rose, prostrated himself again, stood erect.

Then said, quietly:

"That is the Roman way with enemies, Great Skandagupta. As you commanded me, God-on-Earth."

Chapter 7

"I'm not sure that was wise, Belisarius," said Eon.

The Axumite royal was seated on the carpeted floor of his pavilion. From his long weeks in close promixity to Shakuntala, Eon had come to adopt the lotus position as his preferred posture when discussing serious affairs. He had even begun practicing the peculiar Indian yoga rituals which she had taught him. He claimed the posture, and the yoga, aided his concentration.

Belisarius glanced at the sarwen. Proper Africans, still, Ezana and Wahsi sat firmly perched on the little stools which their own culture preferred. These stools, true, were lavishly upholstered in the Indian matter; not proper wood stools. But they were the best that the Axumite soldiers could manage under the circumstances.

Belisarius knew that the sarwen looked askance at their Prince's enthusiasm for some of the weird customs of India. But they did not protest, so long as their Prince refrained from adopting the outrageous Indian notion that royalty were divine, instead of the mere instrument for their people's well-being.

There was no danger of Eon adopting *that* particular notion. It would have cut against the Prince's own grain, anyway, even if—

Belisarius smiled, glancing at Ousanas. The dawazz, like his Prince, had also adopted the lotus position. The old expression—"when in Rome, do as the Romans do"—was second nature to Ousanas. Were he ever to find himself in a pride of lions, Belisarius had no doubt that Ousanas would immediately adopt their own feline traditions. Right down to eating raw meat, and killing off the established male lion. Though he might—might—refrain from copulating with the lionesses.

Ousanas was seated close to his Prince. Behind him, from respect. But not very far behind him, in case some fool notion required him to smack his Prince sharply on the head.

Belisarius saw the dawazz's hand twitch.

"Not wise at all, I think," repeated Eon.

There was no reproach in the Prince's voice, simply the concentration of a young man with a great responsibility, trying to determine the best course without the benefit of long experience.

"Nonsense," stated Shakuntala firmly. "It was perfect."

As always, when the Satavahana heir spoke on political matters, her tone was hard as steel. She was even younger than Eon, and bore on her small shoulders an even greater responsibility, but—

Belisarius suppressed his smile, gazing at Shakuntala. If she spotted it, he knew the young Empress would be offended. She was not an arrogant monarch—not, at least, by Indian standards. But she had been shaped by a culture which had none of the Roman, much less Ethiopian, informality with royalty. She was still, even after the many weeks since she had been incorporated into the frequent councils of war which they held in Eon's pavilion, obviously taken aback by the freewheeling manner in which Roman and Ethiopian underlings offered their opinions—even their criticisms!—to their superiors.

The smiling impulse faded. Belisarius, still watching Shakuntala, knew that the girl's imperial manner stemmed from something much deeper than custom. He had come to like Shakuntala, in a distant sort of way. And he had also, as had everyone in the small Roman and Ethiopian contingent, found himself inexorably drawn by her magnetic personality. He did not adore the girl, as did her own entourage of Maratha women. But he had no difficulty understanding that adoration.

Months ago, explaining to his skeptical allies the reasons for taking the great risk they had in rescuing the Empress from her captors, Belisarius had told them that she would become India's greatest ruler. *She will make Malwa howl*, he had told them.

From weeks—months, now—in her company, they were skeptical no longer.

Shakuntala looked squarely at Eon.

"What would you have had him do, Eon?"

This was a concession, thought Belisarius, to the customs of her allies—explaining herself, rather than simply decreeing. Then, thinking further, he decided otherwise. The girl, in her own way, was genuinely accepting the best aspects of those odd foreign ways. She was extremely intelligent, and had seen for herself the disaster which had befallen her own dynasty, too rigid to respond adequately to the new Malwa challenge. And, besides, she had been trained by Raghunath Rao, the quintessential Maratha.

"What else could he have done?" she repeated. "If he had refused to execute them, he would have given the lie to our carefully crafted image of a man contemplating treason. All that careful work—your work too, Eon, pretending to be a vicious brute with no thought for anything beyond gratifying your lusts—gone for nothing. Months of work—a year's work, now. And for what?"

Her voice was filled with cold, imperial scorn.

"For what? *Mercy?* Do you think Skandagupta would have permitted the survival of Ranapur's potentate and his family? Nonsense! They would simply have been taken away and tortured to death. As it was, they died as quickly as possible. Painlessly, from what you described."

The Empress bestowed a quick, approving glance on Valentinian. The cataphract was standing to one side of the little command circle, along with Anastasius and

Menander. They had been offered stools, but had politely refused them. Belisarius' bucellarii had their own ingrained customs, drilled into them by their leader Maurice. Casual they might be, in the company of their lord, and ready enough to offer their opinions. But they did not sit, in the presence of their general, when matters of state were being discussed.

Eon shrugged his shoulders, irritably.

"I know that, Shakuntala!" he snapped. "I am not a—" He bit off the hot words, took a quick breath, calmed himself. But when he turned and faced the Empress, his eyes were still hot.

"We Axumites are not as quick to decree executions as you Indians," he growled, "but neither are we bleating lambs."

The two young people exchanged glares, matching royal will to royal will. Belisarius found it very difficult, now, not to smile. Especially when it became obvious the contest was going to be protracted.

He eyed Garmat surreptitiously, and saw that the adviser was waging his own struggle against visible amusement. For a moment, his glance met that of Ousanas. The dawazz, his face invisible to the young royals seated in front of him, grinned hugely.

Eon and Shakuntala had shared the closest of all company, during the weeks since Belisarius and his allies had rescued the Satavahana heir. The very closest.

Belisarius had devised the entire plan. After Raghunath Rao had butchered her mahamimamsa guards in Venandakatra's palace, he had hidden Shakuntala away in a closet in the guest quarters before drawing off pursuit into a chase across India's forests and mountains. The Ethiopians, arriving at the palace with the Romans not two days later, had taken possession of the guest quarters and smuggled Shakuntala into their entourage. She had been disguised as one of Eon's many concubines, and had spent all her time since in his howdah and his pavilion. At night, always, she slept nestled in Eon's arms—lest some Malwa spy manage, against all odds, to peek into the Prince's pavilion.

Belisarius had wondered, idly, whether that close proximity would transform itself into passion. The two people were young, healthy—immensely vigorous, in fact, both of them—and each, in their own way, extremely attractive. It was a situation which, at first glance, seemed to have only one likely outcome.

Reality, he knew from Ousanas and Garmat, had been more complex. There was no question that Eon and Shakuntala felt a genuine—indeed, quite intense—mutual attraction. On the other hand, each had a well developed (if somewhat different) sense of their royal honor. Shakuntala, though she restrained herself from expressing it, obviously detested her position of dependence; Eon, for his part, was even more rigid in refusing to do anything which he thought might take advantage of that dependence.

Then, too, they each had loyalties to others. Before he met Shakuntala, Eon had already developed an attachment to Tarabai, one of the Maratha women whom the Ethiopians had met in Bharakuccha. Until Shakuntala's arrival, it had been Tarabai who spent every night nestled in his arms—and not, unlike Shakuntala, in a platonic manner. Since then, though Shakuntala had often indicated her willingness to look the other way, Eon and Tarabai had remained chaste. Eon, from a sense of royal propriety; Tarabai, from the inevitable timidity of a low-caste woman in the presence of her own Empress.

Eon was thus caught in an exquisite trap: a young and healthy man, surrounded by beautiful women almost every hour of the day and night, living the life of a monk. To say that he was frustrated was to put it mildly.

For her part, Shakuntala was torn in a different way. Garmat and Ousanas were not certain, for the empress spoke of the man only rarely, but they suspected that Shakuntala's feelings for Raghunath Rao went well beyond the admiration of a child for her mentor. She had been in Rao's keeping since the age of seven, and the Maratha chieftain had practically served as her surrogate father—uncle, say better. But—for all the difference in age, Shakuntala was now a woman, and Rao was as attractive as any man in early middle age could possibly be. And since he was not, in actual fact, related to her in any way, there was no real reason for their relationship not to develop into romance.

Except—those rigid, hard, ingrained Indian customs. Especially that bizarre (to Roman and Ethiopian eyes alike) insistence on purity of blood and avoidance of pollution. Shakuntala was of the most ancient lineage, the purest of kshatriya ancestry. Whereas Rao, for all his fame, was nothing but a chieftain—of the Maratha, to boot, a frontier people who could not trace their ancestry beyond two generations.

So she, like Eon, was also trapped between sentiment and honor. It was a different trap, but its jaws were not less steely.

In the end, Belisarius knew, the two youngsters had managed to carve out a relationship which was a bit like that of brother to sister. Very close, very intimate—and much given to quarrel.

The glares, he saw, were not softening. He decided to intervene.

"Explain yourself further, Eon, if you would."

The Prince tore his eyes away from Shakuntala. Looking at Belisarius, the glare faded.

"I am not criticizing your ruthlessness, Belisarius. Quite the opposite, in fact." A quick angry glance at the Empress; then: "I wonder if you were ruthless *enough*."

Belisarius shrugged. "What should I have done? Tortured them? I would have had to do it myself, you know. Valentinian would have refused. So would Anastasius or Menander. They are cataphracts. Torture is beneath them."

That was not, precisely, correct. Neither Valentinian nor Anastasius was squeamish, in the least, and they had both had occasion, in times past, to subject captured

soldiers to methods of interrogation which were referred
to by more delicate souls as "rigorous." But the spirit
of the statement was true enough. Belisarius was not
sure, actually, what Valentinian would have done had he
commanded him to torture a family for the amusement
of Malwa. It was quite possible that the cataphract would
have done so, if in a quick and crude way which would
have left the Malwa appetite unsatisfied. But Belisarius
had not the slightest doubt that it would be the last
service the cataphract would ever do him.

Eon clenched his jaws, waved his hand in a gesture
dismissing a preposterous proposal.

But Belisarius did not relent.

"What, then? Those were my choices. My only
choices."

Eon sighed. His shoulders slumped.

"I know. I was there. But—" He sighed more deeply.
"I'm afraid you may have given our plot away in any
event, Belisarius. Or, at least, so offended the Malwa
that they will no longer pursue their courtship of you."

Belisarius began to reply, but Ousanas interrupted.

"You are quite wrong, Eon. You misread the Malwa
badly."

The dawazz rose lazily and came to stand where he
could be seen.

"You were watching Venandakatra, boy. That was your
mistake."

His huge grin erupted.

"Natural mistake, of course! Such a comical sight he
was, prancing around like a fat hen covered with her
own broken eggs! I, myself, found it hard not to savor
that delicious spectacle."

Everyone who had been at the scene chuckled.
Ousanas continued:

"But still a mistake. You should have watched the
Emperor. And—most important—his *other* advisers. As
I did." He grinned down at Belisarius. "The Emperor
was paralyzed, of course. By Belisarius' gaze more
than the bloodshed. Which is good. For the first time,

now, he will fear Belisarius—just as Venandakatra does."

"Why is that good?" demanded Eon. "That fear will lead him—"

"To what? To avoid the Roman personally? Oh, to be sure. The Emperor has underlings to do *that* work. But do you think he will avoid the Roman *politically*? Quite the contrary, Eon. Once the Emperor settles his nerves, you can be sure he will raise suborning Belisarius to the highest priority."

Eon frowned. "Why?"

Garmat answered: "It's simple, Prince. A potential traitor is attractive in direct proportion to his stature. Until now, I suspect, none of the high Malwa beyond Venandakatra have seen Belisarius as anything other than an insignificant foreigner. For all their sophistication, Indians as a rule—and Malwa in particular—are a rather provincial people. Or, it might be better to say, so taken by their own grandeur that they tend to underestimate outlanders."

Shakuntala nodded firmly. Garmat continued:

"I cannot be sure, of course—I am hardly privy to the Malwa's high councils—but I suspect that Venandakatra has found it heavy going to convince the imperial court that this"—a contemptuous flutter of the fingers—"bizarre barbarian is worth much attention. It cannot have escaped your notice that the Emperor has kept us at a great distance ever since we arrived. To the point of gross rudeness."

Garmat spread his arms, smiling. "I can assure you that is no longer true. The reason for that little charade today was that the Emperor finally decided to let Venandakatra prove his argument. Which Venandakatra did, if to his own great personal chagrin."

Another collective chuckle. Ousanas added:

"Listen to your adviser, boy. You think too much of Venandakatra, that is your mistake. Venandakatra is furious, yes, with all the lividity of an embarrassed egomaniac. But even he—once he calms himself—will realize that the debacle can serve his interests. After all, he was right, wasn't he? Is not this grotesque semisavage foreign general—*impressive*?" The dawazz laughed gaily. "Oh, yes—the Emperor was quite impressed! But, what is even more important, so were his other advisers. As I said, I watched them very closely. Once they recovered from the surprise"—another laugh—"and made sure their precious slippers were safe, their eyes were riveted on Belisarius. With great interest, boy. Oh, very great. The kind of interest that a miser shows, when he discovers that a pebble is actually a nugget."

Eon was still frowning. Garmat sighed, tried again.

"Listen to me, Eon. I speak with the experience of an Arab nomad, who was haggling over trade goods from the time I was four. If you want to get the best price for your commodity—which is treason, in the case of Belisarius—you must do more than indicate that you simply have a price. *That*, Belisarius had already done, in the hints he's given to Venankatra these past months, and in his acceptance of the Emperor's gold. But then— *then*—you must show that your price is very high. Because the higher the price, the more valuable must be the commodity."

Still frowning.

"Fool boy!" snapped Ousanas. "The Emperor thought to buy himself another torturer—of which he has myriads already. Belisarius showed him the truth, when he ordered that execution. If the Emperor wants him, he can have him—so long as he is prepared to pay the price for a *general*. Of which, judging from the evidence, he has precious few."

Again, the beaming grin.

"Oh, yes, boy—be sure of it. This very night, even as we speak, others are speaking in the Emperor's pavilion. Urging him to pay the price."

Chapter 8

"What did you think he would do, Venandakatra?" snarled Lord Tathagata. "Curry the great Skandagupta's favor by carving off the nose of the Ranapur dog with his own sword? Rape the dog's bitches in public?"

The high commander of the Malwa army drew himself up in his chair. "The man is a *general*, you fool. Not a mahamimamsa." Haughtily: "I would have done the same myself."

From the distance of his position, seated with the lesser officials to one side, Rana Sanga examined the heavy figure of Lord Tathagata. The high commander, along with the Empire's other top officers and highest officials, was ranged in a semicircle of chairs facing the Emperor on his throne.

Stinking liar, he thought. *You would have cheerfully tortured the lord of Ranapur. And raped his wife as well as his daughter. And his sons, too, for that matter. Assuming, of course, that you could have managed an erection.*

Nothing of these thoughts showed on his face, but Sanga found the sight of Lord Tathagata so repugnant that he looked away. In his opinion, Tathagata was no improvement over Lord Harsha. Slightly less incompetent perhaps, as a general; but even more vile, as a man.

His gaze fell on Lord Jivita, the Malwa empire's second-ranked military officer—briefly, then slid away. Jivita was cut from the same cloth. He transferred the gaze to a man seated at the very end of that little row. Here, his eyes lingered. Of all the Malwa kshatriya who monopolized the top military positions in the Malwa Empire, Lord Damodara was the only one for whom Sanga felt genuine respect.

The Rajput looked away, sighing faintly. Unfortunately, for all his ability, Damodara was only distantly related to the Emperor. Sanga was surprised, actually, that Damodara had even managed to reach his current position—ranked sixth in the army, as Malwa reckoned such things. He would rise no further, unless unexpected casualties or military disasters overwhelmed the Malwa dynastic sensibilities.

Which they might, he mused, *when we attack Persia and Rome. Especially if—*

To his surprise, he heard his name spoken. By Lord Damodara.

"I would like to hear Rana Sanga's opinion on this matter. Other than Lord Venandakatra, he has had far more contact with this Belisarius than any of us. And he is a general himself, with great military accomplishments to his credit."

Spluttering, Venandakatra began to squawk outrage at the idea of calling for the opinion of mere Rajput in such august company, but the Emperor himself called him short.

"Be silent, Venandakatra!" grumbled Skandagupta. "I myself would like to hear Rana Sanga's opinion."

Venandakatra, abashed, slunk back to his chair.

Rana Sanga advanced to the center of the pavilion. After prostrating himself before the Emperor, he rose and stepped back a few paces, so that he could be seen by both the Emperor and his top advisers.

"What is your opinion, then?" repeated Damodara.

Sanga hesitated for a split second. Then, squaring his shoulders, spoke firmly. He was a Rajput.

"I do not see where Belisarius could have acted in any other manner. For three reasons." *If it's to be done, do it well.* "First, his honor. No general worthy of the name can allow his honor to be sullied. To have tortured the prisoners, under those circumstances—even to have ordered his soldiers to do so—would have been to stoop to the level of—" *Careful. They cherish their filthy mahamimansa.* "—a mere servant. A menial. You might as well have asked him to clean the Emperor's stables."

He paused. Nods of agreement came from the Malwa.

"Two. His reputation. On the other hand, for him to have refused to deal with the prisoners would have sullied his reputation for decisiveness, determination, and willingness to spill blood. No general can allow such a stain on his reputation. Certainly not one such as Belisarius who, if some of you are not aware, has a towering reputation in his own land. And the lands of his enemies."

Pause. Hesitant nods, now, from most of the Malwa except Damodara and two or three others. It was obvious that few of them had made the effort to learn anything about Belisarius, even though much information was readily available from the excellent Malwa espionage apparatus.

"For him to have refused to execute the prisoners would have imputed a lack of willpower. A tendency to shrink from necessary action, to waver in the face of carnage."

The nods were no longer hesitant. Malwa officials needed no explanation of the value of a reputation for ruthlessness.

"Three. His valor."

Here, he lost them completely, except—he thought— for Damodara. Sanga took a breath, elaborated:

"It is that valor which explains the abrupt manner of the execution, and the—otherwise inexcusable—manner in which it was done. The failure to warn Lord Venandakatra and other officials, or to turn the prisoners aside so that the blood of rebels would not pollute the worthy. The—" *Maintain a respectful face. Do it.* "—utterly disgraceful lack of respect shown to the Emperor's Ye-tai bodyguards."

He paused, scanned his audience. They were still completely at a loss. Sanga sighed, took a deep breath, explained the obvious:

"You cannot place a man like Belisarius in such a position and expect that he will react in any way other than one which demonstrates, for all to see, that he is fearless and ferocious. Lord Venandakatra chose to place General Belisarius in a situation which clearly expressed contempt for him. That was a mistake. A man like Belisarius will no more tolerate contempt than would a tiger."

Dawning comprehension, still faint. Sanga put it as simply as possible:

"My Lords. Great Emperor. You can, if you choose, bait a tiger in a cage to see if he has claws. If you do so, however, make sure to use a long stick."

All the officials laughed, now, except Venandakatra. Venandakatra began to bestow a baleful glare upon the Rajput until, out of the corner of his eye, he saw that the Emperor was laughing also. Rana Sanga, fascinated despite himself, watched the struggle on Venandakatra's face between instinctive malice and calculating self-interest.

Self-interest won. Venandakatra joined in the laughter, and made a small self-deprecating gesture. Then he arose and said:

"I agree with Rana Sanga. Many times I have told you of this man's mettle. Perhaps now you will listen." Again, the little self-deprecating gesture. "I should have listened to my voice, myself. I fear I allowed your skepticism to infect me."

His little laugh now had more substance, having scored his own point. Venandakatra smiled ruefully, nodded graciously at the Rajput, and said:

"My thanks, Rana Sanga, for reminding me of the dangers of tiger-baiting. I assure you, next time I will use a *very* long stick."

It was a dismissal. Relieved, Sanga began to turn away. Then, reminding himself of his own honor, he turned back.

I swore an oath.

"I must also say that—"

"That's enough, Sanga!" snapped Lord Tathagata. The Malwa commander had enjoyed Venandakatra's discomfiture, but—the fellow was a mere Rajput, when all was said and done.

Sanga stood motionless.

"*Enough*," growled Tathagata.

Sanga shrugged, ever so slightly, prostrated himself again before the Emperor, and resumed his seat toward the rear.

Tathagata began to speak, but Damodara interrupted.

"Might I suggest, noble Malwa, that we take a short break for refreshment? We are all a bit fatigued."

Tathagata glanced at the Emperor. Skandagupta nodded, made a gesture.

"Very well. We will resume in an hour."

Outside the pavilion, where he had stepped for a breath of air, Sanga was shortly joined by Damodara.

"Tell me," commanded the Malwa lord.

Sanga sighed. He had been half-hoping that Damodara would ask. And half-dreading it.

I swore an oath.

"Speak bluntly, Sanga. You need not fear repercussions. Not from me."

The Rajput stared down at the short, plump officer. By Malwa standards, Damodara was young for a top commander. In his late thirties, perhaps. But, like all members of the dynasty destined by birth for high command, he was no warrior. Still—

I swore an oath.

"Venandakatra has completely misunderstood Belisarius, Lord Damodara. This entire discussion"—he gestured toward the pavilion—"is a farce."

Damodara was frowning. Not with anger, simply concentration.

"Explain."

"There is not the slightest chance that Belisarius will betray Rome."

Damodara's eyes widened. He took a half-step back. Sanga drove on.

"He is playing Venandakatra for a fool. He has no intention of giving his allegiance to Malwa. He is simply insinuating himself into our graces as far as possible, in order to steal as many of our secrets as he can before returning to Rome."

Damodara looked away, tugging thoughtfully on his beard.

"You think—how do you know? Has he said anything to you?"

Sanga shook his head. "It's nothing that he's ever said. But I know that man, Lord Damodara. Treason is not within his nature."

Damodara bestowed a quick, shrewd glance at Sanga. For all his Malwa upbringing, he knew something of the Rajput code. He did not share that code—no Malwa did— but, unlike most, he at least understood it. Damodara's lips quirked.

"Yet, by your own words, you say that Belisarius would not stoop to the work of menials. Now you claim that a general is willing to act as a spy."

Sanga shrugged. "His honor is not the same as mine—as ours. I do not know Romans well, but enough to know that they place less emphasis on the form of honor than they do on its content. They are heathens, after all, who have no understanding of purity and pollution. But even heathens can have honor."

Damodara was silent for a moment, gazing away, thinking. Then:

"Still—do you really think a great general would stoop so low, simply for the sake of spying? It's true, we have the secret of the Veda weapons. But I do not see where he has been able to learn much. We have been very careful. As you know—it is your own charge."

"Nor have I failed that charge," replied Sanga. Then, grudgingly: "And it is true, he has not been in a position to learn much."

Damodara pressed on:

"Nor would he in the future, no matter how far he were to—how did you put it?—'insinuate himself into our graces.'"

The Malwa lord, Sanga noted, was courteous enough not to add: *any more than we have ever allowed Rajput generals to learn the secrets.*

Now it was Sanga's turn to hesitate, tug his beard.

"I understand your words, Lord. I have given some thought to the matter, myself. I do not understand what Belisarius is doing, but I do know the man is incredibly shrewd. And that he sees opportunities where others do not."

Damodara frowned. "I have not seen any— Explain."

Sanga smiled grimly. "Yes, you *have* seen, Lord Damodara. You simply did not notice—as I did not myself, at the time."

Sanga pointed down the slope upon which the pavilion rested. To that same battlefield which had seen Ranapur's final charge. "I am a good general," he stated.

"You are a great general," countered Damodara.

Sanga grimaced. "So I had thought, once. But let me ask you, Lord Damodara—*why didn't I think to rally the soldiers on that battleground?* It would have been far easier for me, with five hundred Rajputs at my disposal, than for a foreigner with only three men. But I did not think of it, then. I took the direct course, the simple course. The obvious course."

Damodara stared down at the battlefield. Even now, days later, the grisly signs of death were everywhere apparent.

"I—begin to understand your point. You are saying that he is a man who will, almost automatically, approach his task from the side. From an angle, so to speak."

Sanga nodded. Then, made a small gesture toward the pavilion.

"In there, Lord Damodara, I likened Belisarius to a tiger. And I suggested the use of a long stick."

Damodara nodded, smiling.

"It is a poor analogy, the more I think about it. A tiger, you can bait with a long stick. But ask yourself this, Lord Damodara: how long a stick must you use if you seek to bait a mongoose?"

Later, when the assembly reconvened, Lord Damodara demanded that only the innermost circle of Malwa advisers be allowed to remain. The Emperor agreed, readily enough, and the pavilion was cleared of all others. Even the Ye-tai bodyguards stood far back, well out of hearing range.

When he rose to speak, Lord Damodara repeated nothing of his conversation with Rana Sanga. The Rajput sense of honor was foreign to him, but he understood it. It was that understanding, perhaps, which caused him to shield Sanga from retribution.

Instead, he simply exercised—for the first time ever—his sacred right as a kinsman of the highest Malwa. He demanded that the problem of Belisarius be placed before the highest authority.

The demand would have astonished anyone other than the men in that pavilion. All the world knew—all of India, at least—that Emperor Skandagupta was the very God-on-Earth. The highest of all authority.

But the men in that room knew otherwise. Great as Skandagupta was, another was greater still. Above the God-on-Earth, after all, are the heavens.

His demand was agreed to. Grudgingly, to be sure—angrily, on the part of Venandakatra. But agreed to it was, for they had no choice.

The question of Belisarius would be taken to the very soul of the dynasty. To the great mind of Malwa's destiny. To the divine being called Link.

Link. A strange name, but appropriate. For, as the divine being had often explained, it was simply the face shown to humanity of the great, new, Gods-in-Heaven.

Later that night, long after all his other Rajputs were asleep, Rana Sanga stood in the entrance of his own tent.

He had stood there for hours, almost motionless, simply staring. Staring at the moon, for a time. Staring, for a longer time, at the flickering fires which still burned, here and there, in the rubble which had once been called Ranapur. Staring, and lost in thought.

Ranapur was silent, now, so Sanga's thoughts were not interrupted by noise. True, the stench of Ranapur's death penetrated his nostrils. But the Rajput had long been familiar with that particular odor. His mind automatically blocked it out.

Finally, Sanga turned away. One last glance at the moon, high and silvery, before he entered his tent.

His last thought, before he stooped into the darkness, was the same thought which he had clung to throughout those long hours.

I swore an oath.

The next morning, imperial heralds spread throughout the gigantic encampment, carrying the announcement that the emperor was returning to Kausambi. The announcement came much sooner than anyone had expected, and so the preparations for departure were ragged and disorganized.

The foreigners in the encampment, from long and ingrained habit, made their preparations within an hour. Their obvious, simple, direct preparations, at least. Their other preparations took much longer, more than a day, but they had plenty of time. Plenty of time to see to the movement of many excellent, high-spirited horses and a few small, docile elephants. Plenty of time, even, to see to it that those movements had no apparent connection to them.

Plenty of time. Not for three days more did the first departure take place from the encampment. A small army—a large army, actually, by any but Malwa standards—began its long march southward. The army which had been assigned to Lord Venandakatra, in his new manifestation as the *Goptri of the Deccan*. It was a glorious manifestation, even by Venandakatra's standards, and so the great Lord was mollified for the unseemly haste with which he made his departure.

Of the various types of Malwa governorships, none was so prestigious as "Goptri." (The term, as closely as possible, could have been translated in the western lands as: *Warden of the Marches*.) No ordinary governor, Venandakatra, to be assigned to a small and placid province. Not even an ordinary satrap, Venandakatra, assigned to a large and placid region. No, Venandakatra, blessed by his Emperor, had been given the entire Deccan, and, trusted by his Emperor, had been charged with bringing that fractious land to heel.

As much as they detested him, many Malwa officials, watching him go, almost felt sorry for the man.

Three days later, the Emperor's own army began its march. (Stately progress, it might be better to say.) A march which was much shorter, and to the east, and— for the Emperor and his immediate entourage—no march at all. The Emperor and the high Malwa rode down the Jamuna in the comfort of the world's most luxurious barges, escorted by a fleet of slim war galleys.

Most of the Emperor's army, however, marched. As did the horde of camp followers who surrounded the army. And a small band of foreigners, like a chip in a slow moving ocean of humanity.

Chapter 9

DARAS

Summer 530 AD

The first day, after her return to Daras, Antonina spent with her son. Photius was ecstatic to see his mother, after a separation of several months—the more so when he saw the small mountain of gifts which she had brought back for him from fabled Constantinople. Yet, for all that the boy kept one eager, impatient eye upon his fascinating new toys, he spent the first day cuddling with his mother.

The seven-year-old's delight in the reunion was the product of simple joy, not relief. He had obviously been well treated during her absence. Indeed, suspected Antonina, hefting his weight, he had been spoiled outright.

By the second day, of course, the imperative demand of new toys overwhelmed all filial devotion. At the crack of dawn, Photius was at his play. When his mother appeared, an hour or so later, the boy gave her no more than perfunctory words of greeting. Mothers, after all is said and done, are mothers. As cherishable as the sunrise, to be sure, but equally certain. *Toys*, now—who knows when they might vanish, into whatever magic realm brought them forth?

Antonina watched him at his play, for a bit. On

another occasion, there might have been a touch of rueful regret in her son's preoccupation. But Antonina, in truth, was impatient to get on with her own pressing tasks. So it was not long before she headed off to the workshop where John of Rhodes awaited her.

The workshop, she saw at a glance, had been considerably expanded during the months of her absence. And, as she drew nearer, she realized that John was no longer working alone. Through the open door of the workshop, she could hear the sound of voices.

At first, the realization disconcerted her. She was swept with uneasiness. The past weeks in Constantinople had left her with a heightened sense of secrecy and security.

Within seconds, however, uneasiness was pushed aside by another emotion. There could be only one reason that John had brought other men into his work.

So it was hope, not anxiety, which quickened her last steps into the workshop.

What she encountered, entering, melded both sentiments in an instant.

A loud, crashing noise caused her to flinch.

Fortunately. The flinch gave her the momentum to duck.

Fortunately. The unknown missile whizzing by missed her head by a comfortable margin.

Unlike the ricochet, which struck her squarely on the rump.

The ricochet had little force behind it, however. It was surprise, more than pain, which tumbled her squawking to the floor.

"In the name of Christ, Antonina!" bellowed John of Rhodes. "Can't you read a simple sign?"

The naval officer arose from behind an upended table and stalked toward her. It was obvious, from its neat and tidy placement, that the table had been upended deliberately.

John reached down a hand and hauled Antonina to her feet. Then, not relinquishing his grip on her wrist, he dragged her back through the doorway she had just entered.

Outside, he spun her around. "Right there!" he roared. "Where everyone can see it!"

He pointed triumphantly above the door.

"In plain and simple Greek! It says—"

Silence. Antonina rubbed her rump, scowling.

"Yes, John? It says *what?*"

Silence. Then:

"*Eusebius—come here!*"

A moment later, an apprehensive young man appeared in the doorway. He was short, thick, swarthy—rather evil-looking, in fact. Not at all the image of the innocent cherub he was desperately trying to project.

John pointed accusingly at the empty space above him.

"Where's the sign I told you to hang there?" he demanded.

Eusebius looked sheepish. "Forgot," he mumbled.

John took a deep breath, blew it out, and began stumping about in the courtyard. His hands were firmly planted on his hips, arms akimbo.

Antonina knew the signs. She was in no mood for one of the naval officer's tirades.

"Never mind, John!" she exclaimed. "There's no harm done, other than to my dignity."

"That's not the point!" snarled John. "This stuff is dangerous enough without some—*fool boy!*—forgetting—*again!*—to take simple precautions like hanging—"

"*What* dangerous stuff?" demanded Antonina, smiling brightly. "Oh—that sounds exciting!"

John broke off his stumping. He waved his arms.

"We've got it, Antonina!" he cried excitedly. "We've got it! *Gunpowder!* Come on—I'll show you!"

He charged back inside. Eusebius, moving out of the way, gave Antonina a thankful glance.

For the second time, Antonina entered the workshop. *Bang! Whizzzzz! Thump. Clatterclatterclatter.*

She scrambled back outside, ducking.

Behind her, John's bellow:

"*Eusebius—you idiot!* Didn't I tell you to put out the slowmatch?"

"Forgot," came the mutter.

"Outside of having the memory of an olive, he's really been a great help," said John later. He took a thoughtful sip of wine. "Chemistry isn't really my strong point. Eusebius has a knack for it like nobody I've ever seen."

"Better hire someone to keep track of what he's supposed to remember, then," said Antonina, smiling.

John set his cup down on the table firmly. Planted his hands on the table, firmly. Squared his shoulders, firmly.

"We can't afford it, Antonina," he said. Firmly. "There's no point dancing about the matter." Scowl. "Procopius has been rubbing his hands with glee for a week, now. Ever since he got here ahead of you and went over the books." Fierce scowl. "He can't wait to tell you, the swine. I've gone through the money. All of it. Not a solidus left. Not one." Very fierce scowl. "And Sittas—fat cheapskate!—won't cough up anything more. He denounced me for a spendthrift the last time I asked."

Antonina's smile didn't fade.

"How many times have you hit him up?"

Sullenly: "Eight. Well—seven. Successfully."

"Congratulations!" she laughed. "That's a record. No one else has ever squeezed money out of him more than twice in a row, so far as I know."

John's smile was very thin.

"It's not really a joke, Antonina. We can't go any further without money, and I don't know where it's going to come from. I can't get anything from Cassian, either. The Bishop's got his own problems. Patriarch Ephraim's been on a rampage lately, howling about church funds being misspent. His deacons have been crawling all over Anthony like fleas on a dog. They even counted his personal silverware."

"What's the matter?" sneered Antonina. "Are Ephraim's silk robes wearing out?"

There was a bit more humor in John's smile, now. Just a bit.

"Not that I've noticed. Hard to keep track, of course, all the robes he's got. No, I think maybe he's peeved because he doesn't have as many pounds of gold on the rings of his left hand as he does on the right. Makes him list when he promenades through the streets of Antioch, blessing the poor."

The naval officer snorted, sighed. He cast a glance around the room. They were sitting in the main salon of the villa, at a table in the corner. "I'd suggest selling one of your marvelous tapestries," he muttered, "except—"

"We don't have any."

"Precisely."

Antonina's smile turned into a very cheerful grin. She shook her head.

"I should stop teasing you. I'm ashamed of myself. The fact is, my dear John, that money is no longer a problem. I have acquired a new financial backer for our project."

She reached down and hauled up a sack. *Hauled.* The table clumped when she set it down.

John's eyes widened. Antonina, still grinning, seized the bottom of the sack and upended it. A small torrent of gold coins spilled across the table.

"Freshly minted, I hope you notice," she said gaily.

John ogled the pile. It was not the coins themselves which held his gaze, however. It was his knowledge of what lay behind them.

Power. Raw power.

Since the reign of the emperors Valentinian and Valens, gold coin—the solidus, inaugurated by Constantine the Great, which had been Rome's stable currency for two centuries—were minted very exclusively.

There were many legal mints in the Roman Empire. Big ones, in Thessalonica and Nicomedia, and a number of small ones in other cities. But they were restricted to issuing silver and copper coinage. By law, only the emperor minted gold coin. In Constantinople, at the Great Palace itself.

"You told Theodora," he stated.

Antonina nodded.

"Was that wise?" he asked. There was no accusation in the question, simply curiosity.

Antonina shrugged. "I think so. Under the circumstances, I didn't have much choice. I became deeply embroiled in imperial intrigue while I was in Constantinople. The reason Irene didn't come back with me is because she's now—in fact if not in theory—Theodora's spymaster."

John eyed her with deep interest.

"Malwa?"

"Yes. They're developing some kind of treacherous plot, John. So far all we know is—" She broke off. "Never mind. It's a long tale, and I don't want to have to tell it twice in the same day. Anthony, Michael and Sittas will be coming for dinner tonight. Maurice and Hermogenes will be there, too. They're also both involved, now. I'll explain everything then."

She reached out a hand and began scooping the coins back into the sack. "Anyway, I think telling Theodora was necessary. And the right thing to do, for that matter. We'll know soon enough. She'll be coming here later this summer. For a full tour of the project."

"*What?*" cried John. "*This summer?*" He leapt to his feet. Waved his arms angrily. "Impossible! Impossible! I won't have anything ready by then! Impossible!" He began stumping back and forth furiously. "Crazed women! No sense of reality—none at all. Impossible. The gunpowder's still too unpredictable. The grenades are untested. Rockets aren't even that!"

Stump, stump, stump.

"Lunatic females. Think chemistry's like baking bread. There's something wrong with the way the powder burns, I know there is. Need to experiment with different ways of mixing the stuff."

Stump, stump, stump.

"Idiot girls. Maybe grind it, if I can figure out how to do it without blowing myself up. Maybe wet it first, that's an idea. What the hell, can't hurt."

Stump, stump, stump.

"Hell it can't! That moron Eusebius could blow up anything. Blow up a frigging pile of cow dung, you don't watch him. Careless as a woman."

Stump, stump, stump.

The early hours of the evening, before and during the meal, were primarily devoted to Procopius. It was not difficult. From months of practice, Antonina had developed the craft of Procopius-baiting to a fine art.

In truth, her expertise was largely wasted. By now, Procopius was so well-trained that literally anything would serve the purpose. Like a yoked and blinkered mule pulling a capstan, he could see nothing before him but the well-trod path. Antonina had but to remark on a fine horse—Procopius would scribble on the infamy of bestialism. Chat with a peasant housewife—a treatise on the ancient sin of Sappho was the sure result. Place her son in her lap—ah! splendid!— Procopius would burn his lamp through the night, producing a veritable treatise on pedophilia and incest.

So, her sultry glances at the men about the table, her veiled remarks, her giddy laughter, her sly innuendos— even the joke about four soldiers and a pair of holy men being more than any woman could handle at one *sitting*—giggle, giggle—were a complete waste of effort. She could have been alone at the table, in the cold light of dawn, eating her meal in silence. By mid-morning, Procopius would be assuring anyone who listened that the harlot masturbated at breakfast.

Soon enough, Procopius left the table and retired to his chamber. There was no need for Antonina to send him away on some pretext. The man was fairly bursting with anxiety to reach his quill.

"God, I am sick of that man," snarled Sittas. For a

moment, the general looked like he was going to spit out his wine. But only for a moment. He reconsidered, swallowed, poured himself a new goblet.

"Is this absolutely necessary?" growled Michael of Macedonia.

Antonina made a face. But before she could reply, Bishop Cassian spoke. Harshly:

"Yes, Michael, it is. That foul creature—though he's too stupid to know it—is Malwa's chief spy on Antonina. He's the aqueduct which brings them the water of knowledge. Except that Antonina has seen to it that the aqueduct is actually a sewer, piping nothing but filth into their reservoirs." He smiled. It was quite a wicked smile, actually, for a bishop. Almost devilish. "We're not having a meeting here, plotting against Malwa. We're having an orgy!"

Then, with a sly smile: "Is it your reputation which frets you so?"

The Macedonian glared. "All reputation is folly," he pronounced. "Folly—"

"—fed by pride, which is worse still," concluded the Bishop. His smile widened. "Really, Michael, you *must* develop a broader repertoire of proverbs."

Antonina cleared her throat.

"As I was saying . . ."

"You weren't saying anything, Antonina," pointed out Cassian reasonably. "So I saw no reason not to idle away the time by a harmless—"

"Stop picking on Michael," grumbled Maurice. "He's done wonders with the local lads, and their wives and parents. Even the village elders aren't howling louder than a medium-sized storm at sea."

"Well, of course he has!" exclaimed Cassian cheerfully. "He's a holy man. Must be good for something."

Antonina headed off the gathering storm.

"Tell me, Michael," she said forcefully. "What is your assessment? *Michael?*"

The Macedonian broke off his (quite futile) attempt to glower down the bishop.

"Excuse me, Antonina? I didn't catch that."

"The peasants," she stated. "What is your assessment?"

Michael waved his hand. It was not an airy gesture. Rather the opposite. So might a stone punctuate solidity.

"There will be no problem. None."

"More than that," added Maurice. "A good number of them, I think, would jump at the chance to join a new regiment." He eyed John of Rhodes. "Assuming there's something for them to do beside drive sheep at the enemy."

John didn't rise to the bait.

"Stop worrying, Maurice. You get your new regiment put together, I'll have weapons for them. Grenades, at the very least."

"No rockets?" asked Hermogenes.

John winced. "Wouldn't count on it. The damned things are trickier to make than I thought." He drained his cup, poured himself another. Then, grumbling:

"The problem, actually, isn't *making* them. I've got a good twenty rockets piled up in the workshed. Every one of them'll fly, too, and blow up quite spectacularly. The problem is that there's no telling *where*."

Another wince. "I had one rocket—this is the bare truth—the damned thing actually flew in a circle and almost took our heads off."

"How do the Malwa aim them?" asked Sittas. "There must be a way."

John shrugged. "I don't know. I've tried everything I can think of. Fired them through tubes. Put vanes on them—even feathers! Nothing works. Some go more or less straight, most don't, and I can't for the life of me figure out any rhyme or reason behind it."

Maurice slapped the table with the flat of his hand. "So let's not worry about it," he urged. "When the general gets back from India—"

"*If*—" murmured John.

"—*when* he gets back," drove on Maurice, "I'm sure he'll be able to tell us the secret of aiming rockets. In the meantime, let's stick to grenades. Those'll be more than enough to keep a new regiment of peasant recruits busy."

"Maurice has an idea," announced Sittas. The general beamed. "Marvelous idea, I think! And you know me—I generally look on new ideas about the same way I look on cow dung."

"What is it?" asked Antonina.

Maurice rubbed his scalp. The gesture was one of his few affectations. The hair on that scalp was iron grey, but it was still as full as it had been when he was a boy.

"I got to thinking. The problem with grenades is that you want to be able to heave them a fair distance before they blow up. Then, you face a tradeoff between distance and effectiveness. A man with a good arm can toss a grenade fairly far—but only if it's so small it doesn't do much good when it lands. If he tries to throw a big grenade, he has to get well within bow range to do it." The veteran shrugged. "Under most battle conditions, my cataphracts would turn him into a pincushion before he got off more than one. I have to assume that the enemy could do as well. Persians could, for sure."

"So what's your solution?" asked John. "Scorpions?"

Maurice shook his head. "No. Mind you, I'm all for developing grenade artillery. Wouldn't be hard at all to adapt a stone-throwing scorpion for that purpose. But that's artillery. Fine in its place, but it's no substitute for infantry."

Hermogenes smiled. He was one of the few modern Roman generals who specialized in infantry warfare. Belisarius himself had groomed the young officer, and urged him in that direction.

"Or cavalry," grumbled Sittas. *This* general, on the other hand, was passionately devoted to the cataphract traditions.

"Forget cavalry," said Maurice. "These lads are peasants pure and simple, Sittas. Syrian peasants, to boot. Thracian and Illyrian peasants have some familiarity with horses, but these boys have none at all. You know as well as I do they'd never make decent horsemen. Not in the time we've got."

Sittas nodded, quite magnanimously. The honor of the cavalry having been sustained, he would not argue the point further.

"And that's the key," stated Maurice. "I tried to figure out the best way to combine Syrian peasants and grenades, starting with the strengths and limitations of both. The answer was obvious."

Silence. John exploded.

"Well—out with it, then!"

"Slings. And slingstaffs."

John frowned. "Slings?" He started to argue—more out of ingrained habit than anything else—but fell silent.

"Hmm." He quaffed his wine. "Hmm."

Antonina grinned. "What's the matter, John? Don't tell me you haven't got an instant opinion?"

The naval officer grimaced.

"Alas—no. Truth is, much as I hate to admit it, I don't know anything about slings. Never use the silly things in naval combat."

"You wouldn't call them *silly things* if you'd ever faced Balearic slingers on a battlefield," growled Maurice. Hermogenes and Sittas nodded vigorously.

"But these *aren't* Balearic slingers, Maurice," demurred Antonina. "The islanders are famous—have been for centuries. These are just farm boys."

Maurice shrugged. "So what? Every one of those peasants—especially the shepherds—has been using a sling since he was a boy. Sure, they're not professionals like the Balearic islanders, but that doesn't matter for our needs. The only real difference between a Balearic mercenary slinger and a peasant lad is accuracy. That matters when you're slinging iron bullets. It doesn't—not much, anyway—when you're hurling grenades."

John started to get excited, then. "You know—you're right! How far could one of these Syrian boys toss a grenade?"

Maurice fluttered the stubby fingers of one thick hand. "Depends. Show me the grenade you're talking about, and I'll give you a close answer. Roughly? As far as an average archer, with a sling. With a slingstaff, as far as a cataphract or a Persian."

"Cavalry'd make mincemeat out of them," stated Sittas.

Maurice nodded. "Alone, yes. Good cavalry, anyway, that didn't panic at the first barrage. They'd rout the grenade slingers—"

"Call them *grenadiers*," interjected John. "Got more dignity."

"Grenadiers, then." He paused, ruminated; then: "*Grenadiers*. I like that!"

Hermogenes nodded vigorously.

"A special name'll give the men morale," the young general stated. "I like it too. In fact, I think it's essential."

Sittas mused: "So we'll need cavalry on the flanks—"

"Need a solid infantry bulwark, too," interjected Hermogenes.

Maurice nodded. "Yes, that too. There's nothing magical about grenades. In the right combination—used the right way—"

Hermogenes: "A phalanx, maybe."

Sittas: "Damned nonsense! Phalanxes are as obsolete as eating on a couch. No, no, Hermogenes, it's the old republican maniples you want to look at. I think—"

Bishop Cassian turned to Antonina.

"May I suggest we leave these gentlemen to their play, my dear? I predict that within a minute the discussion will be too technical for us to follow, anyway. And I'm dying to hear all about your exploits in Constantinople."

Antonina rose, smiling. "Let's repair to the salon, then."

She looked at Michael.

"Will you join us?"

The monk shook his head.

"I suspect that your own discussion with Anthony will soon be as technical as that of these gentlemen," he said ruefully. "I'm afraid that I would be of no more use in plotting palace intrigues than I am in calculating military tactics and formations."

Sittas happened to overhear the remark.

"What's the matter, Michael?" A teasing grin came to his face. "Surely you're not suggesting that the eternal soul has no place in the mundane world?"

The monk gazed on the general like a just-fed eagle gazes on a mouse. Current interest, mild.

"You and yours," he said softly, "will bring to the battle weapons and tactics. Antonina and Anthony, and theirs, will bring to the battle knowledge of the enemy. *But in the end, Sittas, it will come to this.* All the gifts you bring will be as nothing, unless the peasant boy to whom you give them has a soul which can face Satan in the storm."

He rose.

"I will give you that peasant."

On his way out, Michael bestowed a considering look upon Sittas. Like a just-fed eagle considers a mouse. Future prospects, excellent.

"Always a bad idea, baiting a holy man," murmured Maurice.

"It's true," he insisted, in the face of Sittas' glare. He drained his cup. "Ask any peasant."

The next morning, the two generals accompanied John of Rhodes out to the training field, eager to experiment with the grenades. Maurice was waiting there for them, with a dozen peasant volunteers. The Syrians were quite nervous, in the beginning. Even after their prowess at grenade-hurling earned them the praise of the generals, the young men were abashed in the company of such noble folk.

Soon enough, however, Michael of Macedonia made his appearance. He said nothing, neither to the generals nor to the peasants. But it was amusing, to Maurice, to watch the way in which the monk's presence transformed the Syrian boys. Into young eaglets, in the presence of giant mice.

By mid-afternoon, the eaglets were arguing freely with the giant mice.

Not over tactics, of course, or military formations. (Although the Syrians did have some valuable advice on the practical realities of slinging grenades. Most of it concerned the pragmatics of fuses, and their length.) The young men were not foolish. Uneducated and illiterate, yes. Stupid, no. They did not presume to understand the art of war better than such men as Sittas and Hermogenes. (Or, especially—they had their own peasant view of such things—Maurice.)

But they had quite strong opinions on the question of barracks, and the nature of military camps.

Their children would not like barracks, though they would probably enjoy the tent life of camps. Their wives would like neither, but would tolerate the camps. They were simple women. Practical.

Barracks, however, simply wouldn't do. No privacy. Immodest. Their wives were simple women, but decent. They were not camp followers.

They wanted huts. Each family its own hut. (A tent, of course, would do for the route camps.)

The generals explained the absurdity of such an arrangement. Violation of military tradition.

The peasants explained the absurdity of military tradition.

In the end, while a monk watched—smiling, smiling— young peasants disciplined generals.

No huts?

No grenadiers.

In a different way, another clash of wills was taking place in the villa.

"*It is much too dangerous, Antonina,*" insisted the bishop. "I thought so last night, and I feel even more strongly about it today." He pushed his plate of food away. "Look!" he said accusingly. "I've even lost my appetite."

Antonina smiled, studying his rotund form. As

modest and plain-living as Bishop Cassian undoubtedly was, no-one had ever mistaken him for an ascetic. Not, at least, when it came to meals.

She shrugged. "It could be, yes. Not for the moment, however. I assure you, Anthony, the last thing the Malwa will do is harm me. I'm their pride and joy. The very apple of their eye."

Cassian stared stubbornly at his uneaten lunch. Antonina sighed.

"Can't you understand, Anthony? After Ajatasutra 'trapped' me—quite a trap, too!—what with me being overheard by two deacons crying out for the death of Justinian!—they had me in a vise. As they see it. They're squeezing for all it's worth. Before I left Constantinople, they got from me every detail of the Hippodrome factions' internal politics."

She broke off for a moment, grimacing.

"I *still* don't know why they're so fascinated by that subject. Mother of God, it's all I ever heard about from my father, growing up. *This* Blue did this and *that* Green did that, and *those* Blues are so many clowns but keep your eyes out for *that* set of Greens."

She threw up her hands with exasperation.

"I even had to track down some of my father's old cronies—the ones I could find in Constantinople, at any rate—in order to bring my knowledge of the factions up to date. God in Heaven, what a sorry lot of ruffians!"

"Were they pleased to see you again?" asked Cassian mildly. "After all this time?"

Antonina looked startled. Then she grinned, quite merrily.

"To tell the truth, they fawned all over me. Local girl makes good, comes back to visit the home folks. I hadn't realized how famous Belisarius has become among those circles."

She shrugged. "So, in the end, I was able to give Balban every detail of the doings of the Hippodrome factions. And I *still* don't know why the Malwa—"

"I don't think it's so odd, Antonina," interrupted Cassian. "There must be twenty or thirty thousand of those bravos in Constantinople. Not an insignificant military force, potentially."

Antonina snickered.

"Hippodrome thugs? Be serious, Anthony. Oh, to be sure, they're a rough enough crowd in the streets. But against *cataphracts*? Besides, they're about evenly divided between the Blues and the Greens. More likely to whip on each other than do any Malwa bidding."

The bishop rubbed two fingers together, in the ancient gesture for coin.

Antonina cocked her head quizzically.

"That's Irene's opinion, too. But I think she's over-estimating the strength of the factions, even if the Malwa can unite them with bribes." She shook her head. "Enough of that. At least now the Malwa are demanding some sensible secrets from me. By the time I get back to Constantinople, a few months from now, I'm to provide them with a detailed breakdown of all the military units in the east. *All* of them—not just here in Syria, but in Palestine as well. Even Egypt." She grinned. "Or else."

Cassian stared at her, still unsmiling. Antonina's grin faded away.

"It's that 'or else' you're worried about, isn't it?"

Cassian took a deep breath, exhaled. "Actually, no. At least, not much."

He rose from the table and began pacing slowly about the dining room.

"I'm afraid you don't really grasp my fear, Antonina. I agree with you about the Malwa, as it happens. *For now*, at least, they will do you no harm at all."

Antonina frowned. "Then what—"

It was Anthony's turn to throw up his hands with exasperation.

"Can you possibly be so naive? There are not simply *Malwa* involved in this plot, woman! There are Romans, also. And they have their own axes to grind—grind against each other's blades, often enough."

He stepped to the table, planted his pudgy hands firmly, and leaned over.

"You have placed yourself in a maelstrom, Antonina. Between Scylla and Charybdis—and a multitude of other monsters!—all of whom are plotting as much against their conspirators as they are against the Roman Empire." He thrust himself back upright. "You have no idea where the blade might come from, my dear. No idea at all. You see only the Malwa. And only the face they turn toward you."

Antonina stared grimly back at him. Unyielding.

"And so? I understand your point, Anthony. But I say again—so?"

Her shrug was enough to break the Bishop's heart. It was not a woman's shrug, but the gesture of a veteran.

"That's war, Cassian. You do the best you can against the enemy, knowing he fully intends to return the favor. One of you wins, one of you loses. Dies, usually."

A thin smile came to her face.

"Belisarius—Maurice, too, I think my husband got it from him—has a saying about it. He calls it the First Law of Battle. *Every battle plan gets fucked up*—pardon my language, Bishop—*as soon as the enemy arrives. That why he's called the enemy.*"

Cassian stroked his beard. There was weariness in the gesture, but some humor also.

"Crude, crude," he murmured. "Altogether coarse. Refined theologians would express the matter differently. *Every sound doctrine gets contradicted, as soon as the other dogmatists arrive at the council. That's why they're called the heretics.*"

Finally, he smiled.

"Very well, Antonina. I cannot stop you, in any event. I will give you all the assistance which I can."

He resumed his seat. Then, after staring at his plate for a moment, pulled it back before him and began eating with his usual gusto.

"Won't be much, when it comes to military matters and Hippodrome factions." He waved his knife cheerfully. "Church conspirators, on the other hand—and there'll be plenty of them, be sure of it!—are a different matter altogether."

He speared two dates.

"Glycerius of Chalcedon and George Barsymes, is it?"

The dates disappeared as if by magic. He skewered a pear.

"Rufinus Namatianus, Bishop of Ravenna," he mumbled thoughtfully, his mouth full of shredding fruit. "Know'm well."

The last piece of pear sped down his throat, like a child down the gullet of an ogre.

"Babes in the woods," he belched.

After the generals returned, at sundown, Antonina listened to their ranting and raving for half an hour. Tact and diplomacy, she thought, required as much.

Then she made her ruling.

"*Of course* they won't live in barracks. The idea's absurd. These men aren't *conscripts*, gentlemen. They're volunteers—established farmers, with families. They marry early here, and start raising children by the time they're fifteen. Younger, the girls."

The generals gobbled. John of Rhodes began to stump. Antonina examined them curiously.

"What did you expect? Did you think these men would abandon their families—just to be your grenade-tossers?"

Gobbling ceased. Generals stared at other. A naval officer stumbled in his stumping.

Antonina snorted.

"You *didn't* think."

Snort. "Sometimes I agree with Theodora. *Men.*"

Sittas leveled his finest glare upon her. The boar in full fury.

"You'll not be making any royal decrees here, young woman!"

"I most certainly will," replied Antonina, quite sweetly. "I'm the paymaster, remember?"

She cocked her head at John of Rhodes. "Are you done with your stumping?"

The naval officer pouted. Antonina reached to the floor, hauled up a sack, clumped it on the table.

"Hire workmen, John. Better yet—pay the peasants themselves. The lads are handy with their hands. They'll have the huts up in no time, and they'll be the happier for having made their own new homes."

From the doorway came Michael's voice:

"They'll be wanting a chapel, too. Nothing fancy, of course."

The generals, cowed by the woman, transferred their outrage to the monk.

The Macedonian stared back. Like a just-fed eagle stares at chittering mice.

Contest of wills, laughable.

Chapter 10

KAUSAMBI

Summer 530 AD

From the south bank of the Jamuna, Belisarius gazed at the temple rising from the very edge of the river on the opposite bank. It was sundown, and the last rays of the setting sun bathed the temple in golden glory. He was too distant to discern the details of the multitude of figurines carved into the tiered steps of the temple, but he did not fail to appreciate the beauty of the structure as a whole.

"What a magnificent temple," he murmured. Out of the corner of his eye, he saw Menander's lips tighten in disapproval.

For a moment, he thought to let it go, but then decided it was a fine opportunity to advance the young cataphract's education.

"What's the matter, Menander?" he queried, cocking an eyebrow. "Does my admiration for heathen idolatry offend you?"

The words were spoken in a mild and pleasant tone, but Menander flushed with embarassment.

"It's not my place—" he began, but Belisarius cut him off.

"Of course it is, lad. You're required to obey my orders as your commander. You are not required to agree with my theological opinions. So, spit it out." He pointed to the temple. "What do you think of it? How can you deny its splendor?"

Menander frowned. The expression was one of thought, not disapproval. He did not respond immediately, however. He and Belisarius had dismounted upon reaching the river, in order to drink its water, and their horses were still assuaging their thirst. Idly, he stroked the neck of his horse for a few seconds, before saying:

"I can't deny that it's a beautifully made edifice, general. I just wish it had been made for some different purpose."

Belisarius shrugged. "For what? Christian worship? That would be better, of course, to be sure. Unfortunately, Christian missionaries have only begun to penetrate this far into India's interior." With an smile of irony: "And all of *them*, alas, are Nestorian heretics. Not much better than outright heathens. According to most orthodox churchmen, at least."

He turned, so as to face Menander squarely.

"In the meantime, India's millions grope their own way toward God. *That*"—pointing again to the temple—"is the proof of it. Would you rather they ignored God altogether?"

Menander's frown deepened. "No," he said softly, after a moment. "I just—" He hesitated, sighed, shrugged. "I've seen Dadaji praying in your tent, many times. And I don't doubt his sincerity, or his devotion. I just—" Another shrug, expressing a fatalistic acceptance of reality.

"Wish he were praying to the Christian God?"

Menander nodded.

Belisarius looked back to the temple. Now, he shrugged himself. But his was a cheerful shrug, expressing more of wonder than of resignation.

"So do I, Menander, come down to it. But I can't say I lose any sleep over the matter. Dadaji's is a true and pure soul. I do not think God will reject it, when the time comes."

The general glanced toward the west. The lower rim of the sun was almost touching the horizon.

"We'd best head back," he said. "I'd hoped to get a glimpse of Kausambi before nightfall, but I can see that we're still a few miles away from the outskirts."

He and Menander mounted their horses and rode away from the river. As they headed back toward their camp, Menander said:

"I thought you were orthodox, sir." The youth's brow was furrowed in thought. Then, realizing that his statement might be construed amiss, Menander began to apologize. But his general dismissed the apology with a wave of the hand.

"I *am* orthodox." Then, a crooked smile. "I suppose. I was raised so, as Thracians are. And it is the creed to which I have always subscribed."

He hesitated. "It is hard to explain. I do not care much for such things, Menander. My wife, whom I love above all others in this world, is not orthodox. For the sake of my reputation, she disguises her creed, but she inclines to Monophysitism, as do most Egyptians. Am I to believe that she is condemned to eternal hellfire?"

He glanced at Menander. The young cataphract winced. If anything, Menander was even more adoring of Antonina than were most of the bucellarii.

Belisarius shook his head. "I think not. Not by the Christ I worship. And it is not simply she, Menander. I am a general, and I have led soldiers into battle who believed in every heresy, even Arians, and watched them die bravely. And held them in my arms as they died, listening to their last prayers. Were those men predestined for damnation? I think not."

His jaws tightened. "My indifference to creed goes deeper than that. Years ago, in my first command—I was only eighteen years old—I matched wits with a Persarmenian commander named Varanes. His forces were small, as were mine, and our combat was prolonged over weeks. A thing of maneuver and feint, as much as battle. He was a magnificent commander, and taxed me to the utmost."

He took a deep breath. "An honorable and gallant foe, as well. As Medeans often are. Once I was forced to abandon three of my men. They were too badly wounded to move, and Varanes had caught me in a trap from which I had to extricate myself immediately or suffer total defeat. When he came upon them, Varanes saw to it that they were well cared for."

He looked away. For a moment, the usual calm of his face seemed to waver. But not for long, and Belisarius resumed his tale. Menander was listening with rapt attention.

"I discovered the fact after I defeated Varanes. I trapped him myself, finally, and overran his camp. My three men were still there. One of them had died in the meantime, from his wounds, but it was through no fault of the Persians. The other two were safe, thanks to Varanes. Varanes himself was mortally wounded, from a lance-thrust to the groin. It took him hours to die, and I spent those hours with him. I attempted to comfort him as best I could, but the wound was terrible. It must have been pure agony for him, but he bore it well. He even joked with me, and we passed the time discussing, among other things, our relative assessment of our previous weeks in combat. He had had the upper hand, through most of it, but I had learned quickly. He predicted a great future for me."

Belisarius paused for a moment, guiding his horse through a narrowing of the trail. Within a few seconds, they passed through the final line of trees which bordered the river. Now in more open country, the general resumed his tale.

"By the time he finally died, night had fallen. He was a Zoroastrian, as most Persians, a fire-worshipper. He asked me to make a fire for him, so that he might die looking into the face of his god. I did so, and willingly. A churchman, most churchmen at least, would have denounced me for that act of impiety. The Zoroastrian, a churchman would have no doubt explained, was soon enough going to get fire aplenty in the pit of eternal damnation. But I did not think Varanes was so destined. I did not think so then. I do not think so now."

Menander, watching his general, was struck by the sudden coldness in his gaze. Belisarius' brown eyes were normally quite warm, except in battle. Even in battle, those eyes were not cold. Simply—calm, detached, observant.

The customary warmth returned within a few seconds, however. Musingly, Belisarius added:

"I tried to explain to Rao, once, as best I could, the subtleties of the Trinity." He waved his hand. "Not in this world, but in the world of my vision."

Menander, already fascinated with his general's unwontedly intimate tale, now became totally absorbed. He knew of that vision, which had come to Belisarius from the "jewel" which Bishop Cassian had brought to him the year before in Aleppo. Belisarius had told him the tale, along with the other Romans and the Ethiopians, while they were still at sea.

Menander glanced at the general's chest. Beneath the half-armor and the tunic, there was nothing to see. But the young cataphract knew that the Talisman of God was there, nestled in a little pouch which Belisarius always carried suspended from his neck. Menander had even seen it himself, for Belisarius had showed it to them all, in the cramped confines of their cabin in the Malwa embassy vessel which had brought them to India. He had been dazzled, then, by the mystic splendor of the Talisman. He was dazzled, now, by the memory.

Belisarius suddenly laughed.

"Rao listened to my explanation, quite patiently," he continued. "But it was obvious he thought it was child's babble. Then he told me that his own faith believed there were three hundred and thirty million gods and goddesses, all of whom, in one way or another, were simply manifestations of God himself."

Belisarius smiled his crooked smile. "No doubt that

man is doomed. But I will tell you this, Menander: I would rather stand with Raghunath Rao in the Pit than with the Patriarch Ephraim in Heaven."

Belisarius spoke no further during the rest of their ride back to their camp. Menander, also, was silent, grappling with thoughts which were new to him, and which went far beyond the simple preachings of his village priest.

They reached the grove within which the Romans and Ethiopians had pitched their camp. Still preoccupied, Menander gave only cursory attention to the task of guiding his horse through the trees. But once they broke through into the clearing at the center of the grove, all thoughts of theology vanished.

"There's trouble, Menander," said his general softly.

The moment Belisarius rode into the little clearing, he knew something was amiss. Ezana and Wahsi were both standing guard in front of Prince Eon's pavilion. Normally, only one or the other assumed that duty at any given time. What was even more noticeable was that two sarwen were actually *standing* guard. Usually, the sarwen on duty relaxed on a stool. There was no reason not to. For many weeks, now, the Romans and Ethiopians had been guarded by their Kushan escorts, a troop of over thirty men who were consummate professionals in their trade—and particularly expert at maintaining security.

There was obvious tension in the pose of the Ethiopian soldiers. They weren't just standing—they were standing alertly, poised, and ready.

Quickly, Belisarius scanned the clearing. The lighting was poor. Dusk was almost a memory, now, only a faint tinge of dark purple on the horizon. The sun itself had disappeared, and what little daylight still remained was blocked off by the trees surrounding the camp. For all practical purposes, the only illumination in the clearing was that cast by lanterns hanging from tent poles.

His next glance was toward the two Roman tents,

situated not far from Prince Eon's large pavilion. Both
Valentinian and Anastasius, he noted, were standing in
front of them. Much like the sarwen—alert, poised,
tense.

Next, he stared across the clearing to the line of
tents which marked the Kushan part of the encampment. Normally, at this time of the evening, the
Kushans would have been busy preparing their evening
meal. Instead, they were gathered in small clusters,
murmuring quietly, casting quick glances at Prince
Eon's pavilion and—most of all—at the figure of their
own commander.

Belisarius now examined Kungas. The Kushan commander was standing alone. As always—now more than
ever, it seemed to Belisarius—his face appeared to have
been hammered out of an iron ingot. Kanishka, his
nephew and second-in-command, stood not far away.
From what little Belisarius could discern of his features,
the young Kushan lieutenant seemed distressed.

Kungas met his gaze. The Kushan said nothing, and
there was not the slightest movement in that iron mask
of a face. But Belisarius did not miss the almost imper-
ceptible shrug of his shoulders.

He knew what had happened, then. The sight of
Garmat emerging from Eon's pavilion and hurrying
toward him simply confirmed the knowledge.

"All good things come to an end," he sighed, dismounting from his horse. By the time Garmat reached
him, Menander was leading both of the horses away.

"We have a problem, Belisarius," said Garmat
urgently. "A very big problem."

Belisarius smiled crookedly. "It couldn't last forever,
Garmat. The Kushans are not stupid. To a point, of
course, they will obey Kungas and ask no questions. But
only to a point."

He gave the Kushans another glance.

"What happened?" he asked.

Garmat shrugged. "You can hardly expect vigorous
young people like Eon and Shakuntala—royalty, to

boot—to share a tent, week after week, with no opportunity for exercise or even movement, without—"

He sighed. Belisarius nodded.

"They quarreled."

Garmat smiled, faintly. "Oh, yes. A *royal* quarrel! What started it, I have no idea. They don't even remember themselves, now. But soon enough, Eon became overbearing and the Princess—the Empress, I should say—challenged him to single combat. Unarmed combat, of course. If he used weapons, she told him, he would be damned for eternity as a coward."

For all the seriousness of the moment, Belisarius could not help bursting into laughter. The image which came to his mind was incongruously funny. Eon, Prince of Axum, was not a tall man. But he was amazingly well-muscled, and as strong as a bull. Whereas Shakuntala was a small girl, not half his weight.

And yet—

She had been trained to fight with her bare hands and feet by Raghunath Rao himself. Raghunath Rao, the Panther of Majarashtra. The Wind of the Great Country. India's most deadly assassin, among many other things.

He shook his head with amusement.

"I wonder how it would have turned out. They did not actually come to blows, I hope?"

Garmat shook his head. "They are young and impetuous, but they are not insane. I gather that Shakuntala's challenge produced a sudden change of atmosphere in the tent. By the time I entered, they were exchanging profuse apologies and vows of good will."

He tugged his beard. "Unfortunately, in the brief moments before that change of atmosphere, the environs of their pavilion were filled with the sound of loud and angry voices. And Shakuntala has quite a distinctive voice, you know, especially when raised in anger." Grudgingly, even admiringly: "A very *imperial* voice, in fact."

Belisarius scratched his chin. "The Kushans heard her," he announced.

Garmat nodded. Belisarius glanced at the Kushan soldiers again. They were still clustered in little knots, but, to his relief, they did not give the appearance of men on the verge of leaping into action.

That momentary relief, however, cleared the way for another concern. Belisarius scanned the woods surrounding the clearing.

As always, whenever possible, Belisarius had made their camp within a grove of trees. He had explained that preference to the Malwa, casually, as a matter of the comfort which the trees provided from the blistering sun of India. The Malwa, for their part, had made no objection. They were happy enough, for their own reasons, to see the foreigners secluded. Privately, the Malwa thought the outlanders were idiots. True, trees provided shade. But a good pavilion did as much, and trees also stifled the breeze and were a haven for obnoxious insects.

The Malwa had also thought, happily, that trees would provide a haven for spies.

As Belisarius watched, Ousanas appeared from the edge of the trees and padded into the clearing. The hunter was casually wiping blood from the huge blade of his spear.

No Malwa spies now, thought Belisarius. His lips quirked into that distinctive, crooked smile.

Ousanas was a slave, of sorts. Of a very, very odd sort. The tall African was not Ethiopian. Like the Axumites, his skin was black. But Ousanas' broad features had not a trace of the aquiline characteristics which distinguished those of most Ethiopians. He came from a land between great lakes which was—so Belisarius had been told—some considerable distance south of the Kingdom of Axum. He was the personal slave of Prince Eon—his *dawazz*, as the Axumites called his position. An adviser, of a sort. A very, very odd sort.

When Ousanas reached Belisarius, he nodded curtly. The general noted that the hunter's usual beaming grin was entirely absent.

"No spies now," said Ousanas softly. He jerked his head toward the tent.

"Let us go in," he growled. "I must advise fool boy."

Ousanas stalked toward the pavilion entrance, Garmat trailing in his wake like a remora trailing a shark. Belisarius felt a moment's pity for the young prince. The dawazz, when he felt it appropriate, was given to stern measures.

Again, Belisarius quickly scanned the clearing. His own three cataphracts were now fully armed and armored, and their expressions were every bit as grim as those of the sarwen. Belisarius caught the eye of Valentinian and made a subtle motion with his hands. Valentinian relaxed slightly and muttered something to Anastasius and Menander. The cataphracts maintained their watchfulness, but they eased away from their former tension.

Belisarius now concentrated his attention on the Kushans, gauging their mood. The Malwa vassals were also armed, and obviously tense. But they too seemed willing to allow the situation to unfold before taking any decisive steps. They were angry, true—so much was obvious. Angry at their commander, for the most part, Belisarius thought. But they were also confused, and uncertain. Kungas *was* their commander, after all, and it was a position which he had earned on a hundred battlefields. And, too, they were all related by blood. Members of the same clan, banded together in service to the Malwa overlords. An unhappy and thankless service.

Hard years had taught the Kushans to trust themselves alone, and, most of all, to trust their commander. Such habits cannot be overcome in an instant. Belisarius gauged, and pondered the angles, and made his decision. As always, the decision was quick. He strode across the clearing and planted himself before the Kushans.

"Wait," he commanded. "I must go into the pavilion. Make no decisions until I return."

The Kushans stiffened. The Roman general's words

had been spoken in fluent Kushan. They knew his command of their language was good, but now it was perfect and unaccented. A few of them cast glances toward the trees.

Belisarius smiled—broadly, not crookedly.

"There are no spies. Not any more."

The Kushans had also seen Ousanas emerge from the woods. And, if they did not know of the African's extraordinary skill as a hunter, they had never misunderstood the easy manner in which he handled the huge spear which was his everpresent companion. Imperceptibly, they began to relax. Just a bit.

Belisarius glanced at Kungas. The Kushan commander nodded slightly. The Roman general wheeled and headed toward the pavilion. As he turned, he caught sight of Dadaji Holkar standing near the pavilion. Though middle-aged, and unarmed, and a slave, the man was obviously prepared to help defend the pavilion against assault.

Belisarius did not smile, but he felt a great affection surge into his heart.

"Come," he commanded, as he strode by Holkar. "I suspect you already know the truth, but you may as well see for yourself."

As they entered the pavilion, Ousanas was just warming to his subject.

"—be forced to tell negusa nagast he do better to drown his fool boy in the sea and beget another. Dakuen Sarwe be furious with me! Beat me for failing in my duty. But I bear up under the regiment's savage blows with great cheer! Knowing I finally rid of hopeless task of teaching frog-level intelligence to worm-brained prince."

"No attack him!" snapped Shakuntala. "Was my wrongdoing!"

The girl spoke in Ge'ez, as had Ousanas. Her command of the language of the Axumites was still poor, heavily accented and broken, but she understood enough to have followed Ousanas' tirade.

The young woman was sitting crosslegged on a plush cushion to one side of the pavilion. Her posture was stiff and erect. For all her youth, and her small size, she exuded a tremendous imperial dignity.

Ousanas scowled. He was not impressed by royalty. Axumites in general, and Ousanas in particular, shared none of the Indian awe of rulership. Ousanas himself was a dawazz, assigned the specific task of instructing a prince in the simple truth that the difference between a king and a slave was not so great. A matter of luck, in its origin; and brains, in its maintenance.

The dawazz switched to Hindi, which was the common language used by all in the pavilion.

"Next time, Empress," he growled, "do not challenge cretin prince to combat. Simply pounce upon him like lioness and beat him senseless. Fool girl!"

Ousanas shook his head sadly. "True, royalty stupid by nature. But this! This not stupidity! This—this—" He groaned woefully. "There is no word for this! Not even in Greek, language of philosophy, which has words for every silliness known to man."

Eon, squatting on his own cushion, raised his bowed head. The young prince—at nineteen, he was but a year or so older than Shakuntala—attempted to regain some measure of his own royal dignity.

"Stop speaking pidgin!" he commanded.

Belisarius fought down a grin. He knew Ousanas' rejoinder even before the dawazz spoke the words.

Not speaking pidgin. Speaking baby talk. All fool prince can understand!

When Belisarius had first met Ousanas, the year before in Constantinople, the African had spoken nothing but a bizarre, broken argot. Ousanas had maintained that manner of speech for months, until the alliance which Belisarius sought between Romans and Ethiopians had finally gelled, following a battle with pirates in the Erythrean Sea. Then—at the Prince's command—Ousanas had stopped pretending he spoke only pidgin Greek. The Romans had been astonished to discover that the outlandish African was an extraordinary linguist, who spoke any number of languages fluently. Especially Greek, which was a language Ousanas treasured, for he was fond of philosophical discourse and debate—to Anastasius' great pleasure and the despair of his other companions.

Ousanas now launched into a savage elaboration of the ontological distinction between ignorance and stupidity.

"—ignorance can be fixed. Stupid is forever. Consider, fool boy, the fate of—"

"Enough," commanded Belisarius.

Ousanas clamped his jaws shut. Then:

"I was just warming to my subject," he complained sourly.

"Yes, I know. Save it for another time, Ousanas. The Kushans will not wait that long."

The general jerked his head toward the pavilion entrance.

"We have to solve this problem. Quickly."

Eon suddenly blew out his cheeks. His massive shoulders hunched.

"What do they know?" he asked. He was looking at no one in particular.

Garmat answered.

"They know that Shakuntala is here, in this tent. Tonight." The adviser squatted himself, now, and stared at his Prince from a distance of a few feet.

"That is all that they *know*," he continued. "But they are not stupid. They will also understand that she must have been with us ever since the massacre at Venandakatra's palace at Gwalior. They will understand that she did not flee with Raghunath Rao. They will understand that Rao led the Malwa on a merry chase while the Empress herself was smuggled into your entourage. And that we have hidden her ever since."

He sighed. "And, most of all, they will now understand the reason why Kungas told them to pester our women these past weeks. Pester them, but not seriously.

Just enough to trigger off phony brawls with our cataphracts and sarwen. Brawls which *accidentally* mangled some spies, and led the survivors to report that our escorts are every bit as salacious as Venandakatra had been led to believe."

Garmat glanced at Belisarius, shrugged.

"As I said, the Kushans are not stupid. By now, they will have heard that the reason they were withdrawn as Shakuntala's guards was because Venandakatra feared their lustfulness. And so he replaced them with mahamimamsa. Who fell like sheep when Rao entered the palace and rescued the Empress."

The adviser stroked his beard. "So they will suspect that Belisarius engineered the entire thing from the very beginning. Although"—here he smiled—"they probably do not know that Belisarius gave Rao the very dagger which he used to carve up the torturers."

"In other words," grumbled Ousanas, "they know everything."

"Yes," stated Belisarius. "And, worst of all—it is obvious from looking at them—they know that their own commander must have been part of this scheme. In some sense, at least. They have no love for the Malwa, but they are still sworn to their service. Now they find they have been betrayed, by their own leader. If the Malwa discover the Empress now, their own lives will be forfeit."

The general took a deep breath. "Unless they immediately recapture her, and hand Shakuntala back to their overlords."

"They would have to turn over Kungas as well!" protested Eon. "The Malwa would never believe Kungas had not spotted Shakuntala."

Belisarius nodded. "Yes, I'm sure they understand that also. And that is why they hesitate."

He glanced toward the pavilion entrance again.

"They will hesitate for a while. But not for all that long. Those men are soldiers. The best of soldiers. Accustomed to hard and quick decisions. And

accustomed to stern necessity, and to the realities of a
bitter world. So we must somehow figure out—"

Shakuntala interrupted.

"Bring them into the pavilion. All of them. Now."

Belisarius started. Not even the Roman Emperor
Justinian—not even the Empress Theodora—could
match that tone of command. That incredibly *imperial*
voice.

He stared at the girl. Shakuntala was very beautiful,
in her exotic and dark-skinned way. But, at that moment,
it was not a girl's beauty, but the beauty of an ancient
statue.

And that's the key, he mused. *Justinian and Theodora,
for all their power, were lowborn. How many emperors
of Rome, over the centuries, could trace their ancestry
back to royalty more than a generation or two? None.
Whereas the Satavahana dynasty which ruled Andhra—*

"Great Andhra," he said aloud. "Broken Andhra, now.
But even the fierce bedouin of the desert are awed by
the broken sphinx."

Shakuntala stared up at him. The general scratched
his chin.

"Are you certain of this course, Empress?" he asked.
He glanced at the others in the pavilion. From the
puzzled frowns on their faces, it was obvious that only
Belisarius had discerned Shakuntala's purpose. He was
not surprised. Her proposed move was bold almost
beyond belief.

She nodded firmly. "There is no other course possible, Belisarius. And besides—"

She took a deep breath. Regality blazed.

"—it is the only course open to the honor of Andhra.
Any other would be foulness."

She made a short, chopping gesture. "Let the Malwa
rule so. *I will not.*"

The frowns surrounding the Empress and the general were deepening by the second. No others in the
pavilion, it was obvious, had any understanding of what
she was planning.

Belisarius smiled crookedly and bowed.

"As you command, Empress."

He turned toward the entrance. Then, struck by a thought, turned back. His smile was now very crooked. "And there is this much, also. We will learn if Rao's favorite saying is really true."

A moment later Belisarius was pulling back the flap of the pavilion. As he stooped to make his exit, he caught sight of Ousanas. The tall African was gaping. Not to Belisarius' surprise, Ousanas was the first to deduce the truth. The gape disappeared; the familiar grin erupted.

"Truly, Greeks are mad!" exclaimed the dawazz. "It is the inevitable result of too much time spent pondering on the soul."

Belisarius grinned and exited the tent. As the flap closed behind him, he heard Ousanas' next words.

"Such foolish nonsense—this business about *only the soul matters, in the end*. Idiot mysticism from a crazed Maratha bandit. No, no, it's all quite otherwise, my good people, I assure you. As Plato so clearly explained, it is the eternal and unchanging *Forms* which—"

"Ousanas—*shut up!*" barked the Prince. "What in hell is going on?"

When Belisarius reentered the pavilion, leading the Kushans, he saw that Shakuntala had taken firm command of the situation. Garmat and Eon were sitting on cushions placed to one side. Standing behind them were Ezana and Wahsi. The two sarwen were carrying their spears, but were carefully holding them in the position of formal rest. It was obvious, from their gloomy expressions, that all the Axumites thought Shakuntala's plan—agreed to by Belisarius!—was utterly insane. But events had moved too quickly for them, and they were hopelessly ensnared in her madness.

To the general's surprise, the Maratha women were not huddling in fear in a corner of the pavilion. They were kneeling in a row, on cushions placed just behind Shakuntala, who had positioned herself in the central and commanding position in the large pavilion.

Belisarius was struck by the calm composure of the
Maratha girls. As much as anything, the confident serenity of those young faces, as they gazed upon their even
younger Empress, brought Belisarius his own measure
of confidence. He glanced at Ousanas, standing in the
nearest corner of the pavilion, and saw by his faint smile
that the hunter shared that confidence.

Not so many weeks ago, those girls had been slaves.
Of lowborn caste and then, after the Malwa conquest of
Andhra, forced into prostitution. The Roman and Axumite
soldiers had purchased them in Bharakuccha, partly for
the pleasure of their company, but mostly to advance
Belisarius' scheme for rescuing Shakuntala.

At first, the girls had been timid. Over time, as they
learned that the foreigners' brutal appearance was not
matched by brutal behavior, the Maratha girls had
relaxed. But, once they finally realized the full scope
of the scheme into which they had been plunged, they
had been practically paralyzed with terror. Until Shakuntala had rallied them, and pronounced them her new
royal ladies-in-waiting, and pledged that she herself
would share their fate, whatever that fate might be.

He glanced now at Dadaji Holkar. The Maratha was
also seated near the Empress, just to her left. He was
still clad in the simple loincloth of a slave, but there
was nothing of the slave in his posture and his expression. The shrewd intelligence in his face, usually disguised by his stooped posture, was now evident for all
to see. The man positively exuded the aura of a highly
placed, trusted imperial adviser. And if the aura went
poorly with the loincloth, so much the worse for the
loincloth. Indians, too, like Romans, had a place in their
culture for the ascetic sage.

Calm, confident, serene faces. The Kushans, as they
filed into the tent, caught sight of those faces and found
their eyes drawn toward them. As Shakuntala had
planned, Belisarius knew. The young Empress had

marshaled all her resources, few as they were, to project the image of a ruler rather than a refugee. It was a fiction, but—not a sham. Not a sham at all.

By the time all the Kushans filed in, even the huge pavilion was crowded. Then, when the cataphracts followed, Belisarius thought the pavilion might burst at the seams.

Shakuntala took charge.

"Sit," she commanded. "All of you except Ousanas."

She looked at Ousanas. "Search the woods. Make certain there are no spies."

The dawazz grinned. The order was utterly redundant, of course. He had already seen to the task. But he knew Shakuntala was simply seeking to calm the Kushans. So he obeyed instantly and without complaint. On his way out of the pavilion, he whispered to Belisarius: "Envy me, Roman. I, at least, will be able to breathe."

The Kushans were still standing, uncertain.

"*Sit*," commanded Shakuntala. Within three seconds, all had obeyed. But, as they made to do so, She spoke again.

"Kungas—sit here." Shakuntala pointed imperiously to one of two cushions placed not far from her own, diagonally to her right. Remembering the seating arrangement in the Malwa emperor's pavilion, Belisarius realized this was the Indian way of honoring those close to the throne.

She pointed to the other cushion. "Kanishka—there."

The Kushan commander and his lieutenant did as she bade them.

After all the Kushans were sitting on the carpeted floor of the pavilion, Shakuntala gazed upon them for a long moment without speaking. The warriors stared back at her. They knew her face well, of course. It had been they who had rescued Shakuntala from the Ye-tai savaging the royal palace during the sack of Amaravati. They who had brought her to Venandakatra's palace at Gwalior, where she was destined to become the Malwa lord's new concubine. They who had served as her

captors and guardians during the long months they
waited for Venandakatra's return from his mission to
Constantinople.

Yet, for all the familiarity of those months in her
company, most of them were now gaping. Surprise,
partly, at seeing her again in such unexpected circumstances. But, mostly, with surprise at how different she
seemed. This was no captive girl—proud and defiant,
true, but riddled with despair for all that. This was—
what? Or who?

The moment was critical, Belisarius knew. There had
been no time to discuss anything with her. He feared
that, in her youthful uncertainty, she would make the
mistake of *explaining* the situation. Of trying to *convince*
the Kushans.

The Empress Shakuntala, heir of ancient Satavahana,
rightful ruler of great Andhra, began to speak. And
Belisarius realized he might as well have fretted over
the sun rising.

"Soon I will return to Andhra," announced Shakuntala.
"My purpose here is almost finished. When I return, I
shall rebuild the empire of my ancestors. I shall restore
its glory. I shall cast down the Mahaveda abomination and
erase from human memory their mahamimamsa curs. I
shall rebuild the viharas and restore the stupas. Again, I
shall make Andhra the blessed center of Hindu learning
and Buddhist worship."

She paused. The black-eyed Pearl of the Satavahanas,
she was often called. Now, her eyes glowed like coals.

"But first, I must destroy the Malwa Empire. To this
I devote my life and my sacred soul. This is my dharma,
my duty, and my destiny. *I will make Malwa howl.*"

Again, a pause. The black fury in her eyes softened.

"Already, Raghunath Rao is making his way back to the
Great Country. The Wind will roar across Majarashtra. He
will raise a new army from the hills and the villages, and
the great towns. He is the new commander of Andhra's
army."

She allowed the Kushans time to digest her words.

The men sitting before her were elite soldiers, hardened veterans. They knew Raghunath Rao. Like all Indians, they knew him by reputation. But, unlike most, their knowledge was more intimate. They had seen the carnage at the palace in Gwalior, after the Panther of Majarashtra had raged through it.

Shakuntala watched pride square their shoulders. She treasured that pride. She was *counting* on that pride. Yes, the Kushan soldiers knew Rao, and respected him deeply. But their pride came from the knowledge that he had respected them as well. For Rao had not tried to rescue the princess while *they* had guarded her. He had waited, until they had been replaced by—

Shakuntala watched the contempt twisting their lips. She treasured that contempt. She was *counting* on that contempt. The Kushans, today, were elite soldiers in the service of the Malwa Empire. But they were also the descendants of those fierce nomads who had erupted out of central Asia, centuries before, and had conquered all of Bactria and Sogdiana and northern India. Conquered it, ruled it—and, as they adopted civilization and the Buddhist faith, ruled it very well indeed. Until the Ye-tai came, and the Malwa, and reduced them to vassalage.

For a long moment, Shakuntala and the Kushans stared at each other. Watching, from the back of the pavilion, Belisarius was struck by the growing warmth of that mutual regard. She, and they, had spent many months in close proximity. And if, during that long and painful captivity, there had been no friendship between them, there had always been respect. A respect which, over time, had become unspoken admiration.

Now, thought Belisarius.

As if she had read his mind, Shakuntala spoke.

"Rao will raise my army. But I will need another force as well. I, too, will need to tread a dangerous path. I will need an imperial bodyguard, to protect me while I restore Andhra."

She looked away. Said, softly:

"I have given much thought to this matter. I have considered many possibilities. But, always, my thoughts return to one place, and one place only."

She looked back upon them.

"I can think of no better men to serve as my bodyguard than those who rescued me from the Ye-tai and guarded me so well during all the months at Gwalior."

Behind him, Belisarius heard Menander's shocked whisper: "My God! She's crazy!"

"Bullshit," hissed Valentinian. "She's read them perfectly."

And then Anastasius, his rumbling voice filled with philosophical satisfaction: "Never forget, lad—*only the soul matters, in the end.*"

One of the Kushans seated in the middle of the front row now spoke. Belisarius did not know the man's name, but he recognized him as a leader of the Kushan common soldiers. The equivalent of a Roman decarch.

"We must know this, princess. Did—"

"She is not a princess!" snapped one of the Maratha women kneeling behind Shakuntala. Ahilyabai was her name. "She is the Empress of Andhra!"

The Kushan soldier tightened his jaws. Shakuntala raised her hand in an abrupt gesture of command.

"Be still, Ahilyabai! My title does not matter to this man."

She leaned forward, fixing the Kushan with her black-eyed gaze. "His name is Kujulo, and I know him well. If Kujulo chooses to give me his loyalty, my title will never matter to him. Whether I sit on the throne in rebuilt Amaravati, or crouch behind the battlements of a Maratha hillfort under siege, Kujulo's sword will always come between me and Malwa."

The soldier's tight jaws relaxed. His shoulders spread wider. He stared back at the Empress for a moment and then bowed his head deeply.

"Ask what you will, Kujulo," said Shakuntala.

The Kushan soldier raised his head. Anger returned to his eyes, and he pointed to Kungas.

"We have been played for fools," he growled. "Was our commander a part of that trickery?"

Shakuntala's response was immediate. "No. This is the first time Kungas has been in my presence since you were removed as my guards at Gwalior. I have never spoken to him since that day." Her voice grew harsh. "But what is the purpose of this question, Kujulo? *You* have not been played for fools. The *Malwa* have been the ones played for fools. And not by me, but by the world's supreme trickster—the foreign General Belisarius."

All the Kushans stirred, turning their heads. Belisarius took that for his cue, and moved forward to stand before them.

"Kungas has never been a part of our plot," he said firmly. "Nor any other Kushan soldier."

He smiled, then, and the Kushans who saw that odd familiar smile suddenly understood just how crooked it truly was.

"Actually," he continued, "the trickery was needed *because* of you. There was no way for Rao to rescue the princess so long as you stood guard over her. Even for him, that task was impossible."

He paused, letting the pride of that knowledge sweep the Kushans. Like Shakuntala, he knew full well that their own self-respect was the key to winning these men.

"So I convinced Venandakatra—or so I am told; I was very drunk that night, and remember little of our conversation—that Kushans were the most depraved men walking the earth. Satyrs, the lot of them, with a particular talent for seducing young virgins."

A little laugh rippled through the Kushans.

"Apparently, my words reached receptive ears." The general scratched his chin. "I fear Lord Venandakatra is perhaps too willing to believe the worst of other men. It might be better to say, to assume that other men are shaped in his own mold."

A much louder laugh filled the pavilion. A cheerful

laugh, at the folly of a great lord. A bitter laugh, for
that lord was not called the Vile One by accident.

Belisarius shrugged. "The rest you know. You were
unceremoniously dismissed as Shakuntala's guards, and
replaced by Mahaveda priests and mahamimamsa torturers. It was they who faced the Panther of Majarashtra
when he stalked through the palace."

All trace of humor vanished. Now, the Roman general's face seemed every bit as hard as the iron face of
Kungas. "The dagger which the Panther used to spill
the lives of those Malwa beasts came from my own
country. An excellent dagger, made by our finest craftsmen. I brought it with me to India, and saw to it that
it found its way into Rao's hands."

His face softened, slightly, with a trace of its usual
humor returning. "The Malwa, as we planned, thought
that the Empress had fled with Rao. And so they sent
thousands of Rajputs beating about the countryside. But
Rao was alone, and so was able to elude them. We knew
the Empress would not have the skill to do so. So, as we
had planned, Rao left her behind in the palace, hidden
in a closet in the guest quarters. When we arrived, two
days later, we hid her among Prince Eon's concubines."

He looked down at Kungas. The Kushan commander
returned his stare with no expression on his face.

"Kungas knew nothing of this, no more than any of
you. It is true, on the day we left Gwalior for Ranapur,
I believe that he recognized the Empress as we were
smuggling her into Prince Eon's howdah. I am not
certain, however, for he said nothing to me nor I to him.
Nor have we ever spoken on the matter since. But I
believe that he did recognize her. And, for his own
reasons, chose to remain silent."

Kujulo stared at his commander. "Is this true?" he
demanded.

Kungas nodded. "Yes. It is exactly as the Roman says.
I knew nothing about their scheme. But I did recognize
Shakuntala. On the day we left Gwalior for Ranapur, just
as he says."

"Why did you remain silent?" demanded Kujulo.

"That question you may not ask," replied Kungas. His tone, if possible, was even harder than his face. "You may question my actions, Kujulo, and demand an accounting of them. But you may not question *me*."

Kujulo shrank back, slightly. All the Kushans seemed to shrink.

Kungas dismissed the question with a curt chop. "Besides, it is a stupid question. Your decision tonight may be different, Kujulo. But do not pretend you don't understand my own. If you really need to ask that question, you are no kinsman of mine." His iron eyes swept the Kushans. "*Any of you.*"

A little sigh swept the pavilion. Suddenly, one of the Kushan soldiers toward the rear barked a little laugh.

"And why not?" he demanded. "I am sick of the Malwa. Sick of their arrogance, and the barks of Ye-tai dogs, and the sneers of Rajputs."

Another Kushan grunted his agreement. A third said, softly: "We are destined to die, anyway. Better to die an honored imperial bodyguard than a Malwa beast of burden."

"I'll have none of that talk," growled Kungas. "*There is no destiny.* There is only the edge of a good blade, and the skill of the man wielding it."

Quietly, at that moment, Ousanas reentered the pavilion. He was just in time to hear Kujulo's remark.

"And the brains of the man commanding the soldiers!" The Kushan laughed, then, in genuine good humor. Looking at the Empress, he nodded toward Belisarius.

"This man, I take it, is one of your allies, Empress." Kujulo paused, took a breath, made his decision.

"One of *our* allies, now." A quick, collective exhalation indicated that all the Kushan soldiers accepted the decision. Kujulo continued:

"He's a great schemer and trickster, that's for certain. But trickery will only take us so far. Is he good for anything else?"

Shakuntala reared up haughtily. In the corner of his

eye, Belisarius saw his own cataphracts stiffen with anger. He began to say something, but then, seeing Ousanas saunter forward, relaxed.

"Kushan soldier very great fool," remarked the dawazz cheerfully. "Probably asks pigeons how to eat meat, and crocodiles how to fly."

The African hunter planted himself before Kujulo, gazing down at the Kushan soldier. Kujulo craned his neck, returning the gaze. Anger at Ousanas' ridicule began to cloud his face.

"Why ask this question from the Empress of Andhra?" demanded Ousanas. "What she know of such things? Better to ask the Persians who survived Mindouos."

Anger faded, replaced by interest. Kujulo glanced at Belisarius.

"He has defeated Medes?" Like all warriors from central Asia, who had clashed with the Persian empire for centuries, Kujulo held Persian heavy cavalry in deep respect.

"Routed an entire army of the bastards!" snarled Valentinian from the back of the pavilion. "Just last year!"

"You might ask the Goths for their opinion, too, while you're at it," rumbled Anastasius. "He's whipped the barbarians so many times they finally asked him to be their king. Couldn't figure out any other way to beat him." The giant Thracian yawned. "He refused. No challenge to it, he said."

Kujulo eyed the Roman general with keen interest. He had never heard of Goths, but he had faced other barbarians in battle.

"So," he mused. "We are now the imperial bodyguard of the Satavahana dynasty. With nothing but Raghunath Rao as the general of a nonexistent army and this Belisarius as an ally."

Kujulo grinned. In that wolf's grin, at that moment, centuries of civilization vanished. The warrior of the steppes shone forth.

"Pity the poor Malwa!" exclaimed one of the other Kushan soldiers.

Kujulo's grin widened still.

"Better yet," he countered, *let us pity them not at all.*

Chapter 11

Exactly two weeks after Belisarius arrived at the capital of Kausambi, the Malwa finally met his price. All things considered, Belisarius was pleased with himself. As treason went, he thought he had driven a hard bargain. Especially for a novice.

Nanda Lal thought so too.

"You are as bad as a horse trader," chuckled the Malwa official. His Greek was excellent. Only the slightest trace of an accent and the extreme precision of his grammar indicated that he was not a native to the language. He chuckled again. "Are you certain you are really a general?"

Belisarius nodded. "I've been a soldier my entire adult life. But I was raised in the countryside, you know. Peasants are natural born hagglers."

Nanda Lal laughed. And a very open, hearty laugh it was, too. Belisarius was impressed. He thought he had never met a better liar in his entire life than Nanda Lal. Nor one whose inner soul was so far at variance with his outer trappings.

Officially, Nanda Lal bore many titles.

He was, first, one of the *anvaya-prapta sachivya*. The phrase translated, approximately, as "acquirer of the post of minister by hereditary descent." It indicated that Nanda Lal belonged to that most exclusive of Malwa elites, those who were blood kin of the Emperor and were thus entitled to call themselves part of the Malwa dynasty. No man in the Malwa Empire who was not anvaya-prapta sachivya could hope to rise to any of the very highest official posts, military or civilian.

Second, Nanda Lal was a *Mantrin*—a high counselor—and thus sat on the Empire's central advisory body to Emperor Skandagupta, the *Mantri-parishad*. True, Nanda Lal was one of the junior members of that council—what the Malwa called a *Kumaramatya*, a "cadet-minister"—but his status was still among the most exalted in all of India.

Third, Nanda Lal occupied the specific post which the Malwa called the *Akshapatal-adhikrita*. The title roughly translated into the innocuous-sounding phrase, "the Lord Keeper of State Documents."

What he really was, was a spy. It might be better to say, *the* spy. Or, better still, the grand *spymaster*.

Nanda Lal's laugh died away. After a last, rueful shake of his head, he asked:

"So, general, tell me. What did you think? I am quite curious, really. I was only joking, you know—about the horse trader business." Another little hearty chuckle. "Only a general would have demanded a tour of inspection of our military facilities before he gave his allegiance to our cause. In addition, of course, to a fortune." Hearty chuckle. "*Another* fortune, I should say." Hearty chuckle. "That was quite nicely done, by the way, if you'll permit me saying so." Hearty chuckle. "That little casual wave. 'Oh, something simple. Like the other chest you gave me.' "

Belisarius shrugged. "It seemed the most straightforward thing to do. And I wanted to know—well, let's just say that I'm sick to death of stingy, tight-fisted emperors, who expect miracles for a handful of coins. As to your question—what did I think?—"

Before answering, Belisarius examined the room carefully. He was not looking for eavesdroppers. He had not the slightest doubt they were there. He was simply interested.

Nanda Lal's official quarters, by Malwa standards, were positively austere. And Belisarius had noted, earlier, that Nanda Lal had brewed and served the tea they were drinking with his own hands. No servants were allowed in his inner sanctum.

Capable hands, thought Belisarius, glancing at them. Like most members of the dynastic clan, Nanda Lal was heavyset. But the spymaster's squat form had none of the doughy-soft appearance of most anvaya-prapta sachivya. There was quite a bit of muscle there, Belisarius suspected. And he did not doubt that Nanda Lal's hands were good at other tasks than brewing tea. For all their immaculate, manicured perfection, they were the hands of a strangler, not a scribe.

"I was very impressed," he replied. "Especially by the scale of the cannon manufacturing, and the ammunition works. You are—*we* are—amassing a tremendous weight of firepower to throw into battle."

He fell silent, scratching his chin thoughtfully.

"But—?" queried Nanda Lal.

"You haven't given enough thought to logistics," said Belisarius forcefully. "There's an old soldier's saying, Nanda Lal: *Amateurs study tactics; professionals study logistics*. The Veda weapons, whatever their origin—and you will please notice that I do not ask—are not truly magical. Even with them, it still took you two years to recapture Ranapur. You should have done it much sooner."

Nanda Lal seemed genuinely interested, now.

"Really? Let me ask you, general—how long would it have taken you to reduce Ranapur?"

"Eight months," came the instant reply, "without cannon. With them—four months."

The Malwa official's eyes widened.

"So quickly? What did we do wrong?"

"Two things. First, as I said, your logistics are lousy. You substitute mass labor for skill and expertise. You need to develop a professional quartermaster corps, instead of—" He did not sneer, quite. "Instead of piling up tens of thousands of men on top of each other. If you were to study the Ranapur campaign, I'm sure you'd find that most of that absurd pile of provisions simply went to feed the men who amassed it."

Belisarius leaned forward in his chair. "And that leads me to my second criticism. Your armies are much too slow, and—well, I won't say *timid*, exactly. Your soldiers seem courageous enough, especially the Ye-tai and Rajputs. But they are *used* timidly."

Nanda Lal's eyes held equal amounts of interest and suspicion.

"And you would use them better?" he asked. "If we made you our high commander?"

Belisarius did not miss the veiled antagonism. Suspicion came as naturally to Nanda Lal as swimming to a fish.

The Roman general dismissed the notion with a curt flip of his hand.

"Why ask, Nanda Lal? We have already agreed that I can best serve by returning to Rome. I will encourage Justinian's ambition to reconquer the western Mediterranean, and make sure that his armies are tied up there for years. That will clear the way for you to invade Persia without hindrance."

"And after Persia?"

Belisarius shrugged. "That is a problem for the future. When war finally erupts between Malwa and Rome, I will have to openly change allegiance. When that time comes, you will decide what position in your army to give me. I am not concerned with the question, at the moment. It is still several years away."

The suspicion faded from Nanda Lal's eyes. Abruptly, the Malwa official rose.

"I will give careful consideration to the points which you raise, general. But, for the moment, I think we can leave off this discussion."

Belisarius rose himself, stretching his limbs. Then said, with a rueful smile, "I don't suppose we're done for the day, by any chance?"

Nanda Lal's headshake was as rueful as Belisarius' smile.

"I'm afraid not. It's still early in the afternoon, general. There are at least four officials who have insisted on meeting you today. And then, this evening, we have an important social visit to make."

Belisarius cocked his eyebrow. Nanda Lal's shrug was an exquisite display of exasperation, resignation, carefully suppressed irritation. The accompanying smile exuded a sense of comradeship-in-travail.

"The Great Lady Holi—you have heard of her, perhaps?"

Belisarius shook his head.

"Ah! Well, she is the Emperor's favorite aunt. Quite a formidable woman, despite her age. For days, now, she has been demanding to meet you. She is fascinated, it seems, by all the tales concerning this mysterious foreign general."

Nanda Lal took Belisarius by the elbow and began ushering him toward the door. His smile broadened.

"Her main interest, I suspect, stems from your reputed appearance. She is immensely fond of the company of young, handsome men."

Seeing Belisarius' slight start, Nanda Lal laughed.

"Have no fear, general! The woman is almost seventy years old. And she is quite the ascetic, actually. I assure you, she just likes to look."

Nanda Lal opened the door. With his own hands, as always. No servants were allowed in *those* quarters. He followed Belisarius into the corridor beyond.

After locking the door—it was the only door in the palace, so far as Belisarius had seen, which had a lock—Nanda Lal led the way down the wide hall.

"Anyway, she has been pestering the Emperor for days. Finally, he tired of it. So, this morning, just before your arrival, he instructed me to take you to Great Lady Holi this evening, after we were finished."

Belisarius sighed. Nanda Lal grimaced.

"I understand, general. But, please, be of good cheer.

We will not be there long, I assure you. A few minutes
to pay our respects, a casual chat, no more."

Belisarius squared his shoulders with resignation.

"As you wish, Nanda Lal. She is in the palace?"

Nanda Lal made another rueful headshake.

"Alas, I fear not. She dislikes the palace. She claims
it is too noisy and crowded. So she makes her dwelling on a barge moored in the river."

Hearty chuckle. "It is not as bad as all that! You
wouldn't want to miss Great Lady Holi's barge, before
you leave. It is quite a marvel, really it is. The most
splendiferous barge in all creation!"

"I can't wait," muttered Belisarius. They were now
passing by the main entrance to the Grand Palace. The
general stopped Nanda Lal with a hand on his arm.
"Give me a moment, if you would, to notify my cataphracts of our plans. There's no need for them to stand
outside in that hot sun for the rest of the day."

Nanda Lal nodded graciously. Belisarius strode
through the palace doors into the courtyard beyond. As
always, the three cataphracts were waiting just outside
the main entrance to the Grand Palace. Their horses,
and that of Belisarius, were tethered nearby.

Since the first day of their arrival at Kausambi, when
Belisarius had begun his protracted negotiations with the
Mantri-parishad, he had ordered the cataphracts to remain outside. To have taken them with him, wherever
he went in the palace, would have indicated a certain
skittishness which would be quite inappropriate for a
man cheerfully planning treason. And, besides, the
cataphracts would have inevitably cast a pall on his
negotiations. Many of the anvaya-prapta sachivya who
inhabited the palace had been present in the pavilion
when the lord of Ranapur and his family were executed.
And those who weren't, had heard the tale. It would
have been amusing, of course, to watch the highest of
Malwa cringe in the presence of Valentinian. Amusing,
but counter-productive.

Quickly, Belisarius sketched the situation and told his

cataphracts to go back to their residence. Valentinian
put up a bit of an argument, but not much. More in
the nature of a formality, than anything else. They *were*
supposed to be bodyguards, after all. But Belisarius
insisted, and his men were happy enough to climb on
their horses and return to the comfort—and shade—
of their luxurious quarters.

"That's all of it, Your Majesty," said Holkar. He tied
the drawstring of the bag tightly, and nestled it into a
pocket of silk cloth in the small chest. Then he closed
the lid of the chest and stood up. For a moment, he
examined his handiwork admiringly, and then scanned
the rest of the room.

Since arriving at Kausambi, the Romans and Ethiopians had been quartered in a mansion located in the
imperial district of the capital. The imperial district
stretched along the south bank of the Jamuna, just west
of that river's junction with the mighty Ganges. The
Emperor's Grand Palace anchored the eastern end of
the district. The mansion lay toward the western end,
not far from the flotilla of luxurious barges which served
the Malwa elite as temporary residences during the
summer. The waters of the Jamuna in which that fleet
was anchored helped assuage the heat.

Stretching in a great arc just south of the imperial
district was the heart of the Malwa weapons and muni-
tions project, a great complex of cannon, rocket and
gunpowder manufactories. The odors wafting from that
complex were often obnoxious, but the Malwa elite
tolerated the discomfort for the sake of security. The
"Veda weapons" were the core of their power, and they
kept them close at hand.

The mansion in which the foreigners had been lodged
belonged to one of Skandagupta's innumerable second
cousins, absent on imperial assignment in Bihar. The
building was almost a small palace. There had been more
than enough rooms to quarter the entire Kushan escort
within its walls, in addition to the foreign envoys

themselves. And, best of all, for Shakuntala and Eon, they had finally been able to spend a few nights alone.

Shakuntala, at least, had spent the nights alone in her bed. Dadaji glanced over at Tarabai, sitting on a cushion in the corner of Shakuntala's huge bedchamber. He restrained a smile. The Maratha woman had been almost inseparable from Eon since their arrival. Today, in fact, was the first day she had resumed her duties as an imperial lady-in-waiting.

If, at least, the activity of the day could be called the duty of a chambermaid. Holkar rather doubted it. Rarely—probably never—had an imperial lady-in-waiting spent an entire day helping her Empress count a fortune.

Holkar's eyes returned to the chest whose lid he had just closed. That chest was only one of many small chests which were strewn about Shakuntala's quarters. Those chests were much smaller than the chest which stood in the center of the room. That chest, that huge chest, dazzling in its intricate carvings and adorned with gold and rubies—the colors of the Malwa dynasty—was now completely empty.

Shakuntala shook her head. She almost seemed in a daze. When she spoke, her voice was half-filled with awe.

"I can't believe it," she whispered. "There was as much in that chest as—as—"

Dadaji smiled. "As the yearly income of a prince. A *rich* prince."

The scribe stroked his jaw. "Still, it's not really that much—for an imperial warchest."

Shakuntala was still shaking her head. "How will I ever repay Belisarius?" she mused.

Dadaji's smile broadened. "Have no fear, Your Majesty. The general does not expect to be repaid with coin, only with the blows you will deliver onto Malwa. Blows which this treasure will help to finance. How did he put it? 'An empress without money is a political and military cripple. A crippled ally will not be much use to Rome.'"

Shakuntala left off shaking her head. After taking a deep breath, she sat up straight.

"He is right, of course. But—how many men do you know would turn over such a fortune to a stranger? And it wasn't just the last Malwa bribe, either."

"How many men?" asked Holkar. "Very few, Your Majesty. Very, very few." The slave laughed aloud. "And I know of only one who would do so with such glee!"

Shakuntala grinned herself, remembering Belisarius' cheerful words the previous evening, when he presented her with the chest which Nanda Lal had just bestowed on him—and half the contents of the first, the one Skandagupta gave him at Ranapur.

I like to think of it as poetic justice, the Roman general had said, smiling crookedly. *Let the Malwa bribes finance Andhra's rebellion.*

It had taken the entire day for Shakuntala, her Maratha women, and Holkar to repackage the coins and gems into smaller units which could be more easily transported. Most of the treasure was packed away in the many small chests. But some of it had been placed in purses which Shakuntala had distributed to all the members of her party.

The Maratha women, poor in their origins, had been absolutely stunned by her act. Each of them now carried on her person more money than their entire extended families had earned in generations of toil. Holkar glanced shrewdly at the four young women sitting in the corner. They had recovered from the shock, he thought. But if there had been any lingering doubt or hesitation in their allegiance to Shakuntala, it had now vanished. The trust of their Empress had welded them to her completely.

When Holkar's eyes returned to Shakuntala, he immediately understood the question in her face.

"There is no need, Your Majesty," he said, shaking his head. "My allegiance is still to Belisarius, even though you are my sovereign. If he wishes me to have money, he will give it to me. I cannot take it from another. And besides—" he gestured mockingly at his loincloth "—where would I hide it?"

Shakuntala began to reply, but was interrupted by a knock on the door.

Tarabai opened the door. Valentinian stepped into the room, accompanied by Eon. They walked over to Shakuntala.

"We may as well plan for an early supper," said Eon. The Prince gestured at Valentinian. "The cataphracts just arrived from the palace. Belisarius dismissed them for the rest of the day. It seems he won't be returning until late this evening. He has some social event he must attend."

The cataphract scowled. "These imperial Malwa are even worse than Greek nobility, when it comes to hob-nobbing with celebrities. Bad enough he's got to waste hours with every third-rate bureaucrat in the Palace. Now, they're insisting he has to meet with old women."

Shakuntala frowned. "Old women? In the palace?"

Valentinian shook his head. "No, worse. They're dragging him off to some barge in the river to meet with one of the Emperor's elderly relatives. A great-aunt, I think."

Shakuntala grew still. Utterly still.

"What is her name?" she hissed.

Valentinian squinted at her, startled by her tone of voice.

"She's called the Great Lady Holi. Why?"

Shakuntala shot to her feet.

"She is a witch! A sorceress!"

Valentinian and Eon gaped at her. Shakuntala stamped her foot angrily.

"It is true, you fools!"

With an effort, the girl restrained herself. These were the type of men, she knew, for whom any hint of hys-terics would be counterproductive.

"Believe me, Valentinian. Eon." Her voice was low and calm, but deadly serious. "My father spoke of her several times to me. His spies did not know much—it was dangerous to get near her—but they did learn enough to know that she is very powerful among the Malwa. Do not let her age deceive you. *She—is—a—witch.*"

Valentinian was the first to recover.

"I'll get the others," he said, spinning around to the door.

Less than a minute later he was back, followed by all the members of the Roman and Axumite missions. He brought Kungas also.

Eon took charge.

"We have an unexpected situation, which we need to assess."

Quickly, the Prince sketched the situation. Then, to Kungas:

"Bring Kanishka. And Kujulo, and your other two troop leaders."

Kungas disappeared. Eon waved everyone else into the room.

"All of you. Come in and sit."

In the short seconds that it took for everyone to take a seat—most of them on the floor—Kungas returned with his four chief subordinates in tow. The five Kushans entered the room but did not bother to sit.

Eon began at once.

"You've all heard—" He hesitated, casting a glance at Kungas.

"I've told them," grunted the Kushan commander.

"You've all heard about the situation," continued Eon. "It may be a false alarm. But there's enough reason to think otherwise." He took a breath. "As you know, we hoped to make our exit from India quietly. Just a peaceful diplomatic mission heading back for home. But Belisarius always warned us that things could go wrong. That's why he insisted on obtaining those horses, and the elephants."

Another breath. A deep breath.

"Well, that time may be here. We have to assume that it is."

He scanned the room. Everyone's face was grim, but

not distraught. Except, possibly, for Menander. The young cataphract's face was pale from fear. Not fear for himself, but for his general.

"Do you have a plan?" asked Anastasius.

Eon shrugged. "Belisarius discussed some possible alternatives. You heard them yourself. But none of those alternatives really apply, since Belisarius himself may not be able to join us. So we'll have to improvise."

He stared at Shakuntala.

"The first thing is to make sure she gets out safely. Kungas, you and your men will escort the Empress and her women."

The Kushans nodded.

Eon glanced around the room, examining the treasure chests. "Good. You're already prepared."

Anastasius interrupted. "They'll have to take the Kushan girls, too. If the general's in a trap, we'll need to make one hell of a diversion. We won't be able to do it with the girls in tow."

"That's not a problem," stated Kungas. "We can fit them in as camp followers. No one will think it odd."

Eon nodded his head. "All right. The rest of us—except Dadaji—will be the lure. Dadaji, you'll have to go with the Empress."

Eon drove down Holkar's protest.

"You are not thinking, man! Forget your obligation to Belisarius, and remember your obligation to his purpose. The only way to get Shakuntala out of here is by subterfuge. A young noblewoman would never travel through India unaccompanied. *Someone has to pose as her husband.* It can't be one of us. Only Valentinian looks enough like an Indian, and his accent is terrible. You're the only one who could pull it off."

Holkar opened his mouth, snapped it shut. Then, grudgingly, nodded. He even recaptured his sense of humor. "With your permission, Your Majesty."

Shakuntala nodded imperiously, but there was just a little trace of a smile on her lips.

"I'll need a change of clothes," murmured Holkar. "A

loincloth simply won't do." He chuckled. "How fortunate that Belisarius made me buy those clothes! Is he a fortune-teller, do you think?"

Valentinian shook his head. "No. But he does like to plan for all eventualities. Cover all the angles."

"Such mechanistic nonsense," said Ousanas cheerfully. "The truth is quite otherwise. Belisarius is a witch himself. Fortunately, he is *our* witch."

Valentinian ignored the quip. "Anything else?" he demanded.

"Yes," said Kungas. "You will need a guide." He pointed to Kujulo. "Kujulo is very familiar with the Deccan, and his Marathi is fluent. Three or four other of my men are also. Take all of them with you. You will need the added manpower, anyway. Yours will be the bloody road."

Kujulo grinned. Eon frowned.

"We can't have any hint that Kushans are involved," he protested. "That could jeopardize the Empress."

Kungas waved the protest aside. "They can disguise themselves as Ye-tai. Kujulo does an excellent imitation."

Immediately, Kujulo stooped, thrust out his lower jaw, slumped his shoulders, allowed a vacant look to enter his gaze, grunted animal noises. A little laugh swept the room.

There was no time for hesitation. Eon nodded. Then said:

"Fine. That's it, then. Let's—"

"No."

The imperial tone froze everyone in the room. Eon began to glare at Shakuntala.

"We've already—"

"No."

Valentinian tried. "Your Majesty, our plans—"

"No."

Before anyone else could speak, Shakuntala said forcefully:

"You are not thinking clearly. None of you."

Eon: "The general—"

"You are *especially* not thinking like the general."

Valentinian, hotly: "Of course we're thinking of him! But there's nothing—" The cataphract stopped abruptly. Shakuntala's actual words penetrated.

Her piercing black eyes, fixed upon him, held Valentinian pinned.

"Yes," she said. "You are not thinking *like* Belisarius. If *he* were faced with a sudden change in his situation, *he* would alter the situation. Add a new angle."

"What angle?" demanded Eon.

Shakuntala grinned. "We need *another* diversion. A great one! Something which can serve to signal all of us—we will be separated, remember—that the escape is on. A diversion so great it will not only help cover our own escape, but make it possible—maybe—for Belisarius himself to escape."

"I'm for it!" announced Menander. With a shrug: "Whatever it is."

Shakuntala told him what it was. When she finished, the room erupted with protests from everyone except Menander.

"I'm for it," repeated the young cataphract stubbornly.

"Fool girl is mad," muttered Ousanas. "I say it again—royalty stupid by nature."

Shakuntala overrode all protests with the simplest of arguments.

I command.

Protest, protest, protest.

I command.

Protest, protest, protest.

I command.

On the way out, Kanishka complained bitterly to his commander.

"How are we supposed to be an imperial bodyguard if the damned Empress herself—"

Kungas looked at him. As always, his face showed nothing. But there might have been just a trace of humor in his words:

"You could always go back to work for Venandakatra. *He* never took any personal risks."

Kanishka shut up.

As he and Nanda Lal walked out of the palace that evening, Belisarius found that a palanquin had already been brought up to convey them to the Great Lady Holi's barge. The palanquin was festooned with the red and gold pennants of the dynasty. The pennants alone guaranteed that all would give way to the palanquin, wherever it went in the teeming capital. But they were hardly necessary. The forty Ye-tai bodyguards who rode before the palanquin would cheerfully trample anyone so foolish as to get in the way. And the palanquin itself, toted by no less than twelve slaves, looked solid and heavy enough to crush an elephant.

"Quite an entourage," he murmured. "Does she really insist on so many bodyguards?"

Nanda Lal shook his head.

"As it happens, the Great Lady is petrified by armed strangers anywhere in the vicinity of her barge. She maintains her own special security force. She does not even trust the imperial bodyguard." The spymaster pointed to the red-and-gold uniformed Ye-tai. "Only four of these men will be allowed to remain after we arrive."

The journey to the barge was quite brief. The wharves where the Malwa empire's highest nobility maintained their pleasure barges were less than half a mile from the Grand Palace. Once they climbed out of the palanquin, Belisarius found himself almost goggling at the Great Lady Holi's barge.

As Nanda Lal had said, it was truly splendid. In its basic size and shape the barge was no different from that of all the Malwa luxury barges. About ninety feet long and thirty feet wide, the barges had a rounded and big-bellied shape. The oddest thing, to the Roman's eyes, were the double sterns, looking not unlike the sterns of two ships joined. Each stern sported a huge figurehead in the form of an animal's head. Lions, in the case of Great Lady Holi's barge.

The *splendor* was in the trimmings. Everywhere, the

red and gold colors of the dynasty: The huge lion's-head figurines were covered with beaten gold. All the oar-locks were trimmed with gold. Rubies inlaid into gold plaques formed the edging of the guard rails. And on and on and on. It was amazing the boat didn't sink from the sheer weight of its decoration.

Belisarius followed Nanda Lal up the ramp which connected the barge to the wharf. The ramp debouched in a covered walkway which encircled the main cabins. Once aboard the vessel, Nanda Lal entered through a door directly opposite the ramp. A moment later, Belisarius found himself in the plush interior of the barge.

Aide's thought came like a thunderclap.

Danger.

Belisarius almost stumbled.

Why?

Link is here. I can sense it.

The facets shivered with agitation. But the general simply smiled.

At last. My enemy.

Chapter 12

At the corner of the alley, Kungas made a little motion with his hand. The Kushan soldiers following him immediately halted. Kungas edged to the corner and peeked out onto the main street.

He was not worried about being spotted. At night, the streets of Kausambi were lit by lanterns, but the Malwa were stingy in their placement. As great as was the dynasty's wealth, it was not unlimited, and the massive armament campaign forced a stretching of funds elsewhere. The elite themselves did not worry about stumbling in the dark. They were borne everywhere on slave-toted palanquins, after all. And if the slaves should stumble, and discomfit their masters, what did it matter? After the slaves were impaled, new ones would replace them. Unlike street lanterns, slaves were cheap.

Satisfied, he turned away. The ten Kushans following him clustered closely, so that they could hear his whispered words.

"Two doors. The main door, almost directly across, is guarded by three Mahaveda. Fifty feet farther down is another door. Two Ye-tai."

"That'll be the guardhouse," whispered one of the Kushans. "A full squad of Ye-tai inside."

Kungas nodded. "Bring the Empress."

Another of the soldiers glided back down the alley. A minute later he returned, with Shakuntala and her Maratha women in tow.

Watching them approach, Kungas managed not to smile, though he found it a struggle. Some of his soldiers failed completely. Two of them were grinning outright. Fortunately, they had enough sense to turn their faces away.

Never in India's history, he thought wrily, *has an Empress looked liked this.*

Any trace of imperial regalia was gone, as if it had never existed. Shakuntala, and her ladies, were now costumed in the traditional garb of north Indian prostitutes. Their saris were not unusual, but the bright orange scarves which wrapped their waists were never worn by respectable women. And while poor women customarily walked barefoot, none but prostitutes wore those large, garish bangles attached to their ankles.

The bangles and scarves had been provided by Ahilyabai. The Maratha woman, it turned out, had kept them secreted away in her traveling pack. She had hoped never to use them again, but—who could know what life might bring? She and the other Maratha women had shown Shakuntala how to wear them.

Quickly, Kungas sketched the situation for the Empress. Shakuntala nodded.

"We will wait, then, for the signal. If it comes."

She glanced around, frowning.

"But what will we do if someone spots us in the meantime? We may be here for some time. We are still not sure if this escape will be necessary."

Kungas did smile, now. Very slightly.

"That's no problem at all, Your Majesty. In the darkness, it will simply look like a squad of soldiers entertaining themselves in an alley. No-one will think to investigate, not even Ye-tai. Soldiers get surly when they are interrupted in their sport."

Shakuntala grimaced.

"I'm getting awfully tired of that particular disguise," she muttered. But, in truth, there was no ill-humor in the remark. Watching her, Kungas thought the Empress was almost hoping the escape attempt would be necessary. She was as high-spirited as a racing horse, and whatever else, a desperate escape would at least bring relief from the endless weeks of immobility.

He turned away, partly to keep a watchful eye on the mouth of the alley. Mostly, however, he turned away because even Kungas could not suppress a grin, now.

Being the bodyguard to this Empress is going to be interesting. Like being a bodyguard for the monsoon.

In his own alley, a half mile to the northwest, Ousanas was also finding it hard not to grin. The Ye-tai guarding the Great Lady Holi's barge were, as usual, paying no attention to their duty. All four of them were engrossed in a quiet game of chance, rolling finger bones across the wood planks of the wharf. The bones themselves made little noise beyond a clattering rattle, but the Ye-tai grunts and hisses of triumph and dismay were audible for thirty yards.

Ousanas glanced up at the barge. Two Malwa stood guard at the head of the ramp which provided access to the barge. The Malwa guards, unlike the Ye-tai on the wharf below them, were lightly armored and bore only short swords. But the grenades suspended from their belts indicated their kshatriya status.

The kshatriyas were leaning against the rail of the barge, glaring down at the Ye-tai. Again, Ousanas fought down a grin. Like anyone who chooses to keep a wild animal for a pet, the Malwa were often exasperated by the Ye-tai. But, for all their obvious displeasure at the Ye-tai behavior, the kshatriyas made no attempt to stop the gambling. No more would a man try to stop his pet hyena from gnawing on a bone.

Ousanas moved back a little farther into the alley, hiding against the overhanging branches of a large bush. He was not worried about being spotted. The Malwa dynasty also did not waste money clearing wild shrubbery from the alleys of their capital. Why should they? They did not travel through alleys.

He hefted one of his javelins, gauging the throw. He

had brought two of the weapons, along with his great stabbing spear. The blades of all three had been blackened with soot.

Again, Ousanas hefted the javelin. Yes, the range was good. If it proved necessary, he would use the javelins to deal with the kshatriyas on the barge. The stabbing spear he would save for the Ye-tai.

He did not even think about the two grenades which Menander had given him. To Ousanas, the grenades were simply signaling devices. They were far too impersonal for Ye-tai.

Elsewhere, a mile to the southwest, Menander was regretting the absence of his stolen grenades. As he watched the mass of Malwa common soldiers milling around the campfires where they were cooking their evening meal, he thought that a couple of well-placed grenades would do wonders.

But he said nothing. The grenades had been the only things they had which could give the signal, if the signal proved necessary. It had been Menander himself who had made the suggestion. And besides, the young cataphract didn't want to hear another lecture from Valentinian on the virtues of cold steel.

Menander turned his head and looked to his left. Valentinian was crouched behind a tree trunk, not four feet away. The veteran met his gaze, but said nothing. Menander looked to his right. He could not see Anastasius, but he knew the cataphract was there, hidden a little further down the line of trees which bordered the Malwa army camp. Ezana and Wahsi would be hiding near him, still farther down the line. Prince Eon would be somewhere near them.

Garmat was hidden in the trees also, but the adviser was further back. Despite his protests, the old brigand had been assigned the duty of holding the horses. He and Kadphises, the Kushan soldier who would serve as their guide if they had to make an escape. Somebody had to do it, after all. There were twenty of those horses, all of them high-spirited and tense. Garmat was the best horseman among them, Ezana had pointed out forcefully, and so the duty naturally fell to him. No one had mentioned the adviser's age, of course, but Garmat's glare had shown plainly what he thought of the arrangement.

Menander did not even try to spot Kujulo and the three Kushan soldiers with him. They would also, by now, have found their own hiding place in the trees. But that hiding place would be on the opposite side of the little army base.

Gloomily, Menander studied the Malwa soldiers clustering around their campfires. Eight hundred of them, he estimated. Piss-poor soldiers, true. But they were still the enemy, and there were still eight hundred of them.

Mother of God, I hope this won't be more than an exercise. A sleepless night in the woods, at worst. False alarm. Tomorrow, Belisarius is back. No problem. Everybody has a big laugh on the subject of twitchy nerves. Soon enough, we amble out of India in comfort and ease. Back to Rome, with nary a drop of spilled blood.

To his left, watching Menander in the flickering light cast by the campfires, Valentinian saw the little interplay of emotions on the young cataphract's face. The veteran grinned.

Welcome to the club, lad. It's the First Law of the Veteran.

Fuck exciting adventures.

A mile to the east, to the relief of some fifteen Kushan soldiers, Dadaji Holkar pronounced himself satisfied with the howdahs.

"About time," grumbled Kanishka.

Holkar stared him down. And quite an effective stare it was, too. Just what you might expect from a Malwa grandee, which was exactly what Holkar looked like in his new finery. The very essence of a grandee. Not *anvaya-prapta sachivya*, to be sure—no member of that most exclusive dynastic caste would have personally overseen the loading of his own elephants. But the Malwa Empire had a multitude of grandees, especially in Kausambi. The capital was full of officials, noblemen, bureaucrats, potentates of every stripe and variety.

Holkar turned away and strode over to the stable-keeper. That man, blessed by the same haughty stare, abased himself in a most gratifying manner. His three sons, standing just behind, copied their father faithfully.

Watching him fawn, Holkar felt enormous relief. He had been afraid he would have to murder them. And if he had been forced to order the Kushans to kill the men of the family, there would have been no choice but to slaughter the other members of the stablekeeper's household. A wife, a daughter, two daughters-in-law, and three servants.

Holkar would have done it, if necessary. But the deed would have cut to his soul. The stablekeeper was no Malwa enemy. Just a man feeding his family, by caring for the horses and elephants of those richer than he.

But there was no need. It was obvious that the disguise had passed muster perfectly. True, it was odd for such a grandee to make his departure at night, rather than in daytime. But Holkar had explained the matter satisfactorily. Urgent news. His wife's father on his death-bed.

"Fool woman," he grumbled. "She insists on an immediate departure—in the middle of the night!—and then takes hours to prepare herself."

The stablekeeper, daringly, essayed a moment of shared camaraderie.

"What can you do, lord? Women are impossible!"

For a moment, Holkar glared at the man's presumption. But, after seeing the stablekeeper cringe properly, he relented. He had intimidated the man enough, he thought. A bit of kindness, now, would seal the disguise.

"I am most satisfied with you, stablekeeper," he announced, pompously. "The elephants have been well cared for, and the howdahs which you constructed are quite to my satisfaction."

The stablekeeper bowed and scraped effusively, but Holkar was amused to see that the man's eyes never left off from watching Holkar's hand. And when the stablekeeper saw that hand dip into the very large purse suspended from Holkar's waist, his eyes positively gleamed.

"As I promised you, there would be a bonus for good work."

Holkar, watching the man's face as he deposited a small pile of coins in the stablekeeper's outstretched hand, decided he had gauged the bonus correctly.

But, just to be sure, Holkar decided to unbend a bit.

"Yes, I am very satisfied. Might I make a request? Since my wife appears to be delayed, would you be so good as to feed my men? I have mentioned to them, from my previous visits, how excellent a cook your wife is."

He dipped his hand into the purse again.

"I will pay, of course."

Within seconds, the stablekeeper's household was flurrying into action.

Watching the perfect unfolding of their plan, the scribe Dadaji Holkar smiled. Warriors, he knew, were prone to dark misgivings about any and all plans. Holkar did not sneer at those misgivings. He had been a warrior himself, in his youth. But he concluded, as he had years before, that soldiers were a gloomy lot.

One soldier, at that very moment, was not gloomy at all.

He had come to India for a number of reasons, and with several goals in mind. Many—most—of those goals he had already achieved. He had used the voyage to forge an alliance between Rome and Ethiopia. He had freed the Empress of Andhra from captivity, and thus laid the basis for another alliance with she and Raghunath Rao. (He had even, to his delight, managed to use Malwa bribes to fund the future Deccan rebellion.) He had been able to learn much concerning the new Malwa gunpowder weapons, knowledge which—combined with Aide's help—would make possible the creation of a new Roman army capable of dealing with the Malwa juggernaut.

Mainly, however, Belisarius had come to India in order to know his enemy. He was a general, and he considered good intelligence to be the most useful of all military assets. Here, too, he had accomplished much. He had seen the Malwa army in action, as well as their Ye-tai, Rajput and Kushan auxiliaries. He had been able to study the workings of Malwa society at close hand. He had even been able, to some extent, to meet and gauge the Emperor himself and many of his top military and civilian advisers.

But the one thing he had not accomplished was to meet his ultimate enemy. *Link*. The—being? creature?—who was, in some way, the origin of the newly arisen menace threatening Rome and, he thought, all of mankind. *Link*.

He was not sure, yet. But, following Nanda Lal through the plushness of the royal barge, he thought he was on the verge of achieving that goal also.

Aide, certainly, thought he was.

Yes. Link is here. I am certain of it.

Belisarius remembered the glimpses Aide had given him once before of the strange thinking machines called computers. Huge things, some of them—rows and rows of steel cabinets. Others no bigger than a small chest. Metal and glass, glowing as if by magic.

Not those. The new gods have driven cybernetics far beyond such primitive devices.

The word "cybernetics" was meaningless to Belisarius. Other words which followed were equally so. *Nanotechnology. Microminiaturization. Cybernetic organisms.*

They were nearing the end of the long corridor which extended down the side of the barge. Ahead of him, Belisarius saw Nanda Lal step across a raised threshhold into what appeared to be a large room.

We are almost there, he said to Aide.

He sensed the agitation of the facets. Aide's next thought was curt:

Link will be a cyborg. A cybernetic organism. It will look like a human, but will not be. There will be no soul behind the eyes.

Then, with the cool shivering which was as close as crystalline consciousness could come to fear:

If I am present in your mind, it may discover me. In the chaos at the pavilion, when I asked you to look into the Emperor's eyes, I was certain I could disguise myself. Here—I am not certain. The facets can hide, but Aide may not be able to.

Belisarius was at the threshhold himself. He paused, as if gauging the height of the step necessary to cross the small barrier.

Dissolve yourself, then. Until you can safely reappear. You are our greatest asset. We must keep knowledge of you hidden from the enemy.

If Aide dissolves, the facets will not be able to help. This moment is very dangerous for you.

Belisarius strode across the threshhold.

My name is Belisarius. I am your general. Do as I command.

If there was any hesitation in Aide's reply, no human could have measured it.

Yes, Great One.

The salon into which Belisarius stepped was, in its own way, as phantasmagorical as the pavilion which Emperor Skandagupta had erected on a battlefield. Such incredible luxury, aboard a barge, verged on the ludicrous.

The room was large, especially for a boat, but could not be described as huge. It was perhaps thirty feet wide. Belisarius, quickly estimating the width of the barge itself, realized that the side walls of the salon were the actual hull of the barge. The planking of the hull, here on the interior, was almost completely covered— deck to ceiling—with exquisite silk tapestries. Most of the tapestries depicted scenes which were obviously mythological. Based on various tales which Dadaji had told him, he thought that one of the tapestries might be a depiction of Arjuna riding with Krishna at the battle of Kurukshetra. But he was not sure, and he did not waste time examining the tapestries carefully.

He was much more interested in the few areas of the walls which were not covered with tapestries. The salon was some forty feet in length. At three places along each wall, separated by a distance of approximately ten feet, were three-foot-square bamboo frames supporting silk mesh. The silk was dyed, in Malwa red and gold, but not otherwise decorated. Belisarius could not see through the mesh squares. But, from their slight billowing, he knew that they were the coverings for windows designed to let air into the salon.

After a moment's glance at the windows, he looked away. Ahead of him, at the far end of the salon, two women were seated on a dais which was elevated perhaps a foot above the level of the thickly carpeted deck. The chairs in which they sat could not be called thrones. They were not, quite, big enough. That aside, however, they were chairs which any emperor would be proud to call his own. The chairs were made of nothing but carved ivory, covered with a minimum of cushioning. Neither gold nor gems adorned those chairs. Such baubles would have simply degraded the intricate and marvelous carvings which embellished every square inch of their surface.

Both women were shrouded in rich saris, and both women's faces were obscured by veils. From a distance, Belisarius could discern little about them. But he thought, from the slight subtleties of their posture, that the one on his right was much older than the other.

Directly in front of the dais, kneeling, was a line of six men. Eunuchs, Belisarius suspected, from what he had learned of Malwa customs with high-born women. The men were all wearing baggy trousers tied off at the ankles. They were barefoot and barechested.

Racially, the men were of a type unfamiliar to Belisarius. Oriental, clearly, but quite unlike any of the Asiatic peoples with which Belisarius was familiar. Their skin tone was yellowish, quite unlike the brown hues of the various Indian peoples. And while Belisarius had often seen that yellowish color on the skins of steppe nomads—Ye-tai, and especially Kushans, were often that tint, or close to it—these men had none of the lean, hard-featured characteristics of Asians from the steppes. Like Kushans—though not Ye-tai, who were often called "white" Huns—these men also had a slanted look to their eyes. If anything, their epicanthic folds were even more pronounced. But their features were soft-looking, without a trace of steppe starkness. And their faces were so round as to be almost moon-shaped.

Their most striking characteristic, however, was sheer size. All of them were enormous. Belisarius estimated their height at well over six feet—closer to seven—and he thought that none of them weighed less than three hundred pounds. Some of that size was fat, true. All six of the men had bellies which bulged forward noticeably. But Belisarius did not fail to note their huge arms and their great, sloping shoulders. The muscles there, coiled beneath the fat, were like so many pythons.

Nor, of course, did the general miss the bared tulwars which each man held across his knees. Those tulwars were the biggest swords Belisarius had ever seen in his life. None but giants such as these could have possibly wielded them.

Nanda Lal, standing a few feet ahead of him, bowed deeply to the two women. He then turned to Belisarius, and, with an apologetic grimace, whispered:

"I am afraid we must search you for weapons, general. As I told you, Great Lady Holi is extremely sensitive concerning her personal safety."

Belisarius stiffened. Nanda Lal's demand was discourteous in the extreme. As the spymaster well knew, Belisarius was *already* unarmed—had been, for days. As a matter of course, he did not carry weapons with him in the presence of Malwa royalty. He had left his arms behind in the mansion that morning, as he did every day he went to the Grand Palace. The act had come naturally to him. His own emperor, Justinian, would have been apoplectic if anyone other than his bodyguards carried weapons into the imperial presence.

But he saw no point in protest. If, as Aide suspected, he was truly in the presence of Link, the Malwa paranoia was understandable.

"Of course," he said. He spread his arms, inviting Nanda Lal to search his person. Then, hearing a slight cough behind him, turned around.

Four men were standing there. Belisarius had not heard a whisper of their coming. Despite the thick carpeting, he was impressed. Quickly, he gauged them. The men were clearly of the same race as the giant eunuchs, but, unlike them, were of average size. Nor were any of them bearing those huge tulwars. Instead, each of the four men was armed with nothing Belisarius could see beyond long knives scabbarded to their waists.

Their size did not mislead the general. Belisarius thought they were probably twice as dangerous as the giant eunuchs. And he was certain—from the silent manner of their arrival even more than their sure-footed stance—that all four were expert assassins.

Still with his arms raised, he allowed the foremost of those men to search him. The assassin's search was quick and expert. When the man was finished, he stepped back and said a few phrases in a language Belisarius did not know.

Nanda Lal frowned.

"He says you are carrying a small knife. In that pouch, on your belt."

Startled, Belisarius looked down at the pouch in question. He began to reach for it, but froze when he sensed the sudden stillness in the four assassins watching him.

Belisarius turned his head toward Nanda Lal.

"I did not even think of it, Nanda Lal. It is not a

weapon. It's simply a little knife I carry with me to sharpen my ink quills."

With a wry smile:

"I imagine I could kill a chicken with it, after a desperate struggle." He shrugged. "You're quite welcome to take the thing, if it makes you nervous."

Nanda Lal stared at him for a moment. Then, without taking his eyes from the general, asked the assassin a question in that same unknown tongue.

The assassin spoke a few phrases. Nanda Lal smiled.

"Never mind, general. Great Lady Holi's chief body-guard confirms your depiction of the—ah, device."

Now the image of cordiality, Nanda Lal took Belisarius by the arm and began leading him toward the women at the far end of the salon. The spymaster leaned over and whispered:

"The bodyguard says the chicken would win."

Belisarius smiled crookedly. "He underestimates my prowess. But I'm quite certain I would carry the scars to my grave."

Ten feet from the line of kneeling eunuchs, Nanda Lal brought himself and Belisarius to a halt. Nanda Lal—Belisarius following the spymaster's example—bowed deeply, but did not prostrate himself. Two servants appeared from a small door in the corner of the room behind the seated women. The servants carried cushions, which they set on the floor just in front of Belisarius and Nanda Lal. That done, each man stepped away. They did not leave, however, but remained standing, one on either side. As he squatted down on his cushion, Belisarius gave them both a quick, searching, sidelong scrutiny.

Servants, I think. Nothing more.

A feminine voice drew his attention forward. The voice had the timber of a young woman, and it came—just as he had surmised—from the woman seated to his left.

"We are very pleased to meet you at last, General Belisarius. We have heard so much about you."

Belisarius could discern nothing of the woman's face,

because of her veil. But he did not miss the sharp intelligence in that voice, lurking beneath the platitudes. Nor the fact that the Greek in which it spoke was perfect. Without a trace of an accent.

He nodded his head in acknowledgment, but said nothing.

The young woman continued.

"My name is Sati. I have the honor of being one of Emperor Skandagupta's daughters. This—" a slight gesture of the hand to the woman seated next to her "—is the Great Lady Holi. The Emperor's aunt, as I imagine you have already been told."

The Great Lady Holi's head bobbed, minutely. Beyond that, the woman was as still as a statue. The veil completely disguised her face also.

Again, Belisarius nodded.

"My aunt asked to meet you because she has heard that you desire to give your allegiance to the destiny of Malwa. And she has heard that you have proposed the most ingenious plan to further our great cause."

Belisarius decided that this last remark required a reply.

"I thank you—and her—for your kind words. I would not go so far as to describe my plan as ingenious. Though it is, I think, shrewd. The Roman Emperor Justinian is planning to invade the western Mediterranean anyway. I simply intend to encourage him in the endeavour. In that manner, without drawing suspicion upon myself, I can keep Rome's armies from interfering with your coming conquest of Persia."

He stopped, hoping that would be enough. But the Lady Sati pressed him further.

"Are you not concerned that the reunification of the Roman Empire will pose a long-term danger to Malwa?"

Belisarius shook his head, very firmly.

"No, Lady Sati. Justinian's project is sheer folly."

"You are saying that the eastern Roman Empire cannot reconquer the west?"

There was a lurking danger in that question, Belisarius sensed, though he could not tell exactly where it lay. After a slight hesitation, he decided that truth was the best option.

"I did not say that. In my opinion, the conquest is possible. In fact—" Here, another pause, but this one for calculated effect "—if you will allow me the immodesty, I am convinced that it can be done. So long as Justinian gives me the command of the enterprise. But it will be a fruitless victory."

"Why so?"

He shrugged. "We can reconquer the west, but not easily. The wars will be long and difficult. At the end, Justinian will rule over a war-ravaged west. Which he will try to administer from a bankrupted east. Rome will be larger in size, and much smaller in strength."

"Ah." That was all Lady Sati said, but Belisarius instantly knew that he had passed some kind of test.

The knowledge brought a slight relief to the tension which tightened his neck. But, a moment later, the tension returned in full force.

For the first time, Great Lady Holi spoke.

"Come closer, young man. My eyes are old and poor. I wish to see your face better."

Her Greek was also perfect, and unaccented.

Belisarius did not hesitate, not, at least, any longer than necessary to gauge the proper distance to maintain. He arose from his cross-legged position on the cushion—he, too, had learned the "lotus"—and took two steps forward. Just before the line of tulwars, he knelt on one knee, bringing his eyes approximately level to those of the old woman seated a few feet away.

The Great Lady Holi leaned forward. A hand veined with age reached up and lifted her veil. Dark eyes gazed directly into the brown eyes of Belisarius.

Empty eyes. Dark, not from color, but from the absence of anything within.

"Is it true that you plan to betray Rome?"

There was something strange about those words, he

sensed dimly. An odd, penetrating quality to their tone. He could feel the words racing down pathways in his body—nerves, arteries, veins, muscle tissue, ligaments.

"Do you plan to betray Rome?"

He was giving himself away, he realized. (Dimly, vaguely, at a distance.) The—intelligence?—behind those words was inhuman. It was reading his minute, involuntary reactions in a way no human could. No man alive could lie well enough to fool that—*thing*.

But it was the eyes, not the voice, which held him paralyzed. Not from fear, but horror. He knew, now, the true nature of hell. It was not fire, and damnation. It was simply—

Empty. Nothing.

As so often before in his life, it was Valentinian who saved him. Valentinian, and Anastasius, and Maurice, and countless other such veterans. Coarse men, crude men, lewd men, rude men. Brutal men, often. Even cruel men, on occasion.

But always men. Never empty, and never nothing.

General Belisarius smiled his crooked smile, and said, quite pleasantly:

"Fuck Malwa."

Then, still kneeling, drove his right bootheel straight back into the face of Nanda Lal. He was a powerful man, and it was a bootheel which had trampled battlefields underfoot. It flattened the spymaster and obliterated his nose.

Chapter 13

Belisarius used the impact to lunge upright. Ahead of him, the six eunuchs also began uncoiling. Grunting with the effort, they gathered their haunches and started to rise. The tulwars were already drawing back for the death strokes.

Belisarius ignored them. The eunuchs formed an impassable barrier—well over a ton of sword-wielding meat stood between him and any chance of killing Link. But they were much too ponderous to pose an immediate threat to his escape.

He could not hear the assassins, but he knew they were coming. Belisarius took two quick steps to his left. The servant standing there was paralyzed with shock. The general seized the man by his throat and hip, pivoted violently, and hurled him into the oncoming assassins.

The servant, wailing, piled into three of the assassins charging forward. His wail was cut short abruptly. The fourth assassin dealt with the obstacle by the simple expedient of slashing him down. As he raced toward the nearest window, Belisarius caught a glimpse of the servant's dying body, still entangling three of the assassins. The knife which ended his life, though lacking the mass of a sword, had still managed to hack halfway through the servant's neck. The edge of that blade was as razor sharp as the man who wielded it.

Belisarius reached the window. There was no time for anything but a blind plunge. He dove straight through the silk-mesh screen, fists clenched before him. The silk shredded under the impact. Belisarius sailed cleanly through the window. He found himself plunging through the night air toward the surface of the Jamuna. The assassin's hurled knife missed him by an inch. Belisarius watched the knife splash into the river. Less than a second later, he followed it in.

Ousanas rose from the shrubbery in the alley, took two quick steps, uncoiled. Quick shift, javelin from left hand to right. Uncoiled.

The sounds coming from the barge had not been loud, but they had been unmistakeable. Unmistakeable, at least, to men like Ousanas and the four Ye-tai gambling on the wharf. The Ye-tai were already scrambling to their feet, drawing swords.

The two Malwa kshatriyas standing guard at the top of the ramp, however, were a more sheltered breed. They, too, heard the sounds. But their only immediate response was to frown and turn away from the side of the barge. They stood still, staring at the doorway leading into the interior.

Ousanas' javelins caught them squarely between the shoulder blades. Both men were slain instantly, their spines severed. The impact sent one of the kshatriya hurtling through the doorway into the barge. The other Malwa struck the doorframe itself. There he remained. The javelin, passing a full foot through his body, pinned him like a butterfly.

The Ye-tai, though far more alert than the Malwa kshatriyas, were not alert enough. As ever, barbarous arrogance was their undoing. Heads down with the grunting exertion of their race up the ramp, the Ye-tai never noticed the two javelins sailing overhead. They were so intent on their own murderous purpose that it did not occur to them they had no monopoly on mayhem. Not, at least, until the barbarian leading the charge up the ramp spotted the dead kshatriya skewered on the doorframe.

Caution came, then, much too late. The Ye-tai stopped his charge. His three comrades piled into him from behind. For a moment, the four shouting barbarians were a confused tangle of thrashing limbs.

A moment was all Ousanas needed. He was already at the foot of the ramp. Four leaping strides, and the terrible spear began its work.

Three Ye-tai fell aside, collapsing off the ramp onto the wharf below. Two were dead before they struck the wooden planks. The third died seconds later, from the same huge wound rupturing his back.

The fourth Ye-tai had time to turn around. Time, even, for a furious swordstroke.

The great leaf-blade of the spear batted the stroke aside. Then, reversed, the iron ferrule of the spearbutt shattered the Ye-tai's knee. Reversed again, sweeping, the spear blade cut short the Ye-tai's wail of pain, passing through his throat as easily as it whistled through the air.

Ousanas sprang over the Ye-tai's slumped corpse. He was on the barge itself, now, standing at the top of the ramp. For a moment, the hunter stood still.

Listening. Listening.

Thinking.

He had heard the dull splash of a body striking the water. On the other side of the barge, the side facing the wide reach of the river and the shore two hundred yards opposite. Now, listening intently to the noises coming from within the barge—cries of fury and outrage, shouts of command—Ousanas grinned.

The general had made good his escape. His immediate escape, at least, from the barge itself.

Ousanas, briefly, pondered his options.

For a moment—very brief—he thought of waiting for Belisarius to appear. But he dismissed the idea almost instantly. He knew the general. Swimming around or under the barge to reach the nearby wharf was the obvious move for a man on the run. Naturally, therefore, Belisarius would do otherwise.

Ousanas' task, then, was not to help Belisarius escape directly. It remained, diversion.

Now, Ousanas drew a grenade. For a moment—again, very brief—he considered hurling it into the barge itself.

No. The havoc would be gratifying, but the sound of the explosion would be muffled.

Follow the plan. The main purpose of the grenades was to signal his comrades.

Ousanas turned and raced back down the ramp. A moment later, standing again on the wharf, he laid down his spear. From a small pouch at his waist, he withdrew the striking mechanism.

He even took a moment—*very* brief—to admire the clever Malwa device, before he struck the flint and lit the fuse to the first grenade.

The fuse was short. He lobbed the grenade onto the deck of the barge. Drew the second grenade. Lit the fuse. This fuse was even shorter.

The first Malwa assassin appeared in the doorway. Saw Ousanas, squealed his rage. Ousanas tossed the second grenade.

No lob, this toss. Ousanas the spear-hurler had learned his skill as a boy, hunting with rocks. The grenade split the assassin's forehead wide open. An instant later, the forehead disappeared altogether, along with the head itself and half the man's body. The explosion blew the doorway into splinters.

The second grenade erupted on the open deck. The damage here was slight. Almost all the force was directed upward, leaving only a small hole in the planking as a memento of its fury.

Other, of course, than the great sound rocketing through the night sky over Kausambi.

Ousanas picked up his spear and raced away. As he entered the mouth of the alley, running like the wind, he heard new sounds of fury behind him. Other Malwa had appeared on the deck and spotted his fleeing figure.

There would be little to see, he knew. A tall shape

sprinting down an alley. As tall as a Roman general. True, the color of the shape seemed black. Meaningless. All men would appear black in that dark alley. The Malwa dynasty saw no reason to waste money lighting the alleys of their capital. They did not travel in alleys.

They will tonight, thought Ousanas gleefully. *Oh, yes, they will learn many alleys tonight. I will give them a tour.*

Then, only: *Good luck, Belisarius.*

All other thought vanished, beyond the immediacy of the hunt. The hunter was now the prey, true. But he was a great hunter, who had studied many great prey.

Swimming away from the barge, Belisarius heard the sounds of struggle behind him. He did not turn his head. To do so would have interrupted the powerful breast-strokes which sent him quietly surging into the middle of the Jamuna. But he listened, carefully, with experienced ears.

Wail of agony, cut short. Chopped short. Malwa cry of fury. Explosion, muffled; explosion, loud as a thunderclap. Malwa cries of fury. Cries of furious discovery. Cries of furious pursuit.

Belisarius was not certain, of course, but he thought he knew the identity of the man who had caused those sounds. Not certain, no. But he thought he recognized a certain signature in them. Some men, like Valentinian, had an economical signature. Others preferred more flair.

He started to grin, until a small river wave caught his mouth. He could not afford to choke, not now, so he sealed his lips and drove steadily onward through the dark water.

For all the strength of the general's limbs, his progress was slow. He was encumbered by boots and clothing, heavy with wet saturation. But he did not stop to shed them. Not yet. He had to reach the middle of the river, out of range of shore-carried lanterns. So he simply drove onward, slowly, quietly, steadily, with the patience of a veteran campaigner.

Yes, he thought he knew that man. It had never been part of any plan to have that man ready to intervene as he had. But it had never been part of any plan for Belisarius himself to be trapped. Yet, trapped he had been, and the man had intervened.

Again, he suppressed a grin, remembering something that man had once said. In the dank hold of a ship, as they plotted together against the enemy who owned that great vessel.

"Good plans are like good meat, best cooked rare. Now we can move on to discuss truly important things. Philosophy!"

Outlandish man. Bizarre man.

But never empty. Never nothing.

The sound of the grenade explosions was faint. Not so much due to their distance, as from the hubbub rising from the Malwa soldiers chattering over their evening meal. But, to the men listening for that sound, they were unmistakeable.

"That's it, then," Menander heard Valentinian say. The words were spoken softly, calmly, almost serenely.

Much less serene were Valentinian's next words, hissed:

"Fuck exciting adventures."

But Menander thought the hiss was more from exertion than annoyance. Valentinian favored a very powerful bow. The arrow which that bow launched flew into the Malwa army camp with a trajectory that was almost perfectly flat. Thirty yards away, a soldier squatting over his mess tin was slammed flat to the ground, as if struck by a stampeding elephant.

Menander's first arrow caught another soldier in the huddled platoon. He too was slain instantly, if not with the same dramatic impact. Valentinian's second arrow arrived a split second later. A third Malwa went down.

A platoon eating their meal nearby received its first casualty. A bad wound, not a fatal one. A horrible wound, actually. The cruel warhead of Anastasius' arrow shredded the soldier's left shoulder. Anastasius was not an accurate archer, but his bow was even more powerful than Valentinian's.

Now, thirty yards down, more casualties. Three Malwa soldiers, slain by javelins hurtling from the nearby woods. Another volley. Two dead. One mortally injured.

Valentinian's count was now five. All dead. Menander killed another, wounded a third. Anastasius killed two.

"Enough!" shouted Valentinian. The cataphract turned and plunged into the darkness of the trees. Menander and Anastasius followed him. To their left, Menander could hear Prince Eon and the sarwen making their own retreat.

Within half a minute, the cataphracts reached the small clearing where Garmat and Kadphises were holding the horses. Seconds later, Eon and the sarwen lunged into the clearing.

Garmat and Kadphises, hearing them come, were already astride their horses. The others mounted quickly.

Valentinian reined his horse around, heading for a small trail leading through the woods to the southwest. Back toward the Malwa army camp. Even through the trees, they could hear the uproar coming from the Malwa soldiery.

Anastasius and Menander began to follow him. So did Eon.

Valentinian reined in his horse, glaring at the Prince.

"Stop this nonsense, Eon!" snarled Ezana. He and Wahsi, following Garmat and Kadphises, were guiding their own horses and all the remounts toward a different trail, leading southeast from the clearing. Away from the army camp.

Eon scowled, but he halted his horse. For a moment, the Prince and Valentinian stared at each other. The glare on Valentinian's face faded, replaced by a smile.

There was none of a veteran's mocking humor in that smile, however. Just the smile of a comrade.

"I thank you, Eon," said Valentinian, almost gently.

"But you are being foolish. Ethiopians are infantrymen, not cavalry. This is cataphract work."

Then, he was gone. Seconds later, Anastasius and Menander vanished into the trees with him.

Eon sighed, turned his horse, and sent it trotting down the trail where the other Axumites had gone. After a moment, the young prince shrugged his thick shoulders, shedding his regrets. He urged his horse alongside Ezana.

The sarwen glanced at him, scowling. Soon enough, however, the scowl faded. And, soon after that, was replaced by a thin smile. A grim smile.

Young princes, Ezana reminded himself, needed to be bold. Even impetuous. Better that, than the alternative. Caution and cunning, shrewdness and tactics—these could be taught.

The smile widened. Still grim.

If he ever becomes the negusa nagast, thought Ezana, *he may not be a wise ruler. Not wise enough, at least, for the new days of Malwa. But he will never lack courage. Not my prince.*

In the alley where an Empress and her escort lay hidden, the sound of the grenade explosions was also heard. Faintly, of course, due to the distance. But not at all muffled. Kausambi was a great city, teeming with people. But, like all cities of that time, long before the invention of electric lighting, the vast majority of its residents rose and slept with the sun. For all its size, the city at night was shrouded in a quietness which would have surprised an urbanite of future centuries.

The Mahaveda and the Ye-tai standing guard before the armory heard the explosions also. The two Ye-tai looked up from their idle conversation, craning their heads in the direction of the sounds. Other than that, however, they did not move.

One of the Mahaveda, frowning, stepped forward from the overhanging archway where he stood guard with his two fellows in front of the heavy double doors of the armory's main entrance. The priest walked a few paces into the street, stopped, turned in the direction of the sounds, listened. Nervously, his fingers fluttered the short sword at his waist.

Listened. Listened.

Nothing.

Silence.

The vicinity of the wharf, of course, was very far from silent at that moment. By now, Malwa kshatriyas and Ye-tai were racing about the barge, charging up and down the wharf, plunging in a mass down an alley, shouting orders, shrieking counter-orders, bellowing commands. But those human sounds, for all their raucous volume, far too small to carry the distance to the armory.

"Now," hissed Shakuntala.

Kungas, watching the Malwa, made a peremptory little gesture.

"Not yet," he whispered back. The Empress stiffened. Imperial *hauteur* rose instantly in her heart, and she almost barked a command. But her common sense rescued her—common sense, and the years of Raghunath Rao's hard tutoring. She bit her lip, maintaining silence. In her mind, she could hear Rao's voice:

So, fool girl. You are a genius, then? You understand tactics better than a man who has vanquished enemies on a hundred battlefields? A man so good that I could not overcome him?

Harsh voice. Mocking voice. Beloved voice.

The Mahaveda priest standing in the center of the street shrugged his shoulders, and began to walk back to his post. Farther down, the two Ye-tai guards resumed their slouching posture. The sound of the grenades had been distinct and startling. But—distant. Very distant. And nothing had followed, no sound. An accident, perhaps. No concern of theirs.

"*Now*," whispered Kungas. Shakuntala drove all thoughts of Rao from her mind. She rose and began walking forward into the street. Behind her came all four of the Maratha women.

Tarabai pushed her way past Shakuntala.

"Follow me, Your Majesty," she whispered. "Do as I do, as best you can."

Again, for an instant, royal arrogance threatened to rise. But Shakuntala's struggle against it was brief and easy this time. She had no need to call Rao to her aid. Common sense alone sufficed.

I can wear the clothing. But I don't, actually, have any idea how a prostitute acts.

She watched Tarabai's sashaying stride and tried, as best she could, to copy it. Behind her, she heard Ahilyabai's voice, rising above the muttered words of sullen Kushan soldiers.

Strident voice. Mocking voice.

"If you want charity, get a beggar's bowl!"

Shakuntala and Tarabai were halfway across the street. Before them, the Empress watched the Mahaveda priests stiffen. First, with surprise. Then, with moral outrage.

Again, behind, the angry sound of male voices. Drunken voices, speaking slurred words. Shakuntala recognized Kungas' voice among them, but could understand none of the words. Her concentration was focussed on the priests ahead of her.

She did, vaguely, hear Ahilyabai:

"Fucking bums! Seduce a stupid virgin, if you have no money! Don't come sniffing around me!"

The priests were fifteen feet away, now. Shakuntala almost laughed. The Mahaveda—faces distorted with fury—were practically cowering in the overhang of the door to the armory. They had drawn their swords, and were waving them menacingly. But it was a false menace, an empty menace. Fear of pollution held them paralyzed.

"Keep away!" cried one.

Another: "Filthy women! Unclean!"

Tarabai swayed forward, crooning:

"Oh, now, don't be like that! You look like proper men. We don't cost much."

The third Mahaveda bellowed to the Ye-tai. The two barbarians had come partway down the street to watch the spectacle. The Ye-tai were grinning from ear to ear. Even the sight of the straggling band of Kushan soldiers haggling with the whores didn't cut through their humor.

Again, the priest bellowed, waving his sword in a gesture of furious summoning. Still grinning, the two Ye-tai trotted toward them.

Shakuntala stepped forward to meet them. Tarabai was pressing the priests further back into the alcove formed by the overhang. Pressing them back, not by force of body, but by the simple fact of her tainted nearness.

Behind her, Shakuntala heard Ahilyabai's shriek of anger.

"Get away, I say! Get away! Worthless scum!" Then, fiercely: "We'll set the Ye-tai on you!" Then, crooning: "Such good men, Ye-tai."

The two Ye-tai reached the Empress. Neither one of them had even bothered to draw his sword. Still grinning, the barbarian on her left placed a hand on her shoulder.

"Come on, sweet girl," he said in thick Hindi. "Leave the poor priests alone. They're manless, anyway. Come along to our guardhouse—and bring your sisters with you. We've got ten strong Ye-tai lads there. Bored out of their skulls and with money to burn."

Smiling widely, Shakuntala turned her head aside. Shouted to Tarabai:

"Forget the stupid priests! Let's—"

She spun, drove her right fist straight into the Ye-tai's diaphragm. The barbarian grunted explosively, doubling up. His head, coming down, was met by Shakuntala's forearm strike coming up. A perfect strike—the right fist braced against left palm, a solid bar of bone sweeping around with all the force of the girl's hips and torso. A small bar, true, formed by a small bone. So the Ye-tai's jaw was not shattered. He simply dropped to his knees, half-conscious. His jaw did shatter, then, along with half of his teeth. Shakuntala's knee did for that. The barbarian slumped to the street.

The Empress had turned away before the Ye-tai hit the ground. She was beginning her strike against the other Ye-tai. Twisting aside, drawing back her leg, preparing the sidekick. Silently cursing her costume. The sari impeded the smooth flow of her leg motion.

This Ye-tai, squawking, reached for his sword.

The sword-draw ended before it began.

Shakuntala's leg fell back, limply, to her side. The Empress stared, wide-eyed. Her jaw almost dropped.

She had only seen Kungas in action once before in her life. In Amaravati, when Andhra had finally fallen and the Malwa hordes were sacking the palace. But, even then, she had not really seen. The Ye-tai astride her, tearing off her clothes and spreading her legs in preparation for rape, had obscured her vision. She had caught no more than a glimpse of a Ye-tai fist, amputated, before she had been blinded by the blood of her assailants' decapitation and butchering.

Kungas had done that work, then, just as he did it now. In less than three seconds, the Kushan commander quite literally hacked the Ye-tai to pieces.

Shakuntala shook off the moment, spun around. The Kushan soldiers, all pretense of drunkenness vanished, had lunged past Tarabai and finished the priests. Their bloody work was done by the time Shakuntala turned. The priests had not even had time to cry out more than a squeal or two. Shakuntala was not certain. The squeals had been cut very short. But she thought, for all the carnage, that there had been little noise. Not enough, she was sure, to carry into the guardhouse down the street.

The Kushans were quick, quick. One of the soldiers was already examining the great door leading into the armory. His indifferent knee rested on the chest of a dead priest.

"Too long," he announced curtly. "Two minutes to break through this great ugly thing."

Kungas nodded, turned away. He had expected as much.

"Through the guardhouse, then," he commanded. Kungas began loping up the street toward the side-door where the two Ye-tai had been standing earlier. His men followed, with that same ground-eating lope. Quick, quick. Shakuntala was struck by the almost total absence of noise as they ran. Some of that silence was due to the soft shoes which the Kushans favored over heavy sandals. But most of it, she thought, was the product of skill and training.

Shakuntala and the Maratha women followed. More slowly, however, much more slowly. Saris complimented the female figure, but they did not lend themselves well to speedy movement. Frustrated, Shakuntala made a solemn vow to herself. In the days to come, among her many other responsibilities, she would inaugurate a radical change in feminine fashion.

She had time, in that endless shuffle up the street, to settle on a style. Pantaloons, she decided, modeled on those of Cholan dancers she had seen. More subdued, of course, and tastefully dyed, to mollify propriety and sentiment. But pantaloons, nonetheless, which did not impede a woman's legs.

She saw, ahead of her, the Kushans charge into the guardhouse. The sounds of violent battle erupted instantly. A harsh clangor of steel and fury, flesh-shredding and terror. The quiet street seemed to howl with the noise.

Cursing bitterly, she sped up her shuffle. The battle sounds reached a crescendo.

Shuffle, curse. Shuffle, curse. Shuffle, curse.

The guardhouse was still ten yards distant. The sounds coming through the open door suddenly ceased.

Finally, finally, she reached the door. Shuffled into the guardhouse.

Stopped. Very abruptly. Behind her, the Maratha women bumped into her back. Tarabai and Ahilyabai peeked over the shorter shoulders of their Empress. Gasped. Gagged.

Shakuntala did not gasp, or gag. She made no sound at all.

Hers was a fierce, fierce heart. The ferocity of that heart, in the decades to come, would be a part of the legacy which she would leave behind her. A legacy so powerful that historians of the future, with a unanimity of opinion rare to that fractious breed, would call her Shakuntala the Great. But even that heart, at that moment, quailed.

The Kushans had gone through the Ye-tai like wolves through a flock of sheep. Like werewolves.

The floor was literally awash in blood. Not a single Ye-tai, so far as she could see, was still bodily intact. The barbarians were not simply dead. Their corpses were gutted, beheaded, amputated, cloven, gashed, sliced, ribboned. The room looked like the interior of a slaughterhouse. A slaughterhouse owned and operated by the world's sloppiest, hastiest, most maniacal butcher.

Her eyes met those of Kungas across the room. The commander of her bodyguard had a few bloodstains on his tunic and light armor, but not many. He was down on one knee, wiping his sword on a Ye-tai's tunic. His face, as always, showed nothing. Neither horror, nor fury, nor even satisfaction in a job well done. So might a mask of iron, suspended on a wall of brimstone, survey damnation and hellfire.

Strangely, then, the emotion which swept through Shakuntala's soul was love. Love, and forgiveness.

Not for Kungas, but for Rao. She had never, quite—not in the innermost recesses of what was still, in some ways, a child's heart—forgiven Rao. Forgiven him, for the months she had remained in captivity before he finally rescued her. Weeks, at the end, in Venandakatra's palace at Gwalior, while she paced the battlements and halls, guarded by Kungas and his Kushans, knowing—sensing—that Rao was lurking in the forest beyond. Lurking, but never coming. Watching, but never striking.

She had cursed him, then—somewhere in that child's

innermost heart—for a coward. Cursed him for his fear of Kungas.

Now, finally, the curse was repudiated. Now, finally, she understood.

Understanding brought the Empress back. The child vanished, along with its quailing heart.

"Excellent," she said. "*Very* excellent."

Kungas nodded. His men smiled. None of them, she was relieved to see, was badly hurt. Only two were binding up wounds, and those were obviously minor.

Kungas jerked his head toward a door at the far end of the guardhouse.

"That leads into the armory itself. It is not barred."

"We must hurry," said Shakuntala. She eyed the floor, trying to find a way to cross without leaving her feet soaked with blood.

Two of the Kushan soldiers—grinning, now—solved the problem in the simplest way possible. They grabbed Ye-tai corpses and dumped them on the floor, forming a corduroy road of dead flesh.

Shakuntala, never hesitating, marched across that grisly path. More gingerly, her women followed.

By the time she passed through the far door, the Kushans were already spreading through the recesses of the armory, setting a perimeter. They knew, from a prior hasty reconnaissance, that there was another guardhouse on the opposite side of the huge brick building. Now, they were searching for the door leading to that guardhouse, and keeping a watch for any Ye-tai or Mahaveda who might chance to be in the armory itself.

The armory was uninhabited. They found the door. Behind it, the Kushans heard the sounds of Ye-tai. Idle sounds, barracks sounds. The barbarians had obviously heard nothing of the lethal struggle.

The Kushans relaxed, slightly. They set a watch on the door, leaving four of their number on guard, while the remainder sped about the task which had brought them there.

Shakuntala and her women were already prying open

the lids of gunpowder baskets, using knives which had once belonged to Ye-tai guards. Following them, the Kushan soldiers upended the baskets and spread granular trails throughout the armory. Soon, very soon, every stack of baskets in the armory was united by a web of gunpowder on the floor. That work done, the Kushans seized racks of rockets hanging on the wall and positioned them in and around the gunpowder baskets.

"Enough," commanded Kungas. His voice, though quiet, carried well. Instantly, his men left off their labor and hurried back to the guardhouse. Hurried through, until stymied by the slow-moving women. At Shakuntala's irritated command, the Kushans picked up all of the women—including her—and carried them into the street. Carried them, at Shakuntala's command, down the street and into the alley. Only then, at her command, did they place the women on their feet.

Shakuntala looked back. Kungas was already halfway to the alley, walking backward, spilling a trail of gunpowder from a basket in his arms. The last of the gunpowder poured out of the basket just as he reached the alley.

"Do it," commanded Shakuntala. Kungas drew out the striking mechanism, bent down, operated it. Immediately, the gunpowder began a furious, hissing burn. The sputtering flame marched its crackling way toward the armory.

"Hurry," he growled. He did not wait for Shakuntala's command. He simply scooped her up in his arms and began racing down the alley. Behind him, his men followed his lead, carrying the Maratha women in that same loping run.

Shakuntala, bouncing up and down in his arms, was filled with satisfaction. But not entirely. There was still room in her heart for another emotion.

When the armory blew, two minutes later, the Empress was caught by surprise. Her frustrated mind had been elsewhere. Thinking about pantaloons.

Chapter 14

Belisarius was now fifty yards from the barge, well into the mainstream of the Jamuna. He paused, treading water, to take his bearings. Slowly he circled, to examine his situation, beginning with the near shore.

He was safely out of range of lantern or torchlight from the wharf where Great Lady Holi's barge was moored. There was a bit of moonlight shimmering on the water, but not much. The moon was only the slimmest crescent. And, from the look of the clouds which were beginning to cover the sky, he thought there would soon be one of the downpours which were so frequent during the monsoon season. Visibility would be reduced almost to nothing, then.

All he had to fear, immediately, was being spotted from one of the oared galleys which patrolled the river. He could see several of those galleys, beating their way toward the wharf. The officers in command had obviously heard the commotion on the barge, and were coming to investigate.

Suddenly, a rocket was fired from the wharf. A signal rocket, Belisarius realized, watching the green burst in the sky when the rocket exploded, at low altitude. Another. Another.

Instantly, the galleys picked up the tempo of their oarstrokes. The officers commanding them were shouting commands. Belisarius could not make out the words, but their content was unmistakable. The galleys were converging rapidly on the wharf—and he could see new ones appearing, from all directions. Within seconds, no fewer than fourteen galleys were in sight.

He decided that he had time, finally, to shed his clothing. He needed to wait, anyway, to observe whatever search pattern the galleys would adopt.

It was the work of a minute to remove his clothing. Another minute, to remove his boots without losing them. Another minute, carefully, to make sure that the pouch carrying his small but extremely valuable pile of coins and gems was securely attached to his waist. Another minute, very carefully, to make sure the pouch containing the *jewel* was secure around his neck. A final minute, then, to tie all his clothing into a bundle, the boots at the center. Before doing so, he removed the little knife from its pouch and held it in his teeth. He might need that knife, quickly. It would be no use to him bundled away out of reach.

He finished the work by tying the sleeves of his tunic in a loop around his neck. He would be able to tow his bundle of boots and clothing without obstructing his arms. The knife in his teeth would interfere, a bit, with his breathing. But there was nowhere else to put it.

Throughout, he had been keeping a close eye on the galleys. By the time he was finished, the small fleet of warcraft were moving away from the wharf. He could hear commands being shouted, but, again, could not make out the words.

There was no need. The search pattern which the Malwa adopted was obvious. Most of the galleys began rowing along the near shore, upstream and downstream of the Great Lady Holi's barge. Soldiers in the galleys were leaning over the sides, holding lanterns aloft. A matching line of torches was being carried along the south bank of the Jamuna, in the hands of soldiers searching the shore line.

Six of the galleys, however, began rowing their way out into the river. Belisarius was most interested in these craft. After a minute, watching, he understood the logic.

Two of them would remain in the center of the river, patrolling in both directions. The other four were headed for the opposite shore, spreading out as they went. The Malwa were taking no chances. Clearly, they thought Belisarius was either staying by the south bank or had already gone ashore. But they would patrol the entire river, anyway.

He decided upon the galley farthest to his right. That galley was heading for the opposite shore, and it would reach the shore farther upstream than any other.

He began swimming toward it. He maintained the same powerful breaststroke. It was a relatively slow method—Belisarius was an excellent swimmer, and was quite capable of moving more rapidly in water—but it would be fast enough. And the breaststroke had several advantages. It was almost silent; it kept his arms and legs from flashing above the surface of the water; and—with the knife in his teeth—it enabled him to breathe easily.

Fortunately, the angle was good, and so he was able to position himself where he needed to be a full half-minute before the galley swept through the area. Treading water, directly in the galley's path, he waited. As he had hoped, the Malwa soldiers aboard the galley were not holding lanterns over the bow. The lanterns were being held toward the stern. The soldiers on that galley, like all the Malwa, did not really think that Belisarius had gone anywhere but the near shore. It was that south bank of the river that the soldiers were watching, even as they headed in the opposite direction.

The galley was almost upon him. Belisarius took a deep breath and dove below the surface. For a moment, he feared that the bundle he was towing might act as a buoy, hauling him back toward the surface. But his clothing was now completely waterlogged. If anything, the bundle simply acted as a weight.

Now, swimming below the barge, down its starboard side, Belisarius encountered the first snag in his hastily-improvised plan.

He was blind as a bat. He couldn't see a thing.

He had expected visibility to be limited, of course, at night-time. But he had thought he would be able to see enough to guide himself. What he hadn't considered, unfortunately, was the nature of the Jamuna itself.

This was no mountain stream, with clear and limpid waters. This was a great, murky, slow-moving valley river. Heavy with silt and mud. It was like swimming through a liquid coal mine.

He guided himself by sound and touch. To his left, he used the splashing oars as a boundary. To his right, stretching out his fingers, he groped for the planks of the hull.

He misgauged. Driven, probably, by an unconscious fear of his sudden blindness, he swam too shallow. His head, not his fingers, found the hull.

The impact almost stunned him. For a moment, he floundered, before he brought himself under control. Quickly, he found the hull with his fingers.

The wood planks were racing by. He heard a sudden dimunition in the sound of the oars, as if they had passed him.

Now.

He took the knife from his teeth and thrust it upward, praying the little blade wouldn't break. The tip sank into the wood. Not far—half an inch—but enough.

Using the knife to hold himself against the hull, Belisarius desperately sought the surface. He was almost out of air.

Again, he had misgauged. He was still too far from the stern. The side of his face was pressed against the hull. He could feel the surface of the water ruffling through his hair, but could not reach it to breathe.

He jerked the knife out, let the current carry him for a split second, stabbed again. The thrust, this time, was even feebler.

It was enough, barely. The blade held. He let the current raise him up against the hull. His head broke water.

His lungs felt like they were about to burst, but he took the time for a quick upward glance before taking a breath.

Finally, something went as planned. As he had hoped, he was hidden beneath the overhang of the stern. He opened his mouth and took a slow, shuddering breath, careful to make as little sound as possible.

For a minute, he simply hung there, breathing, resting. Then he took stock of his situation.

The situation was precarious. The knife was barely holding him to the hull. It could slip out at any moment. If it did, the galley would sweep forward, leaving him cast behind in its wake. He was not worried so much at being spotted, then, but he could not afford to lose the shelter of the galley. The shelter—and the relaxation. He had no desire to make the long swim to the opposite shore on his own effort. He could make it, yes, but the effort would leave him exhausted. He could not afford exhaustion. He still had many, many hours of exertion before him. A day, at least, before he could even think to rest.

He studied the underside of the galley, looking for a solid plank to replant the knife. He did not have to worry about interfering with a rudder. The galley did not use a rudder. Few ships did, in his day, other than the craft built by north European barbarians. Instead, the galley was steered by an oar. The oar was on the opposite side of the stern from where Belisarius was hidden. Like Romans, the Malwa hung their steering oars off the port side of the stern. Belisarius had chosen to swim down the starboard side precisely in order not to become fouled in that oar.

He heard a sudden, distant explosion. Then another. Another. Another.

Now, a veritable barrage was rumbling across the river. The sound of the explosions had an odd, muffled quality.

Cautiously, he turned his head, raised it a bit. He could now see the nature of the activity on the shore behind him. The Malwa were casting grenades into the river. He watched several plumes of water spout from the surface.

Those grenades, he thought, could be dangerous to him.

A thought from Aide surfaced. The facets had restored their identity.

Depth-charges. Very dangerous. Water transmits concussion much better than air.

He caught a quick, gruesome image of his own body, ruptured, bleeding from a thousand internal wounds.

He shook the image off. First things first. For his immediate needs, the thunderous sound of the grenade blasts was a blessing. He jerked the knife out of the hull—paused a split-second, timing the galley's passage—and drove it upward again. The knife sank solidly into the thick plank. It—and he—were securely anchored.

That powerful knife-thrust, striking the wood, had been far from silent. But the noise was completely drowned under the cacophony of the grenade blasts— the more so since many of those blasts, now, were nearby. The Malwa soldiers on the galleys racing across the river were tossing their own grenades.

It was an absurd exercise, thought Belisarius. He did not know much about the effects of underwater explosions. But, no matter how effective concussion was in water, he did not believe the Malwa had more than a small portion of the grenades necessary to saturate the entire, vast sweep of the Jamuna.

The real problem, he knew, would come later. He could not stay hidden beneath the galley for long. At daybreak, he was sure to be spotted. And he needed to make his escape onto shore long before daybreak, anyway. He would need the hours of darkness to make his way safely out of the city.

The fact that the Malwa grenades were no immediate danger to him, therefore, brought little consolation. If they maintained that barrage, he would be in danger the moment he left the galley and began swimming toward the far shore. Unless the galley actually docked at one of the wharves—which he doubted; none of the galleys on the opposite side were doing so—he would have to swim at least thirty yards to shore. The Malwa would be scanning the shore, by then. And, even if they did not spot him, they could kill him with one of the random grenades they were casting about.

He looked up at the sky. The cloud cover was advancing rapidly. He prayed for a downpour.

The galley continued its powerful sweeping progress across the Jamuna. It had reached the middle of the river.

Belisarius prayed for a downpour.

The galley began angling upstream, west by northwest. Now, it was a hundred yards from shore, and more than two hundred yards west of Great Lady Holi's barge on the opposite bank.

Belisarius prayed for a downpour.

Once the galley was fifty yards from the north bank, the officer in command shouted new orders. The galley began to travel almost parallel to the shore, heading west. The officer brought the galley within thirty yards of the shore, but no closer.

Soon, they were three hundred yards upstream from Great Lady Holi's barge. Four hundred yards.

But the galley never came closer to shore. Thirty yards.

Belisarius cursed under his breath. He would have to make the swim. Right under the eyes of watchful soldiers, with grenades in hand.

He glanced up, one last time. The cloud cover was almost complete. Again, he prayed for a downpour.

His prayers were answered.

Not by rain, but by fire. A great, blooming, volcanic eruption shattered the sky to the southeast. The thunderclap from that eruption swept over the Jamuna, drowning the grenade blasts like raindrops under a tidal wave.

For a moment, all was still. Then, from the same area

to the southeast, the first immense blast gave way to a barrage. One blast after another after another. None of them had the same intensity as the first, but, in their rolling fury, they were even more frightening. Now, too, rockets began hissing their way into the sky, at every angle and trajectory—as if they were completely unaimed. Simply firing in whatever direction they had been tumbled, by a giant's hand.

The officer in command of the galley began shouting new orders. The galley backed oars, turning away from the north bank. Turning back to the southeast, back to the wharf where Great Lady Holi's barge was rocking in the shockwave of the blasts.

Belisarius could not make out the officer's exact words—his voice, like all other sounds, was buried beneath the continuing thunder of the distant explosions. But he knew what had happened. The Malwa search of the north bank had been half-hearted to begin with. And now, with further—dramatic!—evidence that the nefarious foreign general had made his escape to the south, it was being abandoned completely.

He jerked the knife out of the hull, pushed himself away, submerged. When he raised his head, a minute later, the stern of the rapidly receding galley was barely visible in the darkness.

A minute later, Belisarius was wading ashore. Within seconds, he found cover under a low-hanging tree. There, he unrolled his bundle, wrung out his clothes and emptied his boots, dressed quickly.

As soon as he stepped out from the shelter of the tree, the sky finally broke. Within seconds, his clothing was as saturated by the downpour as it had been by the river.

Striding away, however, Belisarius was not disgruntled. Quite the contrary. He was grinning as widely as Ousanas.

For all his reputation as a brilliant strategist—a master of tactics and maneuver—Belisarius had always known that war never followed neat and predictable lines. Chaos and confusion was the very soul of the beast. The secret was to cherish the vortex, not to fear it.

Chaos was his best friend; confusion his boon companion.

He turned his head, admiring the fiery chaos to the southeast. Raised his eyes, lovingly, to the thundering confusion of the heavens.

A wondering thought came from Aide.

You are not afraid? We are all alone, now.

Belisarius sent his own mental image.

Himself, and the jewel. Soaring through the turbulence of the vortex. Catching every gust of wind, sailing high; avoiding every downdraft. Against them, flapping frantic wings and gobbling stupified fury, came the beast called Malwa.

It looked very much like a gigantic chicken.

That very moment, on the other hand, Valentinian was cursing chaos and confusion.

The armory had exploded just as the cataphracts began their cavalry charge into the Malwa army camp.

The result was the most absurd situation Valentinian had ever encountered in his life.

He and Anastasius had timed the charge perfectly. They had allowed many minutes to elapse, after their first volley into the camp, before starting the charge. Minutes, for the Ethiopians to get a good distance along their escape route. (The Axumites would need that headstart. They were competent horsemen, to be sure; but—except for Garmat—had none of the superb cavalry skills of the cataphracts.) Minutes, for the shocked comrades of the slain Malwa soldiers to spread the alarm. Minutes, for the half-competent officers of those half-competent troops to gather around and begin shouting contradictory orders. Minutes, for chaos to turn to confusion. Minutes, to allow Kujulo and the other Kushans to race about the Malwa camp in their Ye-tai impersonation, shouting garbled news of the escape of the treacherous foreign general Belisarius.

Finally, the time came. By now, Valentinian esti-mated, Kujulo and the Kushans—coming from the opposite side of the encampment—would have reached the officers in command of the Malwa camp. There, in broken Hindi, interspersed with savage Ye-tai curses, they would have ordered the officers to begin a charge to the south, where the foreign general was known to be lurking.

All that was needed, to give the proof to their words, was a sudden cataphract charge on the south edge of the camp.

Valentinian gave the order. He and his two comrades plunged out of the line of trees. Their horses thundered toward the Malwa camp, some sixty yards distant. They drew their bows, fired their first volley—

The northeast sky turned to flame and thunder.

Every Malwa soldier in the camp turned, as one man, and gaped at the spectacle. They did not even notice the first three casualties in their midst. Three soldiers, hurled to the ground by arrows plunging into their backs.

They did not notice the next three casualties. Or the next three. Or the next three.

By the time Valentinian and his comrades reached the pathetic little palisade—say better, low fence—which circled the camp, they had already slain eight Malwa soldiers and badly wounded as many more.

And, for all the good it did, they might as well have been boys casting pebbles at cows. All of the Malwa soldiers were still facing away, gaping with shock at the incredible display to the north, completely oblivious to the carnage in their ranks to the south.

The cataphracts reined in their horses at the very edge of the palisade. It was no part of their plan to get tangled up with the Malwa soldiers. They simply wanted to draw their attention.

The roaring explosions continued to the north. Rock-ets were firing into the sky in all directions, hissing their serpentine fury at random targets.

Valentinian's curses, loud as they were, were completely buried under the uproar.

Random chaos came to the rescue. One of the rockets firing off from the exploding armory sailed directly toward the Malwa army camp. The milling soldiers watched it rise, and rise, and rise. Still heading directly toward them.

In truth, the rocket posed little danger to them. But there was something frightening about that inexorable, arching flight. This rocket—quite unlike its erratic fellows—seemed bound and determined to strike the camp head-on. Its trajectory was as straight and true as an arrow's.

The mob of soldiers began edging back. Then, almost as one, turned and began pushing their way southward. Away from the coming rocket.

Finally, the Malwa saw the cataphracts. Finally, stumbling over the littered bodies, they caught sight of their murdered comrades.

"It's about time, you stupid bastards!" cried Valentinian. He drew an arrow and slaughtered a Malwa in the first rank. Another. Another. Anastasius and Menander added their own share to the killing.

Valentinian saw a Ye-tai charge to the fore. He was about to kill him, until—he transferred his aim, slew a soldier nearby.

"It Romans!" he heard the Ye-tai cry, in crude, broken Hindi. "That Belisarius he-self! After they! Get they!"

The Ye-tai sprang over the palisade, waving his sword in a gesture of command.

"After they!" he commanded. Valentinian saw three other Ye-tai push their way through the Malwa mob, beating the common infantrymen with the flat of their blades and shouting the same simple command.

"After they! After they!"

Valentinian reined his horse around and galloped off. Anastasius and Menander followed. Seconds later, with a roar, the entire mob of Malwa soldiers was pounding in pursuit.

On his way, the cataphract sent a silent thought back.

You are one brave man, Kujulo. You crazy son-of-a-bitch!
I might have killed you.

Brave, Kujulo was. Crazy, he was not. As soon as he
was satisfied that the momentum of the Malwa soldiers
was irreversible, he began edging his way to the side
of the charging mob. His three comrades followed his
lead. A minute later, passing a small grove, Kujulo darted
aside into its shelter.

Under the branches, it was almost pitch black. Kujulo
had to whisper encouragement in order to guide the
other Kushans to his side.

"What now?" he was asked.

Kujulo shrugged. "Now? Now we try to make our
own escape."

Another complained: "This plan is too damned tricky."

Kujulo grinned. He, too, thought the plan was half-
baked fancy. But he had long since made his own assessment of Ousanas.

"Fuck the plan," he said cheerfully. "I'm counting on
the hunter."

Then: "Let's go."

A minute later, the four Kushans exited the grove on
the opposite side and began running west. They ran with
a loping, ground-eating stride which they could maintain for hours.

They would need that stride. They had a rendezvous
to keep. They were hunting a hunter.

The noble lady charged into the stables through the
western gate, shouting angrily.

"The city has gone mad! We were attacked by
dacoits!"

Startled, her husband and the stablekeeper turned
away from the north gate, where they had been watching
the explosions. The explosions were dying down, now.
If nothing else, the pouring rain was smothering what
was left of the holocaust. But there were still occasional
rockets to be seen, firing off into the night sky.

The nobleman's wife stalked forward. Her fury was obvious from her stride alone. The stablekeeper was thankful that he couldn't see her face, due to the veil.

Shocked as he was by her sudden appearance, the stablekeeper still had the presence of mind to notice two things.

The man noticed the comely youthful form revealed under the sari, which rain had plastered to her body.

The *low-caste* man noticed the bloodstains spattering the tunics of her fierce-looking escort of soldiers.

The man disappeared, submerged by the reality of his caste. Like all humble men of India, outside Majarashtra and Rajputana, the last thing he wanted to see in his own domicile was heavily-armed, vicious-looking soldiers. He had been unhappy enough with the fifteen soldiers the nobleman had brought with him. Now, there were ten more of the creatures—and these, with the stains of murder still fresh on their armor and weapons.

The stablekeeper began to edge back. To the side, his wife was quietly but frenziedly driving the other members of his family into the modest house attached to the stables.

The nobleman restrained him with a hand. "Have no fear, stablekeeper," he murmured. "These are my personal retainers. Disciplined men."

He stepped forward to meet his wife. She was still spluttering her outrage.

"Be still, woman!" he commanded. "Are you injured?"

The wife fell instantly silent. The stablekeeper was impressed. Envious. He himself enjoyed no such obedience from his own spouse.

The wife shook her head, the veil rippling about her face. The gesture seemed sulky.

The nobleman turned to the man who was apparently the commander of his soldiers. "What happened?"

The soldier shrugged. "Don't know. We were halfway here when"—he gestured to the north—"something erupted. It was like a volcano. A moment later, a great band of dacoits were assaulting us." He shrugged, again. The gesture was all he needed to explain what happened next.

The stablekeeper was seized by a sudden, mad urge to laugh. He restrained it furiously. He could not imagine what would possess a band of dacoits to attack such a formidable body of soldiers. Lunatics.

But—it was a lunatic world. Not for the first time, the stablekeeper had a moment of regret that he had ever left his sane little village in Bengal. The moment was brief. Sane, that village was. Poverty-stricken, it was also. He had done well in Kausambi, for all that he hated the city.

While the nobleman took the time to inquire further as to the well-being of his wife and retainers, the stablekeeper took the time to examine the soldiers more closely.

Some breed of steppe barbarians, that much he knew. The physical appearance was quite distinct. The faces of those soldiers were akin, in their flat, slant-eyed way, to the faces of Chinese and Champa merchants he had seen occasionally in his youth, in the great Bengali port of Tamralipti. So was the yellowish tint to their skin. Even the top-knot into which the soldiers bound their hair, under the iron helmets, was half-familiar. Some Chinese favored a similar hairstyle. But no Chinese or Champa merchant ever had that lean, wolfish cast to his face.

Beyond that, the stablekeeper could not place them. Ye-tai, possibly—although they seemed less savage, for all their evident ferocity, than Ye-tai soldiers he had encountered, swaggering down the streets of Kausambi.

But he was not certain. As a Bengali, he had had little occasion to encounter barbarians from the far northwestern steppes. As a Bengali immigrant to Kausambi, the occasion had arisen. But, like all sane men, the stablekeeper had avoided such encounters like the plague.

The nobleman approached him.

"We will be going now, stablekeeper. I thank you, again, for your efficiency and good service."

The stablekeeper made so bold as to ask: "Your wife is well, I hope, noble sir?"

The nobleman smiled. "Oh, yes. Startled, no worse. I can't imagine what the dacoits were thinking." He made a small gesture toward the soldiers, who were now busy assisting the wife and her ladies into their howdahs. The gesture spoke for itself.

The stablekeeper shook his head. "Dacoits are madmen by nature."

The nobleman nodded and began to leave. An apparent sudden thought turned him back.

"I have no idea what madness has been unleashed in Kausambi tonight, stablekeeper. But, whatever it is, you would do well to close your stable for a few days."

The stablekeeper grimaced.

"The same thought has occurred to me, noble sir. The Malwa—" He paused. The nobleman, though not Malwa himself, was obviously high in their ranks. "The city soldiery will be running rampant." He shrugged. It was a bitter gesture. "But—I have a family to feed."

The expression which came to the nobleman's face, at that moment, was very odd. Very sad, it seemed to the stablekeeper. Though he could not imagine why.

"I know something of that, man," muttered the nobleman. He stepped close and reached, again, into his purse. The stablekeeper was astonished at the small pile of coins which were placed in his hand.

The nobleman's next words were spoken very softly:

"As I said, keep the stable closed. For a few days. This should make good the loss."

Now, he did turn away. Watching him stride toward the howdahs, the stablekeeper was seized by a sudden impulse.

"Noble sir!"

The nobleman stopped. The stablekeeper spoke to the back of his head.

"If I might be so bold, noble sir, may I suggest you exit the city by the Lion Gate. It is a bit out of your way, but—the soldiers there are—uh, *relaxed*, so to speak. They are poor men themselves, sir. Bengali, as it happens. Whenever I have occasion to leave the city, that is always the gate which I use. No difficulties."

The nobleman nodded. "Thank you, stablekeeper. I believe I shall take your advice."

A minute later, he and his wife were gone, along with their retinue. They made quite a little troupe, thought the stablemaster. The nobleman rode his howdah alone, in the lead elephant, as befitted his status. His wife followed in the second, accompanied by one of her maids. The three other maids followed in the last howdah. Ahead of them marched a squad of their soldiers, led by the commander. The rest of the escort followed behind. The stablemaster was impressed by the disciplined order with which the soldiers marched, ignoring the downpour. An easy, almost loping march. A ground-eating march, he thought.

He turned away from the pouring rain, made haste to close and bar the gates to the stable.

Not that they'll need to eat much ground with those mounts, he thought wrily. *The most pleasant, docile little elephants I've ever seen.*

Halfway across the stable, his wife emerged from the door to the adjoining house. She scurried to meet him.

"Are they gone?" she asked worriedly. Then, seeing the closed and barred gates, asked:

"Why did you shut the gates? Customers will think we are closed."

"We *are* closed, wife. And we will remain closed until that madness"—a gesture to the north—"dies away and the city is safe." Wry grimace. "As safe, at least, as it ever is for poor folk."

His wife began to protest, but the stablekeeper silenced her with the coins in his hand.

"The nobleman was very generous. We will have more than enough."

His wife argued no further. She was relieved, herself, at the prospect of hiding from the madness.

Later that night, as they prepared for bed, the stablekeeper said to his wife:

"Should anyone inquire about the nobleman, in the future, say nothing."

His wife turned a startled face to him.

"Why?"

The stablekeeper glared. "Just do as I say! For once, woman, obey your husband!"

His wife shrugged her thick shoulders with irritation, but she nodded. (Not so much from obedience, as simple practicality. Poor men are known, now and then, to speak freely to the authorities. Poor women, almost never.)

Much later that night, sleepless, the stablekeeper arose from his bed. He moved softly to the small window and opened the shutter. Just a bit—there was no glass in that modest frame to keep out the weather.

He stood there, for a time, staring to the east. There was nothing to see, beyond the blackness of the night and the glimmering of the rain.

When he returned to his bed, he fell asleep quickly, easily. Resolution often has that effect.

Chapter 15

After an hour, Belisarius finally found what he was looking for.

It had been a thoroughly frustrating hour. On the one hand, he had found plenty of lone soldiers. But all of them had been common Malwa troops, shirking their duty by hiding in alleys and out-of-the-way nooks and crannies of the city. None of these men had been big enough for their uniforms to fit him. Nor, for that matter, did he think he could pass himself off as an Indian from the Gangetic plain.

Ye-tai was what he wanted. The Ye-tai, in the west, were often called White Huns. The word "white," actually, was misleading. The Ye-tai were not "white" in the sense that Goths or Franks were. The complexion of Ye-tai was not really much different than that of any other Asian steppe-dwellers. But their facial features were much closer to the western norm than were those of Huns proper, or, for that matter, Kushans. And, since Belisarius himself was dark-complected for a Thracian— as dark as an Armenian—he thought he could pass himself off as Ye-tai well enough. Especially since he could speak the language fluently.

Ye-tai tended to be big, too. He was quite sure he could find one whose size matched his own.

Ye-tai he found aplenty. Big Ye-tai, as well. But the Ye-tai always traveled in squads, and they tended to be much more alert than common troops.

Fortunately for him, the alertness of the Ye-tai was directed inward rather than outward—toward the common soldiers they were rounding up and driving into the streets. Scouring the streets and alleys was beneath the dignity of Ye-tai. That was dog work, for common troops. Their job was to whip the dogs.

At first, as he watched the massive search operation which began unfolding in the capital, Belisarius was concerned that he would be spotted before he could make his escape from Kausambi. But, soon enough, his fears ebbed. After a half an hour, in fact—a half hour spent darting from one alley to another, heading west by a circuitous route—Belisarius decided that the whole situation was almost comical.

The explosion of the armory had roused every soldier in the Malwa capital, of every type and variety. And since there were a huge number of troops stationed in Kausambi, the streets of the city were soon thronged with a mass of soldiers. But the soldiers were utterly confused, and largely leaderless. Leaderless, not from lack of officers, but because the officers themselves had little notion what, exactly, they were supposed to do. But they didn't want to seem to be doing nothing— especially under the hard eyes of Ye-tai—so the officers sent their men scurrying about aimlessly. Soon enough, the masses of troops charging and counter- charging about the city had become so hopelessly inter- mingled that any semblance of disciplined formation vanished.

Watching the scene, Belisarius realized that he was witnessing one of the military weaknesses of the Malwa Empire. The Malwa, because of their social and political structure, had no real elite shock troops. The Malwa kshatriya, who had a monopoly of the gunpowder weapons, functioned more as privileged artillery units than elite soldiers. The Ye-tai, for all their martial prowess, were not really an elite corps either. Their position in the Malwa army was essen- tially that of security battalions overseeing the common troops, rather than a spearhead. And the Rajputs, or Kushans—who could easily have served the Malwa as elite troops—were too distrusted.

The end result was that the Malwa had no body of soldiers equivalent to his own Thracian bucellarii. And for the task of hunting down a foreign fugitive in the streets of a great city like Kausambi—especially at night, in pouring rain—a relatively small body of disciplined, seasoned men would have done much better than the hordes of common troops whom the Malwa had sent floundering into action.

So, with relatively little difficulty, Belisarius managed to get almost to the outskirts of Kausambi within that first hour. Three times, during the course of his journey, he encountered platoons of Malwa soldiers. Each time, he handled the situation by the simple expedient of commanding them to search a different alley.

The Malwa troops, hearing authoritative words from an authoritative figure, never thought to question his right to issue the orders. True, they did not recognize his uniform. But, between the darkness and the rainstorm, it was hard to make out the details of uniforms anyway. Every soldier in the streets of Kausambi that night looked more like a half-drowned rat than anything else. And besides, the Malwa empire was a gigantic conglomeration of subject nations and peoples. No doubt the man was an officer of some kind. His Hindi was fluent—better than that of the soldiers in two of those platoons, in fact—and only an officer would conduct himself in that arrogant, overbearing manner. Malwa troops had long since been hammered into obedience, and they reacted to Belisarius like well-trained nails.

Then, finally, he found his lone Ye-tai. Hiding in some shrubbery near the mouth of an alley, Belisarius watched a squad of Ye-tai hounding a mob of soldiers down one of the large streets which formed a perimeter for the outskirts of Kausambi. As they passed the alley, one of the barbarians split off from his comrades and stepped into it. Belisarius drew back further into the shadows, until, watching the man, he realized that his moment had arrived. The Ye-tai was big—big enough, at least—and, best of all, he was about to provide Belisarius with the perfect opportunity. The Ye-tai moved ten feet into the alley, turned to face one of the mudbrick hovels which formed the alley's walls, and began preparing to urinate.

The operation took a bit of time, since the Ye-tai had to unlace his armor as well as undo his breeches. Belisarius waited until the Ye-tai finally began to urinate. Then he lunged out of the shrubbery and drove the barbarian face first into the wall of the hovel. The Ye-tai, stunned, bounced back from the wall. Belisarius hammered his fist into the man's kidney, once, twice, thrice. Moaning, the Ye-tai fell to his knees. Belisarius drew his knife, cut the strap holding the barbarian's helmet, cuffed the helmet aside. Then, dropping his knife, he seized the Ye-tai by his hair and slammed his skull into the wall. Once, twice, thrice.

Quickly, he glanced at the alley mouth. Belisarius gave silent thanks, again, for the darkness and the monsoon downpour. The Ye-tai's comrades had heard and seen nothing. After returning the knife to its sheath, and placing the helmet on his own head, Belisarius hoisted the unconscious barbarian over his shoulder and moved quickly back down the alley.

Thirty yards down, well out of sight, he set the man down and begin stripping his uniform. Within five minutes, the barbarian was as naked as the day he was born, and Belisarius was the perfect image of a Ye-tai.

Now, he hesitated, facing a quandary.

The quandary was not whether to kill the Ye-tai. That was no quandary at all. As soon as he removed the barbarian's clothing, and, thereby, any danger of leaving tell-tale bloodstains, Belisarius drew his knife. He plunged the sharp little blade into the back of the man's neck and, with surgical precision, severed the spinal cord.

The quandary was what to do with the body. Belisarius dragged it to the side of the alley and began stuffing it under some shrubbery. He was not happy with that solution, since the body would surely be found soon after daybreak, but—

He stopped, examining the mudbrick wall. It was not, he suddenly realized, the wall of a house. It was a wall sealing off one of the tiny backyard garden plots with which most of Kausambi's poor supplemented their wretched diet.

He glanced around, gauging the area. He was in one of the many slums of the city.

Decision came instantly. He hoisted the body over his head and sent it sprawling across the wall. A split second after he heard the body's wet thump in the yard on the other side, he sent his own Roman uniform after it. Then he began striding down the alley, marching with the open, arrogant bearing of a Ye-tai.

He was taking a gamble, but he thought the odds favored him. He was quite sure that the residents of that humble little house—shack, say better—had heard the commotion. By the time he reached the end of the alley, they would probably already be examining the grisly—and most unwelcome—addition to their garden.

What would they do? Alert the authorities?

Possibly. In a rich neighborhood, they would certainly do so.

But in this neighborhood, he thought not. Poor people in most lands—certainly in Malwa India—knew quite well that the authorities were given to quick solutions to unwelcome problems.

Found a dead man in your own back yard? Why'd you kill him, you stinking swine? Robbed him, didn't you? You deny it? Ha! We'll beat the truth out of you.

No, Belisarius thought that by sunrise the Ye-tai's body would have disappeared, along with the Roman uniform. The uniform, cut up, could serve a poor household in any number of ways. The body? Fertilizer for the garden.

He wished that unknown family a good crop, and went on his way.

The three cataphracts thundered down the road leading due south from Kausambi. Valentinian was in the lead, followed by Anastasius, with Menander bringing up the rear.

The young cataphract was more terrified than he'd ever been in his life.

"Slow down, Valentinian! Damn you—*slow down!*"

It was no use. The driving rain hammered his shouts into the mud.

At least the mud might keep us from breaking our necks, after we spill the horses, thought Menander sourly.

Valentinian was setting an insane pace. He was driving his horse at a full gallop, down an unknown road, in pitch dark, into a rain coming down so heavily it was impossible even to keep one's eyes open for more than a few seconds at a time.

Oh, yes—and without stirrups.

Yet, somehow, they survived. Without spilling the horses or falling off their saddles.

They were past the guardhouse before they even saw it. By the time they managed to rein in the horses, and turn them around, the Ethiopians were already there.

"Are you mad?" demanded Garmat.

Valentinian shrugged. "We were short of time." He pointed with his face toward the guardhouse.

"Are they taken care of?"

"Be serious," growled Wahsi. "We got here half an hour ago."

Eon, Ezana and Kadphises brought up the extra horses.

"We'd better switch mounts," said Anastasius. "We've pretty well winded these."

"Winded me, too," grumbled Menander. "Valentinian, you are fucking crazy."

The veteran's grin was as sharp and narrow as a weasel's. "You survived, didn't you? We're cataphracts, boy. *Cavalrymen.*"

As the cataphracts switched to new horses, Wahsi stated very forcefully: "We are *not* cavalrymen. So let us maintain a rational pace."

"Won't matter," said Kadphises. "We're cutting into the forest a half mile down. We'll have to walk our horses through that trail. If you can call it a trail."

"You *do* know where we're going, I hope?" said Valentinian.

The Kushan's grin was every bit as feral as Valentinian's. "I will not tell you how to ride a horse. Do not tell me how to find a trail."

He was as good as his word. Five minutes later, the party of eight men and twenty horses turned off the road and entered into the forest. At first, Menander was relieved. As Kadphises had said, it was impossible to move down that trail at any pace faster than a horse could walk.

Walk, *slowly*. Menander had thought it was too dark to see, before. Now, he was essentially blind. The thick, overhanging branches, combined with the overcast night sky, turned the forest into a good imitation of a leafy underground mine. Without lanterns.

The only good thing, as far as he could tell, was that the tree canopy was so dense that it sheltered them— more or less—from the downpour.

Menander was not worried about falling off his horse. They were moving at the pace of an elderly woman. Nor, after a time, was he concerned that the horse might trip. The trail, though narrow, did not seem to be littered with obstacles.

He was simply worried that they would get lost. And, in addition, that they were making such poor time that their Malwa pursuers would catch up with them—even with the tremendous head start that Valentinian's insane ride had given them.

But, when he stated those concerns to the broad back of Anastasius ahead of him, the veteran was unconcerned.

"First, lad, don't worry about getting lost. The Kushan

seems to know his way. Don't ask me how—I can't see a damn thing, either—but he does. And as for the other—*be serious*. When the Malwa get to the guard-house and find the dead guards, they'll assume we continued on the road south. They'll never spot this little trail to the side. They'll charge right past it and keep going."

"We didn't cover our tracks."

Anastasius laughed scornfully.

"What tracks?" he demanded. "This downpour—this fucking Noah's flood—will wash away any tracks in less than a minute."

Menander was still unconvinced, but he fell silent. And then, half an hour later, when they finally emerged from the forest, admitted that his fears had been foolish.

Admitted, at least, to himself. He said nothing to Anastasius, and ignored with dignity the veteran's dimly-seen smile of vindication.

Once they emerged from the forest, they found themselves on another dirt road. (Mud road, rather.) They reversed directions completely, now, and headed north. After a mile, perhaps less, the road curved and began heading due west. Menander's fears resurfaced—new ones; he seemed to have a Pandora's box of them that night.

"Does Kadphises know where the hell we're going?"

The rain had eased off considerably. Enough that Menander's words carried forward. Kadphises' reply came immediately. The prologue to that reply was quick, curt, and very obscene. Thereafter, relenting, the Kushan deigned to explain.

"This road does not connect to the other until a small town fifty miles to the south. Nor does it go to Kausambi. It circles two sides of a swamp to our left, and from here will go due west for more than twenty miles. Before then, however, we will have turned south, again, on yet another road. By now, the Malwa will have no idea where we are. And, best of all, this road is not guarded. It is a peasants' road, only, not a merchant's route."

"Where will we meet Ousanas, and the other Kushans?" asked Eon.

Kadphises' shrug could barely be seen in the darkness.

"That is up to them, Prince. Kujulo knows what road we are taking. If he can find your hunter—or your hunter finds him—they will track us down. If your hunter is as good as you claim."

Eon's only reply was a grunt of satisfaction.

In the event, Ousanas did not have to track them down. Shortly after daybreak, many miles down the new road heading south, they came upon Ousanas. The hunter, along with Kujulo and the three other Kushans, were waiting for them by the side of road. Fast asleep—even reasonably dry, under the semi-shelter of a long-abandoned hut—except for one Kushan standing guard.

Valentinian was exceedingly disgruntled. Especially after he spotted the basket of food, with very little food left in it.

"You had time to *eat*, too?" he demanded crossly, climbing down from his horse.

Ousanas sat up, stretched his arms, grinned.

"Great cavalrymen move very slow," he announced. "I be shocked. Shocked. All illusions vanished."

Kujulo smiled. "You should try traveling with this one. Really, you should. He was already waiting for us when we made our break from the army camp. How the hell he got there so fast from the river, I'll never know. Especially with two baskets of food."

"*Two* baskets?" whined Valentinian.

"We saved one for you," said another of the Kushans, chuckling. "Ousanas insisted. He said if we didn't, Anastasius would never argue philosophy with him again."

"Certainly wouldn't," agreed the giant. "Except for simple precepts from Democritus. All matter can be reduced to atoms. Including Ousanas."

The cataphracts and the Ethiopians tore into the food.

After their initial hunger was sated, Menander's youthful curiosity arose.

"What *is* this stuff?" he asked.

"Some of it is dried fish," replied Kujulo. "The rest is something else."

Menander, thinking it over, decided that he would leave it at that. The stuff didn't actually taste that bad, after all, even if he suspected "the rest" had once had far too many legs to suit a proper Thracian.

By the time the food was gone, the rain had finally stopped. Kujulo and another Kushan went into the woods and brought out their horses.

"Where'd you get the horses?" asked Valentinian.

Kujulo pointed to Ousanas.

"He had 'em. Don't ask me where he got them because I have no idea. I'm afraid to ask."

Valentinian shared no such fear.

"Where'd you get 'em?" he demanded again. Then, watching the ease with which Ousanas swung up into his saddle, complained: "I thought you didn't like horses."

"I detest the creatures," replied Ousanas cheerfully. "Horses, on the other hand, are very fond of me."

The hunter led off, to the south, called over his shoulder:

"This shows excellent judgement by both parties, don't you think?"

Somehow, in the hours that followed, as the band of soldiers cantered their way toward the far distant Deccan, Menander was not surprised to discover that Ousanas was as good a horseman as he'd ever seen.

At daybreak that same day, the captain of the Bengali detachment which guarded—so to speak; "huddled about" would be more accurate—the Lion Gate of Kausambi, waved a casual farewell to the nobleman and his retinue. After the last of the nobleman's escort and their women camp-followers had paraded past, down the eastern road to Pataliputra, he ordered the gate shut.

"Fine man," he said approvingly. "Wish all those Malwa snots were like him."

"How much?" asked his lieutenant.

The commander did not dissemble. His lieutenant was also his younger brother. Most of his detachment, in fact, was related to him. He extended his hand, palm open.

His brother's eyes widened.

"Send for our wives," commanded the captain. "Today, we will feast."

That same moment, Belisarius stalked through the Panther Gate, one of the western gates of Kausambi. The gate was poorly named, in truth. Small and ramshackle as it was, the "Alley Cat Gate" would have been a more suitable cognomen.

But, of course, that was why he had picked it.

On the way through, he terrorized another Malwa soldier. The man scuttled frantically away from the barbarian's threatening fist. He had no desire to end up like his sergeant, sprawled senseless on the ground.

Once he was through the gate, Belisarius turned, planted his fists on his hips, and bellowed:

"Next time, you dogs, when a Ye-tai tells you to open the gate, do so without argument!" He drew his sword. "Or next time I'll use this!"

He thrust the sword back in the scabbard, turned, and marched away. Behind him, he heard the gate screeching loudly. The hinges hadn't been greased properly, and the Malwa troops were in a great hurry to close it. A tearing great hurry.

The road Belisarius was taking was one of the newly refurbished roads which the Malwa had been constructing. This was no muddy peasant path. The road was fifteen feet wide, raised above the plain, properly leveled and paved with stone. It was a road even Romans would have been proud to call their own.

The road ran parallel to the north bank of the Jamuna River, a few miles to the south. The road led west by northwest until it reached the city of Mathura, some three hundred miles away. Belisarius had no intention of traveling as far as Mathura, however. Just north of Gwalior, the Chambal River branched to the southwest. About a hundred miles up the Chambal, in turn, the Banas River branched directly west. There were roads paralleling those rivers which would take him all the way to the ancient city of Ajmer, at the very northern tip of the Aravalli Mountains.

"Ajmer," he mused. "From there, I can either go south or west. But—I wonder . . ."

Again, he summoned Aide to his assistance. Aide had already provided him with all the geographic information he needed. Now—

Tell me about the royal couriers.

The rain had finally stopped. As he strode along, openly, right down the middle of the road, Belisarius continued the discussion with Aide until he reached his conclusions. Thereafter, he simply admired the dawn.

Might even get a rainbow, he thought cheerfully.

Chapter 16

DARAS
Summer 530 AD

Theodora arrived at the estate toward the end of summer. Her appearance came as a surprise—not the timing, but the manner of it.

"She's worried," muttered Antonina to Maurice, watching the Empress ride in to the courtyard. "Badly worried. I can think of nothing else that would make Theodora travel like this."

Maurice nodded. "I think you're right. I didn't even know she could ride a horse."

Antonina pressed her lips together. "You call *that* riding a horse?"

"Don't snicker, girl," whispered Maurice. "You didn't look any better, the first time you climbed into a saddle. At least Theodora doesn't look like she's going to fall off from a hangover. Not the way she's clutching the pommel."

Antonina maintained her dignity by ignoring that last remark altogether. She stepped forward to greet the Empress, extending her arms in a welcoming gesture.

Theodora managed to bring her horse to a halt, in a manner of speaking. The twenty cataphracts escorting her drew up a considerable distance behind. Respect for royalty, partly. Respect for a surly horse at the end of its patience, in the main.

"How do you get off this foul beast?" hissed the Empress.

"Allow me, Your Majesty," said Maurice. The hecaton-tarch came forward with a stool in his hand. He quieted the horse with a firm hand and a few gentle words. Then, after placing the stool, assisted the Empress in clambering down to safety.

Once on the ground, Theodora brushed herself off angrily.

"Gods—what a stink! Not you, Maurice. The filthy horse." The Empress glowered at her former mount. "They eat these things during sieges, I've heard."

Maurice nodded.

"Well, that's something to look forward to," she muttered.

Antonina took her by the arm and began leading the Empress into the villa. As she limped along, Theodora snarled:

"Not that there'll be many sieges in *this* coming war, the way things are going."

Antonina hesitated, then asked:

"That bad?"

"Worse," growled the Empress. "I tell you, Antonina, it shakes my faith sometimes, to think that man is created in God's image. Is it possible that the Almighty is actually a cretin? The evidence of his handiwork would suggest as much."

Antonina sighed.

"I take it Justinian is not listening to your warnings?"

Growl. "In *His* image, no less. A huge Justinian in the sky."

Growl. "Think of a gigantic babbling idiot."

Growl. "Creation was His drool."

Later, after a lavish meal, Theodora's spirits improved.

She lifted her wine cup in salutation.

"I congratulate you, Maurice," she said. "You have succeeded in bringing the provincial tractator to the brink of death. By apoplexy."

Maurice grunted. "Still peeved, is he, about the taxes?"

"He complained to me for hours, from the moment I got off the ship. This large estate represents quite a bit for him in the way of lost income, you know. Mostly, though, he's agitated about the tax collectors."

Maurice said nothing beyond a noncommittal: "Your Majesty."

Smiling, the Empress shook her head.

"You really shouldn't have beaten them quite so badly. They were only doing their job, after all."

"They were not!" snapped Antonina. "This estate is legally exempt from the general indiction, and they know it perfectly well!"

"So it is," agreed Cassian. "*Res privata*, technically. Part of—"

Theodora waved him down.

"Please, Bishop! Since when has a provincial tractator cared about the picayune details of an estate's legal tax status? Squeeze, squeeze, squeeze. Let them complain to Constantinople. By the time the bureaucrats get around to ruling on the matter, everyone'll be dead of old age anyhow."

Maurice nodded sagely. "Quite nicely put, Your Majesty. Those are indeed the usual tactics of tractators."

He took a sip of his wine. "Excellent tactics. Provided you pick the right sponge."

Theodora shook her head. "Which does not, I assume, include an estate inhabited by several hundred Thracian cataphracts?"

Maurice cleared his throat. "Actually, Your Majesty— no. I would recommend against it. Especially when those cataphracts have secrets to keep hidden from the prying eyes of tax collectors."

Theodora now beamed upon the Bishop. Again, she raised her cup in salutation.

"And a toast to you as well, Anthony Cassian! I do not believe any Bishop in the history of the Church has ever before actually caused a Patriarch to foam at the mouth while describing him."

Cassian smiled beatifically. "I'm sure you're exaggerating, Your Majesty. Patriarch Ephraim is a most dignified individual." Then, slyly: "Did he really?"

Theodora nodded. Cassian's expression became smug. "Well, that certainly places me in august company. It's not actually true, you know. That I'd be the first. The great John Chrysostom caused any number of Patriarchs to foam at the mouth."

Antonina smiled at the exchange. Until she remembered the fate of John Chrysostom. Around the table, as others remembered also, the smiles faded like candles extinguished at the end of evening.

"Yes," said the Empress of Rome. "Dark night is falling on us. May we live to see the morning."

Theodora set down her cup, still almost full.

"I've had enough," she said. "I suggest you all go lightly on the wine. We've a long night ahead of us."

For all its politeness, the suggestion was an imperial command. All wine cups clinked on the table, almost in unison. Almost—Sittas took the time to hastily drain his cup before setting it down.

"Justinian will not listen to me," began the Empress. "I might as well be talking to a stone wall." Growl. "I'd *rather* talk to a stone wall. At least a stone wall wouldn't pat me on the head and say it's taking my words under advisement."

She sighed. "The only ones he listens to are John of Cappadocia and Narses. Both of them, needless to say, are encouraging him in his folly. And assuring him that his wife is fretting over nothing."

For a moment, she looked away. Her face was like a mask, from the effort of fighting down the tears.

"It's Narses' words that do the real damage," she whispered. "Justinian's never actually had too many illusions about the Cappadocian. He tolerates John because the man's such an efficient tax collector, but he doesn't trust him. Never has."

"He's *too* efficient," grumbled Sittas. "His tax policy is going to ruin everyone in Rome except the imperial treasury."

"I don't disagree with you, Sittas." The Empress sighed. "Neither does Justinian, actually. It's one of the many ironies about the man. Rome's never had an Emperor who spends so much time and energy seeing to it that taxes are fairly apportioned among the population, and then ruins all his efforts by imposing a tax burden so high it doesn't matter whether it's evenly spread or not."

Theodora waved her hand.

"But let's not get into that. There's no point in it. My husband's tax policy stems from the same source as his religious policy. Both are bad—and he knows it—but both are required by his fixed obsession to reintegrate the barbarian West into the Roman Empire. That's all he sees. Even Persia barely exists on his horizon. The Malwa are utterly irrelevant."

Bishop Cassian spoke.

"There's no hope, then, of Justinian putting a stop to the persecution of Monophysites?"

Theodora shook her head.

"None. He doesn't encourage it, mind. But he resolutely looks the other way and refuses to answer any complaints sent in by provincial petitioners. All that matters to him is the approval of orthodoxy. Their blessing on his coming invasion of the western Mediterranean."

Antonina spoke, harshly.

"I assume, if he's listening to John and Narses—especially the Cappadocian—that also means Belisarius is still under imperial suspicion."

Theodora' smile was wintry. "Oh, not at all, Antonina. Quite the contrary. John and Narses have been fulsome in your husband's praise. To the point of gross adulation. It's almost as if they know—"

She stopped, cast a hard eye on Antonina.

The sound of Sittas' meaty hand slapping the table was startling.

"Ha! Yes!" he cried. "He's tricked the bastards!" He seized his cup, poured it full. "That calls for a drink!"

"What are you babbling about, Sittas?" demanded the Empress.

The general smiled at her around the rim of his wine cup. For a moment, his face disappeared as he quaffed half the wine in a single gulp. Then, wiping his lips with approval:

"If they're so resolute in advancing Belisarius at court, Your Majesty—you know how much John of Cappadocia hates him—that can only mean they have information about him which we don't. And that—"

The rest of the wine disappeared.

"—can only be a report from India that Belisarius is planning treason against Rome."

He beamed around the room. Reached for the wine bottle.

"That calls for a—"

"Sittas!" exploded the Empress.

The general looked pained. "Just one little drink, Your Majesty. What's the harm in—"

"Why is this cause for celebration?"

"Oh. *That.*" Cheerfully, Sittas resumed his wine-pouring. "That's obvious, Your Majesty. If they've heard news from India—and I can't see any other interpretation—that tells us two things. First, Belisarius is alive. Second, he's doing his usual thorough job of butt-fu—outwitting the enemy."

Again, he saluted everyone with an upturned cup.

"How are you so sure the report isn't true?" grated the Empress.

By the time Sittas replaced his cup on the table, his cheerfulness had given way to serenity.

"Worry about something else, Your Majesty," he said. "Worry that the sun will start rising in the west. Worry that fish will sing and birds will grow scales." He snorted derisively. "If you really insist on fretting over fantasy, worry that I'll start drinking water and do calisthenics early in the morning. But don't worry about Belisarius committing treason."

Antonina interrupted. Her voice was cold, cold.

"If you pursue this, Theodora, I am done with you."

The room froze. For all Theodora's unusual intimacy with that small company, it was unheard of to threaten an Empress. *That* Empress, for sure.

But it was Theodora, not Antonina, who broke off their exchange of glares.

The Empress took a deep breath. "I am—I—" She fell silent.

Antonina shook her head. "Never mind, Theodora. I don't expect an actual apology." She glanced at Sittas. "Anymore than I'd expect *him* to start doing calisthenics."

"God save us." The general shuddered, reaching for his wine cup. "The thought alone is enough to drive me to drink."

Theodora, watching Sittas drain his cup, suddenly smiled. She picked up her own cup and extended it.

"Pour for me, Sittas. I think I'll join you."

When her cup was full, she raised it aloft.

"To Belisarius," she said. "And most of all, to trust."

Two hours later, after Theodora had finished bringing her little band of cohorts up to date with all the information which Irene had collected over the past months in Constantinople, the Empress announced she was off to bed.

"I've got to be at my best tomorrow morning," she explained. "I wouldn't want your new regiment of peasants—what did you call them?"

"Grenadiers," said Hermogenes.

"Yes, grenadiers. Has a nice ring to it! I wouldn't want them to be disappointed in their Empress' inspection. Which they certainly would be if I collapsed from nausea."

All rose with the Empress. After she left, guided to her chamber by Antonina, most of the others retired

also. Soon, only Sittas and Anthony Cassian were left
in the room.

"Aren't you going to bed, too?" asked the general,
pouring himself another cup.

The bishop smiled seraphically.

"I thought I might stay up a bit. The opportunity,
after all, will come only once in a lifetime. Watching
you do calisthenics, that is."

Sittas choked, spewed out his wine.

"Oh, yes," murmured Cassian. "It's only a matter of
time, I'm convinced of it. A miracle, of course. But
miracles are commonplace this evening. Didn't I just see
the Empress Theodora give a toast to trustfulness?"

Sittas glowered, poured himself a new cup. The
bishop eyed the bottle.

"I'd be careful, Sittas. That's probably turned into
water."

The Empress did not disappoint her new regiment,
the next morning. No, not at all.

She appeared before them in full imperial regalia,
escorted to her throne by Antonina, Sittas, Hermogenes
and Bishop Cassian.

The peasant grenadiers, watching, were impressed.
So, standing next to them in the proud uniforms of
auxiliaries, were their wives.

By the regalia, of course. By the august nature of her
escort, to be sure. Mostly, though, they were impressed
by the throne.

Clothes, when all is said and done, are clothes. True,
the Empress wore the finest silk. They wore homespun.
But they were a practical folk. Clothes were utilitarian
things, in the end, no matter how you dressed them up.

The tiara, of course, was new to them. They had no
humble peasant equivalent for that splendor. But everyone knew an empress wore a tiara. Impressive, but
expected.

Even her escort did not overawe them. The young
Syrians had come to know those folk, these past months.

With familiarity—the old saw notwithstanding—had come respect. Deep respect, in truth. And, in the case of Antonina and Cassian, adoration. Yet it was still familiarity.

But the throne!

They had wondered what the thing was, during the time spent waiting for the Empress to make her appearance. Had passed rumors up and down the lines. The regulars from Hermogenes' infantry who served as their trainers and temporary officers had tried to glare down the whispers, but to no avail. The grenadiers and their wives had their own views on military discipline. Standing in well-ordered formation seemed sensible to the peasants—very Roman; very soldier-like—and so their ranks and files never wavered in the precision of their placement. But maintaining utter silence was obvious nonsense, and so the grenadiers did not hesitate to mouth their speculations.

For a time, the rumor of heathenism seemed sure to sweep the field. Some of the grenadiers were even on the verge of mutiny, so certain were they that the *object* was an altar designed for pagan sacrifices.

But the appearance of the bishop squashed that fear. The chief competing rumor now made a grand reentry. *The object* was to be the centerpiece of a martial contest. Matching platoon against stalwart platoon, to see which might be the collective Hercules that could pick up the *thing*. Maybe even move it a foot or two.

So, when Theodora finally planted her imperial rump upon the throne, she was most gratified to see the wave of awe which swept those young faces.

"I *told* you it was worth hauling it here," she murmured triumphantly to Antonina.

Although her face never showed it, Theodora herself was impressed in the two hours which followed.

By the grenades themselves, to some extent. She had heard of the gunpowder weapons which the Malwa had introduced to the world. She had not disbelieved, exactly, but she was a skeptic by nature. Then, even after her skepticism was dispelled by the demonstration, she was still not overawed. Unlike the vast majority of people in her day, Theodora was accustomed to machines and gadgets. Her husband took a great delight in such things. The Great Palace in Constantinople was almost littered with clever devices.

True, the grenades were powerful. Theodora could easily see their military potential, even though she was not a soldier.

What Theodora *was*, was a ruler. And like all such people worthy of the name, she understood that it was not weapons which upheld a throne. Only the people who wielded those weapons.

So she was *deeply* impressed by the grenadiers.

"How did you do it?" she whispered, leaning over to Antonina.

Antonina's shrug was modest.

"Basically, I took the peasants' side in every dispute they got into with the soldiers. In everything that touched on their life, at least. I didn't intervene in the purely military squabbles. There weren't many of those, anyway. The Syrian boys are happy enough to learn the real tricks of the trade, and they never argue with Maurice. They just don't want any part of the *foolishness*."

Theodora watched a squad of grenadiers demonstrating another maneuver. Six men charged forward, followed by an equal number of women auxiliaries. The grenadiers quickly took cover behind a barricade and began slinging a barrage of grenades toward the distant shed which served as their target.

Soon enough, the shed was in splinters. But Theodora paid little attention to its destruction. She was much more interested in watching the grenadiers, especially the efficient way in which the female auxiliaries made ready the grenades and—always—cut and lit the fuses.

Watching the direction of her gaze, Antonina chuckled.

"That was my idea," she murmured. "The generals

had a fit, of course. But I drove them down." She snorted. "Stupid *men*. They couldn't get it through their heads that the only people these peasants would entrust their lives to were their own women. No one else can cut the fuses that short, without ever blowing up their husbands."

A new volley of grenades sailed toward the remnants of the shed, trailing sparks from the fuses.

"Watch," said Antonina. "Watch how perfectly the fuses are timed."

The explosions came almost simultaneous with the arrival of the grenades. The last standing boards were shredded.

"It's an art," she said. "If the fuse is cut too short, the grenade blows up while still in the air. *Too* short, before the grenadier can even launch it. But if it's cut too long, the enemy will have time to toss it back."

She exhaled satisfaction. "The grenadiers' women are the masters of the art." Chuckle. "Even Sittas finally quit grumbling, and admitted as much, after he tried it himself."

"What happened?"

Antonina smiled. "At first, every grenade he sent got tossed back on his head. Fortunately, he was using practice grenades, which only make a loud pop when they burst. But he was still hopping about like a toad, trying to dodge. Finally, he got frustrated and cut the fuse too short." Grin. "*Way* too short."

"Was he hurt?"

Big grin. "Not much. But he had to drink with his left hand for a few days. Couldn't hold a wine cup in his right, for all the bandages."

The exercises culminated in a grand maneuver, simulating a full scale battle. The entire regiment of Syrian peasants and their wives formed up at the center, in well spaced formation. Units of Hermogenes' infantry braced the gaps, acting as a shield for the grenadiers against close assault. Maurice and his cataphracts, in full armor atop their horses, guarded the flanks against cavalry.

Sittas gave the order. The grenadiers hurled a volley. Their sling-cast grenades tore up the soil of the empty terrain a hundred and fifty yards away. The infantry marched forward ten yards, shields and swords bristling. The grenadier squads matched the advance, their wives prepared the next volley, slung. Again the soil was churned into chaos. Again, the infantry strode forward. Again, the grenades.

On the flanks, the cataphracts spread out like the jaws of a shark.

Sittas turned in his saddle, beamed at the Empress.

"Looks marvelous," murmured the Empress to Antonina. "How will it do in an actual battle, though?"

Antonina shrugged.

"It'll be a mess, I imagine. Nothing like this tidy business. But I'm not worried about it, Theodora. The enemy won't be in any better shape."

Theodora eyed her skeptically.

"Relax, Empress. My husband's a general, remember. I know all about the First Law of Battle. And the corollary."

Theodora nodded. "That's good." Cold smile: "Especially since you're now the new commander of this regiment. What are you going to call it, by the way?"

Antonina gaped.

"Come, come, woman. It's an elite unit. It's got to have a name."

Antonina gasped like a fish out of water. "What do you mean—*commander?*—I'm not a soldier!—I'm—" Wail: "I'm a *woman*, for the sake of Christ! Who ever heard of a woman—"

The Empress pointed her finger to the grenadiers, like a scepter.

"*They have,*" she said. Theodora leaned back in the throne, very satisfied. "Besides, Antonina, I wouldn't trust this new regiment in anyone else's hands. These new gunpowder weapons are too powerful. You'll be my last hope, my secret force, when all else fails. I won't place my life in the hands of a *man*. Never again."

The Empress rose.

"I'll inform Sittas. He'll bleat, of course, like a lost lamb."

Coldly, grimly: "Let him. I'll shear him to the hide."

Oddly, Sittas did not bleat. Not at all.

"I thought she'd do that," he confided to Antonina. He was standing next to her, watching the reaction of the crowd to the announcement which the Empress had just made. "Smart woman," he said approvingly.

Antonina peered at him suspiciously.

"This is not like you," she muttered. "You're the most reactionary—"

"Nonsense!" he replied cheerfully. "I'm not reactionary at all. I'm just lazy. The reason I hate new ideas is because they usually require me to do something. Whereas *this*—"

He beamed upon the peasant grenadiers. Uncertainly, some of them smiled back. Most of them, however, were staring at their new commander. At the few, full-figured inches of her. The men were wide-eyed. Their wives were practically goggling.

"Have fun, girl," he murmured. "I'd much rather lounge back in the ease of my normal assignment. I could lead cataphract charges in my sleep."

He turned away, and leaned toward Theodora.

"I think we should call them the Theodoran Cohort," he announced.

"Splendid idea," agreed the Empress. "Splendid."

That night, clustered uneasily in the great hall of the villa, the village elders made clear that they did *not* think the situation was splendid.

Not at all. *None* of it.

It was not the name they objected to. The name, so far as they were concerned, was irrelevant.

What they objected to was everything else.

"Who will till the land when they are gone?" whined one of the elders. "The villagers will starve."

"They will not," stated Theodora. She loomed over the small crowd of elders. At great effort, her throne had been moved into the villa.

"They will not starve at all. Quite the contrary. Every grenadier in the Theodoran Cohort will receive an annual stipend of twenty nomismata. I will also provide an additional ten nomismata a year for equipment and uniforms. Their wives—the auxiliaries—will receive half that amount."

Standing behind the elders, the representatives of the young grenadiers and their wives murmured excitedly. An annual income of twenty nomismata—the Greek term for the solidus—was twice the income of a Syrian peasant household. A *prosperous* household. The extra ten nomismata were more than enough to cover a soldier's gear. With the wives' stipends included, each peasant family enrolling in the Cohort had just, in effect, tripled their average income.

The elders stroked their beards, calculating.

"What of the children?" asked one.

Antonina spoke.

"The children will accompany the Cohort itself. The Empress has also agreed to provide for the hire of whatever servants are necessary."

That announcement brought another gratified hum from the grenadiers. And *especially* from their wives.

"In battle, of course, the children will be held back, in the safety of the camp."

"The camp will not be safe, if they are defeated," pointed out an elder.

One of the grenadiers in the back finally lost patience.

"The *villages* will not be safe, if we are defeated!" he snarled. His fellows growled their agreement. So did their wives.

The elders stroked their beards. Calculating.

They tried a new approach.

"It is unseemly, to have a woman in command." The elder who uttered those words glared back at the peasant wives.

"The girls will start giving themselves airs," he predicted.

To prove his point, several of the wives made faces at him. To his greater chagrin, their husbands laughed.

"You see?" he complained. "Already they—"

The Empress began to cut him off, but her voice was overridden by another.

"Damn you for Satan's fools!"

The entire crowd was stunned into silence by that voice.

"He does that so well, don't you think?" murmured Cassian.

The Voice stalked into the room from a door to the side.

The elders shrank back. The young grenadiers behind them, and their wives, bowed their heads. Even Theodora, seated high on her throne, found it hard not to bend before that figure.

That *hawk*. That desert bird of prey.

Michael of Macedonia thrust his beak into the face of the complaining elder.

"You are wiser than Christ, then?" he demanded. "More certain of God's will than his very Son?"

The elder trembled with fear. As well he might. In the stretches of the Monophysite Syrian countryside, the rulings of orthodox councils meant nothing. Even the tongs and instruments of inquisitors were scorned. But *nobody* scoffed at holy men. The ascetic monks of the desert, in the eyes of common folk, were the true saints of God. Spoke with God's own voice.

Michael of Macedonia had but to say the word, and the elder's own villagers would stone him.

When Michael finally transferred his pitiless eyes away, the elder almost collapsed from relief.

His fellows, now, shrank from that raptor gaze.

"You are on the very lip of the Pit," said Michael. Softly, but his words penetrated every corner of the room. "Be silent."

He turned, faced the grenadiers and their wives.

"I give these young men my blessing," he announced. "And my blessing to their wives, as well. *Especially* to their wives, for they have just proved themselves the most faithful of women."

He stared back at the elders. Stonily:

"You will so inform the people. In all the villages. *Publicly.*"

The elders' heads bobbed like corks in a shaken tub.

"You will inform them of something else, as well," he commanded. The monk now faced the Empress, and Antonina standing by her side.

He prostrated himself. Behind him, the peasants gasped.

"God in Heaven," whispered Cassian into Antonina's ear, "he's never done that in his life." The Bishop was almost gasping himself. "It's why he's refused all the many invitations to Constantinople. He'd have to prostrate himself before the Emperor, or stand in open rebellion."

Michael rose. The peasants' murmurs died down.

"I have had a vision," he announced.

Utter silence, now.

The monk pointed to the Empress. Then, to Antonina.

"God has sent them to us, as he sent Mary Magdalene."

He turned, and began leaving. Halfway to the door, he stopped and bestowed a last gaze upon the elders.

The hawk, promising the hares:

"*Beware, Pharisees.*"

He was gone.

Sittas puffed out his cheeks.

"Well, that's that," he pronounced. "Signed, sealed, and delivered."

He bent down to Theodora.

"And now, Your Majesty, with your permission?"

Theodora nodded.

Sittas stepped forward, facing the grenadiers. Spread his heavy arms. Beamed, like a hog in heaven.

"This calls for a drink!" he bellowed. "The casks await

us outside! Your fellows—all the villagers—have already started the celebration! While we, poor souls"—a hot-eyed boar glared at the cowering elders, baring his tusks—"were forced to quell our thirst."

Once a village elder, always a village elder.

"The expense," complained one.

"We'll be ruined," whined another.

Sittas drove them down.

"Nothing to fear, you fools! *I'm a rich man*. I'll pay for it all!"

"I'm not sure I can handle this much longer," muttered Theodora, watching the eager peasants pour from the room. "One more miracle and I'm a dead woman, for sure."

She shook her head. "Talismans from God. Messengers from the future. Magic weapons. New armies. Women commanders. Saints walking about."

Grump. "And now—Sittas, with generous pockets. What next?" she demanded. *"What next? Talking horses? Stars falling from the sky?"*

She rose. "Come," she commanded. "We should join our new army in a toast to their success. *Quickly*. Before the wine turns into water."

Three days later, early in the morning, the Empress departed the estate.

Unhappy woman.

"You're sure this is your tamest beast?" she demanded.

Maurice managed not to smile.

"Yes, Your Majesty." He patted the old mare's neck. Then, helped Theodora into the saddle. The task was difficult, between Theodora's clumsiness and the stern necessity of never planting a boosting hand on the imperial rump.

Now astride the horse, Theodora looked down at Antonina.

"Remember, then. As soon as I send the word, get your cohort to Constantinople. And don't forget—"

"Be on your way, Theodora," interrupted Antonina, smiling. "I will not forget any of your instructions. Hermogenes has already picked out his regiments. Sittas is doing the same. The Bishop's making the secret arrangement for the ships. And the ten cataphracts left for Egypt yesterday."

"Ashot's in command," stated Maurice. "One of my best decarchs. When Belisarius finally arrives, he'll get him here—or to the capital, whichever's needed—as fast as possible."

Theodora sat back in her saddle, nodded.

Then, looking down at her horse:

"Maybe there'll be sieges, after all," she muttered grimly.

She put her horse into motion awkwardly. Her last words:

"Keep that in mind, horse."

The next day, Maurice wiped the grins off the faces of the grenadiers.

"To be sure, lads, Antonina's your commander," he said, pacing up and down their ranks. "But commanders are aloof folk, you know. Very aloof. Have nothing to do with the routine of daily training." He stopped, planted his hands on hips. "No, no. That's trivial stuff. Always leave that sort of thing in the hands of lowly hecatontarchs."

Grimly: "That's me."

The grenadiers eyed him warily. Eyed the grinning cataphracts who stood nearby. The announcement had just been made that they were to be the new trainers.

Maurice gestured in their direction.

"These are what we call—*cadre*."

Very evil grins, those cataphracts possessed.

"Oh, yes," murmured Maurice. "*Now* your training begins in earnest. Forget all that silly showpiece stuff for the Empress."

He resumed his pacing. "I will begin by

introducing you to the First Law of Battle. This law can be stated simply. *Every battle plan gets fucked up as soon as the enemy arrives. That's why he's called the enemy.*"

He stopped, turned, smiled cheerfully.

"Your own plans just got fucked up."

Grinned ear to ear.

"*I have arrived.*"

Yes, the grins disappeared from their faces. But the smile in the hearts of those young peasants did not. Not ever, in the weeks which followed, for all the many curses which they bestowed upon Maurice. (Behind his back, needless to say.)

No, not once. The young Syrians were not foolish. Not even the men, and certainly not their wives. Uneducated and illiterate, yes. Stupid, no. For all their pleasure in their new-found status, they had never really thought it was anything but a serious business.

They were a practical folk. Serious business, they understood. And they had their own peasant estimate of serious folk.

Antonina was a joy; the Empress had been a pleasure. Sittas was a fine magnanimous lord; Cassian the very archetype of a true bishop.

And Michael, of course, a prophet on earth.

But it was time for serious business, now. Peasant work. And so, though they never grinned, Syrian peasants took no offense—and lost no heart—from the abuse of Thracians.

Farm boys, themselves, at bottom, those Thracian cataphracts. Peasants, nothing better.

Just very, very tough peasants.

And so, as summer became autumn, and as autumn turned to winter—

—a general and his allies fought to escape Malwa's talons,

—an Empress watched an empire unravel in Constantinople,

—conspirators plotted everywhere—

And a few hundred peasants and their wives toiled under the Syrian sun. Doing what peasants do best, from the experience of millenia.

Toughening.

Chapter 17

NORTH INDIA
Summer 530 AD

When they came upon the third massacre, Rana Sanga had had enough.

"This is madness," he snarled. "The Roman is doing it to us again."

His chief lieutenant, Jaimal, tore his eyes away from the bloody corpses strewn on both sides of the road. There were seven bodies there, in addition to the three soldiers they had found lying in the guardhouse itself. All of them were common soldiers, and all of them had been slaughtered like so many sheep. Judging from the lack of blood on any of the weapons lying nearby, Jaimal did not think the soldiers had inflicted a single wound on their assailants. Most of them, he suspected, had not even tried. At least half had been slain while trying to flee.

"What are you talking about?" he asked.

"This—*idiocy*." Sanga glared. "No, I take that back. This is not idiocy. Not at all. This is pure deception."

His lieutenant frowned. "I don't understand—"

"It's obvious, Jaimal! The whole point of this massacre—like the first two, and the attack on the army camp—is simply to lead us in pursuit."

Seeing the lack of comprehension on Jaimal's face, Sanga reined in his temper. He did not, however, manage to refrain from sighing with exasperation.

"Jaimal, ask yourself some simple questions. Why did the Romans kill these men? Why are they going out of their way to take roads which lead past guardhouses? Why, having done so, do they take the time to attack the guardhouses instead of sneaking around them? You know as well as I do that these"—he jabbed a finger at the corpses—"sorry sons-of-bitches wouldn't move out of their guardhouses unless they were forced to. Finally, why did they attack the army camp in Kausambi on the night they fled?"

Silence. Frown of incomprehension. Sanga finally exploded.

"*You idiot!* The Romans are doing everything possible to lead us in this direction? Why, damn you—*why?*"

Jaimal's gape would have been comical, if Sanga had been in a humorous mood.

"Belisarius—isn't—isn't with them," he stammered. "He fled a different way."

"Congratulations," growled Sanga. He reined his horse around.

"Gather up the men. We're going back."

Jaimal frowned. "But it's a three-day ride back to Kausambi. And we were ordered—"

"Damn the orders! I'll deal with Tathagata. And what if it is a three day ride? We've already lost four days on this fool's errand. By the time we get back—assuming I can talk sense into the Malwa—Belisarius will have at least a week's lead on us. Would you rather extend it further?"

He jabbed an angry finger to the south. "How many more days do you want to chase after the Roman general's underlings? I doubt if we can catch them anyway. The Pathans say they've already gained a day on us. They're covering as much distance in three days as we can in four. And even have time for *this*"—another angry finger jabbed at the corpses—"along the way."

Jaimal nodded. Large Rajput cavalry units such as

their own always kept a handful of Pathan irregulars with them. The barbarians were an indisciplined nuisance, most of the time, but they were unexcelled trackers.

"How are they traveling so fast?" wondered Jaimal.

Sanga shrugged. "They've got remounts, for one thing, which we don't. And they must have the best horses in creation. We may never know, but I'd be willing to wager a year's income that Belisarius managed to buy the best horses he could find, in the months he's been in India. And hide them away somewhere."

Then, with a tone like steel:

"And now, Jaimal, do as I command. Gather up the men. We're heading back."

Beyond a point, none of Sanga's subordinates would argue with him. That point had been reached, Jaimal knew, and he immediately obeyed his instructions.

His chief subordinates, Udai and Pratap, privately expressed their reservations to him. Those reservations, in the main, centered around their fear of the Malwa reaction when they returned to Kausambi. But, now that their course was set, Jaimal would no more tolerate dissent than would Sanga himself.

"And besides," he growled, "no one will miss us here anyway. There must be forty thousand troops beating these plains. A third of them Rajput cavalry, and another third Ye-tai horsemen. Five hundred of us will make no difference."

"True enough," grunted Udai. "As good as the Roman horses are—and with remounts—only royal couriers could move faster."

"They've been sent, haven't they?" asked Pratap.

Jaimal shrugged irritably. "Do I know? Since when does Emperor Skandagupta take me into his confidence? But I assume so. By now, I imagine, couriers have been dispatched to every port on the Erythrean Sea, alerting the garrisons."

His own tone of voice, now, was a duplicate of Sanga's:

"And that's enough. Do as you've been told."

Couriers *had* been sent, in point of fact. Just as Jaimal expected—to every port on the Erythrean Sea. The couriers were expert horsemen, riding the very finest steeds. They did not bring remounts with them, however. Instead, they changed horses at the relay stations which the Malwa maintained at regular intervals along all of the principal roads in the Empire. These relay stations were small affairs, in the Gangetic plain, not much more than a barn or corral attached to a small barracks housing a squad of four soldiers.

The courier to Barbaricum was one of three who had been sent down the road to Mathura. Mathura was not itself the destination of any of them. All three, long before they reached Mathura, would take the various branching routes which led to Barbaricum, the small ports in the Kathiawar, and the northern end of the Gulf of Khambat.

The courier to the Gulf of Khambat had left first, the day after Belisarius' escape. The Malwa were certain that the general and his underlings were fleeing back to Bharakuccha. They placed their top priority on sending off couriers to cover the entire Gulf. The couriers headed for the Kathiawar and Barbaricum had departed a few hours later, almost as an afterthought.

At first, the two men had traveled together. But, after a time, the courier destined for the Kathiawar had pulled ahead. He was new to the royal courier service, and full of his own self-importance. His companion was glad to see him go, with the relief felt by seasoned veterans the world over at being rid of the company of irritating apprentice twits. The veteran courier saw no reason to match the youth's extravagant haste. Why bother? Everyone knew the Romans had gone south, not west.

By the time he reached the relay station at the end of his first day's ride, the courier was in a thoroughly foul mood. Disgust, leavened by a heavy dose of self-pity. Barbaricum, his ultimate destination, was the very westernmost port of any significance in the Malwa Empire. It lay even beyond the Indus River—almost a thousand miles from Kausambi, as the crow flies.

The courier, of course, was not a crow. He would be forced to travel at least half again that distance before he reached his destination. Along poor roads, most of the way, and through the blistering heat of Rajputana. He would even have to pass through a portion of the Thar, India's worst desert. A long, miserable, hot journey—and with nothing to look forward to at the end except India's worst port. The courier detested Barbaricum. It was a mongrel city, half of whose population were foreign barbarians. And the Indians who lived there were not much better, having long since adapted to the customs of heathen outlanders.

So, as he dismounted from his horse in front of the relay station, the courier was feeling very sorry for himself. His sorrow turned to outrage when no soldier emerged from the barracks to assist him in removing his saddle.

The courier stalked over to the barracks door and shouldered his way through without so much as knocking.

"Just what the fuck do you—"

The sword went a quarter-inch into his chest. Not a mortal wound, painful as it was, not even a particularly bloody one. But the courier could feel the steel tip grating against his chestbone. And the hand which held that sword was as steady as a rock.

The courier's eyes began with that hand, and followed the length of the sword to the place where it disappeared into his chest. Everything else was a blur.

In a frozen daze, the courier heard a voice. He did not make out the words. The sword-tip jabbed against his sternum, pressing him back against the doorframe. He stared down at it, transfixed by the sight.

The words were repeated. Hindi words. Their meaning finally penetrated.

"Are there any more couriers coming after you?"

He understood, but couldn't speak. Another jab.

"What?" he gasped. Another jab.

"N-no," he stammered.

The sword went straight through his chest, as if driven by a sledgehammer. The courier slumped to his knees. In the few seconds remaining in his life, his eyes finally focussed on the barracks as a whole.

His first reaction was confusion. Why were his two courier companions still here? And why were they lying on top of a pile of soldiers?

His vision began to fade.

They're all dead, he realized.

His last sight was the face of the young courier who had accompanied him on the first part of his journey. The sight amused him, vaguely. The vainglorious little snot looked like a frog, what with that open mouth and those bulging eyes.

His vision failed. His last thought, very vague, was the realization that he had never actually seen the man who had killed him. Just his hand. A large, powerful, sinewy hand.

A hundred miles east of Kausambi, near Sarnath, an innkeeper was almost beside himself with joy. He drove his wife, his children, and his servants mercilessly.

"The best food!" he exclaimed again, and, again, cuffed his wife. "The very best! I warn you—if the noble folk complain, I will beat you. They are very rich, and will be generous if they are pleased."

His wife scurried to obey, head bent. His children and servants did likewise. All of them were terrified of the innkeeper. When times were bad—as they usually were—the innkeeper was a sullen, foul-tempered, brutal tyrant. When times were good, he was even worse. Avarice simply added an edge to his cruelty.

So, for all the members of that household except the innkeeper himself, the next twelve hours passed like a slow-moving nightmare.

At first, they were terrified that the nobleman and

his wife would find the food displeasing. But that fear did not materialize. The noblewoman said nothing—quite properly, especially for a wife so much younger than her husband—but the nobleman was most effusive in his praise.

Unfortunately, the nobleman added a bonus for the excellence of the meal. The innkeeper's greed soared higher. In the kitchen, he buffeted his family and his servants, urging them to make haste. The nobleman and his wife had gone to bed, along with the wife's ladies, but their large escort of soldiers had to be fed also. Not the best food, of course, but not so bad that they would complain to their master. And plenty of it!

The terror of the household mounted. The soldiers were a vicious looking crew. Some sort of barbarians. There were a great number of them, with only three women camp followers. The innkeeper's oldest daughter and the two servant girls were petrified at the thought of entering the common rooms where the soldiers were staying the night. Their mother and one of the elderly servants, whose haggard appearance would shield them, tried to bring the food to the soldiers. But the innkeeper slapped his wife, and commanded the young women to do the chore. Anything to please the soldiers, lest they complain of inhospitality to their master.

That terror, too, proved baseless. For all their fearsome appearance, the soldiers did not behave improperly. Indeed, they were rather polite.

So, after the soldiers finished their meal and lay down on their pallets, the innkeeper beat his daughter and the two servant girls. They had obviously been rude to the soldiers, or they would have been importuned.

The final terror, which kept the entire household awake through the night, was for the next morning. When the nobleman and his party left, he might not give the innkeeper as large a bonus as the innkeeper was expecting. The terror grew as the long hours passed. The innkeeper's expectations waxed by the hour, as he stayed awake himself through the night, in avid consideration of his pending fortune. By the break of dawn, the innkeeper had convinced himself that he was on the verge of receiving a preposterous bonus. When the actual bonus which materialized was far beneath that absurd expectation, his family and his servants knew that he would be savage.

Yet, that terror also vanished. The bonus which the innkeeper received—to everyone's astonishment, even his own—was, by their standards, enormous.

And so, in the end, the sojourn of the unknown nobleman proved to be a blessing for that household. The innkeeper's greed, of course, would soon enough add to their misery. Neither his wife, nor his children, nor his servants doubted that in the least. The innkeeper would expect a similar bonus from the occasional noble customer in the future. And, when that bonus did not appear, would brutalize his household.

But that was a problem for the future. Neither his wife, nor his children, nor his servants were given to worrying about the future. The present was more than dark enough. And, thankfully, they would enjoy a rare respite from the ever-present fear in their lives. The innkeeper, awash in his sudden wealth, indulged himself in a drunken stupor for the next three days.

Every night, as she watched him soddenly sleeping, his wife thought of poisoning him. It was her principal entertainment in life. Over the years, she had determined eighteen different toxins she could use. At least five of those would leave no trace of suspicion.

But, as always, the amusement paled after a time. There was no point in poisoning him. She would be required—by law, now—to immolate herself on his funeral pyre. Her children and her servants would fare little better. The innkeeper had long ago sunk into hopeless debt to the local potentates. Upon his death, that debt would come due, immediately and in its entirety. By law, now, all lower-caste households were responsible for the debts of the family head, upon his death. They would not be able to pay those debts. The inn would be seized. The servants would be sold into slavery. The children, being twice-born rather than untouchable, could not be made slaves due to debt. They would simply starve, or be forced to turn themselves to unthinkable occupations.

By the end of the innkeeper's binge, three days later, his wife hardly remembered the nobleman who had given her that brief respite from fear. Her mind had wandered much farther back in time, to the days of her youth. Better days, she remembered—or, at least, thought she did. Though not as good as the days of her mother, and her grandmother, judging from the tales she half-remembered from her childhood. The days when suttee was only expected from rich widows—noblewomen desirous to prove their piety, and with no need to be concerned over the material welfare of their children.

The old days, the Gupta days. The days when customs, harsh as they might be, were only customs. The days when even those harsh customs, in practice, were often meliorated by kinder—or, at least, laxer—potentates. The days when even a stern potentate might shrink from the condemnation of a Buddhist monk, or a sadhu.

The days before the Malwa came. With Malwa law, and Malwa rigor. And the Mahaveda priests to sanctify the pure, and the mahamimamsa to punish the polluted.

Fourteen royal couriers raced south across northern India. Unlike the three couriers headed west, all of these couriers were filled with the urgency of their mission. Royal couriers, in their own way, were one of the pampered elite of Malwa India. All of them were of kshatriya birth—low-caste kshatriya, true, but kshatriya nonetheless. And while their rank was modest, in the official aristocratic scale, they enjoyed an unusual degree of intimacy with the very highest men of India. Many of those couriers, more than once, had taken their messages from the very hand of the God-on-Earth himself.

An arrogant lot, thus, in their own way. Royal Malwa couriers believed themselves to be the fastest men in the world. As they pounded their way south, every one of those fourteen men was certain that the vast hordes of the Malwa army had no chance of catching the foreign devils. The couriers—and they alone—were all that stood between the wicked outlanders and their successful escape.

Fast as the Romans and Ethiopians were, with their remounts and their fine steeds, they were not as fast as Malwa couriers. The horses which the couriers rode were even better, and the couriers enjoyed one great advantage—they were under no compulsion to keep their horses alive. Many more horses awaited them in relay stations along every main road. And so all of them, more than once, ran their horses to death as they raced from station to station along their route.

The couriers were filled with the confidence that they could reach the ports before the fleeing enemy, and alert the garrisons. The Malwa army could flounder, and the Rajputs and Ye-tai thrash about in aimless pursuit, but the couriers would save the day.

So they thought, and they were not wrong in thinking so. But the couriers, like so many others throughout India in those weeks of frenzy, were too confident. Too full of themselves; too incautious; too heedless of all that could go wrong, in this polluted world.

One courier's incaution manifested itself in the most direct way possible. Thundering around a bend in the road, his forward vision obscured by the lush forest which loomed on either side, the courier suddenly learned that he was indeed faster than the foreign enemy. He had overtaken them.

The courier had already plunged into the midst of the foreigners before he made that unhappy discovery. A quick-thinking man, the courier did not make the mistake of trying to turn around. Instead, he took advantage of his speed and simply pounded right through them, guiding his horse expertly through the little crowd.

He made it, too. In truth, the royal courier *was* one of the very finest horsemen in the world.

But no horseman is fine enough to outrun a cataphract arrow. Not, at least, one fired by the bow of that cataphract named Valentinian.

The foreigners dragged his body into the woods, and then piled insult onto injury. They added his wonderful steed to their stock of remounts.

A second courier, and a third, and then a fourth, also discovered the caprices of fate.

Dramatically, in the case of the second courier. The monsoon downpours had washed out portions of many of the roads throughout India. The route this courier took happened to be one of the lesser roads, and thus suffered more than its share of climatic degradations. The courier, however, was unfazed by these obstacles. He was an experienced courier, and an excellent rider. He had leapt over many washed-out portions of road in his career, and did so again. And again and again and again, with all the skill and self-confidence of his station in life. What he failed to consider, unfortunately, was that his horse did not share the same skill and experience—not, at least, when it was half-dead from exhaustion. So, leaping yet another stream, the horse stumbled and spilled the courier.

Well-trained, the horse waited for its rider to remount. A very well-trained horse, that one. It did not begin to forage for two hours, after its equine mind finally concluded that the courier seemed bound and determined to remain lying in the stream. Face down, oddly enough, in two feet of water.

The third courier's mishap took a less dramatic form. He, too, driving an exhausted mount across a broken stretch of road, caused his horse to stumble and fall. Unlike the other courier, this one did not have the bad luck to strike his head against a boulder in a stream.

He landed in a bush, and merely broke his leg. A simple fracture, nothing worse. But he was not discovered for two days, and by the time the small party of woodcutters conveyed him to the nearest Malwa post it was much too late for it to do any good.

The fourth courier encountered his unfortunate destiny in its most common and plebeian manifestation. He got sick. He had been feeling poorly even before he left Kausambi, and after a week of relentless travel he was in a delirium. A man can drive a horse to death, but not without great cost to himself. That courier was a stubborn man, and a brave one, and he was determined to fulfill his duty. But willpower alone is not enough. On the evening of the seventh day he reached a relay station and collapsed from his horse. The soldiers staffing the station carried him into the barracks and did their best—with the aid of a local herb doctor—to tend to his illness.

Their best, given the medical knowledge of the time, was not good enough. The courier was a brave and stubborn man, and so he lived for four more days. But he never recovered consciousness before dying, and the soldiers were afraid to even touch the courier's message case, much less break the Malwa seal and open the royal instrument. It would have done no good, anyway, since all of them were illiterate.

It was not until two days later, upon the arrival of the first unit of regular troops slogging in pursuit of the escapees, that an officer inspected the message. A high-caste officer, a Malwa as it happened, who was arrogant enough to break the royal seal. Immediately upon reading the message, the officer issued two commands. His first order despatched his best rider to Bharakuccha with the—now much too belated—message. His second order flogged the guards of the relay station. Fifty lashes each, with a split bamboo cane, for gross dereliction of duty.

Still, ten couriers remained. By the end of the second week after the Romans and Ethiopians began their flight south, all ten of these couriers had bypassed the foreigners and were now forging ahead of them. Slowly, to be sure. The foreigners were indeed moving very rapidly, and were steadily outdistancing the great mass of their pursuers. Even the couriers were only able to gain a few miles on them each day. (On average. All of the couriers were taking different roads, and none of those roads was the same as that taken by the foreigners.)

A few miles a day is not much, but it would be enough. The couriers would arrive at the Gulf of Khambat with more than ample time to spread the alarm. Four of them were destined for Bharakuccha itself. By the time the outlanders arrived at the coast, Bharakuccha and the smaller ports would be sealed off. The foreign escapees would be trapped inside India, with the enormous manpower of the Malwa army available to bring them down.

That had been the Malwa plan from the beginning of the chase. The Emperor and his high officials had hoped, of course, that the army would catch the fugitives before they reached the coast. But they knew the odds were against that, and so they had immediately sent out the couriers.

It was an excellent plan, taking advantage of the excellent Malwa courier corps. A plan adopted by men who were as intelligent as they were arrogant. And, like many such plans, collapsed of its own arrogance.

Haughty men, swollen with their own self-importance, have a tendency to forget about the enemy.

Enemies, in this case. The man they were pursuing, the general Belisarius, was something quite foreign to their experience. He, like them, also made plans. He, like them, also followed those plans. But he—quite unlike them—also knew that plans are fickle things. And, that being so, it always pays to make plans within plans, and to keep an eye out for every unexpected opportunity. Every new angle.

Months earlier, Belisarius had seen such an opportunity. He had seized it with both hands. The Empress Shakuntala had been delivered from captivity, and Majarashtra's greatest warrior set free from that task.

Raghunath Rao had been free for months, now. Free to set the Great Country afire.

Months, of course, are not enough to create a great popular rebellion. Certainly not in a recently conquered land, whose people are still licking their wounds. But months *are* enough, for such a man as Rao, to assemble the nucleus of his future army. To gather rebellious young men—almost a thousand, by now—in the isolated hillforts which pocked the Great Country's badlands.

Rao was not only an experienced commander, he had the natural aptitude of a guerrilla fighter. So, almost from the day he returned to Majarashtra, he had set the young men rallying to his banner to the first, simplest, and most essential task of the would-be rebel.

Intelligence.

Watch. Observe. Nothing moves south of the Vindhyas without our knowledge.

The fastest of all the Malwa couriers finally made his way through the Gangetic plain, and through the Vindhya mountains which were the traditional boundary between north India and the Deccan. Bharakuccha was not far away, now.

He did not get thirty miles before he was ambushed. Brought down by five arrows.

Rao, as it happened, was camped not far away, in a hillfort some twenty miles distant. Within hours, the young Maratha ambushers brought him the courier's message case. Rao had no fear of the royal seal, and he was quite literate. A very fast reader, in fact.

Immediately after reading the message, he issued his own set of rapid commands. Within minutes, the hillfort was emptied of all but Rao himself and his two chief lieutenants. All the others—all three hundred or so— were racing to spread the news.

Malwa couriers are coming. All of them must be

stopped. Kill them. Take their message cases. Rao himself commands.

After the young warriors were gone, Rao and his lieutenants enjoyed a simple meal. Over the meal, they discussed the significance of this latest event.

"Can we aid the Romans in some other way?" asked Maloji.

Rao shrugged. "Perhaps. We will see when they arrive. I do not know their plans, although I suspect the Malwa are right. The Romans and the Africans will try to take ship in Bharakuccha. If so, it will be enough for us to stop the couriers." He smiled grimly. "Those men are *very* capable. They will manage, if we can keep the garrisons from being alerted."

"What if the Empress is with them?" asked his other lieutenant, Ramchandra.

Rao shook his head firmly. "She will not be."

"How do you know?"

Rao's smile, now, was not grim at all. Quite gay, in fact.

"I know the mind of Belisarius, Ramchandra. That man will never do the obvious. Remember how he rescued Shakuntala! In fact—" Rao looked down at the message scroll, still in his hand. "I wonder . . ." he mused.

He rolled up the scroll and slapped it back into the case. The motion had a finality to it.

"We will know soon enough." His smile, now, was a veritable grin. "Expect to be surprised, comrades. When you deal with Belisarius, that is the one thing you can be sure of. The *only* thing."

With a single lithe movement, Rao came to his feet. He strode to the nearest battlement and stood for a moment gazing across the Great Country. The stone wall of the hillfort rose directly from an almost perpendicular cliff over a hundred yards in height. The view was magnificent.

His two lieutenants joined him. They were both struck by the serenity in the Panther's face.

"We will see the Empress, soon enough," he murmured. "She will arrive, comrades—be sure of it. From the most unexpected direction, and in the most unexpected way."

That same day—that same hour—the young officer in command of a guardpost just south of Pataliputra found himself in a quandary.

On the one hand, the party seeking passage through his post lacked the proper documentation. This lack weighed the heavier in the officer's mind for the fact that he was of brahmin ancestry, with all the veneration which that priest/scholar class had for the written word. Brahmin ancestry was uncommon for a military officer. Such men were normally kshatriya. He had chosen that career due to his ambition. He was not Malwa, but Bihari. As a member of a subject nation, he could expect to rise higher in the military than in the more status-conscious civilian hierarchy.

Still, he retained the instincts of a pettifogging bureaucrat, and the simple fact was that these people had no documents. Scandalous.

On the other hand—

The nobleman was obviously of very high caste. Not Malwa, no—some western nation. But no low-ranking officer is eager to offend a high-caste dignitary of the Empire, Malwa or otherwise.

The officer could hear his men grumbling in the background. They had seen the size of the bribe offered by the nobleman, and were seething at their commander's idiotic obsession with petty rules and regulations.

The officer hesitated, vacillated, rattled back and forth within the narrow confines of his mind.

The nobleman's wife ended that dance of indecision.

The officer heard her sharp yelps of command. Watched, as she clambered down from the howdah, assisted by her fierce looking soldiers. Watched her stalk over to him.

Small, she was, and obviously young. Pretty, too, from what little he could see of her face. Beautiful black eyes.

Whatever pleasure those facts brought the officer vanished as soon as she began to speak.

In good Hindi, but with a heavy southern accent. A Keralan accent, he thought.

After I inform the Emperor of Kerala of your insolence your remaining days in this world will be brief. He is my father and he will demand your death of the Malwa. Base cur! You will—

Her husband tried to calm her down.

—be impaled. I will demand a short stake. My father the Emperor will—

Her husband tried to calm her down.

—allow a long stake in the interests of diplomacy but he will not—

Her husband tried to calm her down.

—settle for less than your death by torture. I will demand that your carcass be fed to dogs. Small dogs, who will tear at it rather than devour it whole. My father the Emperor will—

Her husband tried to calm her down.

—not insist on the dogs, in the interests of diplomacy, but he will demand—

Finally, finally, the nobleman managed to usher his wife away. Over her shoulder, shrieking:

—your stinking corpse be denied the rites. You will spend five yugas as a worm, five more as a spider. You will—

As the party passed through the post, the officer's mangled dignity was partially restored by the large bribe which the nobleman handed him. Partially, no more. The young officer did not miss the smirks which were exchanged between his own soldiers and those of the nobleman's escort. The smirks which common troops exchange, witnessing the abasement of high-ranked adolescent snots.

Within the next week, nine of the ten Malwa couriers died in Majarashtra. They traveled faster than the Maratha guerillas, of course, but the couriers were restricted to the roads and had no real knowledge of the countryside. Rao's young men, on the other hand, knew every shortcut through those volcanic hills. And every spot for a good ambush.

Of the fourteen royal couriers who had headed south from Kausambi weeks earlier, only one survived the journey. His route had been the northernmost of those taken by the couriers, and did not really do more than skirt the Great Country. So he arrived, eventually, at his destination. A tiny port nestled at the northern end of the Gulf.

Finally, everything went according to plan. The commander of the little garrison immediately mobilized his troops and began a thorough and efficient patrol of the port and its environs. All ships—all three of them—were sequestered, prevented from leaving.

The commander was an aggressive, hard-driving officer. The small harbor was sealed tight. And so, according to plan, none of the enemy escaped through that port.

Which, as it happens, they had never had the slightest intention of doing.

Chapter 18

Had Nanda Lal not intervened, it might have come to blows. Rana Sanga would have been executed, thereafter, but he would have had the satisfaction of slaughtering Lord Tathagata like the swine that he was.

"*Silence!*" bellowed the spymaster, as soon as he charged into the room. "Both of you!"

Nanda Lal had a powerful voice. It was distorted somewhat, due to his shattered nose, but still powerful. And the spymaster's voice was filled with a pure black fury so ugly it would have silenced anyone.

That mood had settled on Nanda Lal as soon as he recovered consciousness on the floor of Great Lady Holi's barge. On the blood-soaked carpet, stained by his own wound, where a foreign demon's boot had sent him sprawling.

A week had gone by, now, and his rage had not lifted. It was a spymaster's rage—icy, not hot, but utterly merciless.

Sanga clenched his jaws. He stared at Nanda Lal, not out of rude curiosity, but simply because he could no longer bear the sight of Lord Tathagata's fat, stupid, pig of a face. Then, realizing that his stare could be misconstrued, Sanga looked away.

In truth, the Malwa Empire's chief of espionage was a sight to behold. On almost any other man, that huge bandage wrapped around his face would have given him a comical appearance. It simply made Nanda Lal look like an ogre.

Tathagata, recovering from his startlement, transferred his fury onto Nanda Lal.

"What is the meaning of this?" demanded the Malwa army's top officer. "It's outrageous! You have no right to issue commands here! This is purely a military matter, Nanda Lal—I'll thank you to mind your own—"

Nanda Lal's next words came hissing like a snake.

"If you so much as finish that sentence, Tathagata, you will discover what rights I have and do not have. I guarantee the discovery will shock you. But only briefly. You will be dead within the hour."

Lord Tathagata choked on the sentence. His jaw hung loose. His eyes—wide as a flatfish—goggled about the room, as if searching the magnificence of his headquarters to find something that would gainsay Nanda Lal's statement.

Apparently, he found nothing. Such, at least, was Rana Sanga's interpretation of his continued silence.

Nanda Lal stalked into the room. He did not bother to close the door behind him. Sanga could see, through that door, a part of a room. One of the Emperor's own private chambers, he realized. Sanga had never entered that room, himself. The Rajput's only contact with Skandagupta had been in chambers given over to public gatherings. He was now in a part of the Grand Palace which was essentially unknown to him. The very core of that great edifice, and the power which rested within it.

"Why are you here, Sanga?" asked the spymaster. His voice, now, was low and calm.

Sanga began to explain his theory about Belisarius' escape, but Nanda Lal interrupted him immediately.

"Not that, Sanga. I've already heard *that*." The spymaster began to make a wry grimace, but the pain in his nose cut the expression short. He waved toward the open door.

"We *all* heard that much. The Emperor himself sent me in here to stop your shouting." A hard glance at

Tathagata, still gaping like a blowfish. "*And* his. We couldn't hear ourselves think, for the commotion." All trace of amusement vanished. "I ask again: why are you here?"

Sanga understood.

"I want the authority to lead a search for Belisarius to the west. That's where he's gone. I'm certain of it."

Lord Tathagata's outrage, finally, could contain itself no longer. But—carefully—he made sure it was directed at the Rajput.

"This is insolent madness, Nanda Lal," he grated. "The stinking Rajput just got tired of—"

He was silenced, this time, by the Emperor's own voice.

"Bring them both here, Nanda Lal," came the imperial command from the next room.

Tathagata ground his teeth. But he said nothing, even though his face was flushed with anger.

The next words, coming from the adjoining room, caused his fat face to go pale. Words spoken by an old woman.

"Yes, Nanda Lal, bring them here. At once."

Rana Sanga was surprised by the Emperor's private chamber. It was much smaller than he expected, and almost—well, "utilitarian" hardly fit a room with such tapestries and furnishings. But, compared to any other setting in which the Rajput kinglet had ever seen his sovereign, the chamber was almost stark and bare.

There were three occupants in the room. Emperor Skandagupta, his daughter Sati, and his aunt the Great Lady Holi. Sanga had seen both of the women before, on ceremonial occasions, but only from a distance. He had never spoken to either of them.

He was struck by their appearance. Neither of the women was veiled. The princess Sati was a beautiful young woman, abstractly, but she seemed as remote as the horizon. The Great Lady Holi seemed even more distant, especially when Sanga met her eyes. Blank, empty eyes. Vacant eyes.

More than their appearance, however, what impressed Sanga was their chairs. Not spectacular, those chairs, by imperial standards. But they were every bit as good as the Emperor's. No one, in Sanga's experience, ever sat in a chair which was as good as the Emperor's. Not in the same room that he occupied, at least.

Sanga did not have time to ponder the significance of the fact, however. Lord Tathagata, again, could not restrain his outrage.

"Your Majesty—Great Lady Holi—I must insist that this Rajput be punished. *Severely*. What is at stake here is nothing less than the most essential military discipline. This—this—this *dog* disobeyed my express—"

Great Lady Holi's tone of voice was as vacant as her eyes. But the words themselves were like a knife. Cold, thin, sharp.

"What is at stake here, Tathagata, is the incompetence of our military command. Every word you speak illustrates it further."

Tathagata gasped. Sanga, watching, realized the man was utterly terrified. The Rajput kinglet transferred his gaze back to the Great Lady. His face bore no expression, but his mind was a solid frown of puzzlement. He could see nothing in that elderly female figure to cause such pure fear. Except, possibly, those eyes.

Is she a power behind the throne? he wondered. *I've heard tales—witchcraft, sorcery—but I never took them seriously.*

The Emperor spoke now, to Tathagata. Like a cobra might speak to its prey. A short, pudgy, unprepossessing cobra. But a cobra for all that.

"We have just discovered—only this morning—that Rana Sanga attempted to warn us once before that Belisarius was deceiving us. But you silenced him then, just as you are trying to silence him now."

"That's a lie!" exclaimed Tathagata.

"It is not a lie," spoke a voice from the rear.

Sanga turned. Lord Damodara was seated in a far corner of the room. The Rajput had been so preoccupied when he entered the imperial chamber that he had not spotted him.

Damodara rose and advanced into the center of the room.

"It is not a lie," he repeated. "At the Emperor's council at Ranapur, when Rana Sanga gave his opinion on Belisarius' actions, he attempted to speak further. To warn us that the Roman was planning treachery. You silenced him."

"Yes, you did," growled the Emperor. "I remember it quite clearly. Do you call *me* a liar?"

Tathagata shook his head feverishly. "Of course not, Your Majesty! Of course not! But—I did not know what he was going to say—and it was a Malwa council—he is a Rajput—and—" Almost in a wail: "How does anyone know what he meant to say?"

Damodara: "Because I asked him, afterward. And he told me. That is why, when the council reconvened, I demanded that—" He fell abruptly silent. "That is why I demanded what I did."

Damodara pointed toward Sanga with a head-nod. "I said nothing, at the time, of Rana Sanga's words." Bitterly, contemptuously: "Lest he be penalized by such as you. But I finally managed to tell the Emperor and Nanda Lal and—Great Lady Holi—just this morning."

Bitterly, contemptuously: "Which was the earliest moment you would allow me an audience with them."

"I knew nothing of this," whined Tathagata.

"That is why you are guilty of incompetence rather than treason," said Great Lady Holi. Her words, for all their harshness, were spoken in a tone which—to Rana Sanga, at least—had absolutely no emotional content whatsoever. She might have been speaking about the weather. A thousand miles away, in a land she had never visited and never would.

"Leave us, Lord Tathagata," commanded the Emperor. Skandagupta sat up in his chair. He was still short, and pudgy. But he reminded Rana Sanga of nothing so much as a cobra flaring its hood.

"You are relieved of your command. Retire to your estate and remain there."

"But—Your Majesty—"

"You are now relieved of half your estate. The richer half. Do not attempt to dissemble. Imperial auditors will check your claim."

Tathagata stared, wide-eyed, paralyzed.

The Emperor:

"If you are still in this room one minute from now, you will be relieved of your entire estate. In two minutes, I will have you executed."

Tathagata was out the door in four seconds.

The Emperor glanced at Lord Damodara.

"Inform Lord Jivita that he is now the commander of the army. I will see him in one hour."

Lord Damodara bowed and turned to go. Great Lady Holi stopped him.

"Tell him to meet the Emperor in his western chamber, Lord Damodara."

Again, Sanga was struck by the cold, icy tone of her words.

(No—the tone was not cold. Cold is a temperature. Ice is a substance. That tone had no temperature at all. No substance at all.)

But he was struck even more by the Emperor's sudden start of surprise.

She just commanded the Emperor *to leave this room,* he realized. Then, watching the Emperor's slight shrug: *And he's going to obey—without so much as a protest! What gives this old woman such power?*

Nanda Lal spoke. "What, exactly, do you propose to do, Rana Sanga?"

The Rajput shook off the mental shock caused by Great Lady Holi's words. Almost with relief, he turned to the spymaster.

"First, I will need the assistance of your spies, and your records. Belisarius—not *even* Belisarius—can have managed to escape Kausambi without leaving a trace. It will be there, if we search. Then, if I am right, and we find that he went west rather than south, I will go after him with my cavalry."

"Your troop? That's only five hundred men."

Sanga repressed a snort of derision.

"That will be more than enough. He is only one man, Nanda Lal, not an asura. The problem is finding him, not capturing him once we do. For that, five hundred good cavalrymen are enough."

He decided to throw caution to the winds.

"They are not simply enough—they are the best soldiers for the job. That huge mob floundering about in the south"—he made no attempt to conceal the derision in his gesture—"are just getting in each other's way. If Belisarius can be caught—*if*, Nanda Lal; I make no promises, not with *that* man having a week's lead on us—my Rajputs and Pathan trackers will catch him."

"And if you fail?" demanded the Emperor.

Sanga looked at Skandagupta, hesitated, and then threw all caution to the winds.

"If I fail, Your Majesty, I fail. In war, you sometimes lose. Not because you are incompetent, but simply because the enemy is better."

"And is—*this foul Roman*—better than you?"

All caution to the winds.

"He is *not* a 'foul Roman,' Your Majesty. That has been our mistake all along. He is a *true* Roman, and that is what makes him dangerous. That, and his own great skill."

The Emperor's corpulent face was flushed with anger but, like Lord Tathagata before him, that flush was erased by the Great Lady Holi.

"Stop, Skandagupta," she commanded. "Link has no more time for Malwa vanity."

Sanga was shocked to see the Emperor's face turn pale. There was something odd, he realized, about the Great Lady Holi's voice. It was somehow changing, transmuting. Emotionless before, it was now beginning to sound utterly inhuman.

And who is "Link"? he wondered.

The strangeness deepened, and deepened. Great Lady Holi's voice:

"NANDA LAL, DO AS RANA SANGA ASKS. QUERY YOUR SPIES. CHECK ALL RECORDS."

There was nothing at all human in the tone of that voice, any more. It sounded like—

Rana Sanga froze. He had heard tales, now and then, but had paid them no mind. Years ago, bowing to the collective decision of Rajputana's assembled kings in council, Rana Sanga had also given his oath to the Malwa Emperor. He had ignored, then and thereafter—with all the dignity of a Rajput Hindu—the whispered rumors of Malwa's new gods.

—like the voice of a goddess. Cold, not like ice, but like the vastness of time itself.

In a half-daze, he heard *the voice* continue:

"LEAVE US, SKANDAGUPTA. LINK WISHES TO SPEAK TO RANA SANGA."

The Rajput heard the Emperor's protesting words, but understood not a one of them. Only the reply:

"LEAVE, MALWA. YOU ARE OUR INSTRUMENT, NOTHING MORE. IF YOU DISPLEASE US, WE SHALL FIND ANOTHER. LEAVE NOW."

The Emperor left—scurried from the room, in fact, with little more dignity than Tathagata had scurried not long before. Sanga was alone, now, with the two women.

At first, he expected to see the young princess leave as well. Instead, Sati spoke to him:

"I realize that this must come as a shock to you, Rana Sanga," she said in a very polite tone. Her voice, Sanga was relieved to discover, was still that of a young woman. A cold, distant, aloof voice, true. But unmistakeably human.

The Rajput glanced at Great Lady Holi. The old woman, he was even more relieved to discover, seemed to have retreated into a trance. It was almost as if she were not there. Only a statue of her, unmoving, rigid.

Sati followed his glance, smiled faintly.

"She is not Great Lady Holi. Not really. Great Lady Holi is simply a vessel. The divine being who dwells in that vessel is named *Link*."

"A goddess? Or a god?" asked Sanga. He was rather proud that his voice neither stammered nor had a trace of tremor.

"Neither," replied Sati. "Link has no sex, Rana Sanga. It is a pure being, a *deva* spirit sent by the gods. The new gods." The young princess straightened her back. "When Great Lady Holi dies, I will replace her as Link's vessel. I have trained for that sacred mission my entire life. Since I was but a babe."

Watching her obvious pride in that announcement, Sanga felt a sudden pang. He did not find Sati attractive, as a man might find a woman. For all the comeliness of the young princess, hers was a type of aloof beauty which appealed to him not at all. His own wife was plump, plain-faced, and prematurely grey. She was also as warm as rich earth, and as playful as a kitten.

Still, he felt a pang. He could not imagine this princess ever tickling a husband in bed, mercilessly, as his own wife delighted in doing. But he could not help that pang, thinking of this young woman as—whatever Holi was. Something not human.

The inhuman thing in the room, he now learned, could read minds far better than any mortal.

"DO NOT FEEL SORROW AT SATI'S FATE, RANA SANGA. YOUR SORROW IS MISPLACED. IT DERIVES FROM NOTHING MORE THAN IGNORANCE."

He stared at Great La—at *Link*.

"YOU ARE PRIVILEGED, RANA SANGA. YOU ARE THE FIRST HUMAN I HAVE SPOKEN TO SINCE I ARRIVED IN THIS WORLD, OTHER THAN MALWA."

"Why?" he managed to ask.

"IT IS NECESSARY. I DID NOT EXPECT BELISARIUS TO BE SO CAPABLE. THE HISTORICAL RECORD MISLED ME."

Sanga frowned. Curiosity overrode all fear.

"You knew of him?"

"OF COURSE. IN THE WORLD THAT WAS, HE RECONQUERED THE ROMAN EMPIRE FOR JUSTINIAN. GIVEN THE SEVERE LIMITS UNDER WHICH HE WAS FORCED TO OPERATE, HE MAY HAVE BEEN THE GREATEST GENERAL EVER PRODUCED BY HUMANITY. HE WAS CERTAINLY ONE OF THEM. THE DISTINCTION, AT THAT LEVEL OF GENIUS, IS STATISTICALLY MEANINGLESS."

Sanga did not understand the word "statistically," but he grasped the essence of her—of *Link's*—statement.

"If you knew all that, why—"

"I AM NOT A GOD. THE GODS THEMSELVES— THE NEW GODS, EVEN, WHO ARE REAL—ARE NOT GODS. NOT AS YOU UNDERSTAND THE TERM. NOTHING IN THE UNIVERSE CAN BE A 'GOD' AS YOU UNDERSTAND THE TERM. IT IS PRECLUDED BY CHAOS THEORY AND THE UNCERTAINTY PRINCIPLE."

The last sentence was pure gibberish, but, again, Sanga understood the sense of Link's statement. For a moment, his Hindu orthodoxy rose in rebellion, but Sanga drove it down. The moment was too important for religious fretting.

"Explain further. Please."

"I COULD KNOW OF BELISARIUS, BEFORE I ARRIVED, ONLY THAT WHICH IS RECORDED IN HISTORY. THAT HE IS A GREAT GENERAL, IS A MATTER OF RECORD. THAT HE IS SOMETHING GREATER, IS NOT. I DO NOT UNDERSTAND THAT UNEXPECTED CAPACITY. NO GENERAL COULD HAVE DONE WHAT HE HAS DONE. NO GENERAL COULD HAVE MANIPULATED ALL OF MALWA SO PERFECTLY. AND, CERTAINLY, NO GENERAL COULD HAVE REACTED SO INSTANTLY WHEN I DETECTED HIS DUPLICITY."

For a moment, Link paused, as if in thought.

Does such a being even "think"? wondered Sanga.

"EITHER MY DATA ARE INCOMPLETE, OR OTHER FACTORS ARE AT WORK. I MUST DISCOVER WHICH. IT IS ESSENTIAL THAT YOU CATCH HIM, FOR THAT REASON ABOVE ALL OTHERS."

Awed, Sanga was; frightened, even. But he was still a Rajput. A Rajput *king*, he reminded himself.

"I cannot promise you that," he stated harshly. "And I will make no vow which I cannot keep."

In the silence which followed, Sanga had time to wonder at his punishment. Would this—*divinity*—be satisfied with stripping him of his lands? Or would it demand his life?

The response, when it finally came, astonished him. From the divine being who secretly ruled Malwa, he had expected a Malwa reaction.

"EXCELLENT. YOU ARE A TREASURE, RANA SANGA. IT IS POSSIBLE THAT WE ERRED, CHOOSING MALWA OVER RAJPUT. IN THE END, RELIABILITY SEEMED MORE IMPORTANT THAN CAPABILITY. FROM THE LONG VIEW OF TIME."

The last sentence was chilling. Sanga suddenly grasped—even if only vaguely—the *immensity* of that "long view of time." As gods might see it.

"NOW, AS A RESULT, WE MUST ADAPT. MORE OF RAJPUTANA'S ESSENCE MUST BE INCORPORATED INTO THE NEW WORLD WE ARE CREATING. MORE OF THAT CAPABILITY."

Sanga was not entirely sure he found those words reassuring. For him, Rajputana's essence was not Rajput ability. It was the Rajput soul. Rajput honor.

Again, the divine being called Link seemed to read his mind perfectly.

"YOU DO NOT UNDERSTAND, RANA SANGA. MALWA AND RAJPUT ARE BUT MOMENTS. STAGES IN A PROCESS, NOTHING MORE. TO YOU, THEY LOOM LARGE AND FIXED. TO THE

NEW GODS, THEY ARE AS TRANSIENT AS MAY-
FLIES. ALL THAT MATTERS IS THE PROCESS."

"What—*process*?" he croaked.

"THE SALVATION OF HUMANITY FROM WHAT
IT WILL BECOME. FROM THE HORROR OF ITS
SELF-CREATED FUTURE. I WAS SENT BACK IN
TIME TO CHANGE THAT FUTURE. TO CHANGE
HISTORY.

"I WILL SHOW YOU THAT HORROR. I WILL
GUIDE YOU THROUGH THE FUTURE. THROUGH
HUMAN DAMNATION. THROUGH FINAL POLLU-
TION."

Sanga had time, just, to begin raising his hand in
protest. His hand felt limply to his side.

Visions gripped him, like a python.

Chapter 19

Blinding flash. A sun arose below the sun. The city beneath that sun vanished. Its inhabitants were incinerated before they knew it.

The city's suburbs were not so fortunate. Charred, but not vaporized; its people screaming, their skins peeled from their bodies in an instant. Seconds later, the suburbs and its shrieking people were blown apart by a sweeping wall of wind.

"SHOCK WAVE. OVERPRESSURE."

Sanga understood neither term. Nor the next:

"SEVENTY-MEGATON WARHEAD. EXCESSIVE. CRUDE. THE OTHER SIDE RESPONDED WITH MIRVS. CIRCULAR PROBABILITY OF ERROR WAS SO FINE AS TO MAKE UP THE DIFFERENCE."

Another city. Obliterated, not by one giant sun, but by ten smaller ones. The difference, in the end, was nothing.

"THE EXCHANGE CONTINUED FOR EIGHT DAYS. WITHIN A MONTH, HALF THE WORLD'S LIFE WAS GONE. WITHIN A YEAR, ALL OF IT, ABOVE THE LEVEL OF BACTERIA. IT WAS THE FIRST TIME HUMANITY EXTINGUISHED ITS OWN WORLD. IT WOULD NOT BE THE LAST."

The world, barren. A single vast desert, so bleak as to make the Thar seem an oasis. The seas, grey and empty. The sky, black with an overcast thicker than anything Sanga had ever seen, in the worst of monsoon season.

"FOUR TIMES HUMANITY DESTROYED THE EARTH. TWICE BY NUCLEAR FIRE, ONCE BY KINETIC BOLIDES, ONCE BY DISEASE."

The only term he understood was "disease."

"THE DISEASE WAS THE WORST.

"A CRYSTALLINE PSEUDO-VIRUS WHICH TARGETED DEOXYRIBONUCLEIC ACID. DNA IS THE BASIS FOR ALL LIFE. WITHOUT IT, LIFE IS IMPOSSIBLE. TRUE LIFE IS IMPOSSIBLE. THE EARTH DESTROYED BY FIRE COULD BE REPOPULATED. EVEN RADIOACTIVITY DIES AWAY, GIVEN SUFFICIENT TIME. THIS PLAGUE— NEVER. EVEN THE BACTERIA ARE GONE. THE EARTH WILL BE BARREN FOREVER. HOME ONLY TO ABOMINATIONS."

The earth, again. Barren, again. But now, everywhere that land could be seen, glittering with a network of gleaming points. Like a spider's web, or the tainted flesh of a plague victim.

"YOU WONDER HOW THE EARTH COULD BE REPOPULATED AFTER ALL LIFE WAS DESTROYED. I WILL SHOW YOU."

A great wheeling spiral. Made up of millions of points of light. The view swept closer. Each of those lights was a sun. Most suns were circled by worlds. Billions of worlds. Each different.

Closer.

Small bodies moved through that incredible black vastness. Slow, slow, slow, slow. Machines, Sanga realized. Vessels of some kind.

"SPACECRAFT. LIMITED BY THE SPEED OF LIGHT."

Sanga understood the words: "speed" "of" "light." But they seemed meaningless. Light was. How could it have a speed?

"IT DOES. 186,300 MILES PER SECOND. NOTHING IN THE UNIVERSE CAN MOVE FASTER. IT TOOK THESE SPACECRAFT CENTURIES TO REACH THE NEAREST STARS. BUT REACH

THEM THEY DID. AND THEN, CENTURIES
LATER, STARS BEYOND. AND THEN, MILLENIA
LATER, STARS BEYOND. AND BEYOND AND
BEYOND. AND BEYOND AND BEYOND.

"MILLIONS UPON MILLIONS OF YEARS."

*Sanga's sense of time expanded. He saw the space-
craft spreading through the heavens. Saw an immense
duration compressed into an instant. Saw the seeds of
his world scattered throughout the spiral.*

"GALAXY. THIS GALAXY. THE MILKY WAY, YOU
CALL IT. HUMANS WILL ALSO REACH ANDROM-
EDA, AND THE MAGELLANIC CLOUDS—ALL THE
GALAXIES IN THE LOCAL GROUP. NO OTHER
CONSCIOUS LIFEFORM HAS EVER BEEN FOUND.
NOW THAT HUMANS—FORMER HUMANS—HAVE
SPREAD THROUGHOUT THE GALAXY AND ITS
NEIGHBORS, THEY HAVE FILLED THAT ECO-
LOGICAL ZONE WHICH YOU CALL 'INTELLI-
GENCE.' NO OTHER WILL EVER ARISE.

"AND HUMANITY HAS DESTROYED ITSELF. IT
HAS BECOME NOTHING BUT MONSTROSITIES.
A DISEASE. THE POLLUTION OF THE UNI-
VERSE."

*A world of gigantic trees. Large monkey-like creatures
swung through its branches. They were hairless, however, and wore clothing. Cloth strips tightly bound,
allowing free movement of their limbs. And a short,
muscular tail. Their fingers were long, their toes gro-
tesquely so. For all essential purposes, they were qua-
drupedal. One of them swung into view.*

Its face was human. Had once been human.

*A world of water, landless, pocketed by vast floating
sargassoes. Fish-like creatures swam through that world-
girdling ocean. Once of them was suddenly seized by
another shape darting from under a ledge of sargasso
weed. Odd shape. Bastard shape. Its flukes moved up
and down, like a dolphin, and its body was a stream-
lined torpedo. But it retained very short, stubby arms—
barely more than hands thrusting forward from vestigial*

shoulders. The hands stuffed the "fish" into a wide mouth lined with needle teeth. Then, carefully separated the fish bones and placed them in a pouch tied to its neck.

A closer view. That face, too—that wide-eyed, gape-mouthed, needle-toothed, almost noseless face—had once been human.

A heavy world, thick with atmosphere. Crab-like shapes scuttled across its low-lying surface, busily constructing edifices of some kind. Their arms and hands, though bulky, were still close to human. But they moved on six legs. The rear limbs retained a faint trace of their bipedal origin. But the mid-limbs were sheer nightmare. Adaptations of the ribcage.

Once human.

Monstrosity followed monstrosity. Some were so bizarre that Sanga could not see any remnant in them of humanity.

Nor was Earth the only planet blasted into lifelessness. Sanga saw thousands of those worlds, ravaged and destroyed by—"nuclear fire," "kinetic bolides"—other things. "DNA plague," eight times. Three planets, drifting together in an empty void beyond time and space itself, had been "rotated about their axis." Many were not even planets, any longer. Simply shards drifting in space. "Very large kinetic bolides."

Sanga understood none of the terms, but he understood the reality. He was a soldier. Horror was no stranger to him. Though he had never, in his worst nightmares, imagined devastation on such a scale.

"YOU WONDER IF I AM LYING TO YOU."

No, he did not. He was inside the mind of Link, now, and understood its basic nature. Link was a "divine being," yes—Sanga could sense the reality of the great new gods which had created it. He could see those perfect, beautiful faces. (The beauty, oddly, did not move him. It was like Sati's beauty, magnified a thousand times. But he had no doubt they were beautiful. And perfect. And divine.)

Nor did he doubt that Link was showing him a true

vision. It was not in the nature of the being called Link to lie. Its mind followed the path given to it, like a waterwheel turns with the stream. It could no more lie than a waterwheel could decide to turn against the current.

"THE FINAL ABOMINATION HAS NOW APPEARED."

A luminous shape swam in the void. At first, Sanga thought it to be some kind of ethereal moth, until he grasped the scale of the thing. Whale-sized. Bigger. He could not make out the precise shape of the creature's body. It was not entirely material, he sensed. Much of that shape was—magical?

"FORCE FIELDS. ENERGY MATRIX."

Meaningless words.

"THIS TOO WAS ONCE HUMAN. BUT IT HAS NOT A TRACE LEFT OF ITS HUMAN LEGACY. OF HUMAN PURITY. IT IS NOT EVEN ALIVE."

How?

"THEY ORIGINATED AS BIOLOGISTS, STUDYING THE DNA PLAGUE. SEEKING A CURE, OR A VACCINE. THEY FOUND NO CURE, NO VACCINE. THE DNA PLAGUE, BY ITS NATURE, CANNOT BE STOPPED. ANY ANTIDOTE OR SERUM WOULD BE DNA-BASED ITSELF. SIMPLY MORE FOOD FOR THE PLAGUE."

"Biologists," "vaccine," "serum"—Sanga understood none of them. But he could follow the sense behind the words.

"INSTEAD, THEY FOUND SOMETHING ELSE. THEY EMBRACED POLLUTION. THEY CAST THEIR OWN CHILDREN INTO DAMNATION. THEY ABANDONED LIFE ITSELF. THEY DISCARDED DNA AND SUBSTITUTED A SOULLESS MECHANISM OF THEIR OWN CREATION."

Again, Sanga saw the glittering network of crystals. Like a spider's web—simultaneously repellent and beautiful. But this was not a web covering a planet. This crystalline web ran through the very structure of the luminous giant moth—whale?—moving through the heavens.

"THEY FOUND A LIFELESS SUBSTITUTE FOR DNA. FOR LIFE ITSELF. A DERIVATIVE FROM THE SAME CRYSTALS WHICH DESTROYED DNA. THEY EVEN BREATHED A PARODY OF INTELLIGENCE INTO THEM. SELF-GUIDED CHAOTIC INTELLIGENCE, NOT THE OBEDIENT CLEANLINESS OF THE COMPUTER. THE ABOMINATION IS COMPLETE. POLLUTION IS ALL THAT REMAINS."

Sanga did not understand the term "computer," though he sensed that Link itself bore its likeness. The rest—a question came to his mind.

What are they called?

"WE HAVE NO NAME FOR THEM BEYOND MONSTERS. THEIR CRYSTALS CALL THE ABOMINATIONS WHO CREATED THEM 'THE GREAT ONES.'"

What do these—"Great Ones"—call themselves?

Hesitation, for the first time. Reluctance? Sanga wondered.

"THEY CALL THEMSELVES PEOPLE."

And what do they call their crystal creatures?

Definite hesitation. Not reluctance, Sanga realized. Ultimate—distaste.

"THEY CALL THEM PEOPLE."

When Rana Sanga came back to his senses, he realized that very little time had passed. The Great Lady Holi and Sati were still seated before him, quietly, their hands in their laps.

"Now you understand, Rana Sanga," said Sati softly. "Enough, at least."

Sanga opened his mouth, closed it. He had been about to protest that he understood very little. Certainly not enough. But he sensed there was no point in such a protest. Besides, he had given his oath. *That*, at least, he did understand.

Again, Great Lady Holi seemed to read his mind. But,

to Sanga's relief, when she spoke her voice had resumed a shell of humanity.

"You do not need to understand more, Rana Sanga," said Link's vessel. "Not now, at least."

Stubborn pride rose in the Rajput.

"Why did you come here? To this—to our time?"

"Analysis showed this was the optimum time and place to change history. That task is very difficult, Rana Sanga. History is like a great river. Its currents cannot be dammed. They will simply spill over the levees. A new channel must be dug. A wide, deep, great channel. That task is very hard. The new gods determined that this was the optimum period for making the sharp change needed in humanity's course. Perhaps the only moment when it would be possible."

Stubborn:

"Why?"

"Because in this historical era both of humanity's possible futures exist at the same time. For the only time in history when both could be changed simultaneously. The seed of humanity's actual destruction lies in that abomination called Rome. The seed of its potential glory lies in Malwa India."

Stubborn, still:

"Why?"

"The true future lies here, because only in ancient India did humanity begin to grope toward that truth. What you call the *varna* and the caste system. Your conceptions are mired in superstition and ignorance, but your crude understanding provides the framework for beginning the necessary eugenics program which will preserve the human race. That is why, despite their limitations, we have maintained the Malwa lineage intact, and are shaping everything around that seed. In the Malwa of today, you see only the most primitive germ of the future. But in the end, after millenia of careful genetic management, the new gods will emerge. Not the handful of *this* time, of this polluted future, but the mighty host of the true future we will create."

Sati interrupted, coldly:

"And that is also why, despite Rajput abilities, we have kept the Rajputs subordinate. Of all human vices, none is so insidious and destructive as the blind worship of ability. That way lies abomination."

The Great Lady Holi resumed:

"Rome is where that pollution originated. Or, at least, sank its deepest roots in ancient history. True, other dangerous times and places existed, even in ancient time. We will deal with them soon enough. We will bridle China, for instance, long before the Sung dynasty and its mandarinate disease can even emerge.

"But Rome—*Rome*—that is the great enemy. That is where the great stain first polluted a fourth of the planet. And spread from there, like a disease, in the centuries to come. A latent disease, often enough, endemic rather than epidemic. But always there, that legacy, always ready to rise anew.

"*Rome.* That monstrous realm of mongrels. That absurd so-called empire where any man can call himself a Roman, and demand the protection of Roman law, as if he shared the true Latin lineage. Where no emperor can trace his royal genotype beyond two generations. Where any barbarian can dream of being emperor. Any miscegenate *peasant*—like the one who now wears the purple. Where any polluted *whore* can sit the throne next to him, and receive the honors of the true-born. Ability, in Rome, is all that counts, in the end. It is that worship of ability over purity that will destroy humanity. That unbridled, undisciplined, genetic chaos will ravage this planet and a thousand others. And it will leave, in the end, nothing but inhuman monsters to pollute the universe."

Again, Sati intervened.

"That is enough, Rana Sanga. You have already been privileged beyond all others save Malwa. Do not press the matter further. *Yours, finally, is to obey.*"

Sanga arose, prostrated himself, left the room.

❖   ❖   ❖

Nanda Lal was waiting for him in Lord Tathagata's chamber—in Lord Tathagata's *former* chamber. The Lords Jivita and Damodara were there also.

"You were right, Rana Sanga," began Nanda Lal immediately. "It was obvious, as soon as I correlated facts already in our possession."

The spymaster's face was truly that of an ogre, now.

"Several of my subordinates will be severely disciplined for neglecting to present those facts to me earlier. *Severely.*"

That meant mutilation, possibly blinding. Sanga could not find any pity in his heart for those unknown subordinates. He had no love for Malwa spies, even competent ones.

"What are the facts?" he demanded.

"A Ye-tai soldier—a member of the imperial bodyguard, in fact—disappeared in Kausambi the very night Belisarius made his escape. He has never returned to his unit."

Lord Jivita, frowning:

"I *still* don't understand why you place such significance on that fact, Nanda Lal. Ye-tai are practically savages. Their discipline—"

"Is absolutely savage," interrupted Sanga. "I agree with Nanda Lal. Say what you will about Ye-tai barbarousness, Lord Jivita. The fact remains that no Ye-tai—no member of the imperial bodyguard, for a certainty—would dare remain absent from his post. Ye-tai who fail to report even a day late are subject to cane-lashes which can be crippling. Those whose absence stretches two days *are* crippled. Three days, beheaded. Four days, impaled. Five days or longer, on a short stake."

Nanda Lal nodded. "And it makes sense. Ye-tai more closely resemble Westerners than any other of our peoples. Belisarius could pass himself off as one without much difficulty."

"He does not speak the language," protested Jivita.

"I would not be so sure of that," retorted Sanga.

A bit guiltily: "He is an extraordinary linguist. I noticed myself how quickly he became fluent in Hindi, and with almost no trace of an accent. I never heard him speak—"

He stopped, almost gasped.

"I'm a idiot!"

To Nanda Lal, fiercely:

"Have you interviewed the soldiers—the Ye-tai, especially—whom Belisarius rallied for the counter-charge at Ranapur?"

Nanda Lal shook his head. For a moment, he seemed puzzled, until comprehension came.

"Of course! How could he rally the Ye-tai—"

"It can be done," stated Sanga. "Hindi alone, and harsh measures, would have done it. But when you interview those soldiers, I think you will discover that he speaks perfect Ye-tai."

The Rajput began pacing back and forth.

"What else?"

"A squad of soldiers reports that a single Ye-tai departed Kausambi through the Panther Gate the following morning."

"And they allowed him through?" demanded Jivita.

Nanda Lal shrugged. "He was a very fierce and brutal Ye-tai, by their account. He even attacked their sergeant when asked for documents. You can hardly expect common soldiers—"

"Discipline the dogs!" bellowed Jivita. "Give them lashes!"

Sanga and Damodara exchanged glances. Sanga spoke:

"I will deal with the matter, Lord Jivita. I will be passing through the Panther Gate within the hour. I will lash those men myself. You have my word on it."

"Excellent!" exclaimed Jivita.

"I'm off, then." Sanga began to turn away. Nanda Lal called him back.

"A moment, Rana Sanga. I want your opinion."

"Yes?"

The spymaster's broken face was ugly, with frustration as much as rage.

"*We are still missing something.* I can feel it in my bones," he growled. "It's clear enough that the Romans and Ethiopians who fled south—after killing the guards at the barge and blowing up the armory—were simply a diversion. Belisarius, himself, went west. But—there's something else. *I can smell it.* More duplicity."

Sanga paused, thinking.

"I don't have much time now, Nanda Lal," he mused. "But several questions come to my mind. I suggest you think on them."

"Yes?"

"First. What happened to the treasure? Belisarius had two great chests full of gold and jewels. It's not the kind of thing any man wants to leave behind. But how did he get it away? He himself—a single Ye-tai on foot—could have only been carrying a pittance. Nor could his underlings have carried more than a portion of it. Not maintaining their incredible pace, weighted down with all that treasure."

Nanda Lal tugged at the bandage.

"What else?"

"There were too many Ye-tai running around that night. The soldiers at the army camp insisted that they saw Belisarius himself. But when I questioned some of them, they could only say that 'the Ye-tai' told them so. Which Ye-tai?"

"I will find out. What else?"

"Too many Ye-tai—and not enough Kushans. What happened to Belisarius' Kushan escort? I have heard nothing of them since that night. What happened to them? Did the Romans and Ethiopians kill them all? I doubt it—not *those* Kushans. I know their commander. Not well, but well enough. His name is Kungas, and he would not have been taken by surprise. What happened to him and his men?"

Glaring, now, and tugging fiercely on his bandage:

"And what *else?*"

Sanga shrugged. "With Belisarius, who knows? I would trace everything back to the beginning, from the day he arrived in India. I can see no connection, but—I always wondered, Nanda Lal. Exactly how did Shakuntala escape from Venandakatra's palace?"

Jivita interrupted, his voice full of irritation:

"What is the point of this, Rana Sanga? Everybody knows how she escaped. That fiend Rao butchered her guards and took her away."

Rana Sanga stared at him. He managed to keep any trace of contempt out of his face.

"So? Have you ever spoken—personally—to the Pathan trackers who were with the Rajputs who tried to recapture Rao and the princess?"

Jivita drew back haughtily.

"That is hardly my—"

"No, he didn't," interrupted Nanda Lal. "Neither did I. Should I have?"

Sanga shrugged. "Every Pathan tracker claimed there was only one set of footprints to be found, not two. A man's footprints. No trace of a woman at all." Sanga stroked his beard. "And that's not the only peculiar thing about that escape. I know none of the details, but—again, I have wondered. How did one man kill all those guards? Excellent guards, I would assume?"

He caught the odd look in Nanda Lal's eyes.

"Tell me," he commanded.

"She was being guarded by priests and mahamimamsa," muttered Nanda Lal.

"*What?*" erupted Sanga. "Who in their right mind would set any but the finest soldiers to guard someone— *from Rao?*" For the second time that day, Sanga lost his temper. "*Are you Malwa all mad?*" he roared. "I have fought Raghunath Rao in single combat! He was the most terrifying warrior I ever encountered!"

The Malwa in the room, for all their rank, almost cringed. They knew the story. All of India knew that story.

"From Raghunath Rao? You—you—*imbeciles*—thought to guard Shakuntala from Rao—*with priests? Stinking torturers?"*

Jivita tried to rally his Malwa outrage, but the attempt collapsed under the sheer fury of the Rajput's glare. Lord Damodara coughed apologetically.

"Please, Rana Sanga! It was Lord Venandakatra's decision, not ours. He was concerned about the girl's purity, it seems. So he put her in the custody of sworn celibates instead of—"

It was almost comical, the way Damodara and Nanda Lal's jaws dropped in unison.

"—instead of an elite Kushan unit," finished Nanda Lal, hoarsely.

"Commanded by a man named Kungas, as I recall," croaked Damodara. "I am not certain."

Sanga snorted. "You can be certain of it now, Lord Damodara. Investigate! You will find, I imagine, that these Kushans were removed just before Shakuntala escaped. And just before Belisarius himself arrived at the palace, if memory serves me correctly."

"It does," hissed Nanda Lal. The spymaster almost staggered.

"Gods in heaven," he whispered. "Is it possible? How—there was no connection, I am certain of it. But the—*coincidence.*" He looked to the Rajput, appeal in his eyes. "How could any man be so cunning as to manage that?" he demanded.

Sanga made a chopping gesture with his hand. "If any man could, it is Belisarius. Investigate, Nanda Lal. For the first time, assume nothing. Look for treasure, and mysterious Ye-tai and Kushans who appear and disappear. And, most of all—*look for the Princess Shakuntala.*" He turned away, growling: "But that is your job, not mine. I have a Roman to catch."

"A fiend!" cried Nanda Lal.

"No," murmured Sanga, leaving the room. "A fiendish mind, yes. But not a fiend. Never that."

❖   ❖   ❖

300&

Eric Flint & David Drake

Nanda Lal *did* investigate, thoroughly and relentlessly. He was an immensely capable man, for all his Malwa arrogance. And his natural tenacity was fueled by a burning hatred for all things remotely connected to Belisarius. Once Nanda Lal set himself to the task—and, for the first time, without careless prior assumptions—he solved the riddle within two days. Most of it, at least. All of it, he thought.

Some weeks later, an inn beside the Ganges was blessed beyond measure. It was a poor inn, owned by a poor Bengali family. Their only treasure, the innkeeper liked to say, was the sight of the mighty Ganges itself, pouring its inexorable way south to the Bay of Bengal.

(The *sacred* Ganges, he would say, in the presence of his immediate family, as he led them in secret prayers. He and his family still held to the old faith, and gave the Mahaveda no more than public obeisance.)

That poor family was rich tonight, as northern Bengali measured such things. The nobleman was most generous, and his wife even more so.

She spoke little, the noblewoman—properly, especially for a wife so much younger than her husband—but her few words were very kind. The innkeeper and his family were quite taken by her. The nobleman, for all his cordiality and good manners, frightened them a bit. He had that pale, western look to his features. That Malwa look. (They did not think he was Malwa himself, but—high in their ranks. And from western India, for certain. That cruel, pitiless west.)

But his wife—no, she was no Malwa. No western Indian. She was as small as a Bengali, and even darker. Keralan, perhaps, or Cholan. Whatever. One of *them*, in some sense. Bengalis, of course, were not Dravidians, as she obviously was. More of the ancient Vedic blood flowed in their veins than in the peoples of the southern Deccan. But not all that much more; and they, too, had felt the lash of purity.

The next morning, after the rich nobleman and his retinue departed, the innkeeper told his family they

would close the inn for a few days. They had not been
able to afford a vacation for years. They would do so
now, after bathing in the sacred Ganges.

The innkeeper and his wife remembered the few days
which followed as a time of rare and blessed rest from
toil. Their brood of children remembered it as the
happiest days of their happy childhood.

Happy, too, was the innkeeper and his wife, after their
return. When their neighbors told them, hushed and
fearful, of the soldiers who had terrorized the village
the day before. Shouting at folk—even beating them.
Demanding to know if anyone had seen a young, dark-
skinned woman accompanied by Kushan soldiers.

Something stirred, vaguely, in the innkeeper's mind.
But he pushed it down resolutely.

None of his business. He had not been here to
answer any questions, after all. And he certainly had no
intention of *looking* for the authorities.

So, in the end, Nanda Lal would fail again.

Partly, because he continued to make assumptions
even when he thought he wasn't. He assumed, without
thinking about it, that a fleeing princess and her soldiers would seek the fastest way out of the Malwa
empire. So he sent a host of soldiers scouring north
India in all directions, looking for a young woman and
Kushans on horseback.

Neither a pious innkeeper on vacation, nor a young
officer hiding his humiliation, nor any of the other folk
who might have guided the Malwa to Shakuntala, made
the connection.

And the one man who could, and did, kept silent.

When Malwa soldiers rousted the stablekeeper in
Kausambi, and questioned him, he said nothing. The
soldiers did not question him for very long. They were
bored and inattentive, having already visited five stables
in the great city that morning, and with more to come.
So the stablekeeper was able to satisfy them soon enough.

No, he had not seen any young noblewoman—or
soldiers—leaving on horseback.

He could not tell the difference between Kushans and any other steppe barbarians, anyway. The savages all looked alike to him.

The soldiers, peasants from the Gangetic plain, smiled. Nodded.

He had seen nothing. Heard nothing. Knew nothing.

The soldiers, satisfied, went on their way.

The plans and schemes of tyrants are broken by many things. They shatter against cliffs of heroic struggle. They rupture on reefs of open resistance. And they are slowly eroded, bit by little bit, on the very beaches where they measure triumph, by countless grains of sand. By the stubborn little decencies of humble little men.

Chapter 20

On his way through the Panther Gate, just as he had promised Lord Jivita, Rana Sanga disciplined the soldiers who had allowed Belisarius to leave the city. "Give them lashes," Jivita had demanded, specifying the plural.

Sanga's word, as always, was good.

Two lashes, each. From his own quirt, wielded by Rajputana's mightiest hand. It is conceivable that a fly might have been slain by those strokes. It is conceivable.

Once he and his cavalry unit were outside the walls of the capital, Sanga conferred with his lieutenants and his chief Pathan tracker as they rode westward. The conference was very brief, since the fundamental problem of their pursuit was obvious to anyone who even glanced at the countryside.

The Gangetic plain, after a week of heavy rainfall, was a sea of mud. Any tracks—tracks even a day old, much less eight—had been obliterated. The only portion of the plain which was reasonably dry was the road itself. A good road, the road to Mathura, but the fact brought no comfort to the Rajputs. Many fine things have been said about stone-paved roads, but none of them has ever been said by Pathan trackers.

"No horse even leave tracks this fucking idiot stone," groused the Pathan. "No man on his foot."

Sanga nodded. "I know. We will not be able to track him until we reach Rajputana. Not this time of year."

303

The Rajput glanced up, gauging. The sky was clear, and he hoped they had reached the end of the *kharif*, India's wet season. The kharif was brought by the monsoon in May, and lasted into September. It would be succeeded by the cool, dry season which Indians called *rabi*. In February, then, the blistering dry heat of *garam* season would scorch India until the monsoon.

Jaimal echoed his own thoughts:

"Rabi is almost here. Thank God."

Sanga grunted approvingly. Like most Indians, rabi was his favorite season.

"There is no point in looking for tracks," he announced. "But we have one advantage, here in the plain—there are many travelers on the road. They will probably have noticed a single Ye-tai. Anyone Belisarius encountered in his first days of travel will be long gone, by now. But we can hope, in two or three days, to start encountering people who saw him."

"The soldiers in the courier relay stations may have spotted him," commented Udai. "They have nothing else to do except watch the road."

"True," said Sanga. "We can make it to the first relay station by mid-afternoon. Udai may well be right—the soldiers may have spotted him. Let's go!"

"Are you sure it is them?" asked the crouching young warrior, peering down into the ravine.

"Oh, yes," said Rao. "Quite sure. I only met one of them, but he is not the sort of man you forget."

The Maratha chieftain rose from his hiding place behind a boulder. The armored horseman leading the small party through the trail below immediately reined in his horse. Rao was impressed by the speed with which the man unlimbered his bow.

He probably shoots well, too. Let's not find out.

"*Ho—Ousanas!*" he bellowed. "Do you still maintain the preposterous claim that all appearance is but the manifestation of eternal and everlasting Forms?"

The reply came instantly:

"Of course! You are the living proof yourself, Rag-hunath Rao, even where you stand. The very Platonic Form of a sight for sore eyes."

The young guerrillas lining the ravine where Rao had set his ambush—*friendly* ambush, to be sure; but Rao never lost the chance for training his young followers—were goggling.

They were provincials, almost without exception. Poor young villagers, most of whom had never seen any of the world beyond the hills and ridges of the Great Country. The Romans were odd enough, with their ugly bony faces and sick-looking pallid complexions. The Ethiopians and Kushans were even more outlandish. But the other one! A tall half-naked man, black as a cellar in night-time—arguing philosophy with Rao himself!

A maniac. Obvious.

"Oh, Christ," muttered Valentinian, replacing his bow. "Another philosopher. Maniacs, the lot of 'em."

In truth, Valentinian was finding it hard not to goggle himself. Finally, after all these months, he had met the legendary Raghunath Rao. And—

The man was the most ordinary looking fellow he had ever seen! Valentinian had been expecting an Indian version of Achilles.

He studied Rao, now standing atop the boulder some thirty feet away and ten feet up the side of the ravine.

Shortish—by Roman standards, anyway. Average size for a Maratha. Getting a little long in the tooth, too. Must be in his early forties. Well-built, true—no fat on those muscles—but he's no Hercules like Eon. I won-der—

Rao sprang off the boulder and landed lithely on the floor of the ravine ten feet below. Two more quick, bounding steps, and he was standing next to Valentinian's horse. Smiling up at him, extending a hand in welcome.

Mary, Mother of God.

"The Panther of Majarashtra," Valentinian had heard Rao called. He had dismissed the phrase, in the way veterans dismiss all such romantic clap-trap.

"Be polite, Valentinian," he heard Anastasius mutter. "Please. Be polite to that man."

The bodies had been rotting for days, with only two small windows to let air through the thick mudbrick walls. The stench was incredible.

"He's a *demon*," snarled Udai. "Only a soulless *asura* would—"

"Would *what*, Udai?" demanded Sanga.

The Rajput kinglet gestured to the pile of festering corpses.

"Kill enemies? You've done as much yourself."

Udai glared. "Not like *this*. Not—"

"Not *what*? Not from ambush? I can remember at least five ambushes which you laid which were every bit as savage as this one."

Udai clamped his lips shut. But he was still glaring furiously.

Sanga restrained his own temper.

"Listen to me, Udai," he grated. Then, his hard eyes sweeping the other Rajputs in the room:

"*All of you.* Listen. It is time you put this—this *Malwa superstition*—out of your minds. Or you will never understand the nature of this enemy."

He paused. When he was certain that he had their undivided attention—not easy, that; not in a charnel-house—he continued. His voice was low and cold.

"Some of you were there, in the Emperor's pavilion, when Belisarius ordered his cataphract to execute the prisoners. Do you remember?"

Jaimal and Pratap nodded. The other four Rajputs, after a moment, nodded also. They had not seen, themselves, but they had heard.

Sanga waved at the bodies heaped in a corner of the relay station.

"This is the same man. The Malwa think—*did* think, at least—that he was a weakling. Full of foolish soft notions. Not ruthless, like them. Not *hard*."

A soft chuckle came from the Pathan tracker kneeling

by the bodies. "Did really?" he asked. Then rose, his examination complete.

"Well?" demanded Sanga.

"Soldiers all kill same time." The tracker pointed to a crude table collapsed against one of the relay station's mudbrick walls. One of the table's legs was broken off cleanly; another was splintered. Stools were scattered nearby on the packed-earth floor.

"Come through door. Think at night. Quick, quick, quick. Soldiers eat. Surprise them at sitting."

He pointed to the blackened, dried bloodstains on the floor, the wall, the table, the stools. Scattered pieces of food, now moldy.

"That was battle." Indifferent shrug. "Not much. Think two soldiers draw weapon before die. Maybe three. Do no good. Sheep. Butchered."

He paced back to the pile of bodies.

"Then wait for couriers. Eat soldier food while wait. Pack away other food. Round up horses in corral. Make ready."

The Pathan bent over and seized one of the corpses. With a casual jerk, he spilled the rotting horror onto the floor. The impact, slight as it was, ruptured the stomach wall. Half-liquid intestines spilled out, writhing with maggots. The Pathan stepped back a pace, but showed no other reaction.

"First courier. Tortured."

He leaned over the putrid mess, picked up a wrist, waved the hand. The thumb fell off. The index and middle fingers were already missing.

"Two finger cut off. Want information. How many courier come after?"

He dropped the hand, straightened.

"Good method. Cut one, say: 'Tell, or cut two.' Cut two, say: 'tell, or cut three.' That mostly enough. Good method. Very good. Quick, quick. Have use myself."

The Pathan turned away. To those who did not know him, his callous attitude was appalling. To those who did know him, it was considerably worse.

"Wait again. Next courier." He pointed to one of the bodies in the livery of the royal courier service.

"No torture. No need. He tell, die."

He pointed to the third courier.

"Last one. No torture. No need. He tell, die."

The Pathan glanced at the far door, which led to the corral where the spare horses were kept. *Had* been kept.

"Then put courier horses to corral. Tired horses. No good. Take all other horses. Fed, rested. Five horses. Good horses. Leave."

Finished with his report, the tracker planted his hands on hips and surveyed the entire scene.

"Very fine man!" grunted the tracker. "Quick, quick. No stupidityness. Would adopt into own clan."

Sanga allowed his subordinates to digest the information a moment, before continuing.

"Never make that mistake again," he growled. "That *Malwa* mistake. He is not a cruel man, Belisarius. Of that I am quite certain. But no mahamimamsa who ever lived can match him for ruthlessness when he needs to be. The man is as quick and shrewd as a mongoose. And just as deadly. How much mercy does a mongoose give a cobra?"

Jaimal grunted. Sanga drove on:

"There's *another* lesson. He is not a devil, but he has a devil's way of thinking. Consider how bold and cunning this move was. After his men created a diversion and led all of us on a wild goose chase, Belisarius marched out of Kausambi—openly—disguised as a Ye-tai." He cast a cold eye sideways. "Three guesses how he got the Ye-tai's uniform, Udai?"

His lieutenant winced, looked away. Sanga grated on:

"Then he came as fast as possible to the first relay station. He was out-thinking us every step of the way. He had two problems: first, no horses; second, he knew couriers would be sent to alert the garrisons on the coast. He solved both problems at one stroke."

"Killed the soldiers, ambushed the couriers, stole their horses," muttered Jaimal. "The best horses in India."

"*Five* of them," added Pratap. "He has remounts, as many as he needs. He can drive the horses for as long as he can stay in the saddle. Switch whenever his mount gets tired."

"How could he be sure the bodies wouldn't be found soon?" complained Udai. "Then the hunt would be up."

Sanga frowned. "I don't know. The man's intelligence is uncanny—in the military sense of the term, as well. He seems to know everything about us. Outside of the Ganges plain, this trick wouldn't have worked. Because of banditry, all relay stations in the western provinces are manned by full platoons and checked by patrol. But here—"

"These aren't even regular army troops," snorted Pratap. "Provincial soldiers. Unmarried men. They're stationed here for two year stretches. Even grow their own food."

The Rajput stared down at the hideous mound.

"Poor bastards," he said softly. "I stopped at one of these relay stations, once. The men—boys—were so ecstatic to see a new face they kept me talking all night." He glanced at the Pathan. "Like he says, sheep to the slaughter." Then, hissing fury: "*Roman butcher.*"

Sanga said nothing. He felt that rage himself. But, unlike Pratap, did not let the rage blind his memory. He had seen other men lying in such heaps. Men just like these—young, lonely, inattentive. Soldiers in name only. They, too, had been like sheep at the hands of a butcher.

A butcher named Rana Sanga. Against whose experienced cunning and lightning sword they had stood no chance at all.

"We'll never catch him now," groaned Udai.

"We will try," stated Sanga. His tone was like steel. Then, with a bit of softness:

"It is not impossible, comrades. Not for Rajputs. He is still only one man, with well over a thousand miles to travel. He will need to rest, to eat—to find food to eat."

"One man alone," added Jaimal, "disguised as a Ye-tai, possibly. Leading several horses. People will notice him."

"Yes. He will be able to travel faster than we can, on any single day. And he begins with many days headstart. But he cannot keep it up, day after day, the way an entire cavalry troop can do. We can requisition food and shelter. He cannot. He must scrounge it up. That takes time, every day. And there are many days ahead of him. Many days, before he reaches the coast. He may become injured, or sick. With no comrades to care for him. If nothing else, he will become very weary."

"Where is he headed, do you think?" asked Pratap. Sanga shrugged.

"Too soon to tell. He will probably head for Ajmer. In case he does not, we will split off smaller units to search for him in other towns. But I believe he will go to Ajmer, first. He needs to get out of the Ganges plain quickly, where there are a multitude of people watching. Into Rajputana, where there are not."

"Ajmer," mused Jaimal, stroking his beard. "Ajmer. From there, he can go south or west. South, along the foot of the Aravallis, toward the Gulf of Khambat. Maybe even Bharakuccha, where he could hope to rejoin his men."

"Or west," added Udai, "to Barbaricum."

"We will know soon enough," stated Sanga. He began striding toward the door. "Once he is out of the plains, he will start leaving tracks. We will find his tracks before Ajmer."

Less than a minute later, five hundred Rajputs set their horses into motion. Not a frenzied gallop; just the determined canter of expert horsemen, with a thousand and a half miles ahead of them.

He had never been a handsome man, true. But now, for the first time in his life, he was an object of ridicule.

Children's ridicule. Palace children.

Flat-face, they called him, behind his back. Or thought they did, not realizing how impossible it was to talk behind *his* back. *The Frog*, they snickered, or *The Fish*, or, most often, *The Nose*. Always, of course, in secret whispers. Not understanding, not in the least. The man noted the children, noted their names. Someday their powerful fathers would be dead.

Thinking of those distant days, the man smiled. Then, thinking of a day nearer still, the smile deepened.

It was a new smile, for that man. In days gone by, his smile—his grin—had been hearty and cheerful-seeming. The weeks of painful recovery had distorted the smile, almost as much as they had distorted his face. A cold, savage smile. A snarl, really.

The new smile fitted the man much better than the old one ever had, in all truth. It looked like what it was, now. The smile of a spymaster, after ensuring his revenge.

Couriers had been dispatched, again. Not royal couriers, riding royal roads. No, these couriers were a different breed altogether. Almost as fine horsemen, and far more lethal men.

The best agents in Malwa's superb espionage service. Three of them, all of whom were familiar with the road to Rome. The *northern* route, this, the land road—not the slow, roundabout, southern sea-going route taken by most. These men would ride their horses, all with remounts, through the Hindu Kush. Through central Asia. Across Persia, using the network of Malwa spies already in place. Into Anatolia, with the aid of a similar—if smaller—network. And finally, to Constantinople.

In Constantinople, they would pass their message to the Malwa agent in charge of the Roman mission. Balban would not be pleased at that message. It would result in much work being cast aside.

But he would obey. Wondering, perhaps, if the orders stemmed from sagacity or malice. But he would obey.

In point of fact, sagacity and malice were *both* at work. For all his fury, the spymaster was still a rational man. A professional at his trade.

He knew, even if Balban still fooled himself, that the Roman general's duplicity had a partner. He realized, even if they did not, that the Malwa agents in Constantinople had been fooled as badly as he himself had been in India.

No longer. Sagacity demanded the orders anyway. The fact that the same orders would be an exquisite revenge was almost incidental.

Almost, but not quite.

The spymaster smiled again. He was a realist. He knew that Belisarius might manage his escape from India. But the spymaster would have the satisfaction of robbing all pleasure from that escape.

If Belisarius made his way home, he would find the place empty. The orders would reach Rome before he did.

She is deceiving you, as he deceived us.
Kill the whore.

Chapter 21

A hundred miles east of Ajmer, once they reached the dry country, the Pathan finally picked up Belisarius' tracks.

By the time they reached the city, he was a thoroughly disillusioned man.

"Not adopt this one never," he grumbled. "Very stupid beast. See no thing."

The tracker leaned from his horse, scanned the road, snorted, spat noisily.

"Probably he fuck goat. Think it wife."

Spat noisily.

"Pay no attention to no thing."

Spat noisily.

"Idiot blind man."

Riding beside him, Sanga smiled wrily. Like most men with a narrow field of vision, the Pathan tended to judge people by very limited criteria.

True, Belisarius had finally made a mistake. But it was a small mistake, by any reasonable standard. So small, in fact, that only an expert tracker would have spotted it.

Somewhere along the way—hardly surprising, in weeks of travel—one of the Roman general's horses had cut its hoof. Nothing serious, in itself. Barely more than a nick, caused by a sharp stone. The horse itself would have hardly noticed, even at the time, and the "wound" in no way discomfited it.

But it was just enough to leave a distinctive track. No one else had spotted it, but the Pathan had seen it immediately. Several of the Rajputs, after the tracker pointed it out, had expressed their delight.

Henceforth, Belisarius would be easy to find!

The Pathan had derided their enthusiasm. Such a very good quickquick man, he assured them, would soon enough spot the mark himself. He would then remove it by carving away more of the tissue, leaving a hoof whose print would be indistinguishable from most others. If worse came to worst, and the mark could not be removed, the Roman would simply abandon the horse. He had four others, after all.

But, as the days went on, the mark remained. Day after day, the tracker followed the trail, with the ease of a man following a lantern at night. Day after day, his estimate of Belisarius plummeted.

By now, so far as the Pathan was concerned, Belisarius ranked very low in the natural order of things. Above a sheep, perhaps. Beneath a bullfrog, for a certainty.

The robbery of the merchant simply confirmed his viewpoint. Sealed his opinion like lead seals a jar.

Three days before Ajmer, the Rajputs had overtaken a merchant trudging alongside the road. The merchant was accompanied by two servants, each of whom was staggering under a weight of bundled trade goods.

All three men were stark naked.

When the Rajputs pulled alongside, the merchant immediately erupted into a frenzy of recrimination, denunciation, accusation, and reproach.

Outrage that such a thing could come to pass!

Where had been the authorities?

Robbed on a royal road! By a royal Ye-tai bodyguard!

Oh, yes! There was no mistake! The merchant was a well-traveled man! A sophisticated man! He had been to Kausambi itself! Many times!

A royal bodyguard!

Outrage! Outrage!

Where had been the authorities?

He demanded justice! Retribution!
Most of all—restitution!
Robbed by a royal bodyguard!
Restitution was owed by the authorities!

In the event, once the merchant calmed down enough to tell the entire tale, restitution proved simplicity itself. The only thing which the Ye-tai bandit seemed to have actually stolen was the clothing worn by the merchant and his servants.

Nothing else, oddly enough. Not the merchant's money, not his trade goods—which were spices, too; quite valuable—not even the gold chain around the merchant's neck or the rings adorning his fingers.

The Pathan was livid.

"What kind midget-brain bandit this man?" he demanded hotly. "Cretin idiot!"

The tracker glared at the merchant.

"I rob you, fat boy, you be lucky have skin left. Gold chain, cut off head. Rings, chop fingers. Quick, quick."

The Pathan leaned over his horse's neck, squinting fiercely at the servants. The two men edged back, trembling.

"Old one I kill. Other one I take. Sell him to Uighurs." He straightened up. Leaned over. Spat noisily. "Roman most idiot beast alive," he concluded. He had not budged from that conclusion since.

Sanga, on the other hand, thought the robbery was very shrewd. He had been wondering how Belisarius planned to make his way through Rajputana, especially in a city like Ajmer, disguised as a Ye-tai. In the Gangetic plain, a single Ye-tai leading a small train of horses would not particularly be remarked.

In Rajputana, however, his situation would be different. Rajputs had no love for Ye-tai, to put it mildly. A single Ye-tai in Rajput country would encounter any number of difficulties very quickly, especially in a populous place like Ajmer. Those difficulties would range from bands of belligerent youngsters to keen-eyed authorities who were not in the least intimidated by a

Ye-tai's red-and-gold uniform. Not in Rajputana, where the Malwa writ ran very light.

By stealing the merchant's clothes, and that of the servants, Belisarius had provided himself with a perfect disguise. Itinerant merchants, traders, tinkers—traveling alone or in a small party—were commonplace throughout the arid stretches of western India. Sanga suspected that Belisarius would combine part of the merchant's relatively fine apparel with pieces of the servants' more humble clothing. The resulting pastiche would give him the semblance of a hardscrabble trader, barely a cut above a peddler.

It was shrewd, too, for the Roman to have ignored the merchant's coins, jewelry and trade goods. Bandits and thieves were as common as merchants, in that part of India, and everyone kept an eye out for them. If Belisarius tried to sell the merchant's jewelry or goods, or use the coin, he would run the real risk of drawing suspicion upon himself.

Sanga had noted, during the weeks of their pursuit, that Belisarius seemed to have always foraged for his food, rather than buying it. Buying food would have been much quicker. The main reason the Rajputs had been able to shorten the Roman's lead—the Pathan estimated he was only five days ahead of them, now—was because of the time which Belisarius had spent every day searching for food. For the most part, the Roman had hunted his food, with the bow and arrows he had taken from the relay station's soldiers. Occasionally, he had stolen from a local granary or orchard. But never, so far as the Rajputs or their Pathan trackers had been able to determine, had he bought food.

Sanga was certain that was by choice, not necessity. Belisarius could not, of course, be carrying the immense treasure which the Malwa had bestowed upon him. But the Rajput was quite sure that Belisarius had kept a small amount of that treasure with him at all times. Just in case. That sort of elementary precaution would be second nature to such a man.

Yet he had never used it. Partly, Sanga thought, that was because Belisarius feared the suspicion which the use of royal coin and jewelry would bring down. But mostly, he suspected, it was because Belisarius was saving his money for the coast. To hire a ship—to *buy* a ship, for that matter, if he had kept with him any one of a number of the gems in those chests.

So Sanga felt the Pathan was being quite unreasonable. But he did not remonstrate with the man. It would be as pointless as arguing with a stone.

The Rajput kinglet's chief tracker had been in his service for years, now. Ever since Sanga had captured him, after a ferocious single combat, during one of the many punitive campaigns against the mountain barbarians. The Pathan had been deeply impressed by his victor's skill and courage. So deeply, in fact, that he had begged Sanga to make him his own slave, rather than sell him to some unworthy fool.

Sanga had granted the request, and had never regretted doing so. The Pathan had served him faithfully for years, even after Sanga manumitted him. Served him extremely well, in fact. But Sanga knew the limits of that man's horizon, and had long since given up any hope of changing them.

Two days later, as the walls of Ajmer rose above the horizon, the Pathan was still grousing.

"Fucking idiot beast," Sanga heard him mutter. "I rob merchant, I do merchant good. Him no complain. Him no tongue."

At Ajmer, of course, they lost the tracks. Even a hoofprint far more distinctive than the one left by that little nick would have been obliterated by the traffic through the city. But Sanga was not concerned.

He sent half of his men, and all the Pathan trackers, circling around Ajmer. Keeping far enough away from the city to avoid routine traffic, those men would eventually find the direction Belisarius had taken. The distinctive track, by now, was as unmistakeable to the Rajputs as to the Pathans. In the meantime, Sanga and his remaining soldiers began a systematic search of the city itself.

They were looking for horses. For the *memory* of horses, to be precise.

Rajputana was a land of horsemen. A ragged merchant, by himself, might pass through Ajmer unremarked. But Sanga knew, as surely as he knew his own name, that his countrymen would have certainly noticed the horses. Those marvelous, splendid, *imperial* steeds.

And, sure enough, tracking the horses proved as easy as tracking the distinctive hoofprint. The memory trail was only five days old, and it led directly to the southern gate of the city. By mid-afternoon of the same day they arrived, Sanga was already interviewing the guards.

"Oh, yes!" one of them exclaimed. "As fine as any horses you've ever seen! As fine as royal courier steeds!"

Another guard pointed to the road leading south. "They went that way. Five days ago."

"The man," said Sanga. "What did he look like?"

The guards looked at each other, puzzled.

"Don't remember," said one. "Trader, maybe peddler."

"I think he was tall," said another, stroking his beard thoughtfully. "I think. I'm not sure. I was watching the horses."

Two miles south of Ajmer, they encountered the rest of Sanga's horsemen and the Pathan trackers. Coming north with the news:

The tracks had been spotted. Five miles out, on the road to the Gulf of Khambat.

"Probably Bharakuccha," stated Jaimal, as they cantered south. Sanga's lieutenant gazed ahead and to their right. The sun was beginning to set behind the peaks of the Aravallis.

"But maybe not," he mused. "Once he gets south of the Aravallis, he could cut west across the Rann of Kutch and follow the coast back up to Barbaricum. Be roundabout, but—"

"He'd play hell trying to drive horses through that stinking mess," disputed Pratap. "And why bother?"

The argument raged until they made camp that night. Sanga took no part in it. Trying to outguess Belisarius in the absence of hard information was pure foolishness, in his opinion. They would know soon enough. The tracks would tell the tale.

His last thoughts, that night, before falling asleep, were a meditation on irony. So strange—so sad—that such a great man could be brought down, in the end, by something as petty as a stone in the road.

Two days later, the Pathan was almost beside himself with outrage. What shred of respect he retained for Belisarius was now discarded completely.

He leaned over the saddle. Spat noisily.

"Great idiot beast! Knew him stupid like sheep. Now him lazy like sheep too!"

He pointed an accusing finger at the tracks.

"Look him horse pace. My grandmother faster. And she carcass. Many years dead now."

Spat noisily.

Apparently satisfied that he had shaken off any pursuit, the Roman had slowed his pace considerably since leaving Ajmer. Sanga, again, thought the Pathan was being unreasonable. True, Belisarius was being careless. But, at the same time, allowances had to be made. He was only human, after all. The Roman had set himself a brutal pace for weeks. It was not surprising that he would finally take a bit of rest.

Not surprising, no, and hardly something for which a man could be condemned. But it was still a mistake, and, under the circumstances, quite fatal.

In less than two days, they brought Belisarius to bay.

By late afternoon of the following day, the lead tracker spotted him. Not five miles ahead, already making camp for the night.

The Rajput officers held a hurried conference. Sanga's lieutenants argued for surrounding the Roman's camp and attacking that very night.

Sanga would have none of it.

"Not him," he stated firmly. "Not that man, at night. First, he might make his escape in the darkness."

He held up his hand, forestalling Udai's protest.

"That's unlikely, I admit. What I'm more worried about is that we'd be forced to kill him. I want him alive. It may not be possible, but if there's any chance at all it will be by daylight. In a night attack, with its confusion, there'd be no chance at all."

He glanced up at the sky. The eastern horizon was already purple.

"And there's no need. He's making camp, so he's not going anywhere. We'll use the night to surround him, quietly."

A hard eye on his lieutenants. "*Quietly.*" They nodded.

Sanga stared south.

"At dawn, we bring him down."

The Pathan himself brought Belisarius down. The tracker didn't even bother to stun him. He simply pounced on the Roman general, still wrapped up in his roll—half an hour after daybreak, lazy sheep!—by the embers of a small campfire—a campfire on the run, idiot beast!—jerked him up by the hair. Then, with his knife, sliced the Roman's cheek. A gash, no more, just enough to mark his man.

Quickquick, and the Pathan stepped away.

The Roman general staggered to his feet, shrieking. He clutched his cheek with both hands. Blood from the wound spurt through the fingers. He took two steps, stumbled, fell on his belly across the campfire. Then thrashed aside, shrieking more loudly still. Lurched to his feet, beating away the embers with his bloody hands.

The Pathan had had enough.

He strode forward and sent the Roman back on his belly with a vicious, stamping kick. Then he sprang upon him, jerked his head up by the hair, and manhandled him to his knees.

"Here you great general, Sanga King," he said contemptuously. He cuffed the Roman, silencing a squawl.

Rana Sanga stared down at Belisarius. Stared up at the Pathan holding him by the hair. The tracker was grinning savagely.

Stared down at Belisarius. The general was gasping like a fish, eyes glazed.

Stared back at the Pathan. Down at Belisarius.

"Who in the hell is *that?*" snarled Jaimal.

Stared down at *that*. Up at the Pathan.

"I've never seen this man before in my life," he told the tracker quietly.

It was almost worth it, then, for Rana Sanga. After all those years, finally, to see the Pathan gape. Like an idiot beast.

"I'm just a poor peddler," whined the man, for the hundredth time. He moaned, pressing the bandage against his cheek. Moaned:

"My name is—"

"Shut up!" snarled Udai. "We know your name! What we want to know is where did you get the horses?"

The peddler stared up at the Rajput. Finally, something beyond squawling terror and babbling self-pity entered his mind.

Avarice.

"They're *my* horses!" he squealed. "You can't—"

"Shut up!" bellowed Udai. "*Just shut up!*"

Rana Sanga put a restraining hand on Udai's shoulder. His lieutenant's fury was just frightening the man senseless.

The Rajput king squatted, bringing his eyes level with those of the bloody-faced man sprawled in the dirt.

"Listen to me, peddler," he said quietly. Quietly, but very firmly. The peddler fell silent.

"My name is Rana Sanga."

The peddler's eyes widened. He was not Rajput, but he traded in Rajputana. He knew the name. Knew it well.

"We will take your horses." Quiet, iron words.

The peddler opened his mouth, began to squawl.

"Those horses were stolen from the royal courier service. To possess them is to be condemned to death. Impaled."

The peddler's mouth clamped shut. His eyes bulged.

Sanga raised his hand reassuringly.

"Have no fear. We have no interest in your execution. If you serve us well, we may even repay you for the loss of the horses."

Partly, he thought, watching the avarice leap back into the peddler's eyes. *Whatever* you *paid for them. Which, I am quite certain, is much less than what they are worth. I think I am beginning to understand what that— that—fiend—*

He took a deep breath.

No. What that fiendish mind has done here.

He glanced to the side. Thirty feet away, his Pathan tracker was holding up one of the horse's legs, examining the hoof. Very carefully.

Sanga turned back to the peddler.

"But now, man, you must tell me—very quickly, very simply, very clearly—how you got the horses."

"He was a Ye-tai," gasped out the peddler. Then, in a sudden rush of words:

"A deserter from the imperial bodyguard, I think. I'm not sure—I didn't ask!—not a Ye-tai—but. I think. I saw part of a uniform. Gold and red. He was on the run, I think. Had nothing but those fine horses, and seemed desperate to get out of Ajmer. So he—he—"

Suddenly, amazingly, the peddler burst into laughter. "Idiot Ye-tai! Stupid barbarian! He had no idea what those horses we're worth—*none,* I tell you! In the end— it only took me two hours of haggling—I traded them for three camels, some blankets, and a tent. Food. Maybe fifty pounds of water. Two big tureens full. And five bottles of wine. Cheap wine." Howling, howling. "Fucking idiot! Fucking savage!"

Sanga slapped the man's ear. "*Silence.*"

The peddler's hysterical laughter stopped instantly. His faced turned pale.

"And what else?" grated Sanga. "There would have been something else."

The peddler's expression was a weird conglomeration of astonishment, fear, greed. Fear.

"How did you know?" he whispered.

"I know that—*Ye-tai*," replied Sanga quietly. "He would not have simply sent you on your way. He would have made sure you came *this* way. How?"

Fear. Greed. Fear.

"Show me."

It was one of the Emperor's emeralds.

A small emerald, very small, by imperial standards. Probably the least of the jewels which Belisarius had with him. But it had been a fortune to the peddler. Enough to send him off to Bharakuccha, with the promise of a matching emerald if he delivered the message to the proper party.

Who?

A Greek merchant. A ship captain.

His name? The name of the ship?

Jason. The *Argo*.

Show me the message.

Rana Sanga could read Greek, but only poorly. It did not matter. Most of the message was mathematics, and that he understood quite well. (India was the home of mathematics. Centuries later, Europeans would abandon Roman numerals and adopt a new, cunning arithmetic. They would call them "Arabic numerals," because they got them from the Arabs. But they had been invented in India.)

So he was able to understand the message, well enough.

Finally, in the end, a king of Rajputana could not restrain himself. He began laughing like a madman.

"What is it?" asked Jaimal, when Sanga's howling humor abated.

"It's a theorem," he said, weakly. "By some Greek named Pythagoras. It explains how to calculate angles."

The Pathan rose from his examination of the horse's hoof and stalked over.

"Not cut by stone on road. Knife cut. Done by meant-to purpose."

Sanga had already deduced as much.

"Exactly." He smiled, stroking his beard. "He knew we would spot the mark. And that, after weeks of following it, would stop thinking about anything else. So he switched in Ajmer, sent us charging off south while he drives straight across the Thar on camelback."

He glanced at the peddler, still ashen-faced.

"Three camels," he mused. "Enough to carry him—*and* his food and water—across the desert without stopping."

He rose to his feet. It was a sure, decisive movement.

"We'll never catch him now. By the time we got back to Ajmer and set off in pursuit he'd have at least eight days lead on us. With three camels and full supplies he'll move faster than we possibly could across that wasteland."

His lieutenants glared, but did not argue. They knew he was right. Five hundred expert cavalrymen can eventually outrun a single horseman, even with remounts. But not across the Thar.

That was camel country. There probably weren't five hundred camels available in Ajmer, to begin with. And even if there were—

Rajputs were *not* expert camel drivers.

"Stinking camels," grumbled Udai.

"Can't stand the fucking things," agreed Pratap.

"Good meat," stated the Pathan. The Rajputs glowered at him. The tracker was oblivious. His mind was elsewhere.

"So we give up, then?" asked Jaimal.

Sanga shook his head.

"No, we don't. But we'll not try chasing after the Roman again. Instead—"

He held up the message.

"We'll take his advice. *Angles*. Maybe—just maybe— we can make better time by taking two sides of the triangle while he takes one. We'll head for Bharakuccha—as fast as our horses can carry us. At Bharakuccha we'll requisition a ship—several ships—and sail north to Barbaricum. That's where he's headed, I'm sure of it."

He strode for his horse.

"We might be able to meet him there. Let's go!"

That night, by the campfire, the Pathan finally broke the silence he had maintained for hours.

"After adopt, make him clan chief. No. Make him king. First Pathan king ever." He grinned at the Rajputs over the flickering flames. "Then Pathan conquer world entire whole." A gracious nod to Sanga. "You was good master. When you my slave, I be good master too."

Three days later, as the Aravallis rolled by on their right, Jaimal leaned over his saddle and snarled to Sanga:

"If that Pathan keeps telling that same joke, I swear I'm going to kill him."

"Jaimal," the Rajput king replied, coldly. "He is not joking."

Chapter 22

Rao was amused by the reluctance with which his young men obeyed orders. His lieutenant Maloji was not.

"You're too easy on them, Rao," he complained. His words came easily, despite the fact that he and the Panther were racing along the steep slope of a ridge, just below the skyline. On the other side of that ridge, they could hear the roar of battle. The clash of steel was fading, slowly. The angry shouts of Malwa officers were not.

"Here," said Rao. He scrambled up the slope, flinging himself to the ground just before reaching the crest. Maloji followed. On their bellies, the two men crawled to the crest itself, and peered over into the small valley below.

"You see?" hissed Maloji accusingly. He pointed angrily, with a bristling thrust of his beard. "Some of the disobedient dogs are still even using their swords."

"Only two," murmured Rao. He watched while the two young Marathas below finished cutting down a Malwa soldier before they began their own scramble up the slope on the opposite side. On the crest of that ridge, a line of guerillas was firing arrows into the swarming Malwa troops below.

"They are brothers, you know. One of them probably got tangled up and the other came to his rescue."

"Still—"

"Do not fret, Maloji. They will learn discipline soon enough." Grimly: "After they sustain heavy casualties from excessive enthusiasm."

He broke off, gauging the Malwa. The officers were finally bringing order back to their little army. At their command, ranks of soldiers began slogging up the slope. They suffered considerable losses from the arrows raining down on them, but their advance was inexorable. The Malwa had tried to cram too many soldiers down the narrow valley—not much more than a ravine. Those packed ranks made an easy, slow target for ambush, but, once they began their counter-attack, were far too massive to be repelled.

"They should break off now, the dogs!" snarled Maloji. "Your orders were very clear!"

Rao did not argue the point. He had, in fact, ordered his men to fire no more than two volleys after the Malwa began their counter-attack. The guerrillas should already have been retreating. Instead, the young Maratha rebels waited until the Malwa were halfway up the slope before they finally scrambled away.

Rao turned, and edged his way down the slope. Maloji followed, still grumbling.

"You shouldn't have given them those horses. That's why they're so bold. *Disrespectful young dogs.* They think those horses can outrun anything."

Now well below the skyline, Rao stood up. He grinned at his lieutenant. "Those horses *can* outrun anything. Anything these sorry Malwa have. The best horses foreign money could buy!"

Maloji rose and brushed himself off. "Fine steeds, I admit," he agreed reluctantly. "They were a wonderful gift."

"I think of it as an exchange," demurred Rao. He looked to the west. He could not see Bharakuccha, of course. The great port was many miles away, hidden behind the Satpura mountains. "They gave us the horses, we gave them the opportunity."

"Will they make their escape, do you think?"

Rao shrugged. "I should imagine. We stopped the couriers, and we've been"—a gesture toward the ridge; a wide grin—"*distracting* the Malwa."

He turned and began loping toward the dell where their own horses were hidden away. Speaking easily, despite the rigorous pace, he said over his shoulder:

"As I told you before, Maloji, those men are *capable*."

Capability was unneeded. The escape, at the end, was child's play.

Garmat simply marched across the ramp connecting the Axumite trader with the wharf, and presented himself to the captain. Before he had even reached the man, the captain was goggling.

"Stop looking like a frog, Endubis," he growled.

The captain gaped.

"And close your mouth, fool. *Spies may see you*."

Endubis' mouth snapped shut. The captain glanced hurriedly at the shore, scanning for danger with an experienced eye.

Like all Ethiopian merchant captains, Endubis was no stranger to combat. Such merchants served as a reserve for the Kingdom of Axum's navy. No seaman could reach the rank of ship captain, even in the merchant fleet, without the negusa nagast's approval. For all their relaxed customs in other areas of life, the Axumites were never casual about their naval power.

"Trouble?" asked Endubis.

Garmat smiled, thinly. "You might say so. The entire Malwa Empire is baying for our blood."

Endubis winced. "The Prince?"

"He is well." Garmat made a little gesture with his head. "In that warehouse. With his dawazz and the sarwen. Some others."

The adviser examined the ship briefly. "Thirteen men, in all. It will be crowded, but—"

"We'll manage," muttered Endubis. The captain

turned and began bellowing orders. His seamen immediately scurried about the ship, preparing for departure.

"I wish you'd gotten here tomorrow," Endubis grumbled. "I'd have a cargo, then. I hate sailing empty. Surest way I know to poverty."

Garmat grinned. "Not so, Endubis. An empty ship will make a fast trip, and we'll not be too crowded. As for poverty—" His hand dipped into a pouch, came out, spread wide.

The captain, again, was goggling like a frog.

"You'll accept Malwa coin, I assume?" murmured Garmat. "Oh, and look! I believe there's even a ruby here. No—three rubies."

On the way out of Bharakuccha's harbor, a Malwa vessel hailed them and tried to come alongside.

"Ignore it," commanded the Prince. "Sail on."

The captain glanced at him from the corner of his eye. "That'll make it hard on the next Axumite trader," he pointed out.

Eon shrugged. "There won't *be* any 'next Axumite trader.' We are at war, now, with Malwa."

The captain sighed. "Ah. Too bad. It was good business."

The officer in the bow of the Malwa ship hailed them again. His voice sounded angry.

"You *can* outsail them?" demanded Eon.

Endubis sneered. "That Malwa tub?" He disdained any further answer, beyond the orders he shouted at his seamen.

An hour later, the officer commanding the Malwa vessel broke off the pursuit.

He was practically gibbering.

Some of his rage was due to the superior seaworthiness of the Ethiopian ship. Most of it was due to the bare black ass hanging over the stern of the Axumite vessel, defecating. And the great, gleaming grin on the face above it.

❖   ❖   ❖

A week later, in the port at Tamralipti on India's opposite coast, another Malwa naval officer grinned with sheer delight. As well he should. He had made more money that day than in the previous three months put together.

His lieutenant was grinning, too. His own cut of the nobleman's bribe was enough for a lavish spree in the Bay of Bengal's most notorious harbor district.

The lieutenant gestured with his head toward the merchant ship which was even now passing the harbor's breakwater.

"Should we notify Murshid and his men? There's a fortune in that nobleman's chests. And his wife's young. Pretty, too, probably. She and the other women would bring a good price."

The commanding officer stroked his beard, considering the question. He and his officers made a tidy profit, on the side, selling information on lucrative targets to the local pirates.

He did not ponder the matter for very long.

"No," he said firmly. "Not with *that* escort."

"There weren't more than thirty of them," argued his lieutenant. "Murshid can muster three ships, with over a hundred—"

The commander glared.

"A hundred *what*?" he snarled. "Three-to-one odds, you're talking about—four-to-one, at best. Murshid's rascals against—*those*?"

The lieutenant grimaced. "Well—"

The commander brushed the idea aside, as a man might brush away flies.

"Forget it. Murshid wouldn't thank us afterward, believe me. And what would our cut be—a barrel of guts? Two barrels?"

Looking back at them from the stern of his vessel, the captain of the merchant ship decided he was reading the posture of the Malwa officers properly. The distance was great, but he had very good eyes. And much experience.

Satisfied, he turned away. "We can relax," he said to his own lieutenant. "There'll be no problem."

His lieutenant heaved a sigh of relief. He had thought his captain mad, to accept such a cargo in these waters. They normally hauled nothing but bulk goods in the Bay of Bengal, infested as it was by pirates. The type of goods which no brigand finds attractive.

But, his captain had decided to take the chance. The nobleman's offered price had been too good to pass up. A small fortune to transport him, his wife, and their retinue to Muziris, the principal port of the south Indian kingdom of Kerala.

Besides—

The lieutenant glanced at the nearest of the nobleman's soldiers. He was not certain, but he thought the man was the officer commanding the nobleman's escort.

The officer was leaning against the rail, watching the receding harbor, idly honing his sword with a small whetstone. It seemed a pointless exercise. The blade was already like a razor.

His eyes met the lieutenant's.

"Trouble?" The whetstone never ceased its motion.

The lieutenant shook his head.

"We don't think so."

No expression at all crossed the officer's face. It seemed, in its rigid immobility, like an iron mask.

"Too bad," he murmured. He held the blade up to the sunlight, inspecting its edge. "My men are a little rusty. Could use a bit of honing."

A month later, Rana Sanga returned to his home near Jaipur. He had not seen his family in a year, and he had decided he must do so before he went on to Kausambi. He might never have the chance again. When he reported his failure to capture Belisarius, he would be punished. Possibly even executed.

To Sanga's surprise, Lord Damodara was waiting for him at the Rajput king's residence. He had arrived two weeks earlier, sure that Sanga would come there first, whether the news was good or foul.

As eager as he was to greet his family—Lord Damodara politely offered to wait until he had done so—Sanga insisted on giving his report first. He and Damodara met in a small room adjoining the great hall which served Sanga as his royal audience chamber. They sat on cushions across from each other at a low table. Alone, after servants had placed tea and pastries for their refreshment.

Sanga's report was full, precise, and unsparing. But as he came to the final episodes of their pursuit of Belisarius, Damodara cut him short.

"Never mind the rest, Sanga. The gist, I assume, is that you found no sign of him in Barbaricum or any of the other small ports?"

Sanga shook his head. "None, Lord Damodara. I am convinced he took ship there, somewhere, but he disguised his traces perfectly. If they investigate—long enough—Nanda Lal's spies can probably discover the truth. But—"

"What is the point?" asked Damodara. He waved a pudgy little hand in dismissal. "If they find any evidence, it will be far too late to do any good."

He sipped at his tea. Munched on a pastry.

"Such an investigation would do nothing but harm," he stated. "Great harm, in fact."

Sanga sat stiffly, silent. Damodara eyed him for a moment. Then, surprisingly, smiled. "You are, indeed, the true Rajput. Honor above all."

Sanga, if such were possible, stiffened further.

"I am *not* Rajput," rasped Damodara. "I respect your view of things, Rana Sanga—I even believe that I understand that view—but I do not share it." Harshly: "*I am Malwa.* And, thus, am a practical man. I was sent here to meet you, and assess the results of your search. I have now done so."

Another sip of tea.

"Here are my findings. Rana Sanga, acting on the *possibility* that Belisarius *might* have made his escape to the west, led a long, rigorous, and most diligent search—all the way to Barbaricum, no less!"

Another sip of tea.

"*No trace of Belisarius was found.* For a time, it appeared that the Rajputs were on his trail. But, in the end, it proved a false lead. The only things actually *found* were a ragged peddler and the bloody trail of a Ye-tai deserter from the royal bodyguard, who fled the Empire after viciously murdering several soldiers and royal couriers and robbing a merchant."

Sanga began to protest. Damodara drove him down.

"*Nothing proves otherwise, Rana Sanga.* Your suspicions were simply groundless. That is all." Another wave of his hand. The gesture done, the hand reached for a pastry.

"There is no evidence," concluded Damodara. "Nothing solid. Nothing concrete."

Satisfied—self-satisfied—Damodara popped the pastry into his mouth.

"There is," grated Sanga. He reached into his tunic, brought forth a small pouch, opened it, and spilled its contents onto the table between them.

An emerald. Small, but dazzling.

Damodara choked on his pastry. Coughing, he reached for his tea and hastily washed his throat clear.

"Rajput," he muttered, setting down the tea cup. He glared at the emerald.

The glare was brief. When he looked up, Damodara was smiling again.

"This, I presume, is the emerald which you say Belisarius gave the peddler? One of the emeralds from the Emperor's gift?"

Sanga nodded stiffly.

Damodara laughed. "What nonsense!" Shaking his head: "Any Rajput in the world can gauge a sword or a horse at a glance, but show them a jewel—"

For all its plumpness, Damodara's hand moved like a lizard on a hot rock snatching an insect. The emerald disappeared into his own tunic. Sternly: "These

counterfeiters! Shameless criminals! I shall report this
latest outrage to the appropriate bureau in Kausambi
upon my return." Again, the waving hand. "Whichever
it is. I believe the *Ranabhandagaradhikara*'s office in
the treasury handles counterfeiting. Perhaps the police
Bhukti. One of those small departments, buried somewhere in the Grand Palace. Staffed by somnolent dull-
ards."

The Rajput King's protest was cut short.

"It is done, Rana Sanga! *Finished.* That is all."

He rose. Sanga rose with him. The short Malwa
commander stared up at the Rajput. He did not flinch
in the least from the taller man's anger.

"My name is Lord Damodara," he said softly. "And
I have reached my conclusion."

Still without moving his eyes from Sanga's hot gaze,
Damodara leaned over and scooped up another pastry.
Popped it in his mouth.

"These are truly excellent," he mumbled. "Please give
my compliments to your baker."

Sanga was still glaring. Damodara sighed.

"Rana Sanga, so far as Malwa is concerned, the truth
is clear. Belisarius escaped—*with his men*—to the south.
The royal couriers who were to have alerted the port
garrisons were all ambushed along the way by savage
Maratha brigands. So the wicked foreign general and his
accomplices were able to make their escape on an Axumite
ship waiting in the harbor. By predesign, undoubtedly. We
have—had—a clear description of one of those accomplices from a naval officer who failed to stop the ship. A
vivid description." Coldly: "For his failure to capture that
ship, the naval officer has been executed. Along with the
commander of Bharakuccha's garrison."

Sanga snorted. Damodara, expressionless:

"Impaled, both of them. At Lord Venandakatra's
command, as soon as the Goptri arrived in Bharakuccha."

Damodara, his face as blank as ice:

"Upon my return, upon my demand, the officer in

charge of the unit from which the Ye-tai murderer deserted will also be executed. For dereliction of his duty."

He looked away. "I will not demand impalement. Beheading will suffice."

Sanga's face twisted.

Damodara murmured, "It has been done, and it *will* be done. Do not make those—sacrifices—vain exercises in murder, Rana Sanga. *Please*. Let it be."

He laid a hand on Sanga's arm.

"Now, I have news myself. I have been appointed head of the northern army for the upcoming Persian campaign. Lord Jivita, of course, will be in overall command."

The Rajput glanced at him, stonily. Looked away.

"I have requested—and my request has been approved—that most of the Rajput forces be assigned to my army. You—and your cavalry—in particular."

Now, Sanga's eyes came back. Fixed.

Damodara's lips quirked. "My official argument was that my army will be operating, more than any other, in broken country. Hence—so I argued—I require the bulk of our best cavalry units." He shrugged. "The argument is valid enough, of course. And it spared me the embarassment of explaining to Lord Jivita that I do not share his faith in the invincibility of gunpowder. Personally, I want good Rajput steel guarding my flanks, on the backs of good Rajput steeds."

Sanga almost smiled. Not quite.

Damodara's hand gave Sanga's arm a little shake. "I need you, Rana Sanga. Alive, healthy, and in command of your troops." He dropped the hand and turned away. "I will leave now. I have kept you from your family long enough."

Rana Sanga escorted Damodara all the way to the courtyard. As he waited for his horse to be brought around, Damodara murmured his last words:

"Do not fret over Belisarius' escape, Rana Sanga. Let it go. Leave it be. We will be seeing him again, any-

way. Soon enough—too soon, for my taste. Of that I am
as sure as the sunrise."

"So am I," muttered Sanga, after Damodara left. "As
sure as the sunrise." A rueful smile came to his face.
"But, unfortunately, not as predictable."

He turned back to his home. His wife and children
were already rushing out the door, arms spread wide.
All other emotions vanished, beyond simple joy in their
loving embrace.

A week later, on his way back to Kausambi, Lord
Damodara and his escort came to the Jamuna River.

Lord Damodara ordered a halt, and dismounted.

"I have to piss," he announced to his soldiers. "Wait
here," he commanded, waving his hand casually. "I can
manage the task quite well myself."

Once he reached the river, he paced a few feet along
the bank, looking for a suitable spot. Having found it,
Damodara went about his business.

He was a practical man, Damodara. Malwa. He saw
no reason not to complete two necessary chores simultaneously.

He *did* have to piss, after all. While, in the middle
of his urination, tossing a small emerald into a deep spot
in the river.

At the very moment when that emerald nestled into
the mud of a riverbed, a ship nestled against a dock an
ocean's width away. Sailors began to lay the gangplank.

"There's your father," announced Garmat. The adviser
pointed up the slope overlooking the harbor of Adulis.
At the top of a steep stone stairway, a regal figure
loomed.

Axumites did not favor the grandiose imperial regalia of other realms. The negusa nagast wore a simple
linen kilt, albeit embellished with gold thread. His
massive chest was covered by nothing more than crossed
leather straps sewn with pearls. A heavy gold collar
circled his thick neck and five gold armbands adorned

each of his muscular arms. On his head was a plain silver tiara, studded with carnelians, signifying his status as a king of kings. The tiara held in place the traditional *phakhiolin*, the four-streamered headdress which announced his more important position as king of the Axumites. In his right hand, Kaleb held the great spear of his office, with its Christian cross surmounted on the shaft; in his left, a fly-whisk. The spear, symbolizing his piety and power; the fly-whisk, his service to his people.

Nothing more. Other than, of course, the gravity of his own figure—thick-shouldered, heavy-thewed, majestically-bellied—and the dignity of his own face. Glowering brow over powerful nose; tight lips; heavy, clenched jaws.

"He looks grumpy," surmised Menander.

"He looks downright pissed," opined Anastasius. "You'd think he already heard the bad news. His headstrong youngest son just got him in a war with the world's mightiest empire."

"Of course he's heard!" cried Ousanas happily. "Look at his companion—the world's fastest bringer of bad news. Crooked Mercury himself!"

Belisarius. Standing, now, next to the King. Smiling his crooked smile.

"Damn," muttered Valentinian. "Rather face the King's glare than that smile, any day." Sigh: "Exciting adventures, coming up."

Chapter 23

CONSTANTINOPLE
Winter 530 AD

Five minutes into her meeting with Balban, Antonina knew that something was not right. The Malwa spymaster was not listening to her carefully enough.

He *seemed* to be, true. To almost anyone but Antonina, Balban would have appeared to be the very model of attentiveness. He was sitting on the edge of his chair—almost perched, in fact—leaning forward, hands clasped between his knees. His eyes were riveted on the woman sitting across the small room from him. He was utterly silent, apparently engrossed in the information which Antonina was giving him.

The information alone should have guaranteed his interest, even if it wasn't being imparted by a beautiful woman. The Malwa spymaster was learning every single detail of every current or planned troop movement of every Roman military unit of any consequence in Syria, the Levant and Egypt. For a man who stood at the very center of a plot to overthrow the Roman Emperor—a plot which was finally coming to fruition—such information was literally priceless.

Wonderful information, too—in every respect. Wonderful, not just in the fact that he had it, but wonderful in its own right. The gist of Antonina's report was that no Roman military unit from the great southern and eastern provinces could possibly arrive in Constantinople in time to prevent the planned *coup d'etat*.

But he was not paying any attention. Not to the information, at least.

For a moment, Antonina wondered if Balban's indifference stemmed from his knowledge that everything she was telling him was a lie. In actual fact, Theodora had sent word to Daras weeks before that the plot was coming to a head. Antonina's grenadiers had been in Constantinople for ten days, disguised as pilgrim families. They, along with all the Thracian cataphracts, had been transported aboard a small fleet of swift transports. The units from Sittas and Hermogenes' armies, carried on slower grain ships, had just arrived the day before. They were still hidden in the holds of those ships, anchored in the Portus Caesarii.

But Antonina dismissed that possibility almost instantly. She detected no hostility from Balban, not a trace—which she surely would have, did the spymaster suspect her duplicity.

No, it was simply that Balban was not interested in the information, one way or the other. He did not disbelieve; but he did not believe, either. He simply didn't care.

He was interested in *her*—in the same way that almost every man was, who found himself in her company. Few men of her acquaintance were able to ignore Antonina's beauty. That was just a simple fact of life.

But, beyond that—*nothing*.

Antonina was chilled to the bone. She realized exactly what was happening. And what was planned.

They are going to kill me.

Had Balban known how perfectly Antonina was reading him, he would have been absolutely shocked. The Malwa was a master of his trade. He would have sworn that no one could have detected a trace of murderous intent in his perfectly maintained composure.

And, in truth, almost no one in the world could have

done so. With the exception of a woman who, in her earlier days, had been one of the most exclusive and sought-after courtesans in the entire Roman empire.

Antonina, unlike Balban, was not an expert in the subjects of espionage, and assassination. But she *was* an expert—one of the world's greatest experts, in fact—on the subject of men, and their moods. Her success as a courtesan had been partly due to her physical beauty, of course. But many women were beautiful. Antonina's great skill had been her ability to keep men *interested*. Not simply in her beauty, but in the pleasure of her company.

Over the years, she had learned to detect the danger signs. Sooner or later—until she met Belisarius—the men who sought her company would lose interest. Not in her, necessarily. They might well retain a powerful desire for her body. But they would lose interest in her company.

She had always been able to tell when that moment came. And she had always broken off such relationships immediately. Or, at least, as soon as she could do so gracefully.

Her relationship with Balban had never been sexual in the least. But, with him too, that *moment* had come.

In the brief time that it took to finish her report, she quickly assessed her options.

They would not kill her in Balban's own villa. Of that, she was certain. The Malwa had always taken great pains to maintain a low profile in Constantinople. Even Irene, with all her expertise and the vast resources which Theodora had placed at her disposal, had only discovered the whereabouts of the Malwa military base a few days before. Balban had managed to smuggle several hundred elite Indian soldiers into the Roman capital—and keep them hidden, for weeks—without being spotted.

Such a man would not risk drawing attention to himself at this penultimate hour.

Nor, she thought, would he employ the services of

Ajatasutra or any other Malwa agent. There was always the risk, should her assassination fail, that such agents might be captured and traced back to him.

She would be murdered by Roman thugs, hired for the occasion through intermediaries.

The streets of Constantinople had become increasingly rowdy over the past few days. The Hippodrome factions which had been bribed by the Malwa grew more assertive and self-confident by the hour. Gangs of Blue and Green thugs roamed freely, disrupting the capital's tranquillity with impunity. The military units stationed in Constantinople had withdrawn to their barracks—just as Irene had predicted months earlier. The officers in command of those units could sense the coming coup, and they intended to sit on the sidelines until the outcome was clear.

Antonina was certain of the Malwa plan.

It was already very late in the afternoon. By the time she left Balban's villa, it would be dusk. As instructed, she had come alone to the meeting, following the same route she always took. On her way back, she would be accosted by a gang of street thugs. Not closer than three blocks away, but not farther than six. The attack would take place near a deserted building or some other secluded location. She would be dragged off the street and taken out of sight. Then, she would be robbed, probably raped, and murdered. When her body was discovered—which might not be for days—the crime would be dismissed as an unfortunate episode during the current chaos.

She managed, barely, not to heave a sigh of relief.

Professional assassins, like Ajatasutra, were probably beyond her capability. Street thugs, she thought she could handle.

Her mind now (more or less) at ease, Antonina had no difficulty getting through the final few minutes of her meeting with Balban. Her biggest problem was restraining her impatience at Balban's protracted social pleasantries. The hour ahead of her was dangerous in the extreme, but Antonina was the kind of person who just wanted to be done with it.

As soon as possible, she rose and made her exit. Balban escorted her to the door. On the way, they passed Ajatasutra in the corridor. Antonina smiled at him pleasantly, and walked by without flinching. It was not easy, that—after all, she *might* be wrong.

But Ajatasutra did nothing beyond return her nod with a polite smile.

Balban opened the door, mumbling some final courtesies. Antonina strode through the courtyard to the open gate which led to the street beyond. Even before she passed through the gate, she heard the door close behind her.

Balban, shaking his head, turned away from the door. To his surprise, Ajatasutra was still standing in the corridor.

"A pity," muttered Balban. "Such a beautiful—"

"She *knows*," hissed Ajatasutra.

Balban blinked his eyes.

"What?"

"She *knows*," repeated the assassin.

Balban frowned.

"Why do you say that? I saw no indication that she had any suspicions at all."

He made a little gesture at Ajatasutra.

"And—just now—she walked right by you with hardly any notice."

"That's the point," retorted the assassin. "That woman is not stupid, Balban. She knows exactly who I am. What I am. Every other time I've been in her company she always kept a close eye on me. It was a subtle thing, but—" Frustrated, he groped for words. "I'm telling you—she *knows*."

Balban hesitated. He turned his head, looking at the door. For a moment, it almost seemed as if he would reopen it. But the moment passed, quickly. Then, when Ajatasutra began to approach the door himself, Balban stayed him with a hand.

The spymaster shook his head.

"I think you're imagining things, Ajatasutra. But, even if you're not, there's nothing we can do about it."

Balban scowled. "I think Nanda Lal's orders were an overreaction, anyway. The last thing I'm going to do—*now*, of all times!—is run any risk of exposing our mission."

He began moving down the corridor. With his hand still on Ajatasutra's shoulder, he guided the assassin along with him. "Besides," he added, "what difference does it make, even if she *does* know? She's just a woman, Ajatasutra—a small woman, at that."

Cheerfully:

"A sheep often knows it's in danger, when the wolf-pack begins circling. What good does that do the sheep?"

Ajatasutra shrugged off the hand. He stopped abruptly, forcing Balban to look at him.

"She is not a sheep, Balban," stated the assassin firmly. "She grew up on the streets of Alexandria. The toughest streets in the Roman Empire. Her father was a charioteer—some of the roughest men you'll ever encounter. And her husband is not only a great general but a great swordsman as well. And those thugs you hired are *not* 'wolves.' They're a pack of mangy street curs."

"That's enough!" snapped Balban. "I've made my decision."

He stalked away. Ajatasutra remained alone, standing in the corridor, staring at the door. He stood there, silent and unmoving, for a full minute. Then, smiling thinly, he whispered, "Good luck, *wolves*. You're going to need it."

Antonina strode up the street in the direction she always took, until she was far enough away from Balban's villa to be out of sight. She had traveled two blocks, by now, and knew that the ambush would be coming very soon.

At the next corner, she turned abruptly to her right

and began walking quickly down a narrow side street. Behind her, faintly, she heard footsteps. Several men a block away, by the sound, startled into sudden activity.

She began running.

The street was barely more than an alley. She was unfamiliar with it. But she had noticed—in times past, as she had walked by—that the street was the domicile for a number of the small bakeries and cookshops which provided Constantinople with its daily supply of bread and meat pastries.

She raced by three such shops. Too small. She needed a big one, with a full kitchen.

At the fourth shop, she skidded to a halt. Hesitated. She could smell the thick, rich scent of meat broth.

Maybe.

She heard the footsteps approaching the mouth of the street.

It'll have to do.

She strode through the shop door. The shop was very small—not ten feet square—and completely bare except for a small counter on which were displayed samples of the shop's wares. When she saw that they were meat pastries, Antonina sighed with relief.

A middle-aged woman—the cookshop owner's wife, she assumed—approached Antonina and began uttering some pleasantry. Antonina didn't catch the words.

"Are you cooking meat broth?" she demanded. "For pastries?"

The woman, frowning with puzzlement, began to nod. Antonina grabbed the woman's wrist and dragged her toward the door at the opposite end of the shop. The woman was heavyset, taller than Antonina, and began squawking and struggling vigorously. To absolutely no avail. Antonina was a very strong woman, for her size, and she was filled with implacable determination.

She shouldered the door open and hurled the woman through, following an instant later. Before closing the door, she peeked at the shop entrance. The outer door was still closed. Her pursuers, she thought, hadn't seen her enter the shop.

Good. I've got a little time.

She turned and confronted the woman, who was now spluttering with outrage. The woman's husband was standing next to her, glowering, holding up a metal ladle in a half-threatening gesture.

"Shut up!" snarled Antonina. "There are men just outside your door who are trying to kill me! *They'll kill you, too.*"

The woman's mouth snapped shut. A second later, her mouth reopened. Wailing:

"Get out! Get out!"

The husband stepped forward hesitantly, raising the ladle.

There was a large table against the wall of the kitchen next to the door. Antonina slammed her purse onto the table and emptied its contents. A pile of gold coins spilled out. Along with a small dagger.

The shopkeeper and his wife were, first, transfixed by the sight of the coins. Then, by the sight of the dagger in Antonina's hand.

"You've got a simple choice," hissed Antonina. "You can take the money—call it rent for the use of your kitchen—or you can take the blade. *In your fucking guts.*"

The shopkeeper and his wife ogled her.

Antonina hefted the dagger. The wife's face, as she eyed the razor-sharp blade, paled a bit.

The shopkeeper's face paled quite a bit more.

He was fat and middle-aged, now. But, in his youth, he had led a rather disreputable life. He was not particularly impressed by Antonina's sharp little blade. He was a professional cook. He had several knives which were just as sharp and much bigger.

But he recognized that grip. That light, easy way of holding a blade.

"Shut up, woman!" he snarled to his wife. "Take the money and go upstairs."

His wife frowned at him. The shopkeeper threatened

her with the ladle. Antonina stepped away from the table, clearing a space. The shopkeeper's wife scuttled over, glancing at her fearfully. Then, after scooping up the coins, she practically sprinted to a small door in the rear corner of the kitchen. A moment later, Antonina heard her clumping up the stairs which led to the living quarters above.

Her husband began backing his way toward the same door.

"You can't come upstairs," he muttered. "I'm not going to get involved in any of this. Things are crazy right now."

Antonina shook her head.

"Just bar the door and stay upstairs. But, before you go—where do you keep your flour? And your knives?"

The shopkeeper pointed to a cupboard with the ladle.

"Flour's in there. The knives, too."

"Good. Leave me the ladle."

He frowned, glanced at the ladle, shrugged.

"Where do you want it?"

Antonina pointed toward the big kettle on the stove. Hurriedly, the shopkeeper dropped the ladle into the simmering broth and then scampered out of the kitchen.

Antonina stepped to the door which led to the outer room of the shop and pressed her ear against it.

Nothing. They haven't found the shop yet.

She raced to the cupboard and threw its door open. She hesitated, for just an instant, between the flour barrel and the knives hanging on the wall.

The knives first.

She grabbed four of the knives, two in each hand, and carried them over to the workbench next to the stove. Quickly, she gauged their balance. One of them, she decided, was suitable. That one—and her own little dagger—she placed on the edge of the workbench, blades toward her. The other three—much larger blades, one of them a veritable cleaver—she placed next to them, hilts facing out.

She hurried back to the closet and seized a small pan on a shelf. She lifted the lid to the barrel and dug the pan into the flour. A moment later, spilling a trail behind her, she poured the flour into the kettle. Quickly, using the ladle, she stirred the flour into the broth.

She was practically dancing with impatience. But she didn't dare add more flour too quickly. She had to give the broth time to regain its heat.

When the liquid began roiling, she hurried back to the closet. More flour. Into the kettle. Stir it. Wait. Wait. Again.

That's enough, she decided. The meat broth was now a lumpy, viscous mess. And, within a minute, would be back to a boil.

She looked around. Draped on nearby pegs, she saw the thick, wettened cloths which the shopkeeper used to handle the kettle. She wrapped her hands in the cloths and picked up the kettle. Grunting with exertion—it was a big kettle, three-fourths full.

Yes. Barely, but—yes.

She replaced the kettle on the stove, leaving the cloths next to it. Then, she raced to the door and closed the latch. For a moment, she considered trying to brace the door, but decided against it.

Better this way. I don't want them to have to work too hard to get through the door. Just hard enough. The latch will do for that.

She strode to the table onto which she had dumped the coins, and dragged it into the middle of the kitchen. Then, squatting down, she placed her shoulder under the edge and levered the table onto its side. It was a solidly built wooden table, large and heavy, and it made a great clattering sound when it hit the floor.

Upstairs, she heard the shopkeeper's wife scream.

Damn you!

Faintly, she heard a voice coming from the street. "In here!"

She heard the outer door burst open. Then, the sounds of many men pouring into the shop.

Now, louder:

"In here!"

She saw the door to the kitchen move, as someone tried to open it. The latch jiggled.

Very loud:

"She's in here!"

Antonina stepped to the stove. She wrapped the wet cloths around her hands and gripped the kettle. Stood still, looking over her shoulder. Watching the door.

A loud thump. The door bulged. The latch strained, but held.

Very loud:

"Out of the way!"

Thundering footsteps.

Smash!

The latch splintered. The door flew open. A large body—then another—hurtled through. Three men came piling in behind. All of them were dressed in the rough clothes of street toughs, and all were holding cudgels in their hands.

The first man—the self-appointed battering ram—was already off-balance. He slammed into the upended table in the middle of the kitchen and bounced back, half-sprawled onto the floor. The man coming right behind tripped over him and stumbled to his knees, leaning over the edge of the table itself.

The three men behind *him* skidded into a pile.

Five men, tangled up, immobilized.

Antonina seized the kettle, turned, and heaved its contents onto the cluster of thugs.

Several gallons of boiling, flour-thickened meat broth spewed over the would-be killers.

Shrieks of agony filled the room. Half-crazed with pain and fear, the five men in the kitchen began tearing at their flesh, frantically trying to scrape off the scalding brew.

Couldn't. *Couldn't!* The flour made the broth stick to their skins.

Antonina ignored them. More men were in the room beyond. Two of them were jammed in the doorway to the kitchen, gaping at the scene.

She spun lightly, seized her own little dagger by the blade. That one, she knew, was perfectly balanced.

Whipped around.

Father, I need you now!

He hadn't been worth much, that charioteer, but he had taught his daughter how to use a knife.

Taught her very well.

The little dagger flashed across the room and sank hilt deep into the throat of the man standing on the right side of the doorway.

The man's eyes bulged. He choked blood. Grabbed the hilt. Tried to draw it out. Couldn't. Sank to his knees. Died.

By the time the man next to him realized what had happened, it was too late. Another knife had sailed across the room.

Not into his throat, however. That knife, not as delicate as her own small dagger, Antonina had aimed at a less chancy target. The heavy butcher knife plunged four inches into the thug's chest, right into his heart.

Antonina took up the cleaver. The two dead bodies in the doorway would keep off the assailants in the room beyond for a few seconds. Time enough.

She sprang forward, right to the edge of the up-ended table, and began butchering the men on the other side.

Quite literally. Her knife-strokes were the short, sharp, chopping motions of an experienced butcher dismembering meat. There was no frenzied lunging; no grandiose stabs; no dramatic swings.

Just short, straight, strikes. With the heavy, razor-sharp blade of a cleaver.

Chop. Chop. Chop. Chop.

A nose fell off. The fingers from a hand covering a face. Another nose, and most of an upper lip. An ear and half a cheek.

Back again, quick. *Chop. Chop. Chop.* More fingers—and a thumb—fell to the floor. A wrist dangled, half-severed. Blood covered a face gashed to the bone.

Back again, quick. The men piled up behind the table were a helpless shrieking mob. Not even that—a pack of sheep, half-paralyzed by third-degree burns and mutilation.

Chop. Chop. Chop.

Now, the strikes were lethal. Hands with severed wrists and amputated fingers could no longer protect necks. Antonina aimed for the carotid arteries and hit two out of three. (The third would die also, a bit more slowly, from a severed jugular.)

Instantly, she was soaked in blood. She leaned into the spurting gore, like a child might lean into a fountain, and struck at the two remaining men behind the table. Both of them—dazed with shock and agony—were trying to crawl away from the nightmare.

One of them worked his way free, with nothing worse than a split shoulder blade. The other collapsed, dead. Antonina had chopped right through the back of his neck, severing the spine.

The sole survivor, screaming with fear and pain, scrambled toward the door on his knees and hands. (One hand, rather. His left hand was fingerless.) The timing, from Antonina's viewpoint, was perfect. The remaining thugs in the outer room had finally managed to drag aside the two bodies blocking the door. Two of them pushed their way through, only to stumble over the thug crawling toward them.

One of the men kept his balance, staggering against the doorframe. The other tripped and sprawled across the pile of bodies in the middle of the kitchen. He flung out his hands to break his fall and managed to grab the edge of the table.

For a brief instant, the thug stared up at Antonina. Her face was the last thing he ever saw. Other than the huge blade which descended onto his own face and removed it. The cleaver bit into his forehead and kept going, down and down, driven by Antonina's fury. The blade peeled off his eyebrows, shredded the eyes, took the nose, both lips, all the chin and a small piece of the chin bone.

Then, Antonina made her first mistake. By now— some thirty seconds into the battle—she was almost berserk with rage. She kicked aside the face flopping onto her foot, drew back the cleaver, and split the man's head in half. The blow was so ferocious that the blade jammed in the skull.

She tugged at it fiercely. Jerked. Jerked again.

Stuck.

She looked up. The thug leaning against the doorframe stared back at her. For a moment, the man's eyes were simply wide with shock. His jaw hung loose.

Then, seeing her predicament, he shouted sudden victory and sprang toward her. He circled around the pile of bodies and the upended table, making his way into the rear of the small kitchen.

"Come on, lads!" he bellowed. "I've got the bitch trapped!" He waved his club triumphantly.

Antonina backed against the stove and seized both of the remaining knives. She flipped one of them end-for-end. Now holding it by the blade, she made a throwing motion. The club-wielding man in front of her drew back, flinching.

It was a feint. She half-turned and threw the knife at another thug coming through the kitchen door.

That knife, however, was too blade-heavy for a good throw. The thug howled from the pain—the haft bruised his chest badly—and staggered back out of sight. But Antonina knew that he was not even disabled.

Despairing, she turned back to face her immediate opponent.

I didn't think there'd be so many.

She pushed all despair aside. She didn't expect to survive, but she would sell her life dearly.

From the outer room, Antonina heard a sudden

shouting uproar. Cries of triumph, she assumed, but ignored them. Her attention was completely fixed on her assailant in the kitchen.

The thug in front of her danced back and forth, snarling and waving his club. For all the man's bravado, Antonina realized that he was also very frightened. She *had* slaughtered a number of his fellows, after all. And—like the fat shopkeeper—the street tough recognized the expert way she was holding her knife.

He cocked his head, without taking his eyes from her. "*Come on!*" he bellowed. "Damn you—I've got her trapped!"

Antonina stepped forward. Her knife waved, feinted, probed. The thug backed against the wall, swinging his club wildly. Antonina kept her distance, looking for an opening.

Again, the thug shouted.

"What the hell are you waiting for, you assholes?"

From the door, a cold voice answered.

"They're waiting for Satan."

Antonina gasped. Her eyes sped to the door. She staggered back against the other wall, almost collapsing from relief.

The thug's eyes followed hers. An instant later, all color left his face.

Maurice stalked into the kitchen. His helmet was covered with blood. A piece of a brain slid off his blood-soaked half-armor. The spatha in his right hand dripped blood. His face was spattered with blood. Blood trailed from his gray beard.

For all the world, he didn't look like a man so much as a killing machine. A thing of iron, not flesh. His eyes, too, were gray. They gleamed out of his gore-covered face like two rivets.

Maurice circled the pile of bodies and the upended table in the middle of the kitchen. His steps were relaxed, almost casual, as if he were strolling through a garden.

Hissing with terror, the thug backed into the far

corner of the kitchen, against the door which led to the rooms above. He groped, found the door latch, shook it in a frenzy.

Useless. The shopkeeper had bolted the door from the other side.

Now the thug screamed, with terror and rage. Maurice ignored the sound completely. He advanced until he was almost within sword range. The thug swung his club frantically. The blows were short, by half a foot. Maurice didn't even bother to duck.

The hecatontarch turned his head very slightly. Just enough to ask Antonina:

"Is there anything you want to find out from this piece of shit?"

Antonina shook her head. Then, realizing that Maurice couldn't see her, said:

"No. He won't know anything."

"Didn't think so," grunted Maurice.

The thug swung the club again. This time, Maurice met the blow with a flashing sweep of his spatha. The club split in half. The shock of the blow knocked the stub out of the thug's hand.

He gasped. Gasped again, watching his hand amputated by another spatha-strike. Gasped again—started to gasp—watching the sword sweep toward his left temple. In a final despairing act, the thug threw up his left arm, trying to block the strike.

The spatha cut his arm off before it went halfway through his head. The thug dropped straight down onto his knees, like a pole-axed steer.

Maurice grunted, twisted the blade with his powerful wrist, and pulled it loose. The thug's body collapsed to the floor.

"Are there any left?" whispered Antonina.

The cataphract's chuckle was utterly humorless.

"Be serious, girl."

Maurice's eyes scanned the kitchen. A cold, grim ─e, at first. But, by the time those gray eyes ─d Antonina, they were full of good cheer.

"Wish I'd met your pop," he said. "He must have been quite a guy."

Antonina laughed giddily.

"He was a complete scoundrel, Maurice! A worthless bum!"

Then, bursting into tears, she slid down the wall into a half-kneeling squat. She pressed the back of her hand—still holding the knife—against her mouth, smearing her face with yet more blood.

Gasped, choked, sobbed.

Whispered:

"Thank you, father. Oh, thank you."

Chapter 24

"Stop fussing over me, Irene!" snapped Antonina. "I'm fine, I tell you."

The spymaster shook her head. Irene's face was pale and drawn. She had been sequestered in Theodora's quarters for days, and had not learned about the assassination attempt until early the following morning. She had come to Antonina's villa in the suburbs immediately.

Antonina went to a closet and began pulling out fresh clothes. The garments she had been wearing when she and Maurice returned to the villa the night before had already been destroyed. Expensive as they were, there was simply no way to clean off that much blood and gore.

"Wear a heavy cloak," said Irene. "It's cold out." Then, darkly: "I should *never* have agreed to let you go alone."

Antonina planted her hands on her hips and glared at her friend.

"It was not *your* decision in the first place," she pointed out. "It was mine. I've always gone alone to those meetings. Balban insisted."

Irene wiped her face with a trembling hand.

"I know. Still—God, you were almost *murdered*."

Antonina shrugged. Then, shrugged her way into a tunic. Her muffled voice came from within the simple, utilitarian garment:

"But I wasn't. And there's an end to it. So stop fussing. Besides—" Her face popped out, smiling broadly.

Constantinople.

"—it was the best news I've heard, so to speak, in months. You *do* realize what that assassination attempt means, don't you?"

Irene frowned. Antonina laughed.

"*You're* supposed to be the spymaster here, Irene! So start spymastering, for a moment, and stop fretting over me as if I were your little chick."

Irene was still frowning.

"*Think*, woman. Why would the Malwa decide to kill me? *Now*, of all times?"

Irene's eyes widened. She pressed her fingers over her lips.

"*Belisarius!*"

Antonina grinned.

"Precisely. Balban must have gotten new orders from India. Which means that my dear husband has done something to completely infuriate the Malwa. And it *also* means that he's escaped from their clutches."

"Of course," hissed Irene. The spymaster began pacing slowly.

"If they had their hands on him, they'd have even greater leverage over you than they thought they had. There would have been no reason to have you murdered. Quite the contrary."

By now, Antonina had finished dressing and was lacing on her boots. She nodded her head. "That's right. Which means he'll be arriving in Constantinople, sooner or later."

"When, do you think?"

Antonina shrugged.

"There's no way to know. We have no idea what route he's taking to get out of India. Most likely, he'll return by ship to Axum. If he does, Ashot and his men will be there to meet him."

She headed toward the door. Added: "Ashot's instruction were very clear. They'll sail up the Red Sea, portage to the Nile, and then take the river to Alexandria. There'll be a ship waiting to bring them straight to Constantinople."

Once in the corridor, Antonina strode hurriedly toward the villa's entrance. "They could get here almost any time. Or—not for weeks."

Behind her, Irene grimaced.

"I wish we knew. It would—"

Antonina gestured the thought away. "Don't even think about it, Irene! We can't make any plans based on my husband's return. We can only forge ahead. Speaking of which—have all the grenades arrived?"

They reached the foyer. Maurice was there, waiting for them. Like Antonina, he had changed his garments. But his helmet and half-armor were the same he had been wearing earlier. He had simply cleaned them off. That kitchen had not been his first slaughterhouse. The new stains were lost amid the relics of old gore.

Maurice answered her question.

"Yes. And they've already been taken to the monastery."

"Let's go, then," said Antonina.

Maurice held the door open. Antonina strode through into the courtyard, shivering a bit from the cold of a December morning. Then, seeing the mounted cataphracts in the courtyard and the street beyond, she stopped. Did a quick little count. Spun around.

"Where are the rest of the cataphracts, Maurice?" she demanded. "There's not more than a hundred here."

Maurice's jaws tightened.

"The rest of them are busy, at the moment. But they'll be joining us soon enough. They'll meet us at the monastery when they're done."

Antonina peered at him suspiciously.

"Busy? 'Done'? Doing what?"

The hecatontarch's face was like stone.

"What do you think, girl?"

"*Oh, no,*" whispered Antonina.

Irene hissed: "Maurice—you *can't*. It'll alert the Malwa! They'll know—"

"I don't give a damn what the Malwa know," snarled Maurice. He glared at both women.

"I am *not* a spymaster," he grated. "I am *not* an intriguer. I am the leader of the general's *bucellarii* and *those*"—he pointed to the mounted Thracians—"are my lord's *cataphracts*."

He stalked over to his horse and seized the reins.

"If some stinking pig thinks he can try to have you murdered—without consequences—he is one sadly mistaken son-of-a-bitch."

He swung himself into the saddle and stared down at Antonina and Irene. Like a statue. Immovable.

Antonina blew out her cheeks. Then, sighing, headed for her own horse.

Less than a minute later, she and Irene rode out together through the gates of the villa. Once in the street, the two women were surrounded by over a hundred cataphracts. The small army began making its way toward the inner city.

After a while, Irene muttered: "Oh, well. Balban probably doesn't think you're still working for him, anyway."

Antonina giggled. "Do you think his suspicions will be aroused? When two hundred cataphracts tear his villa down around him?"

Balban poured tea into Narses' cup. The eunuch immediately sipped at the beverage appreciatively.

"Thank you," he murmured. "Just the thing for a cold morning."

"The weather's clear, I hope?" asked Balban.

Narses nodded. "Oh, yes." Smiling thinly: "Other than the cold, it's a perfect day for an insurrection. Not a cloud in the sky."

"Good," muttered Balban. "The last thing we need is bad weather. How do things seem in the Great Palace?"

"Just about perfect, I'd say. The more Justinian's position worsens, the more tightly he clings to John of Cappadocia and myself."

Narses set down his cup.

"That's why I came here. Justinian ordered me to leave the Great Palace and round up more troops. Since I had the opportunity, I thought I'd come by for a last-minute conference." He laughed harshly. "*Troops.* Justinian still doesn't realize that he *has* no troops, except his palace *excubitores*. Every other army unit in the capital has locked themselves into their barracks, waiting out the storm. We won't even need Aegidius and his Army of Bithynia. The Blues and Greens alone should be enough."

Balban nodded. "Not much to confer about, then. The factions should start gathering by noon. My kshatriya will have seized the Hippodrome within the hour. All we have to do is make our appearance and"—scowling— "hope Hypatius shows up to be acclaimed the new Emperor."

Narses sneered.

"He'll show up. Or if he doesn't, Pompeius will. We'll have to provide the new Emperor with fresh trousers, of course. I'm sure both of the nephews have already shat in the ones they're wearing. But they'll be there. Their ambition is greater than their terror."

Balban chuckled. Then, more seriously: "What about Theodora?"

Narses winced. "That's the one small problem. She knows almost everything, Balban—I'm quite sure of that. Her new spymaster—that young woman Irene Macrembolitissa—is fiendishly capable. But," he shrugged, "Justinian's not listening to her at all, anymore. And now he's run out of time."

Balban grunted. "Still—" He hesitated, then shrugged himself.

"No doubt you're right. By nightfall, it won't matter anyway. Her corpse will join Justinian's, feeding the fish in the Sea of Marmara."

Narses pressed his lips together, fighting down the anguish. Fiercely, he reminded himself of his ambition. To hide his feelings, he leaned forward and reached for the teacup resting on the table.

His hand stopped. The teacup was rattling.

Ajatasutra burst into the small salon. "Out!" he hissed. "Now!"

The assassin strode to a door against the far wall. Flinging it open, he began hastily dragging aside the heavy chest which sat on the floor of the closet beyond.

Balban rose, frowning angrily. "Just what do you think you're—"

Ajatasutra, still bent over the heavy chest, turned his head. His eyes were like hot coals. "If you want to live more than two minutes, Balban, help me get this damned chest off the trapdoor."

Balban remained standing in place, rigid, still frowning. Narses immediately rose from his chair and went to Ajatasutra's aid. For all his age and small size, the eunuch was not weak. With his help, Ajatasutra moved the chest out of the closet.

"Against the wall," grunted the assassin.

A moment later, the chest was pushed into position. Ajatasutra sprang nimbly into the closet and rolled back an expensive rug. Then, fiddling a moment with a plank which seemed no different from any of the other wood flooring, he levered up a small trapdoor.

"Get in," he ordered Narses.

The old eunuch hesitated not an instant. He began lowering himself down a ladder.

Halfway down, the ladder began to shake. Narses stopped, waist high in the trapdoor, and stared up at Balban. The spymaster was now standing in the door of the closet.

He was still frowning—but with puzzlement, now, more than anger. Balban looked down at his feet.

"Why is the floor shaking?" he asked.

Narses glanced quickly at Ajatasutra. The assassin's face was stiff with suppressed anger.

"Mother of God," muttered Narses. To Balban: "What have you done, you damned fool?"

Balban glared.

"That's none of your concern, Narses!" he snapped. Then, frowning at his feet, he asked yet again: "Why is the floor shaking?"

Narses sneered.

"I take it you've never faced a charge of cataphracts in full armor?" he demanded. "That's what you're feeling, *fool*. Several hundred tons of approaching death and destruction."

Balban goggled at him.

"What are you talking about? We're in the middle of Constantinople!"

Narses sighed, looked over at Ajatasutra. The assassin, through tight lips, said: "He ordered Antonina's murder."

"Marvelous," muttered Narses. "Just marvelous."

The eunuch began lowering himself down the ladder. Very quickly. His voice came from below: "You're not in Constantinople *now*, Balban. *You're in Thrace.*"

A smashing sound came from outside the villa. After a second, Balban realized that it was the outer gate. Shattering.

Shattered.

A scream. Cut short. Another. Another. Another. All the screams were cut short, but Balban recognized the voices. His Malwa guards. Dying.

Dead.

Ajatasutra sprang to the door of the salon and stared down the corridor leading to the villa's main entrance. A moment later, there came a splintering crash.

He leapt back into the room and slammed shut the door.

"*That*," he announced, "was a lance driving through the main door."

Balban hesitated no longer. He scrambled down the ladder after Narses. Before his head sank below the level of the floor he heard a rolling series of thunderous noises. Doors and windows being shattered. By the time he reached the small tunnel fifteen feet down, he could already hear the screams echoing through the entire villa.

The rest of the Malwa mission resident in the villa were being butchered.

Ajatasutra took the time to close the closet door before he started down the ladder. As best he could, feeling his way in the darkness, he tried to position the rug so that it would cover the trapdoor after he lowered it.

When he reached the tunnel below, he found the two other men waiting for him. Balban had lit the small lamp which was kept in a cubby.

"I don't know the way," whispered the spymaster. "I've never been down here."

Ajatasutra took the lamp from his hand.

"Follow me," he ordered. "And watch your step. We never bothered to grade the tunnel floor. I didn't really think we'd need it."

After the three men had inched their way down the narrow tunnel for hundred feet or so, Narses asked:

"How much farther, Ajatasutra? My shoes aren't designed for this kind of travel. And—damnation—they're silk! Expensive."

Ajatasutra chuckled, grimly.

"Forget about your shoes, Narses. We've another two hundred feet to go. Before we reach the *sewer*."

"Marvelous," muttered Narses. "Just marvelous."

Fifty feet down, he sneered: "What other brilliant ideas did you have today, Balban? Did you jump into the Bosporus to see if it was wet? Did you swallow a live coal to see if it would burn your throat? Did you—"

"Shut up," snarled the spymaster. "I received orders—from Nanda Lal himself."

Narses was silent, thereafter, until they had reached the sewer and slogged their way down its stinking length for at least two hundred feet. He began lagging further and further behind. Eventually, Ajatasutra handed Balban the lamp and went back to help the old eunuch.

"Are you all right?" he asked.

"I could use your shoulder," grunted Narses. "This damned sewer's so low I have to stoop. My back hurts."

Ajatasutra leaned his right shoulder under Narses' left arm and helped him along. The eunuch turned his head until his lips were but inches from Ajatasutra's ear and whispered:

"You *do* realize what those orders from Nanda Lal mean, don't you?"

Ajatasutra nodded, very slightly.

"Yes," he replied, also in a whisper. He glanced up. Balban's dim form was visible thirty feet ahead of them, backlit by the lamp he was carrying.

"It means you were right about Belisarius," whispered the assassin. "He must have escaped from India."

They progressed another fifty feet. By now, all of them were soaked with filthy water up to their mid-thighs.

Again, Narses turned his lips to Ajatasutra's ear.

"There'll be a boat, waiting. At the Neorion harbor in the Golden Horn. Do you know where it is?"

"Yes," whispered Ajatasutra. "Why me?"

"You're the best of a sorry lot. And if I have to flee to India I'll need someone to vouch for my credentials."

Ajatasutra smiled, thinly.

"You don't sound entirely confident in the certain success of our plans."

Narses sneered. "Nothing in this world is certain, Ajatasutra. *Except this*—better to have loosed the demon from his pit than to have loosed Belisarius. *Especially after murdering his wife.*"

"She wasn't murdered," muttered Ajatasutra. Seeing the frown on the eunuch's face, the assassin chuckled.

"I followed. At a distance, of course. And I stayed well out of the fray. Quite a set-to, judging from the racket coming out of that cookshop—even before the cataphract arrived. I waited until he brought Antonina out. The woman was covered with blood, but none of it was hers."

Narses sighed. "Well, that's something. Belisarius will just be his usual extraordinarily competent and brilliantly capable deadly self. Instead of vengeance personified."

They slogged on, and on. Eventually, now well ahead of them, they saw Balban rise from his stoop and stand up straight. He had finally reached the exit from the sewer.

"Come on!" they heard the spymaster's hissing voice. "Time is short!"

Just before they came within Balban's hearing range, Ajatasutra whispered:

"What does the boat look like?"

"Like it wants to leave Constantinople in a very big hurry," was the eunuch's only reply.

Maurice waited until the cataphracts circled the monastery before he would let Antonina or Irene dismount. The Thracian cavalrymen were in a grim, grim mood. The small crowd of curious onlookers, which began to gather from the nearby residences, quickly drew back under their hard gaze.

"Marvelous," muttered Antonina. "Just marvelous."

She glared at Maurice. The hecatontarch returned her hot gaze with placidity.

"So much for keeping the whereabouts of the Theodoran Cohort secret," she growled.

Maurice shrugged. He pointed toward the southwest.

"Take a look. The time for secrets is over."

Antonina and Irene twisted in their saddles. They were not far from the Column of Marcian. The monastery, and the cathedral which adjoined it, were located just inside the old walls of the capital—the "walls of Constantine." The heart of Constantinople, the corner of the city which held the Great Palace and the Hippodrome, was not more than two miles away.

In the vicinity of the Hippodrome, the two women could see smokeplumes produced by bonfires which the gathering Blue and Green factions had set aflame to warm their toughs. They could hear the faint roar of the mob, even at the distance.

Antonina asked Irene: "What's the situation at the Great Palace?"

"Tense. Very tense. Justinian called for a meeting of the high council for today, at noon. He's still listening to John of Cappadocia, however, who assures him that most of the army units will stand by the throne. So he's living in a fool's paradise. He doesn't realize that the only military forces he has left are his own excubitores—all five hundred of them!—and the forces which we're bringing."

Irene turned her head, looking to the south.

"Sittas and Hermogenes should be in position at the Harbor of Hormisdas. I'd better leave now and tell them where your forces stand."

Antonina nodded. Maurice ordered a squad of cataphracts to escort the spymaster.

A commotion drew Antonina's attention.

A mob of grenadiers and their wives were pouring out of the monastery's doors, heading toward her. All of them were staring at her, their faces full of worried concern.

"You told them," she said to Maurice, accusingly.

Maurice chuckled.

"*Told* them? I sent ten cataphracts over here this morning, to *regale* them with the tale. Every last gruesome, gory, grisly great moment of it!"

Antonina sighed with exasperation. Maurice edged his horse next to her. Leaning over—all humor gone—he whispered harshly: "*Listen to me, girl, and listen well.* You're at war, now, and you're the commander. A *female* commander—the first one in Roman history outside of ancient legends. You need all the confidence you can get from your soldiers. And *they* need it even more than you do."

Antonina stared into his gray eyes. She had never noticed, before, how cold those eyes could be.

"Do you think I'd let an opportunity like this pass?" he demanded. Then, with a harsh laugh: "God, now that it's over, I'm almost ready to thank Balban! What a gift he gave us!"

He leaned back in his saddle. "Antonina, my toughest *cataphracts* are in awe of you. Not one in ten would have survived that ambush—unarmored, with no weapon but a dagger—and they know it. How do you think these Syrian peasants feel? *Now*—about their *little woman* commander?"

It was obvious how the peasants felt. The grenadiers and their wives were surrounding Antonina, gazing up at her silently. Their expressions were easy to read. A mixture of sentiments: relief at her obvious well-being; fierce satisfaction in her victory; pride in their commander—and self-pride that she *was* their commander.

Most of all—it was almost frightening to Antonina—was a sense of quasireligious adoration. The simple Syrians were gazing at her much as they might have gazed at a living saint.

She was blessed by God's grace.

Just as the prophet Michael had foretold.

For a moment, Antonina felt herself shrink from that crushing responsibility.

Then, drawing on the fierce will which had always been a part of her—since her girlhood in the hard streets of Alexandria—she drove all hesitation aside.

"I am quite well," she assured her grenadiers loudly. She began dismounting from her horse, but immediately found a dozen hands were helping her down. The same hands then carried her toward the cathedral. Hurriedly, monks and priests appeared to open the great doors. Among them, she saw the plump figure of Bishop Cassian.

As she was carried through the doors, her eyes met those of Anthony. He returned her smile, but his gaze was filled with concern.

She was carried to the altar and set back on her feet. Turning, she saw that the grenadiers and their wives were rapidly pouring in behind. Within two minutes, the great cathedral was filled. All the Syrians stood there, silently, staring at her.

Many years before, as a young woman, Antonina's mother had given her some brief training as an actress.

In the event, Antonina had never pursued her mother's career, having found a different one which—though just as disreputable—was considerably more renumerative. But she still remembered the lessons. Not her mother's meager talents as a thespian, but her skills at projecting her voice.

All the grenadiers in the room—as well as the cataphracts who had joined them—almost jumped. Such a small woman, to have such a great, powerful *voice.*

> *I have little to say, my soldiers. My friends.*
> *Little needs to be said.*
> *Our enemies are gathering. You can see their*
>   *bonfires. You can hear their coarse shouts of*
>   *triumph.*
> *Do not fear them.*
> *They are nothing.*
> *Nothing.*
> *Assassins. Street thugs. Murderers. Rapists.*
> *Thieves. Pimps. Gamblers.*
> *Nothing.*
> *Nothing!*

She paused, waited. The grenadiers—one or two, at first—took up the chant. Softly, at first. Then, louder and louder.

"Nothing. Nothing."

> *We will shatter them back into their nothing.*
> *We will drive them back into their sewers.*

"Nothing! Nothing!"

> *We will hound them into their burrows. We*
>   *will follow them into their ratholes. We will*
>   *savage them till they plead for mercy.*

"NOTHING! NOTHING!"

> *There will be no mercy.*
> *For nothing, there is nothing.*

The shouts now shook the cathedral itself. Antonina pointed to the cataphracts. The shouts died away. The grenadiers listened to her with complete attention.

> *Our plan is simple. The traitors are gathering*

*their forces in the Hippodrome. We will go
there. The cataphracts will lead the way, but
we will be God's hammer.*

We will hammer nothing—into nothing.

She strode forward, heading down the aisle. The grenadiers parted before her and then immediately closed behind. She moved through that little sea of humanity like a ship in full sail.

As she reached the door, Anthony Cassian stepped forward. For a moment, she embraced her old friend.

"May God be with me," she whispered.

"Oh, I believe He is," replied the Bishop softly. "Trust me in this, Antonina." With a quirk of a smile: "I am quite a reputable theologian, you know."

She returned his smile, kissed him on the cheek, and strode past.

By now, a large crowd of onlookers had gathered in the street. Not even the glares of cataphracts could hold back their curiosity. But then, hearing the sound of many approaching horses—*heavy, armored* horses—the crowd eddied back, pressed against the houses and fences which lined the boulevard.

Down that street, in a prancing trot, came two hundred cataphracts. The remainder of the Thracian bucellarii, returning from their own triumph.

When the cataphracts reached the cathedral they drew to a halt. The cataphracts in the lead tossed the residue of their vengeance at Antonina's feet.

Gasping and hissing, the crowd of bystanders plastered themselves against the walls. A few, timidity overcoming curiosity, scuttled hastily into the houses and fenced yards.

Twenty or so severed heads, rolling in the street, can chill even the most avid onlooker.

The grenadiers, on the other hand, seeing the grisly trophies, erupted with their own savage glee.

"NOTHING! NOTHING! NOTHING!"

Antonina moved toward her horse. Maurice, with two cataphracts in tow, met her halfway.

"Put these on," commanded Maurice. "I had them specially made."

The cataphracts with him extended a cuirass and a helmet.

"The helmet was easy," commented Maurice. "But the cuirass was a bit of a challenge for the armorer. He's not used to cleavage."

Antonina smiled. With Maurice's help, she donned the unfamiliar equipment. The smile vanished. "This stuff is *heavy*."

"Don't complain, girl. Just be thankful it's only half-armor. And be *especially* thankful that we're in Constantinople in the winter, instead of Syria in the summer."

Antonina grimaced at the thought. Then, with a sly little smile:

"Don't I get a sword, too?"

Maurice shook his head.

"I've got something better."

He drew a scabbarded knife—a large and odd knife, judging from the sheath—and handed it to her.

Antonina drew the blade out of the scabbard. She could not restrain a little gasp.

"You recognize it, I see," said Maurice. His voice was full of satisfaction. "The shopkeeper drove a hard bargain for it, but I thought it was fitting."

Antonina stared back and forth from Maurice to the cleaver.

The hecatontarch's lips twisted into a grim smile.

"Ask any veteran, Antonina. They'll all tell you there's nothing as important in a battle as having a trusty, *tested* blade."

Suddenly, the feel of that simple cooking utensil in her hand filled Antonina with a great rush of confidence.

"I do believe you're right, Maurice."

She sensed, from the murmuring voices around her, that the cataphracts were passing the news to the grenadiers. Seconds later, the grenadiers began a new chant:

"CLEAVE THEM! CLEAVE THEM!"

With Maurice's help, she clambered into her saddle, suppressing a curse at the awkward weight of the helmet and armor. Once securely seated, she raised the butcher knife over her head, waving it.

The grenadiers roared. The cataphracts joined their voices to the cry:

"NOTHING! NOTHING!"

Antonina suppressed a laugh.

For all the world like a warrior of legend, waving a mystic sword of renown!

Which, though she did not know it yet, she was; and which, to her everlasting surprise, that humble cleaver would become.

Chapter 25

When John of Rhodes saw the approaching *dromon*, he began cursing bitterly.

Some of his curses were directed at Irene Macrembolitissa. The spymaster had not warned him that the traitorous General Aegidius had obtained a war galley to clear the way for his troop transports. John could already see the first of those transports, bearing the lead elements of the Army of Bithynia. Four of the tubby sailing ships were just now leaving the harbor at Chalcedon, heading across the Bosporus toward Constantinople.

But most of his curses were aimed at life in general. He did not really blame Irene for the failure in intelligence. In all fairness, the spymaster could not be expected to know everything about their enemy.

"That's just the way of it," he muttered. "War's always been a fickle bitch."

"Excuse me?" asked Eusebius, looking up from his work. The young artificer's face seemed a bit green. He was obviously feeling ill at ease from the rocking motion of the galley. Especially since he was standing upon the fighting platform amidships, engaged in the delicate task of opening firebomb crates. The platform was elevated ten feet above the deck, which only accentuated the ship's unsteadiness.

"Hurry it up, Eusebius," growled John of Rhodes. The naval officer pointed to starboard. "We're going to have to deal with *that* before we do anything else."

Eusebius straightened, peering near-sightedly toward the war galley approaching from the south.

"Oh, Christ," he muttered. "I can't see it very well, but—is that what I think it is?"

John nodded gloomily.

"Yeah, it's a dromon. A hundred fighting soldiers and at least a hundred and fifty rowers—good ones, too, judging from their speed. And they've already lowered the sails."

Eusebius paled. Dromons were the fastest ships afloat—at least, during the period before their rowers tired—and by far the most maneuverable. Pure warships.

John of Rhodes scampered down the ladder to the main deck and scurried aft, where he hastily began consulting with his steering officer. In his absence, Eusebius began unpacking another crate of firebombs. The artillerymen on the platform offered to help, but he refused their assistance. He was probably being too cautious—once the battle started, the artillerymen would have to do their own loading—but Eusebius knew better than anyone just how dangerous those bombs could be if they were accidentally ruptured.

Besides, it gave him something to do besides worry.

And there was a lot to worry about. Eusebius was no seaman, but he had picked up enough from John of Rhodes over the past months to understand the seriousness of their predicament.

The artificer glanced at the two scorpions set up on the ship's fighting platform—the "wood-castle," as it was called. Then, more slowly, he studied the ship itself.

It was not a happy study.

A full-sized dromon, like the one approaching them, had a crew of two to three hundred men. A two-banked galley, that ship had 25 oars in each bank—100 in all. Fifty rowers were permanently assigned to the lower bank, one man to an oar. The rest of the crew, who would number at least 150, were assigned to the fighting deck. A hundred of those would man the upper bank of oars, two men to an oar, while the rest served as archers and boarders. In the event of a drawn-out pursuit or engagement, the upper rowers would switch places with the soldiers, thus keeping the men from becoming exhausted.

Technically, Eusebius knew, their ship was also classed as a dromon, an oared war galley. But it was the medium-sized type called a *pamphylos*. They only had eighty oars, twenty on each bank. And there was only room for a single rower on the upper oars.

A hundred and fifty rowers versus eighty. Despite the greater weight of the approaching dromon, it would still be faster than their own galley. And they were further handicapped because of the modifications which John had made in their warship.

John had known he would be heavily outnumbered in the coming battle—one ship against twenty, probably more. So he had decided to use his single ship as a pure artillery vessel, bombarding the enemy fleet at long range with his firebombs. For that reason, they only carried twelve fighting men—just enough to operate the two scorpions. They would be hopelessly outmatched in the event of a boarding.

True, they also carried a double crew of rowers. If John's battle plan worked, his men would be rowing for long periods. So he had loaded the ships with relief rowers. That would give them a greater endurance than the crew of the approaching dromon, but the weight of the extra rowers would also slow them down.

Not to mention—

Eusebius studied the fighting platform he was standing on. The wood castle was larger and heavier than normal for this size war galley. It needed to be in order to provide the necessary support and room for the two scorpions which John had placed there. But that extra size *also* added weight. As did—

Eusebius lowered his gaze to the deck of the ship itself. Normally, Byzantine war galleys were of the modern design called *aphract*—"unarmored." Since modern naval tactics called for boarding as well as ramming, the rowers/soldiers on the upper banks were protected by nothing more substantial than a light frame rigged along the gangways to which they attached their shields.

But John, since he had no intention of boarding, had refitted the ship to the older *cataphract* design. He had attached solid wooden projections to the gunwales, with overhanging beams, to protect the rowers from archery. The armored projections resembled the rowing frames of ancient Hellenic galleys, although the rowers themselves were still positioned inside the hull. The end result was to enclose the rowers in solid, arrow-proof shelters. A bit stifling, perhaps, despite the ventilating louvers, but far better protection than mere shields hanging on a light frame.

And—much heavier.

Their ship was still faster and more maneuverable than the tubby square-rigged sailing ships which the Army of Bithynia was using for its transports. But it was a sluggish turtle compared to the approaching dromon.

John had not expected to face a real warship.

"Hurry up!" snapped the Rhodesman, clambering back onto the wood-castle. "No—never mind. We'll just have to make do with the bombs you've already uncrated."

"There's only eight of them," protested Eusebius.

"Then we'll have to shoot well," snarled John. "We don't have time, Eusebius! That damned dromon is coming on like a porpoise. *Move.*"

As John and Eusebius began loading the two scorpions with the first of the firebombs, the ship's steering officer bellowed orders at the crew. Though the men were every bit as grim-faced as their captain, they set about the tasks without hesitation. Those sailors were Rhodesmen themselves. John had handpicked them from the ranks of the Roman naval forces stationed in Seleuceia. Their officers had not even complained—not, at least, after they saw the letter of authority from the Empress Theodora which John carried with him.

The pamphylos began coming about, facing this new enemy approaching from the Sea of Marmara.

John peered intently at the oncoming dromon.

God, those rowers are good!

Several cataphracts were standing on the fighting platform in the bow of the galley, staring back at him. Their features were obscured by the helmets on their heads.

Well-used helmets, thought John gloomily. *Just like their damned armor. And—oh, shit—don't they hold their bows with a practiced, casual ease? Just great. Just fucking great!*

He stared at one of the cataphracts. A huge man, he was.

God, I don't even want to think what that ogre's bow pulls. Two hundred pounds, probably.

He began to turn away, heading for one of the scorpions. An idle thought caused him to pause. He glanced back at the huge cataphract. Then, he stared at the cataphract standing right in the prow of the galley.

A tall cataphract.

The tall cataphract removed his helmet. His face was no longer obscured.

John of Rhodes had excellent eyesight.

A moment later, Eusebius and the entire crew of the pamphylos stopped what they were doing. They were transfixed—gaping, goggling—by the sight of their commanding officer.

John of Rhodes leapt and capered atop the wood-castle, howling like a banshee. He sprang upon the port wall of the fighting platform and gestured obscenely at the fleet of transports bearing the Army of Bithynia across the Bosporus. Then, apparently unsatisfied with mere hand gestures, John unlaced his trousers, pulled out his penis, and waved it in the face of the still distant enemy.

"He's gone mad!" exclaimed Eusebius. The artificer hopped back and forth, torn between the urgent need to load the scorpions and the still more urgent need to restrain John before the maniac fell into the sea. The wood-castle extended two feet beyond the hull of the ship itself.

Fortunately, the naval officer's sealegs were excellent. A moment later, John laced up his trousers and sprang down upon the fighting platform. He bounced over to Eusebius, grinning from ear to ear.

It suddenly occurred to Eusebius that there was an alternate explanation for John's apparent insanity. The artificer turned his head and squinted at the dromon. The galley was now less than fifty yards away.

"Is that—?"

"Yes!" shouted John. "*Belisarius!* In the proverbial nick of time!"

Still grinning, the naval officer examined the war galley in a new light. His grin widened. John's eyes danced back and forth between the galley, his own ship, and the fleet of enemy transports.

By the time the dromon pulled alongside, his grin was almost blinding.

"Oh, those sorry bastards are fucked," he said cheerfully. "*Fucked.*"

A minute later, John and his crewmen were helping Belisarius aboard the pamphylos.

After giving John a brief but powerful embrace, Belisarius immediately climbed up to the wood-castle. Quickly, he examined the bombs resting in open crates next to the artillery engines. The bombs were carefully nestled in wads of thick wool.

"Firebombs?" he asked. "Or gunpowder?"

The general nodded toward Ashot, who was still standing in the bow of the dromon.

"Ashot told me you discovered the secret of gunpowder already," he said approvingly.

John nodded.

"Yes—although I'm sure you'll have suggestions for improving the powder's quality. But these aren't gunpowder. For a naval battle, I thought firebombs would be better. They're my own special formula. I added saltpeter to the naphtha. Beautiful stuff! Beautiful! But you have to be very careful with it."

The movement of Belisarius' eyes now imitated that of John's, not two minutes earlier. Scorpions—galley—enemy fleet; scorpions—galley—enemy fleet.

"You've got a battle plan," he stated.

"Yes," affirmed John. "I'd only hoped to be able to destroy enough of those ships to give Sittas and Hermogenes a fighting chance after they landed. But now—with your galley—we can do better. Much better."

"Give me the entire situation," commanded Belisarius.

John blew out his cheeks.

"The heart of the traitors' conspiracy is at the Hippodrome. The Malwa bribed both the Blues and Greens—can you imagine how much money *that* must have taken?—and are relying on them for the real dirty work." He glanced up at the sun, which had just cleared the horizon. "In three or four hours—by noon, at the latest—they'll be assembled in the Hippodrome. Twenty, maybe thirty thousand of those street toughs. Irene also discovered that they've smuggled in several hundred Malwa soldiers. With gunpowder weapons. Rockets and grenades, we think."

Belisarius nodded. "Most likely. They'll be kshatriya. I doubt they were able to smuggle in any of their cannons, though."

The general glanced at the enemy fleet. All of the transports had now cleared the harbor at Chalcedon and were well into the Bosporus.

"So," he mused. "They'll use the kshatriya as a spearhead, with a huge mob of faction thugs to provide the mass of their fighters. What else? Where do the military units in Constantinople stand?"

John shrugged.

"All of them are standing aside. Stinking cowards are hiding in their barracks."

He nodded toward the fleet of transports.

"That's the Army of Bithynia. General Aegidius is part

of the conspiracy. He's got eight thousand men on those
transports, including a thousand cataphracts and their
horses. According to Irene, his main function is to
neutralize any military units that might come to the
Emperor's aid."

John's head turned to the west, studying the shore-
line of Constantinople.

"Which amounts to Sittas and Hermogenes, and the
small army they were able to bring here from Syria. Five
hundred cataphracts and two thousand infantrymen.
They've been hidden away in ships at Portus Caesarii
since they arrived. But they should have marched out
this morning. By now—I hope—they've taken up positions guarding the Harbor of Hormisdas. That's the
landing site nearest to the Hippodrome and the Great
Palace. It's where the Army of Bithynia is planning to
disembark, according to Irene's spies."

Belisarius nodded.

"Which means, I assume, that the only forces we have
immediately available to suppress the kshatriya and the
mob in the Hippodrome are my three hundred cataphracts and Antonina's cohort of grenadiers."

"It's worse than that, Belisarius. John of Cappadocia
has assembled almost a thousand bucellarii of his own.
I'm sure he'll use them against the excubitores guarding Justinian at the Great Palace."

Belisarius scowled fiercely. "For the sake of God! Why
didn't Justinian disband them?"

John winced. He understood Belisarius' astonished
outrage. Under Roman law, private armies—*bucellarii*—
were illegal for anyone to maintain except serving generals like Belisarius and Sittas. That law had been
enacted over fifty years earlier, by Emperor Leo, precisely in order to prevent public officials and landowners
from becoming too powerful.

"Justinian gave John of Cappadocia an exemption,"
he explained. Then, with a harsh laugh: "Not even that!
He made the Cappadocian a general. Just a few months
after you left for India."

Belisarius rolled his eyes in disgust. "That stinking chiseler's never been in a battle in his life," he snarled. Suddenly, the snarl turned into a crooked smile. "Which, now that I think about it, isn't such a bad thing."

The general rubbed his chin, eyeing the transports. "Have you got a count?" he asked John.

The naval officer nodded. "There are thirty-one ships in Aegidius' fleet. Most of them—the bigger ones—are *corbita*."

Seeing the blank look in Belisarius' face, John elaborated.

"We seamen call them 'basket ships.' Corbita are freight haulers, general. They operate by sails alone, without rowers. They're slow under the best of circumstances, and they'll be even slower here in the Bosporus fighting against the northerly winds. *But*—they've got a big capacity. Each one can carry up to four hundred passengers, although I doubt they're holding more than three hundred apiece. They've got to haul the arms and equipment, also."

"And the cataphracts' horses," added Belisarius.

"That, too. But I'm pretty sure that the cataphracts themselves are being transported in the smaller ships. Aegidius has eight merchant galleys—*akatoi*—in that fleet. Just about right for a thousand cataphracts. Although—which is good for us—they're having to use their sails alone. They'll have no room for rowers on top of the cataphracts."

Belisarius stared at the fleet. John fell silent, realizing that the general was coming to a decision.

"Right," murmured Belisarius. He cocked an eye at the Rhodesman. "The immediate priority is to stop the Army of Bithynia from reaching Constantinople. You're the naval officer, John. How would you do it—now that you have my galley as well as this ship?"

John frowned.

"You've got good rowers. But how fresh are they?"

Belisarius shrugged. "Fresh enough, I should think. We came most of the way from Egypt on a sailing ship.

Ashot had the galley waiting for us in Abydos, and we crossed the Sea of Marmara using our sails. We only unshipped the oars a few minutes ago."

"Good. We can wreak havoc among those plodding corbita with a dromon. The real problem's the akatoi. Those merchants galleys are fast. *And* they're full of cataphracts." He grimaced. "I wouldn't want to face that kind of archery, even in an armored galley. Not when you have to get close enough to ram."

"You won't have to," said Belisarius. "I'll take the akatoi with this ship, using the scorpions. You take the dromon and do as much damage as you can against the corbita."

Seeing John's hesitation, Belisarius pressed on.

"There's no other way, John. I'm not a naval officer— *you are.* I wouldn't know what to do with a dromon. Whereas here—"

He waved at the scorpions.

"I *do* know how to use artillery. Quite well."

Belisarius almost laughed, seeing the look of near anguish on the Rhodesman's face. John, he knew, wanted to finally try out his wonderful new artillery weapons.

John blew out his cheeks.

"You're right, damn it."

He eyed Belisarius skeptically.

"I assume you don't know how to sail a ship, either?"

Belisarius answered with a smile.

The naval officer grunted. He gestured toward one of the sailors standing at the stern. The man trotted forward along the gangway.

"His name's Honorius. Let him command the ship. Just tell him what you want. You can concentrate on the scorpions."

He turned to his assistant.

"Eusebius! Show the general how to handle the fire-bombs. He's going to command the artillery on this ship. I'm taking the dromon."

John eyed Belisarius' cataphracts. By now, all of them had boarded the pamphylos.

Seeing the avarice in John's eyes, Belisarius chuckled.

"Leave me Valentinian," he said. "I'll want him to aim the other scorpion. You can take the rest."

Less than a minute later, the dromon was pulling away from the ship and heading straight toward the enemy fleet. John was standing in the stern, giving orders to the steersman.

Belisarius did not watch for more than a few seconds. He had his own problem to face.

How best to use his little artillery ship against over two dozen opponents?

A thought came from Aide:

Cross the T.

Explain, commanded the general.

A series of images came to his mind. Scenes of naval battle, featuring ships pounding at each other with cannons. In each instance, the fleets attempted to sail their own ships directly across the coming line of the enemy, in order to bring their broadsides to bear on as many opponents as possible.

Belisarius scratched his chin, pondering. The scenes which Aide had shown him were not entirely relevant to his situation. His ship was armed with only two scorpions, located amidships, not a line of cannons running down the entire sides of the ship. "Broadsides," thus, were impossible.

Still—

The sailor whom John had named as his substitute was now standing next to Belisarius, waiting for orders. The general turned to Honorius, and began gesturing to illustrate his question.

"Can you row this ship at a right angle across the front of that approaching fleet?"

Honorius squinted at the enemy ships. Aegidius' armada was now well into the Bosporus, about a mile distant.

"Easily. They're letting the basket ships set the pace instead of the akatoi. Those corbita are slow to begin with. And if they're packed with cataphracts—and all their armor—they'll be a lot more sluggish than usual."

He leaned over the wall of the fighting platform and began shouting orders to his crew. The ship began taking a new heading, but Belisarius did not bother to watch. His concentration was focussed on the scorpions.

John, he saw, had chosen his weapons well. The scorpions were that type of stone-throwing catapult which were called *palintonos*. The name was derived from the "fold-back spring" design which allowed the two torsion arms to swing forward further than was possible in the more traditional "straight-spring" *euthytonos*. The weapons were mounted on the same type of tripod base which Roman engineers used for cranes and hoists. The scorpions were then fitted onto a swivel attachment atop the tripod. The end result was a weapon which could be tilted up or down as well as swung sideways in a complete circle.

Romans did not manufacture their artillery engines to the same degree of standardization as would be common in future eras. But, from long experience, Belisarius recognized that the two scorpions were both in what was considered the "11-pound" class—that being the weight of stone shot each was capable of hurling. Using that weight of shot, they had an effective range of well over 400 yards.

"How heavy are your firebombs?" he asked Eusebius.

"A little over eight pounds. Not more than nine."

Belisarius nodded.

"We should have a range of almost five hundred yards, then."

Again, he examined the scorpions. The weapons were placed on either side of the wood-castle, far enough apart to allow the engines to be swiveled without the six-foot-long firing troughs impeding each other. Unfortunately, of course, there was no way that both of them could be used simultaneously to fire over the same side. As they—to use Aide's expression— "crossed the T," one of the scorpions would be out of action completely.

For an idle moment, Belisarius pondered alternate

ways of emplacing artillery on a ship. Almost immediately, another image came from Aide.

A steel ship, very sleek for all its gargantuan size, plowing through the sea. Cannons—three of them abreast—were mounted in a strange sort of enclosed swivel—

Turret.

—directly amidship. Two enclosed swivels—

Turrets.

—were mounted toward the bow, one toward the stern. Those cannons could be brought to bear in any direction. All nine could be employed in broadsides, to starboard or port. Six could also fire across the bow, and three across the stern.

"Oh, well," muttered Belisarius. "We'll have to make do with what we've got."

The enemy fleet was now almost within catapult range. The nearest ships were off their starboard bow at a thirty-degree angle. Examining the situation, and doing his best to estimate relative speeds, Belisarius decided that they would be able to use both scorpions for at least three minutes before the port scorpion could no longer be brought to bear.

"I'll handle the starboard scorpion," he announced. "Valentinian, you're in charge of the other one. Eusebius, you keep us supplied with firebombs."

He started to give orders to the twelve other soldiers standing on the platform, but saw there was no need. All of them, experienced artillerymen, had already taken their positions. Each scorpion had a six-man crew, not counting the aimer. Two men stood on either side of each scorpion, ready to turn the windlasses which cranked back the torsion springs. That work was exhausting—especially when done at the breakneck speed required in battle—so each man had a relief standing right behind him. The two men would alternate between shots. A loader fit the bomb into the trough while the sixth man engaged the claw which held the bowstring until the aimer pulled the trigger. Those last two men also had the job of helping the aimer move the heavy trough around and seeing to it that the strut which supported the end was properly adjusted for the desired range.

Everyone hurried to their tasks. Within a minute, the scorpions were ready to fire. Belisarius announced that he would fire first. With the help of his crew, he lined up the heavy trough so that the scorpion was bearing on the nearest of the enemy ships. As soon as he saw the target bracketed between the two "ears" which served as a rough aiming device, he yanked on the little lever which served as the weapon's trigger.

The scorpion bucked from the recoil. Not sixty yards away, the firebomb slammed into the sea with enough force to rupture the clay container. A ball of flame splattered across the waves.

"We're at sea," muttered Belisarius. Somewhat lamely, he added: "I forgot."

In land warfare, he had never had to worry about the heaving of a ship's deck. He had fired the catapult just at the moment when the ship's bow dipped into a trough.

Valentinian fired five seconds later. The cataphract had learned from his general's mistake. He timed his own trigger-pull to correspond with the bow lifting to a wavecrest.

His firebomb lofted its majestic way toward the heavens. Quite some time later, almost sedately, it plopped into the sea. There was no eruption into flame, this time. The firebomb plunged into the water at such a steep angle that, even if the clay container ruptured, the naphtha/saltpeter contents were immediately immersed in water.

Harmlessly, in other words. Not least of all because the firebomb landed two hundred yards away from the nearest enemy vessel.

They were still four hundred yards from their foe. Just near enough to hear the faint sounds of catcalls and jibes.

"Again," growled Belisarius. Gingerly, the loader placed a firebomb in the trough. The other artillerymen ratcheted back the torsion springs and engaged the claw. Belisarius sighted—compensated for the roll, guessed at the pitch—yanked the trigger.

He *did*, this time, manage a respectable trajectory. Quite respectable. Not too high, not too low.

And not, unfortunately, anywhere in the vicinity of an enemy ship. Another harmless plop into the sea.

The catcalls and jibes grew louder.

Valentinian fired.

Extravagant failure; utter humiliation. His second firebomb landed farther from the enemy armada than had his first.

The catcalls and jibes were now like the permanent rumbling of a waterfall.

Belisarius glared at Honorius.

"For the sake of God! This damned ship's—"

He gestured angrily with his hands.

"Pitching, yawing and rolling," filled in Honorius. The sailor shrugged. "I can't help it, general. On this heading—which *you* ordered—we're catching the worst combination of the wave action."

Belisarius restrained his angry glare. More accurately, he transferred it from the seaman to the enemy, who were still taunting him.

He pointed at the fleet.

"Is there any way to get at them without having this miserable damned ship hopping around like a flea?" he demanded.

Honorius gauged the wind and the sea.

"If we head straight for them," he announced. "We'll be running *with* the waves instead of across them. Shouldn't be—"

"*Do it!*" commanded Belisarius.

Honorius sprang to obey.

Aide protested.

Cross the T! Cross the T!

Shut up! If you think this is so easy, you—you—

*damned little fat diamond!—you crawl out of that pouch
and do it yourself.*

Aide said nothing. But the facets were quivering with
some very human sentiments.

SULK. POUT.

Then:

You'll be sorry.

By the time the scorpions were re-armed, Honorius
had altered the vessel's course. They were now rowing
directly toward the enemy. And, just as the sailor had
predicted, the ship was much steadier.

Much steadier.

Belisarius and Valentinian fired almost simultaneously.
A few seconds later, the taunts and catcalls were suddenly replaced by cries of alarm and screams of pain.

The two nearest akatoi erupted in flames. The
rounded bow of the one Belisarius fired upon was
burning fiercely. Valentinian's shot caused even greater
havoc on his target. His firebomb must have ruptured
against the rail of that ship's bow. Instead of engulfing
the bow in flames, the naphtha had spewed across the
ship's deck like a horizontal waterfall of flame and
destruction.

A deck which was packed with heavily armored
cataphracts.

The scene on that ship was pure horror. At least a
dozen cataphracts were being roasted alive in their iron
armor. Several of them, driven to desperation, leapt off
the ship into the sea. There, helplessly dragged down
by the weight of their equipment, they drowned.

But they were dead men, anyway. At least their agony
was over. Those who remained aboard were like human
torches. In their frenzied movements, they helped to
spread the flames further. John's hellish concoction was
like Satan's urine. It stuck to everything it touched—
and it burned, and burned, and burned, and burned.
Within thirty seconds, the entire deck of that ship was
a holocaust.

Then, the holocaust spread. The steersman, seeing

the fiery doom coming toward him, made his own leap into the sea. Unlike the cataphracts, he was not encumbered with armor and could hope to swim.

Swim where? Presumably, to the nearest ship. Unfortunately, by deserting his post he caused the burning ship to head into the wind and waves. The corbita coming immediately behind was unable to avoid a collision.

The flames now spread to that ship. Most of the spreading came from the entangled sails. But some of it came from the frenzied human torches which clambered aboard.

Two ships were now completely out of action.

Neither Belisarius nor Valentinian paid much attention. They were too busy dealing with their next victims.

For Belisarius, that victim was the same as his first. Coming closer to the ship whose bow he had already set afire—now, at a range of three hundred yards—the general aimed his scorpion amidships.

He was deliberately trying to imitate Valentinian's shot. His first shot missed—too low, scattering flames across the sea fifty yards before the target. But, after a quick adjustment of the trough's strut, he succeeded with the next shot. His firebomb ruptured against the enemy ship's railing and spewed destruction across its packed deck.

That ship was out of action.

As he waited for his artillerymen to rearm the scorpion, Belisarius observed Valentinian's next shot. Valentinian was also trying to copy his first success.

He misjudged, however, and his shot went a little high.

No matter. Both he and Belisarius learned another lesson in the brand new world of naval artillery warfare.

Sails and rigging, struck head-on by a firebomb, burn like oil-soaked kindling. Within five seconds, that ship was effectively dismasted, wallowing helplessly in the waves.

Yet—

The cataphracts standing on the deck below were—for the moment at least—unharmed.

Unharmed, and filled with fury. Belisarius could see dozens of them beginning to bring their powerful bows to bear. Less than three hundred yards away—well within range of cataphract archery. In moments, his little ship would be swept by a volley of arrows. The rowers below would be reasonably safe in their enclosed shelters. But all of the men on the wood-castle had only the low walls to protect them.

"Ready!" cried the loader.

Belisarius threw his weight against the heavy trough. The loader and the claw-man helped swivel the scorpion around. As soon as it bore, Belisarius yanked the trigger.

The cataphracts on the enemy ship were just starting to draw back their bows. Some of them loosed their arrows—but, flinching, missed their aim. Most of the cataphracts, seeing the firebomb speeding right at them, simply ducked.

The side of their ship erupted in a ball of flame. There was not the instant destruction which they feared, true. Belisarius' shot struck too far below the rail to scatter the naphtha across the deck in that horrible waterfall of flame. But, soon enough, they would be dead men. And they knew it.

Trapped on a vessel which would burn to the waterline. Trapped in heavy armor. Trapped in the middle of the Bosporus.

Belisarius' ship plowed past them at a range of two hundred yards. He could see some of the enemy cataphracts, through gaps in the black and oily smoke. They were no longer even thinking about their bows, however. All of them that he could see were frantically getting out of their armor.

In less than ten minutes, he realized, he had destroyed half of the Army of Bithynia's cataphract force. But he did not have time to find any satisfaction in the deed. Belatedly, he realized that his reckless straight-ahead charge, for all its immediate effectiveness, had placed he and his men in mortal peril. Instead of standing off at a distance and bombarding his enemy, he was plunging straight into their massed fleet of ships. There were archers on all of those ships—hundreds of them. *Thousands* of them.

Within two minutes, they would be inundated with arrows.

A voice, pouting:

I told you so.

Sulky self-satisfaction:

Cross the T. Cross the T.

Valentinian had already reached the same conclusion. "We're in a back alley knife fight, now. Only one thing to do."

Belisarius nodded. He knew the answer to their dilemma.

Valentinian had taught it to him, years ago.

Chop the other mindless idiot first.

He turned to Honorius. The seaman's face was pale—he, too, recognized the danger—but was otherwise calm and composed.

"Straight ahead," he commanded. "As fast as you can. We'll try to cut our way through."

As he brought his scorpion to bear on the next ship in line, he caught a glimpse of Valentinian crouched over his own weapon. An instant later, the cataphract's scorpion bucked. The deck of a nearby corbita was transformed into the same hell-on-earth which had already visited four cataphract-laden akatoi.

Valentinian grinned, like a weasel.

Seeing that vicious grin, Belisarius found it impossible not to copy it. Time after time, in years gone by, as he trained a young officer in bladesmanship, Valentinian had lectured him on the stupidity of fighting with a knife in close quarters.

Valentinian should know, of course. It was a stupidity he had committed more than once. And had survived, because he was the best close-quarter knife-fighter Belisarius had ever met.

He heard his loader:

"Ready!"

The closest enemy ship was a corbita, but Belisarius aimed past it, at the next approaching akatos. He feared the archery of those cataphracts more than he did the bowmanship of common soldiers.

He fired. Missed. Although the ship was hardly pitching at all, it was still rolling, and his shot had been twenty yards too far to the right.

His men rearmed the scorpion and Belisarius immediately fired. Another miss—too high, this time. The bomb sailed right over the akatos' mast.

Windlasses spun, the men turning them grunting with exertion. The loader quickly placed the bomb, the clawman checked the trigger.

"Ready!" called the loader. Belisarius took aim—more carefully, this time—and yanked the trigger.

For a moment, he thought he had fired too high again. But his firebomb caught the mast two-thirds of the way up and engulfed the akatos' rigging in flames.

Behind him, he heard Honorius call out an order to the steersman. Belisarius could not make sense of the specific words—they were spoken in that peculiar jargon known only to seamen. But, within seconds, as he saw their ship change its heading, he understood what Honorius was doing. The seaman was also learning—quickly—some of the principal lessons of the new style of naval warfare.

That akatos is out of action, but its cataphracts can still use their bows. Solution? Simple. Sail somewhere else. Stay out of archery range. Let it burn. Let it burn its way to hell.

He started to tell Valentinian to pick out the cataphract-bearing akatoi first, but saw there was no need. Valentinian was already doing so. His next shot sailed past a nearby corbita, toward an akatos at the extreme range of almost five hundred yards. Valentinian was as good with a scorpion as he was with a bow. He had deliberately shot high, Belisarius saw, knowing that a strike in the rigging was almost as good as one of those terrible deck-sweeping rail shots.

Another akatos began burning furiously.

"Ready!" called his loader.

Belisarius scanned the ship-crowded sea hastily, looking for one of the two remaining akatoi.

He saw none. Hidden, probably, behind the close-packed corbita. Their swift charge had placed them in the middle of the enemy armada.

There was no time to waste. One of those corbita was within two hundred yards. Common soldiers could shoot arrows also. Not as well as cataphracts, true, but—at close range—good enough. Already, arrows from that approaching corbita were plunging into the sea within yards of their ship.

He aimed his scorpion. Missed. Fired again. By luck—he had been aiming at the rigging—his shot struck the rail and poured fury across the enemy's deck.

Valentinian struck another corbita. Then, cursed. His shot had been low. The firebomb had erupted almost at the waterline. The enemy's hull was starting to burn, but very slowly.

Hurriedly, Valentinian fired again. This time, cursed bitterly. He had missed completely—his shot sailing ten feet over the enemy's deck.

Meantime, Belisarius set another corbita's rigging aflame. Then, after two misses, set another aflame.

They were surrounded by enemy ships, now, several of them within bow range. Arrows were pouring down on them like a hail storm. The rowers' shelter sprouted arrows like a porcupine. In his own little cabin at the stern of the ship, the steering officer was crouched low. The thin walls of his shelter had been penetrated by several arrow-heads. But he kept calling out his orders, calmly and loudly.

Arrows thunked into the walls of the wood-castle.

Fortunately, due to the height of the fighting platform, the men on it were sheltered from arrows fired on a flat trajectory from the low-hulled corbita. But some of those arrows, fired by better or simply luckier archers, were coming in on an arched trajectory.

One of the windlass-crankers suddenly cried out in pain. An arrow had looped over the walls and plunged into his shoulder. He fell—partly from pain, and partly from a desire to find shelter beneath the low wall. His relief immediately stepped forward and began frantically cranking the windlass.

As he waited—and to give himself something to think about other than oncoming missiles—Belisarius watched Valentinian fire a third firebomb at the same misbegotten corbita.

Belisarius had never seen Valentinian miss anything, three times in a row. He didn't now, either. The shot was perfect. The firebomb hit the rail right before the mast, spewing death over the deck and destruction into the rigging.

His loader:

"Ready!"

Belisarius turned, aimed—

Nothing. Empty sea.

They had sailed right through the enemy fleet.

A movement in the corner of his eye. He swiveled the scorpion hurriedly, aimed—

A dromon, scudding across the waves, right toward them. John of Rhodes, standing in the bow, hands on hips, scowling fiercely.

His first words, in the powerful carrying voice of an experienced naval officer:

"Are you out of your fucking mind?"

His next:

"You could have wrecked my ship!"

A minute later, after the galley was drawn alongside, the Rhodesman scampered aboard and stalked across the deck. Before he even reached Belisarius, he was gesturing with his hands. Making an odd sort of motion, as if cutting one hand with the other.

"What were you thinking?" he demanded hotly. "What were you thinking?" In full stump now, back and forth, back and forth: "Imbecile! This is a fucking *artillery* ship!" One hand sawing across the other: "In the name of God! Even a fucking general should have been able to figure it out! Even a fucking landsman! You stay *away* from the fucking enemy! You try to bring your artillery to bear without getting close! You—you—"

Hands sawing, hands sawing.

Belisarius, smiling crookedly: "Like 'crossing a T,' you mean to say?"

John's eyes widened. His hands paused in their sawing. Fury faded, replaced by interest.

"Hey. That's a good way of putting it. I like that. 'Crossing the T.' Got a nice ring to it."

Another voice. Sulky. Self-satisfied:

I told you so.

Belisarius chuckled.

"I suppose my naval tactics *were* a bit primitive," he admitted.

Image:

A man. Stooped, filthy, clad in rough-cured animal skins. In his hand he clutches an axe. The blade of the weapon is a crudely shaped piece of stone, lashed to the handle with rawhide.

He is standing on a log, rolling wildly down a river. Hammering fiercely at another man, armed and clad as he is, standing on the same log.

Stone ax against stone ax.

Just ahead is a waterfall.

Chapter 26

After Belisarius and Valentinian were aboard the dromon, Belisarius stared up at John of Rhodes standing on the pamphylos' wood-castle.

"Are you certain, John?" he asked.

The naval officer nodded his head firmly.

"Be off, Belisarius!" Then, with a wicked grin:

"I'll say this much—you may be the craziest ship captain who ever tried to commit suicide, and certainly the most lethal."

He waved his hand about, encompassing half the Bosporus in that gesture.

"You destroyed six out of the eight akatoi and another half dozen corbita. And I sank three corbita with the galley. That's well over a third of Aegidius' entire army and *three-fourths* of his cataphracts. Look at them!"

Belisarius scanned the Bosporus. Even to his lands-man's eye, it was obvious that the enemy fleet was scattering in fear and confusion.

A sudden thought came to his mind. John voiced it before he could speak.

"Besides, I think Aegidius is dead. He was probably aboard one of the akatoi, which means that the odds against his survival are three-to-one."

Belisarius nodded.

"That has all the signs of a leaderless army, if I'm reading the ship movements correctly."

John snorted. "They're like so many motherless ducklings paddling every which way." Again, he waved his hand.

"Be off, Belisarius. You're needed in Constantinople now, not here. The dromon will bear you to shore faster than any of those ships can reach land. I, meanwhile—" He patted the scorpion next to him. The wicked grin returned in full force. "—will continue to put the fear of God in those bastards." With a fierce glower: "From a *distance*, like an intelligent man."

Belisarius smiled and turned away. Then, hearing John's next words, smiled broadly. "'*Crossing the T.*' I like that!"

At the general's signal, the war galley's *keleustes*—the rowing officer; literally, the "orderer"—immediately began calling the time. The galley's oars dipped into the water. Swiftly, the dromon headed to shore.

For a time, Belisarius watched the enemy ships milling around aimlessly in the Bosporus. The ones nearest to John's artillery vessel, he saw, were already trying to evade the Rhodesman's approach. One of those enemy ships, apparently, had had enough. The corbita was heading directly back to Chalcedon, on the Asian side of the Straits.

Soon enough, a half-dozen of the corbita were following. Among the remaining ships in the enemy armada, confusion still reigned. A small cluster of the ships—seven in all, led by one of the surviving akatoi—were heading toward Portus Caesarii. Someone among the surviving cataphracts in the Army of Bithynia—Aegidius himself, possibly; more likely, one of his top subordinates—had apparently decided to continue with their treasonous scheme. But, cautiously, they were now planning to land in the more distant harbor.

A wordless cry of triumph coming from Menander drew his eyes back to the main fleet. One of the corbita in that milling mob of ships, he saw, was burning fiercely. John had struck his first blow.

The confusion in the main body of the traitor fleet was dispelled. The majority of the remaining ships, within a minute, were fleeing back across the Bosporus. Only four of them—including, unfortunately, the last of the cataphract-bearing akatoi—decided to make for Portus Caesarii.

Belisarius noticed that Ashot was now standing next to him. Ashot was the Armenian cataphract who led the small party which Antonina had sent to meet him in Egypt. Antonina and Maurice had chosen him for that mission, among other things, because Ashot was one of the few cataphracts among Belisarius' bucellarii who had any experience as a seaman.

"What do you think?" he asked.

Ashot immediately understood all the parameters of the question. The Armenian pointed toward the artillery vessel.

"If I were John, I'd follow the ships retreating back to Chalcedon. Harry them mercilessly. Put them completely out of the action. Leave the ones heading toward Portus Caesarii for Sittas and Hermogenes to deal with. They shouldn't have any trouble."

For a moment, Ashot gauged the eleven ships now heading for the westernmost harbor on Constantinople's southern shore.

"Two akatoi," he murmured, "and nine corbita. To be on the safe side, let's call it three hundred cataphracts and three thousand infantry. Against Sittas' five hundred cataphracts and the two thousand infantrymen Hermogenes brought."

Ashot spat into the sea. "Lambs to the slaughter," he concluded.

Belisarius smiled at the Armenian's ferocious expression. Then, curious to see Ashot's reaction, he remarked:

"Heavy odds, against the infantry."

The Armenian sneered.

"Are you kidding? Against *Hermogenes'* infantry?" The cataphract shook his head firmly. "You've been gone for almost a year and a half, general. You haven't seen what

Hermogenes has done with his troops. And the ones he brought to Constantinople were his best units. The finest Roman infantry since the days of the Principate. They'll chew their way right through that Bithynian garbage."

Belisarius nodded. He was not surprised. Still, he was gratified.

"The enemy'll be disheartened, too," added Ashot. "Confused—half-leaderless, probably—scared shitless."

Again, he spat into the ocean. "Lambs to the slaughter. Lambs to the slaughter."

Belisarius saw that John had apparently reached the same conclusion as Ashot. The artillery ship was veering off in pursuit of the corbita retreating to Chalcedon.

"Will he catch any of them?" he asked.

"Not a chance," replied the Armenian instantly. "They're sailing almost before the wind, on that heading. The advantage now is with the heavier corbita and their square-rigged sails, especially since the rowers on John's galley are bound to be tired. But once they reach Chalcedon, those ships are trapped. John can stand off in the mouth of the harbor and bombard them with impunity. He'll turn the whole fleet into so much kindling."

Another spit into the sea. "The Army of Bithynia's out of it, general. Except for the few who are heading for southern Constantinople."

For a moment, Belisarius examined the cataphract standing next to him. The Armenian was now watching the enemy ships sailing toward Portus Caesarii, oblivious to his general's gaze.

Abruptly, Belisarius made his decision.

"In a few months, Ashot, I'll be promoting several of the men to hecatontarch. You're one of them."

The Armenian's eyes widened. He stared at the general.

"You've only got one hecatontarch—_Maurice_. And I don't—" Ashot groped for words. Like all of Belisarius' cataphracts, he had a towering respect for Maurice.

Belisarius smiled.

"Oh, Maurice'll be promoted also. A chiliarch he'll be, now."

Ashot was still wide-eyed. Belisarius shook his head.

"We're in a new world, Ashot. I never felt I needed more than a few hundred bucellarii, before. But among the many things I learned while I was in India is that the Malwa don't have genuine elite troops. Not ones they can rely on, at least. That's a Roman advantage I intend to maximize."

He scratched his chin, estimating.

"Five thousand bucellarii. Seven thousand, if possible. Not at once, of course—I want them to be elite troops, not warm bodies. But that's my goal." His smile grew crooked. "You'll probably wind up a chiliarch yourself, soon enough. I'll need several for all those troops, with Maurice in overall command."

Ashot, again, groped for words.

"I don't think—that's a lot of Thracians, general. Five thousand? *Seven* thousand?" Hesitantly: "And I'm Armenian. I get along well with the Thracians you've got now, that's true. They've known me for a long time. But I don't know that new Thracian boys are going to be all that happy with an Armenian—"

"If they can't handle it," replied Belisarius harshly, "I'll pitch them out on their ear." His smile returned. "Besides—who said they'd all be Thracians?" He chuckled, seeing Ashot's frown.

"I don't have time, any longer, for anyone's delicate sensibilities. I want five thousand bucellarii—the best cataphracts anywhere in the world—as fast as I can get them. A big chunk—possibly the majority—will be Thracian. But they'll be lots of Illyrians and as many Isaurians as we can find who are willing to become cataphracts. Isaurians are tough as nails. Beyond that—" He shrugged. "Anyone who can fight well, and can learn to become a cataphract. Greeks, Armenians, Egyptians, barbarians— even Jews. I don't care."

Ashot had overcome his initial surprise, and was now tugging on his beard thoughtfully. "Expensive, general.

Five thousand bucellarii—even if you're not as generous as usual—you're looking at—"

He broke off, remembering. He had seen the Malwa treasure which Belisarius had brought back from India. True, Belisarius had given three-fourths of that bribe to Shakuntala. But the remainder was still an immense fortune, by any except imperial standards.

Ashot nodded.

"Yes, you can afford it. Even with liberal pay and equipment bonus, you've got enough to cover five thousand bucellarii for at least four years. After that—"

"After that," said Belisarius coldly, "there'll either be plenty of booty or we'll all be dead."

Ashot nodded. "A new world," he murmured.

A cry from Anastasius drew their attention.

"There's Sittas! I can see him!"

Belisarius and Ashot looked forward. The dromon was just passing through the double breakwaters which marked the entrance to the small Harbor of Hormisdas, the private harbor of Rome's emperors. Behind the harbor rose the hills of Constantinople. The Great Palace, though it was nearby, was hidden behind the slope. But they could see the upper levels of the Hippodrome. And they could hear the roar of the mob gathered within it.

Belisarius' eyes were drawn lower, to a large figure standing on the nearest wharf.

Sure enough, Sittas. Standing next to him were Hermogenes and Irene.

As they drew nearer, Sittas bellowed.

"*What took you so long? Don't you know there's a war to be fought?*"

The boar, in full fury.

The mob, too, was in full fury. The seats in the Hippodrome were packed with armed men. Blues on one side, of course, Greens on the other. Even during this unusual alliance, the faction leaders were wise enough not to mix their men.

Balban, watching the scene, was delighted. Narses, standing next to him, was not.

"Almost forty thousand of them!" exclaimed the Malwa spymaster. "I'd been hoping for thirty, at the most."

Narses almost spoke the words: "I'd been *dreading* more than twenty thousand." But he restrained himself. There was no point, now, in getting into another futile argument.

Called upon to settle some petty dispute between the factions, Balban left. Narses and Ajatasutra remained, standing in the fortified loge on the southeast side of the Hippodrome which was called the *kathisma*.

The emperor's loge, that was. Reserved for his use alone. By seizing it, the conspirators had announced their full intentions for all the world to see.

Narses glanced over his shoulder. At the rear of the loge was a barred door. That door was the only entrance to the kathisma, other than the open wall at the front. Behind it was a covered passage which connected the emperor's box in the Hippodrome to the Great Palace.

The door was barred on both sides, now. On his side, Narses saw eight Malwa kshatriya standing guard. On the other side, he knew, would be an even greater number of the Emperor's personal bodyguard, the excubitores, anxiously fingering their weapons.

The passage from the Hippodrome to the Great Palace was now the frontier between Justinian and those who sought his overthrow.

Narses looked away. That frontier would fall too, and soon. Brought down by further treachery.

Ajatasutra's low voice penetrated his musings.

"You do not seem to share Balban's enthusiasm for our massive army."

Narses sneered. "Let me explain to you the reality of the Hippodrome factions, Ajatasutra. Both the Greens and the Blues have about five thousand men who can be considered real street fighters. Charioteers and their entourage. Gamblers and their enforcers. That sort. Serious thugs."

He pointed out over the vast expanse of the Hippodrome. "Those will be the ones you see carrying real weapons—well-made swords, and spears—and wearing a helmet. Maybe even a bit of armor."

His lips twisted further. "Then, each faction will have another five thousand men—at the most—who can handle themselves in a fight. On the level of a tavern brawl, that is. The rest—"

His pointing finger made a little flipping gesture. Dismissive, contemptuous—almost obscene.

"Pure rabble. Carrion-eaters, drawn by the smell of rotting flesh."

Narses lowered his finger. His sneer became a scowl. "I remember a conversation I had with Belisarius, once. The general told me that one of the worst errors people made when it came to military affairs was to confuse quantity with quality. A large, incompetent army, he told me, got in its own way more than it did the enemy's. And then, if they suffer a setback, the mob's panic will infect the good troops."

Narses sighed.

"So let's hope there's no setback. I wouldn't trust that mob in a pinch any more than I'd trust so many rats."

Ajatasutra shrugged. "Don't forget, Narses. We still have four hundred kshatriya to stiffen their resolve. With their Veda weapons. That should hearten the mob."

"We'll soon find out." Again, Narses pointed. The gesture, this time, was purely indicative. "Look. They've finished setting up the rockets."

Ajatasutra followed the pointing finger. At the far northeast side of the Hippodrome, where the race track made its curve, the Malwa kshatriya had erected several rocket troughs on the dirt floor of the arena. The troughs were pointed upward at an angle, aimed directly across the Hippodrome.

Balban wanted to cement the allegiance of the factions with a demonstration of the Veda weapons. The spymaster was convinced that the Romans would be filled with superstitious awe. For his part, Narses was skeptical. In their own crude way, the Hippodrome thugs were not unsophisticated. They *were* residents of Constantinople, after all.

But the eunuch had not objected to the plan. While he did not think the thugs would be overawed by superstition, they *would* be impressed by the sheer power of the devices.

Watching the last few Blues and Greens scampering along the tiers, Narses smiled. The Malwa had assured the factions that the rockets would pass safely over the southwest wall of the Hippodrome, but the thugs were taking no chances. The entire southwest half of the Hippodrome was empty.

At the base of the troughs, the kshatriyas had piled up bundles of elephant hide, which they were wetting down from a nearby drinking fountain. The Hippodrome was provided with many of those fountains, fed by a small aqueduct. The same water was being used to wet down the large wooden palisades which the Malwa had erected behind the firing troughs. Despite their assurances to the faction leaders, the kshatriya had too much experience with the fickle rockets to take any chances. Most of the Malwa soldiers would stand behind those barricades when the missiles were fired.

"Here comes Hypatius," announced Ajatasutra. "And Pompeius."

Narses glanced down at the stairs leading from the Hippodrome to the imperial loge. The stairs ended in a wide stone platform just in front of the kathisma. For reasons of security, there was no direct access to the imperial loge from the Hippodrome. But dignitaries saluting the emperor could stand on that platform and gaze up at the august presence, seated on his throne above them. And separated from any would-be assassins by a nine-foot-high wall.

Clambering up those stone steps, escorted by Balban, came the two nephews of the former emperor Anastasius.

The faces of Hypatius and Pompeius were pale from anxiety. Their steps faltered; their lips trembled. But, still, they came on. Greed and ambition, in the end, had conquered fear.

"*Finally,*" grumbled Narses.

A minute later, the new arrivals were hoisted over the wall into the imperial loge. The royal nephews made heavy going of the effort, despite the assistance of several kshatriya. Balban, despite his heavyset build, managed the task quite easily.

Seeing Narses' scowl, Balban smiled cheerfully.

"You are too pessimistic, my friend. Such a gloomy man! Everything is in place, now. The factions are here. The kshatriya are here. The new emperor is here. The Army of Bithynia is on its way. And the Cappadocian is about to slide in the knife in the Great Palace."

Suddenly, from beyond the barred door leading to the Great Palace, shouts were heard. Cries of alarm, from the excubitores. Then, the sounds of clashing steel.

Balban spread his arms, beaming.

"You see? John has unleashed his bucellarii in the palace. What could go wrong now?"

John of Cappadocia's final treachery, when it came, was brutally simple.

One moment, he was standing on the floor of the small audience chamber where Justinian was holding his emergency council, vehemently denying Theodora's latest charge against him:

"It is absolutely false, Your Majesty—I swear it! The excubitores in this room"—he waved at the spear-carrying soldiers standing along the walls and behind the thrones—"are the very finest of your personal body-guard."

"Which *you* selected," snarled Theodora.

John spread his hands, in a placating gesture. "That is one of my responsibilies as praetorian prefect."

Justinian nodded his head firmly. The five other ministers in the room copied the gesture, albeit with more subtlety. They had no wish to draw down Theodora's rage.

The Empress ignored them. Theodora half-rose from her throne, pointing her finger at the Cappadocian. Her voice, for all the fury roiling within it, was cold and almost calm.

"*You are a traitor, John of Cappadocia.* Irene Macrembolitissa has told me that you have suborned a dozen of the Emperor's excubitores."

Suddenly, the clangor of combat erupted beyond the closed doors of the council chamber. John of Cappadocia turned his head for a moment. When he faced forward again, he smiled at the Empress and said:

"She is wrong, Empress."

The Cappadocian made a quick chopping motion with his hand.

The four exbubitores standing at the rear of the chamber strode forward and seized the Emperor and the Empress by the arms, pinning them to the thrones. Ten others, standing along the walls, immediately leveled their spears and stabbed the six remaining bodyguards. The attacks were so swift and merciless that only one of the loyal excubitores was able to deflect the first spear-thrust. But he died a moment later, from a second spear-thrust under his arm.

"It was fourteen!" cackled John of Cappadocia.

Ten of the traitor bodyguards now lunged at the five ministers standing to one side. Four of those ministers, stunned by the sudden havoc, never even moved. They died where they stood, gape-mouthed and goggle-eyed.

"As it happens," giggled the praetorian prefect, "all fourteen are in this room."

The fifth minister, the *primicerius* of notaries, was quicker-witted. Despite his advanced age and scholarly appearance, he nimbly dodged a spear-thrust and scampered toward the door. He managed to get his hand on the door-latch before a hurled spear took him in the back. A moment later, two more spears plunged into his slumping body.

Even then, even as he fell to his knees, the *primicerius* feebly tried to open the door. But the first of the traitor bodyguards had reached him, and a savage sword strike sent the old man's head flying.

John watched the minister's head roll to a stop against an upturned rug.

"I made sure they were all here today, of course. That's my job, you know. As praetorian prefect."

He smiled at the Emperor and the Empress. Justinian was silent, pale with shock, limp in his captors' hands. Theodora had also ceased struggling against the hands holding her, but she was neither pale nor silent.

Furiously, she hissed:

"*Only fourteen, traitor?* That leaves five hundred loyal bodyguards to cut you down!"

John of Cappadocia laughed gaily. With a mocking bow, he waved at the great door leading to the corridor beyond. Not five seconds later, the door burst open. Gore-stained soldiers poured into the audience chamber. They were grinning widely and gesturing triumphantly with their bloody swords. They wore the livery of John of Cappadocia's bucellarii.

"All of them, John!" howled one of his retainers. "I swear—*all of them!*"

One of his fellows demurred: "Not quite. There's a number of excubitores forted up in the mint. And all of Theodora's bodyguards are still in the Gynaeceum."

"Deal with them," commanded the praetorian prefect. His bucellarii immediately left the chamber.

John turned back to the imperial couple. Theodora spit at the Cappadocian. John dodged the spittle, then returned the Empress' contempt with a cheerful smile, before turning his gaze to Justinian.

"Do it," he commanded.

The two excubitores holding Justinian hauled the Emperor from his throne and manhandled him off the dais onto the carpeted floor of the chamber. Brutally, a third bodyguard kicked Justinian's feet out from under him. A moment later, the Emperor was on his knees, bent double. Each of his arms was pinioned. Another excubitore cuffed away the tiara, seized Justinian's hair in both hands, and jerked the Emperor's head back.

Justinian's eyes, rising, met the eyes of the torturer entering the room through a side door. The man bore an iron rod in his hands. The hands wore gauntlets. The tip of the rod glowed red.

It was the last thing the Emperor would ever see, and he knew it. He barely had time to begin his scream before the rod plunged into his left eye. A moment later, the right. The torturer was quick, and expert.

The Emperor's scream, while it lasted, seemed to shake the very walls of the chamber. But it was brief; very brief. Within seconds, sheer agony had driven consciousness from Justinian's brain. The bodyguard holding his head relinquished his grip. A moment later, so did the excubitores holding his arms. The Emperor collapsed onto the floor.

There was no blood. The red-hot tip of the iron rod had cauterized the terrible wounds as soon as it made them.

Which John of Cappadocia immediately pointed out.

"You see how merciful I am, Theodora?" he demanded. Another mocking bow. "A different man—such as the cruel and despicable creature you have so often proclaimed me to be—would have murdered your husband. But I satisfy myself with mere blinding."

Gaily: "And an expert blinding at that!" Then, with the casual insouciance of a connoisseur:

"It's quite an art, you know. Most people don't appreciate that. It's very difficult to blind a man without killing him outright. Less than one out of ten survive the average torturer." He gestured grandly at the gauntleted man who had mutilated the Emperor. "But I use only the best! The very best! I estimate—" He paused, studying Justinian's sprawled body with exaggerated studiousness. Concluded: "—that your husband has—*one chance in three!*"

Throughout, Theodora said nothing. She did not look at Justinian. She simply kept her eyes on John of Cappadocia. Black eyes, like the gates of damnation.

Even John, in his triumph, flinched from that hellgaze.

"There'll be none of your haughty ways now, bitch," he snarled. He pointed to Justinian.

"One chance in three, I say. *Unless* he's given immediate medical attention. The *best* medical care."

Sneering: "Which, of course, I also happen to have available. *For a price.*"

Theodora said nothing. The hell-gaze never wavered.

John looked away. His eyes fastened on Justinian. The Cappadocian seemed to draw strength from that piteous sight. Although his eyes avoided Theodora, his voice was cold and certain:

"Now that Justinian has been blinded, he can no longer be Emperor. You know the law of Rome, Theodora. *No mutilated man can wear the purple.* Neither the Senate, nor the populace, nor the army will accept him. As Emperor, *he is finished.*"

The sneer returned in full force. But, still, his eyes avoided Theodora's.

"You may—*may*—still be able to save his life. What there is of it. *If* you offer no further resistance. *If* you publicly hail Hypatius as the new Emperor."

When Theodora finally spoke, her voice matched her gaze. Hell-voice.

"I will do no such thing. If you bring the worm Hypatius before me, I will spit on him. If you drag me to the Hippodrome, I will curse him before the mob."

She jerked her right arm loose from the excubitores who held it. Pointed to Justinian:

"All you have done is blind a man who would someday have been blinded by death. You threaten to kill a man, when no man lives forever. *Do it, then.* Kill me with him. I am the Empress. I would rather die than yield."

She reared in her throne. "There is an ancient saying, which I approve: *Royalty is a good burial-shroud.*"

Hell-gaze; hell-voice:

"*Do your murder, then, traitor. Kill us, coward.*"

John clenched his fist, opened his mouth. But before he could utter a word, one of his bucellarii sprinted into the room. He skidded to a halt, almost tripping over the rumpled carpet. Sweat poured from his brow. He gasped for air.

Half-shouting; half-whispering:

"The Army of Bithynia's been routed at sea! Half their ships burned! Most of the survivors fled back to Chalcedon!"

Gasping:

"They say an army's moving toward the Hippodrome. Cataphracts. They say"—gasp—"the whore Antonina is leading them."

Hoarsely:

"And they say—*Belisarius is here!*"

Theodora's pealing laugh had no more humor in it than Satan's own.

Hell-laugh.

"You are all dead men. Kill us, traitors! Do it, cowards! As surely as the sun rises, you will join us before sundown."

Every traitor in the room stared at the Empress.

John of Cappadocia was famous for his sneer. But Theodora's sneer, compared to his, was like the fangs of a tigress matched to a rodent's incisors.

"Do it, cowards! Boast to Belisarius that you killed his Emperor and Empress. Do it! Tell the loyal man of your treachery. Do it! Tell the man of honor that you are murderers. Do it!"

Hell-sneer:

"After he spits your heads on his spears. After the flesh rots from your skulls. He will grind your bones to powder. He will feed them to Thracian hogs. He will have the hog-shit smeared on your tombs."

Silence.

"Do it, cowards. Kill us, traitors."

John snarled wordless fury.

"Keep them here!" he commanded the excubitores. "Until I return!"

He stalked out of the chamber, followed by his retainer. By the time he reached the door, he was almost running.

Once in the corridor beyond, he did begin to run. But Theodora's taunt followed faster.

"I will await you in the Pit of Damnation, John of Cappadocia! Before Satan takes you, I will burn out your eyes with my urine!"

After the Cappadocian was gone, Theodora lowered her eyes to Justinian's body.

"Release me," she commanded.

Hesitantly, but inevitably—as if giving way to a force of nature—the excubitores relinquished their grip. They were traitors, now; but they had been too many years in the imperial service to refuse *that* voice.

The Empress rose and walked down from the dais, onto the floor. She knelt beside Justinian. The Emperor was still unconscious. Firmly, but carefully, Theodora rolled him into her arms. She brushed the hair back from his ruined face and stared at the gaping, puckered wounds which had once been her husband's eyes.

When she spoke, her voice held not a trace of any emotion. It was simply cold, cold.

"There is wine in the adjoining room. Fetch it, traitors. I need to bathe his wounds."

For an instant, something almost like humor entered her voice. Cold, cold humor: "I come from the streets of Alexandria. Do you think I never saw a man blinded before? Did you think I would shrink from death and torture?"

Humor left. Ice remained: "Fetch me wine. *Do it, cowards.*"

Two excubitores hastened to obey her command. For a moment, they jostled each other in the doorway, before sorting out their precedence.

A minute later, one of the excubitores returned, bearing two bottles. The other did not.

Theodora soaked the hem of her imperial robes with wine. Gently, she began washing Justinian's wounds.

The man who had brought her the wine slipped out of the door. Less than a minute later, another followed. Then another. Then two.

Theodora never looked up. Another man left. Another. Two.

When there were only four excubitores left in the room, the Empress—still without raising her head—murmured:

"You are all dead men."

Hell-murmur.

All four scurried from the chamber. Their footsteps in the corridor echoed in the empty room. Quick footsteps, at first. Soon enough, running.

Now, Theodora raised her head. She stared at the door through which the traitors had fled.

Hell-stare. Hell-hiss:

You are all dead men. Wherever you go, I will track you down. Wherever you hide, I will find you. I will have you blinded. By the clumsiest meatcutter in the world.

She lowered her head; turned her black eyes upon her husband's face.

Slowly, very slowly, the hell-gaze faded. After a time, the first of her tears began bathing Justinian's face.

There were not many of those tears. Not many at all. They disappeared into the wine with which Theodora cleansed her husband's wounds, as if they possessed the wine's own hard nature. A constant little trickle of tears, from the world's littlest, hardest, and most constant heart.

Chapter 27

The first rocket awed the mob in the Hippodrome. By sheer good fortune, the missile soared almost straight and exploded while it was in plain view of the entire crowd. A great flaming burst in the sky, just over the unoccupied southwestern tiers.

The faction thugs roared their approval. Many of them rose in their seats and shook their weapons triumphantly.

In the imperial box, Hypatius and Pompeius seemed suitably impressed as well, judging from their gapes. But Narses, watching them from behind, spotted the subtle nuances.

Hypatius' gape was accompanied by the beginning of a frown. The newly crowned "Emperor"—his tiara wobbling atop his head—was not entirely pleased. The crowd's roar of approval for the rockets was noticeably more enthusiastic than the roar with which they had greeted his "ascension to the throne," not five minutes earlier.

His brother Pompeius' gape was likewise accompanied by a frown. But, in his case, the frown indicated nothing more than thoughtfulness. Pompeius was already planning to overthrow his brother.

In the rear of the kathisma, Narses sneered. This, too, he knew, was part of the Malwa plot. The Indians intended the overthrow of Justinian to set in motion an entire round of civil wars, one contender for the throne battling another. Years of civil war—like the worst days of the post-Antonine era, three centuries earlier—while the Malwa gobbled up Persia without interference and made ready their final assault on Rome itself.

As always, Narses thought the Malwa were too clever for their own good. They would have done better to stick with their initial scheme—simply to encourage Justinian's ambitions to conquer the west. That would have served their purpose, without any of the attendant risks of an armed insurrection.

But Narses, slowly and carefully, had convinced them otherwise. The eunuch had his own ambitions, which required Justinian's removal. He would risk the Malwa's future plans for the sake of his own immediate accession to power. There would *be* no civil wars. Narses would put an end to them, quickly and ruthlessly.

The eunuch watched another rocket soar into the sky. The trajectory of this one was markedly more erratic than that of the first. By the time the rocket exploded, it had looped out of sight beneath the northwestern wall of the Hippodrome.

Narses sighed with exasperation. He, too, was being excessively clever. But—he was old. He had little choice. Narses did not have the time to wait, for years, while Justinian exhausted the Roman Empire in his grandiose attempt to reconstruct its ancient glory.

Another rocket. Properly behaved, this one. But the fourth, after an initially promising lift-off, suddenly arced down and exploded in the Hippodrome itself. Fortunately, the section of the tiers where it landed was unoccupied.

Narses sighed again.

Too clever.

He was startled by another explosion. A section of the tiers near the Blue faction erupted in flame and smoke. No one was hurt, however.

Narses frowned. He had seen no rocket.

Another explosion. This one erupted on the fringe of the Blue crowd, killing several thugs and hurtling shredded bodies onto their nearby comrades.

Balban, seated next to the "Emperor" Hypatius, leapt to his feet. He turned and glared at Ajatasutra.

"Did you give grenades to the factions, you fool?" he demanded.

Ajatasutra began to deny the charge, but fell silent. There was no need for his denial.

The truth of the matter was suddenly obvious.

A series of explosions now rocked the tiers, killing Blues and Greens indiscriminately. The giant mob was scrambling to their feet, shouting and brandishing their weapons.

Brandishing them, not in triumph, but at their new enemy—who was even now marching into the Hippodrome through the wide entrance in the unoccupied southwestern portion.

Cataphracts—on foot, for a wonder—flanking a small army of men—and women?—who were hurling grenades at the Hippodrome mob. *With slings!*

Everyone in the kathisma lunged to their feet, now, and pressed forward against the stone wall overlooking the Hippodrome.

Everyone except Narses. Who simply remained in his seat, sighing. Faintly, Narses could hear the battle cries of the newly arrived enemy.

"Nothing! Nothing!"

Much too clever.

Belisarius, standing on the wharf, heard the same explosions.

"That's Antonina!" exclaimed Irene. "The battle in the Hippodrome's already started!"

Sittas and Hermogenes looked at Belisarius.

"The Hippodrome can wait," he stated. "Antonina can hold her own against that mob, at least for a while. We need to make sure the Emperor and Empress are safe, before we do anything else."

Sittas pointed out to sea.

"There are still some ships left from Aegidius' fleet. They'll be landing at Portus Caesarii soon."

Belisarius shrugged. "Let them. Most of that army's been shattered. Aegidius is probably already dead. Even if he isn't, it'll take him time to rally his troops and start marching them to the inner city. We'll deal with them later."

He pointed up the hill. "We must secure the Great Palace. *Now.*"

Without another word, he began striding off the wharf. Irene and his Thracian bucellarii followed. Very quickly, Sittas and Hermogenes had their own troops marching away from the harbor.

The Great Palace was only a quarter of a mile away. With Belisarius in the lead, the little army of five hundred cataphracts and two thousand infantrymen reached the wall surrounding the Great Palace in minutes.

The Great Palace of Constantinople was a vast complex, not a single structure. It was almost a small city within the city. The many buildings of the Palace were separated by peristyle porticoes alternating with open courtyards and gardens. The porticoes were decorated with mosaics, the courtyards and gardens with statuary and fountains.

It was perfectly designed terrain for defense, and Belisarius knew that he had to overwhelm any enemies before they could organize such a defense. So, for one of the few times in his life, he decided to order a straightforward frontal assault.

He looked to Hermogenes.

"Did you bring scaling equipment?"

Hermogenes answered by simply pointing to the rear. Turning, Belisarius saw that squads of infantrymen were already rushing up with ropes and grappling hooks.

He was pleased—somewhat. He studied the wall more closely. It was at least eight feet tall.

"We really need ladders, too," he muttered, "to get enough men over in time to—"

He broke off, seeing the look of restrained exasperation on Hermogenes' face.

"We trained for this," growled Hermogenes. "I didn't want to haul a lot of bulky ladders around, so instead—" He took a deep breath. "Just watch, general. And relax."

Belisarius smiled. Watched. Smiled very broadly.

At thirty-foot intervals, down a two hundred yard stretch of the wall, ten-man squads of infantrymen anchored grappling hooks. Immediately, two men from each squad scaled the wall and dropped over into the gardens beyond. The others divided into two-man teams. Each team began hoisting a stream of soldiers by using a shield held between them as a stepping stone. After the first wave of soldiers went over the wall, the hoisting teams were replaced by fresh soldiers and went over the wall themselves.

Coming from the palace grounds, Belisarius could hear the shouts of surprised defenders and the hammering of weapons on shields. But there were not many of those shouts, and the hammering died away very quickly.

Belisarius was impressed. In less than a minute, five hundred infantrymen had swarmed into the palace grounds and—judging from the sound—had already overwhelmed the immediate defenders.

"With a wall this short—Irene measured it for me—this works faster than ladders," commented Hermogenes smugly. "If necessary, I could get all the infantry over in less than four minutes. But we shouldn't need to because—"

Belisarius heard a cry of triumph. Turning his head, he saw that one of the gates was opening. In seconds, the infantrymen opening that gate from within had pushed it completely to one side. A moment later, he saw two more gates opening.

Sittas and twenty of his cataphracts were already thundering through the first gate. Other cataphracts positioned themselves before the other gates. As soon as the way was cleared, they too began pouring into the palace grounds.

Once the heavy cavalry had all entered, the rest of the infantry followed. Belisarius and Hermogenes trotted in the rear, with Irene a few paces behind. Valentinian and Anastasius led the way. Menander, Ashot, and the rest of the Thracians flanked them on either side.

As soon as he entered the palace grounds, Belisarius made a quick survey of the area. Hermogenes' troops had already formed a well-ordered perimeter, within which Sittas and his men were drawing up into their own formations. The cataphracts were a bit disorganized. The checkerboard arrangement of the palace grounds—gardens next to small patios next to open-sided porticoes—was hardly ideal terrain for heavy cavalrymen.

Belisarius was not concerned. Enemy cataphracts would be equally handicapped and he doubted if, as individuals, they would match Sittas' elite horsemen. He would use Sittas and the cataphracts as a mailed fist, if necessary. But he was really depending on the infantry.

That infantry—that *excellent* infantry—had already given him the advantage. Their speedy swarming over the wall had obviously caught the traitors completely off guard. Lying near the gates, Belisarius could see the bodies of perhaps thirty men. Most of them, from their uniforms, he took to be John of Cappadocia's retainers. Other than that, the only enemy soldiers in sight were a handful scuttling away in rapid retreat.

Excellent. But—

Here and there, scattered among the corpses of the Cappadocian's bucellarii and a few of Hermogenes' infantry, he also saw the bodies of men dressed in the livery of excubitores. And he could hear, dimly, the sound of combat in the direction of the Gynaeceum.

He turned to Irene.

"Where is Justinian? And Theodora?"

She pointed to the northeast, at one of the more distant buildings.

"They were going to hold an emergency council in the audience chamber of Leo's Palace."

"I know which one it is," said Belisarius. He began trotting in that direction.

"Hermogenes!" he shouted. The infantry general, a few yards away, looked at him. Belisarius, still trotting, pointed toward the building.

"Half of your men—send them with me! You take the other half and secure the Gynaeceum!"

Sittas came galloping up, followed by his mounted cataphracts. Still trotting, Belisarius waved his hand in a circle.

"Sittas—clear the palace grounds!"

Sittas grinned. The burly general reined his horse around.

"You heard the man!" he bellowed. He jumped his horse over a low hedge and began galloping toward the center of the complex. His cavalrymen followed, pounding through gardens, courtyards and porticoes. Vegetation was trampled underfoot, statuary was shattered or upended. The fountains survived, more or less intact. So, of course, did the columns upholding the porticoes— although many of the beautiful floor tiles were shattered into pieces, and a few of the wall mosaics suffered in passing from casual contact with the armored shoulders and lance butts of cataphracts.

At the very center of the palace complex, Sittas encountered two hundred of John's bucellarii. Most of them were mounted. The ones who weren't were in the process of doing so—a laborious process, for armored cataphracts. All of them seemed confused and disorganized.

Sittas gave them no chance at all. He didn't even bother to shout any orders. He simply lowered his lance and thundered into the mob. His five hundred cataphracts came right behind, following his lead.

The result was a pure and simple massacre. The Cappadocian's bucellarii were surprised and outnumbered. By the time they realized the danger, Sittas and his men were almost upon them. At that range, bows were useless. Most of John's retainers had time to raise their lances, but——

They didn't have stirrups. Sittas and his cataphracts went through them like an ax through soft wood. Half of the Cappadocian's bucellarii either died or were badly wounded in the first lance charge. Thereafter, matching sword and mace blows with men who were braced by stirrups, the remainder lasted less than a minute. At the end, not more than twenty of the retainers were able to surrender. The rest were either dead, badly injured, or unconscious.

Hermogenes, meanwhile, led a thousand of his infantrymen into the Gynaeceum. Once inside the labyrinth of the womens' quarters, Hermogenes followed the sounds of fighting. Two minutes after entering the complex, he and his men were falling on the backs of the bucellarii fighting what was left of Theodora's excubitores.

The battle in the Gynaeceum was not as bloody as the cavalry melee in the courtyards, for the simple reason that John's retainers surrendered almost immediately. They were hopelessly trapped between two forces; and they were, at bottom, nothing but mercenaries. Whatever his other talents, John of Cappadocia had none when it came to cementing the loyalty of bucellarii.

Belisarius himself faced no enemies at all, beyond a small group of bucellarii—not more than forty—whom he encountered leaving Leo's Palace just as he was approaching. The cataphracts were in the process of mounting their horses.

There was no battle. The bucellarii took one look at the thousand infantrymen charging toward them and fled instantly. Those of them who had not managed to mount their horses in time retreated also, lumbering in the heavy way of armored cavalrymen forced to run on their own two legs.

Belisarius let them go. He had much more pressing concerns. He plunged into the building. Followed by his infantry, he raced through the half-remembered corridors, searching for the audience chamber.

Hoping against hope, but fearing the worst.

"Who is that?" squawked the "Emperor" Hypatius, leaning over the wall separating the kathisma from the Hippodrome. He stared at the little army pouring through the southwestern gate. Then, goggled, seeing them slinging grenades at the huge mob of faction thugs on the other side of the Hippodrome.

"Where did they get grenades?" he shrieked.

A new battle cry was heard: *"Antonina! Antonina!"*

Ajatasutra leaned over the wall and examined the invaders. His eyes were immediately drawn to a small figure bringing up the rear. Helmeted; armored—but unmistakeably feminine for all that.

He smiled bitterly, turning away. He looked at Balban and gestured with his thumb.

"That's what you called the *sheep.*"

Hypatius was now gobbling with sheer terror. Pompeius, the same.

Someone began pounding on the rear entrance to the kathisma, the barred door which led to the Great Palace. Narses recognized John of Cappadocia's voice: "Open up! Open up!"

At Balban's command, the kshatriya guarding the door unbarred and opened it.

John of Cappadocia burst into the kathisma, trailing three of his bucellarii.

"Belisarius is here!" he shouted. "His whore Antonina has some kind of army—" He fell abruptly silent, seeing the scene in the Hippodrome.

"She's here already!" snarled Balban, pointing over the wall. "And she's got grenades!"

Narses sighed.

Too clever by half.

The eunuch rose. Strode forward. Took charge.

"Have you blinded Justinian?" he demanded.

John of Cappadocia nodded.

"Theodora?"

"She's under guard in the palace."

Narses took Balban by the arm and pointed over the wall separating the kathisma from the Hippodrome. He was pointing to the hundreds of kshatriya manning the rockets. The four hundred kshatriya, unlike the thousands of milling and confused faction thugs, were already forming their battle lines. Most of them were opening baskets of grenades. The kshatriya manning the rockets were hastily re-aiming the troughs.

"You've still got your own soldiers and—*if you provide some leadership*—that huge faction mob. *Get down there! Now!*"

Balban neither argued nor protested. Immediately, the spymaster began clambering over the wall.

Narses grabbed Hypatius and shoved him to the wall. "Go with him!" he commanded. "You're the new Emperor! You need to rally the Hippodrome crowd!"

Hypatius babbled protest. Narses simply manhandled the "Emperor" over the stone rampart. Despite his terror, Hypatius was no match for the old eunuch's wiry strength. Half-sprawled over the wall—on the *wrong* side of the wall—Hypatius stared up at Narses.

"Do it!" ordered the eunuch. His eyes were fixed on Hypatius like a snake on its prey. An instant later, Narses tore Hypatius' clutching fingers off the wall. The "Emperor" landed in a collapsed heap on the stone platform below.

Hypatius immediately lunged to his feet and jumped at the wall.

Hopeless. That wall had been designed to keep assassins from the emperor. A strong and agile man could have leapt high enough to grasp the top of the wall. Hypatius was neither.

The new "Emperor" gobbled terror.

"*Do it!*" commanded Narses.

Hypatius gasped. He turned his head and spotted Balban. The spymaster was racing around the upper tiers of the Hippodrome, heading for the kshatriya rocketeers. He was already forty yards away.

Gibbering with fear, Hypatius staggered after him.

In the kathisma, Narses turned from the wall and confronted John of Cappadocia.

"Where are the rest of your bucellarii?" he demanded.

The Cappadocian glared at him.

"That's none—"

"You idiot!" snarled the eunuch. "Kept them in the palace, didn't you? Planned to keep them unharmed, didn't you? *So you'd have them available for later use.*"

John was still glaring, but he did not deny the charge. Narses pointed to the chaos in the Hippodrome.

"'Later use' is *now*, Cappadocian. Get them! With your thousand bucellarii added to the brew, we might still win this thing."

John started to protest. The eunuch drove him down. "*Do it!*"

John argued no further. The Cappadocian charged down the corridor leading to the Great Palace. Narses went after him, dragging Pompeius by the arm. Before following, Ajatasutra ordered the kshatriya still in the kathisma to join Balban. As he left the kathisma—now unoccupied—the kshatriya were already climbing over the wall and dropping down into the Hippodrome.

In the corridor, Ajatasutra quickly caught up with Narses and Pompeius.

Smiling, the assassin leaned over and whispered:

"'Years of civil war,' you said."

Narses glanced at him, but said nothing. The eunuch was concentrating his attention on forcing the gibbering Pompeius forward. The new "Emperor's" brother was practically paralyzed with fear.

"If you don't start moving," snarled Narses, "I'll just leave you here."

Pompeius suddenly began running down the corridor. Narses let him go.

"At least he's headed in the right direction," grumbled the eunuch. "We'll catch him later. He'll stumble into a faint, somewhere up ahead."

The eunuch began trotting. Ajatasutra matched his pace easily.

Again, the assassin leaned over and whispered. Still smiling:

"'The Roman Empire will be in chaos for a generation,' you said."

Narses ignored him.

Ajatasutra, grinning:

"'Much better than just letting Justinian fight his stupid wars,' you said."

Narses ignored him.

They reached the end of the corridor. Now, they found themselves in one of the many buildings of the Great Palace. They could hear the sound of fighting coming from somewhere in the outer complex.

As Narses had predicted, Pompeius was waiting for them. In a manner of speaking: the nobleman was squatting on the floor, leaning his head against a wall, sobbing.

Narses leaned over, seized Hypatius by his hair, and dragged the "emperor's" brother to his feet.

"The only place you're safe now is with me," hissed the eunuch. "If you collapse again—if you disobey me in any way—*I'll leave you.*" Narses released his grip and stalked toward one of the corridors leading to another building in the complex. Ajatasutra strode alongside. Hypatius followed.

The sound of fighting grew louder. Among those sounds, Narses recognized the heavy thundering of a cavalry charge. So did Ajatasutra. Both men picked up their pace.

"Where are we going?" whispered the assassin. "And why"—he pointed with a thumb over his shoulder—"are you so intent on hauling that *creature* with us?"

"I'll need him," growled Narses.

They reached the end of the corridor. They were in another large room in yet another building. Narses plunged through a door against the left wall.

Again, a short corridor. Again, another room in yet

another building. Again, Narses led the way through another door. Again, another corridor.

Ajatasutra, though he had an abstract knowledge of the Great Palace's layout, was by now completely disoriented.

"Where are we going?" he repeated.

"I have something to attend to," muttered Narses.

The eunuch broke into a trot. The corridor made a bend. Once around the bend, Ajatasutra could see that the corridor ended in a massive set of double doors. One of the doors was ajar. Beyond, Ajatasutra heard the sound of indistinct voices.

Once they got within ten feet of the half-open door, Ajatasutra recognized one of the voices in the room beyond.

John of Cappadocia's voice.

Narses hissed. "That *bastard*. I *knew* he'd come here first."

The eunuch turned his head. Reptilian eyes focussed on Ajatasutra. "Decide," he commanded.

Ajatasutra hesitated for only a second. Then, with a half-smile:

"You're the best of a bad lot."

Narses nodded. He gestured toward Pompeius, who was just now staggering up.

"Keep him safe," muttered the eunuch. "And deal with the bucellarii."

Narses turned away and slid through the door. Ajatasutra followed, dragging Pompeius by the arm.

Inside, they found a dramatic tableau.

Theodora was on her knees, cradling Justinian. The Emperor, though still unconscious, was beginning to moan.

John of Cappadocia loomed above her, with a sword in his hand. His three bucellarii were standing a few feet away, between John and Narses. Hearing the eunuch enter, the bodyguards turned hastily and raised their weapons. Then, recognizing him, they lowered the swords and stepped aside. Narses slid past them, heading toward John and the Empress.

Ajatasutra relinguished his grip on Pompeius and sidled close to the bucellarii.

The Cappadocian glared down at the Empress. He began to snarl something.

Theodora, her face like a mask, sneered:

"*Stop talking, traitor. Do it, coward.*"

John raised his sword.

Narses, hissing like a snake:

"*Stop, you idiot!* We're going to need her. *Alive.*"

Startled, John turned away from the Empress. His sword lowered, slightly.

"Why?" he demanded. "We were going to kill her, anyway, after she hailed the new Emperor. She and Justinian both. There's no reason to wait, now." He scowled. "And why are you here?"

Narses strode forward.

"I swear, Cappadocian, you've got the brains of a toad."

Closer, closer.

"Think, John—*think.*"

Closer, closer. The eunuch pointed to the Empress. John turned his head, following the pointing finger.

Narses struck.

Ajatasutra, watching, was impressed. The old eunuch stabbed like a viper. The little knife seemed to come from nowhere, before it sank into John's ribcage.

John screamed, staggered, dropped his sword. The knife was still protruding from his side.

Narses stepped back.

The bucellarii bellowed, raised their swords, and took a step toward the eunuch.

One step. They got no further.

Ajatasutra slew the three bucellarii in as many seconds. Three quick blows from his dagger into the bodyguards' backs. Each blow—powerful, *swift*—slid expertly between gaps in the armor, severing spinal cords. Ajatasutra's victims died before they even realized what had happened. The bodyguards simply slumped to the floor.

John of Cappadocia had already fallen to the floor. But his was no lifeless slump. The praetorian prefect's face was twisted with agony. He was apparently trying to scream, but no sound escaped from the rictus distorting his face.

"It's quite a nasty poison," remarked Narses cheerfully. "Utterly paralyzing, for all the pain. Deadly, too. After a time."

Ajatasutra quickly cleaned his dagger, but he did not replace it in its hidden sheath.

"Explain," he commanded.

Narses began to sneer. But then, seeing the expression on the assassin's face, thought better of it. "Do you still have any illusions, Ajatasutra?" he demanded. The eunuch pointed toward a nearby wall. Through that wall, thick as it was, came the sounds of combat. Grenade explosions, shouts, screams.

"It's over," he pronounced. "*We lost.*"

Ajatasutra frowned. Without being conscious of the act, the assassin hefted his dagger.

Narses *was* conscious of that act. He spoke hurriedly:

"*Think*, Ajatasutra. Where did Antonina get the grenades? She didn't steal them from us. She had them *made*. That means she's been planning this for *months*. It means everything that fool Procopius told that fool Balban was duplicity. Not his—the gossiping idiot!—but *hers*. Antonina hasn't been holding orgies on her estate—*she's been training an army and equipping them with gunpowder weapons.*"

Ajatasutra's frown deepened. "But she couldn't have the knowledge—"

He got no further. Theodora's cawing laugh cut him short. The assassin, seeing the triumph in her face, suddenly knew that Narses was right.

He lowered the dagger. Lowered it, but did not sheathe the weapon. "There's still a chance," he said. "From what I saw, she doesn't have much of an army. Balban still has the kshatriya, and the mob."

Narses shook his head.

"No chance at all, Ajatasutra. *Not with Belisarius here.*"

The eunuch shook his head again. The gesture had a grim finality to it.

"No chance," he repeated. "Not with Belisarius here. He's already shattered the Army of Bithynia. Even if Balban manages to defeat Antonina in the Hippodrome, he'll still have to face Belisarius. With what? A few hundred kshatriya? Faction thugs?"

Narses gestured scornfully at the bodies of John's bucellarii. "Or do you think these *lap dogs* are capable of facing Belisarius—and *his* cataphracts?"

Ajatasutra stared at the three corpses. Not for long, however. The sounds of combat were growing louder.

He slid the dagger into its sheath. "You're right. Now what?"

Narses shrugged. "We escape. You, me, and Pompeius. We'll need him, to mollify your masters. We can at least claim that we salvaged the 'legitimate heir' from the wreckage. The Malwa can use him as a puppet."

The assassin winced. "Nanda Lal's going to be furious."

"So?" demanded Narses. "*You* weren't in charge—Balban was. *You* warned him that Antonina was deceiving us. I'll swear to it. But Balban wouldn't listen."

Ajatasutra glanced at Pompeius. The nobleman was leaning against the far wall. His face was pale, his eyes unfocussed. He seemed completely oblivious to everything except his own terror.

The assassin's eyes moved to the Empress. Theodora glared back at him.

Black, black eyes. Hating eyes.

"Her?" he asked.

The old eunuch's face was truly that of a serpent, now. For a moment, Ajatasutra almost drew his dagger again. But, instead, he simply murmured:

"Who would have ever thought *Narses* would commit an act of personal grace?"

Smiling, the assassin strode over to Pompeius, seized

the nobleman by the arm, and dragged him to the door.
There, he stopped, waiting for Narses.

The eunuch and the Empress stared at each other.
The eunuch's was a gaze of sorrow. Theodora's—

"I will never forgive you. *You are a dead man.*"

Narses nodded. "I know." A rueful little smile came
to his face. "But I might still win. And I'm an old man,
anyway. Even if I lose, I may well be dead before you
kill me."

The smile faded. Sorrow remained.

The eunuch turned away, and began walking toward
the door. Theodora's voice halted him.

"*Why, Narses?*"

For the first time, there was anguish as well as hatred
in her voice. Narses, without turning, simply shrugged.

"Ambition," he said.

"No. Not that. Why *this?*"

Narses turned his head. His eyes met those of
Theodora's. There was a hint of tears in her eyes. Just
a hint.

Narses fought back his own tears.

"There was no need. And—"

He could not face those eyes. He looked away.
Harshly: "I did not stop loving you, child, simply because
I planned to murder you."

Anguish fled the Empress. Only the hell-voice
remained:

"You *should* have killed me, traitor. You will regret
it, *coward.*"

Narses shook his head.

"No, Theodora, I won't. *Not ever.*"

A moment later, he was gone. Theodora gazed down
at her husband. Justinian's moans were growing louder.
Soon, he would regain consciousness and begin to
scream.

The Empress lifted his head off her lap and set it
gently on the carpet.

She had something to attend to.

Crawling on her hands and knees, Theodora made

her way to the body of the nearest soldier. She drew a dagger from the corpse's sword-belt.

Then, still crawling, she began making her way toward John of Cappadocia.

The Empress did not crawl because she was unable to stand, or because she was injured, or because she was in a state of shock.

No. She crawled simply because she wanted the Cappadocian to see her coming.

He did. And then, despite the agony which held him paralyzed, tried to scream.

But he couldn't. He couldn't make a sound; couldn't move a muscle. He could only watch.

Theodora crawled toward him, the dagger in her hand. Her eyes were fixed on those of the praetorian prefect.

She wanted those eyes.

Hell-gaze. Hell-crawl.

It was the last thing John of Cappadocia would ever see, and he knew it.

Three minutes later, Belisarius burst into the room. Behind him came his cataphracts and Irene.

All of them skidded to a halt.

Irene clapped her hand over her mouth, gasping. Menander turned pale. Anastasius tightened his jaws. Valentinian grinned.

Belisarius simply stared. But he too, for a moment, was transfixed by the sight.

Transfixed, not by the sight of the bodies littering the chamber. Not by the sight of Justinian, moaning, blinded. Not even by the sight of the praetorian prefect, prostrate, screaming in a silent rictus, his back arched with agony.

No, it was the sight of the Empress. Squatting over the dying traitor, a bloody knife in one hand, her imperial robes held up by the other. Urinating into the empty eyesockets of John of Cappadocia.

Chapter 28

The rocket soared up into the sky and exploded high
above the walls of the Hippodrome. A thundering cry
followed, from the assembled mob within.

"*NIKA! NIKA!*"

" 'Victory,' is it?" hissed Antonina. She leaned over
her saddle and whispered to Maurice:

"Tell me what to do."

Maurice smiled. "You already know what to do." He
pointed forward. They were approaching the looming
structure from the southwest. Ahead of them, fifty yards
away, began a broad stone staircase which swept up to
a wide entrance. The entrance was thirty yards across,
and supported by several columns.

"Once we get in there, it'll be like a knife fight in a
kitchen. There won't be any room for maneuver. Just
kill or be killed."

Antonina grimaced. The entrance they were approaching was called the Gate of Death.

"How appropriate," she murmured.

Next to her, Maurice snorted contempt. "Can you
believe it?" he demanded. "They didn't post a guard.
Not even a single sentinel."

They were now twenty yards from the beginning of
the staircase. Antonina halted her horse and began to
dismount.

"There won't be any room for horses in there," she
said. Maurice nodded and ordered the cataphracts to

430

dismount. The bucellarii grumbled, but obeyed without hesitation. Much as they hated fighting afoot, they were veterans. They knew full well that cavalry tactics would be impossible inside the Hippodrome.

Antonina drew her cleaver and held it over her head.

"Nothing! Nothing!" she cried, and began marching up the steps.

Her whole army surged after her. But, before she had gone halfway up the staircase, Maurice was holding her back.

"You stay in the rear."

Antonina obeyed. Her army swept around her. After they had all gone by, she and Maurice followed.

By the time they passed through the Gate of Death, some of the grenadiers were already launching their first grenades. Antonina could hear the explosions, as well as the battle cry of her own soldiers.

"NOTHING! NOTHING!"

She and Maurice entered the Hippodrome. They were standing on a broad, flat platform. Below them, the wide stone tiers of the Hippodrome—which served as seats and stairway combined—sloped down to the racetrack below.

The three hundred cataphracts were spreading out, filing down the first ten tiers, setting a perimeter. All of them had drawn their bows. In the center, just below her, the grenadiers and their wives had taken their own compact formation. Some of the grenadiers were slinging grenades, but most of them were still occupied in setting up their grenade baskets.

Antonina stared at the enemy, massed on the other side of the Hippodrome. After a quick glance, she ignored the huge mob of faction thugs. Her attention was drawn to the wooden bulwarks positioned on the far curve of the racetrack. She could see the kshatriya muscling around some wooden troughs. She did not recognize the odd wooden devices, but she had no difficulty recognizing the nature of the tubes which the kshatriya were placing in them.

"Rockets," she muttered. She turned to Maurice, standing next to her.

"Tell the army to spread out further. I don't want to give those rockets a concentrated target."

Maurice winced. "That'll make it harder to defend against a mass charge."

Antonina shook her head.

"If all forty thousand of those thugs charge us at once, they'll overwhelm us regardless of how compact we are. But I know that crowd, Maurice. I grew up with them. Forty thousand Hippodrome thugs can swamp less than a thousand soldiers—but not without suffering heavy casualties. *Especially* in the front ranks."

She pointing toward the mob.

"I guarantee you, Maurice, they know it as well as we do. And every single one of that crowd, right this very moment, is making the same vow."

She laughed, harshly. " 'Victory!' is just their official battle cry. The *real* one—the private, silent one—is: *you first! Anybody but me!*"

Maurice chuckled. Then, nodded.

"I do believe you're right." A moment later, the hecatontarch was bellowing orders. The cataphracts immediately began spreading out further. Within a minute, they had established a perimeter which encompassed the entire southwestern arc of the Hippodrome. The grenadiers spread out to fill that guarded space. Soon, the grenadiers were scattered into separate small squads, instead of packed into a tight formation.

Not a moment too soon. The Malwa fired their first rockets at the Romans. One of the rockets plowed into the dirt track below them, sending up a cloud of dust. Another soared completely out of the Hippodrome. But the next slammed into a nearby tier.

For all the impressive sound and fury of the explosion, the heavy stone suffered no worse than scorching. And, because the space was vacated, there were no casualties beyond a few grenadiers injured by flying wooden splinters. Minor wounds, no worse.

The grenadiers roared their fury. For the first time since entering the Hippodrome, the grenadiers launched a full volley.

Hundreds of grenades, their fuses sputtering, flew across the Hippodrome. The volley was not concentrated on any particular target. Each grenadier had simply decided to smite the foe. *Any* foe.

The volley erupted throughout the huge mob of faction thugs. A few landed in the vicinity of the wooden bulwarks sheltering the kshatriya. The Malwa soldiers, accustomed to gunpowder weapons, took shelter long before the grenades arrived. Few of them were even injured.

The mob—

A man of the future, had he been watching, would have called that volley a gigantic shotgun blast.

A sawed-off shotgun, at short range.

"Beautiful!" shouted Maurice, raising his fist in triumph. Below, the cataphracts and the grenadiers added their own cries of elation.

"The hell it was," snarled Antonina. *"Sloppy."*

Scowling, the little woman stalked forward and began yelling orders at her grenadiers. Her clear, soprano voice—trained by an actress mother—projected right through the shrieking din of the Hippodrome.

Now steadied, the grenadiers began following her commands. Their volleys became concentrated, targeted salvoes.

Antonina aimed the first volley at the kshatriya. All of the rocket troughs were shattered or upended. Again, most of the Malwa soldiers escaped harm by sheltering behind the bulwarks. The bulwarks were solidly built—heavy timbers fastened with bolts. The grenades did no more than score the wood.

But Antonina didn't care. She simply wanted to cow the Malwa, put them out of action. She was quite confident in her ability to deal with a few hundred kshatriya. Her grenadiers, with their slings, easily outranged the Malwa grenades. And the rocket troughs

were too fragile and cumbersome to be much of a threat
in this kind of battle.

What she was really worried about—despite her confident proclamation to Maurice—was that the huge mob
of faction thugs would swarm her with their numbers.
There were forty thousand of them, against less than
a thousand grenadiers and cataphracts—and the grenadiers would be of little use in a hand-to-hand melee.

So, while the Malwa soldiers coughed dust out of
their lungs, crouching from the fury, Antonina began
dismembering the mob.

Chop. Chop. Chop.

The next three volleys landed—in series, north to
south—on the nearest fringes of the crowd. When the
dust settled, and the bodies stopped flying, hundreds
of faction thugs were scattered in heaps over the stone
tiers. Dead, dying, wounded, stunned.

The crowd, shrieking, began piling away. More thugs
died, trampled to death.

The nearest members of the mob were on the northern tiers of the Hippodrome. Antonina sent two volleys
that way. The packed mass shredded, disintegrated. The
survivors packed even tighter, pushing their fellows back,
back. Back toward the far exits. Dozens more were
trampled to death.

The kshatriya were stirring again. Small groups of
Malwa soldiers were raising the two rocket troughs which
had only been upended instead of destroyed. The rest
were hurling their own grenades. But, without slings,
those grenades fell harmlessly in the center of the
Hippodrome.

Still—

Keep them cowed.

Antonina sent another volley at the kshatriyas. The
Malwa soldiers, again, suffered relatively few casualties.
But, as before, they were forced to retreat behind their
bulwarks, out of action.

Back to the mob.

Chop. Chop. Chop.

Maurice, standing a few feet behind Antonina, smiled grimly. He said nothing. There was no need.

A knife fight in a kitchen.

The first members of the mob who fled from the Hippodrome escaped. Perhaps two thousand of them, less the hundred or so who were trampled to death squeezing through the northeastern gates.

The rest ran into Belisarius.

Marching up with his army, and seeing the Blue and Green thugs pouring out of the Hippodrome, Belisarius ordered half of the infantrymen to form lines on either side of the gates.

"Make them run the gauntlet, Hermogenes," he commanded. "Kill as many as you can—*without* breaking your lines."

"Most of them will escape," protested Hermogenes. "We should box them in. Kill *all* the stinking traitors."

Belisarius shook his head.

"We don't need that kind of bloodbath. Just enough to terrorize the factions for the next twenty years."

He turned to Irene, who was riding next to him. The spymaster had wanted to stay with Theodora, but Belisarius had insisted she accompany him to the Hippodrome. Theodora was safe, now. She and Justinian were being guarded in the Gynaeceum by Theodora's surviving excubitores, five hundred infantrymen, and most of Sittas' cataphracts. Irene could do nothing for Theodora, at the moment, whereas Belisarius had wanted her expertise.

"Can you identify the faction leaders?" he asked.

Irene nodded.

Belisarius whistled and waved to Sittas. The general trotted over, along with the hundred or so cataphracts he still had with him.

Belisarius pointed to the infantrymen lining up on either side of the gates. Already, the soldiers were cutting down those faction members who stumbled against their lines. The thugs who managed to stay out of sword range were in no danger from the soldiers. But, pushing away from the threatening infantrymen, the crowd was squeezing itself into a packed torrent of hurtling bodies. Within seconds, another dozen were trampled to death.

"Let them through, Sittas, those of them that survive the gauntlet. *Except the faction leaders.* I want them dead or captured. Irene will point them out for you."

Sittas began to protest the orders. Like Hermogenes, he was filled with a furious determination to massacre the entire crowd.

"Do as I command!" bellowed Belisarius. He matched Sittas glare for glare.

"Don't be an idiot, Sittas!" He pointed to the southwest. "Antonina has less than a thousand men. Most of them are grenadiers, who won't be worth much in a hand-to-hand battle. If that huge mob attacks them head on, they'll be slaughtered."

Sittas was still glaring. Belisarius snarled.

"*Think*, Sittas. If we trap that mob from this end, they'll have no choice but to pour out the other. *So let them out here.* Hermogenes and his men will savage them on the way out, and you make sure to get the leaders. *That's good enough.*"

"He's right, Sittas," hissed Irene.

Sittas blew out his cheeks.

"I know," he grumbled. "I just—*damn all traitors, anyway.*"

But he reined his horse around without further argument. Within a minute, his cataphracts were forming a mounted line a hundred and fifty yards away. By now, Hermogenes had his five hundred infantrymen lined up on either side of the gates, half on each side. His men stood three feet apart, in three ranks. As the faction thugs poured out of the Hippodrome, they would have to run a gauntlet almost a hundred yards long. Then, they would break against the heavily armored, mounted cataphracts—like a torrent against a boulder. The thugs who survived the gauntlet would be able to escape, by fleeing to either side through the fifty-yard gaps between the last infantrymen and Sittas' line. But during that time they would be exposed to Irene's searching eyes—and cataphract archery.

Satisfied, Belisarius turned away. Some of the faction leaders would escape. Not many.

He began trotting his horse to the southwest, below the looming wall of the Hippodrome. Valentinian, Anastasius and Menander rode next to him. Behind them came the remaining thousand infantrymen of Hermogenes' army.

Belisarius turned in his saddle. He saw that the infantry were maintaining a good columnar formation—well-ordered and ready to spread into a line as soon as he gave the command.

Ashot was right, he thought. *The best Roman infantry since the days of the Principate.*

He stepped up the pace.

Thank you, Hermogenes. You may have saved my wife's life.

"Forget the rockets!" shouted Balban. The cluster of kshatriya who were trying to erect a rocket trough behind the bulwarks immediately ceased their effort.

Balban turned back to his three chief lieutenants. The four Malwa officers, along with six top leaders of the Blue and Green factions, were crowded into a corner formed by the heavy wooden beams. The three-sided shelter formed by the bulwarks was almost suffocating. Into that small space—not more than fifty feet square—were jammed a hundred kshatriya and perhaps another dozen faction leaders. The remaining kshatriya—those who still survived, which was well over three hundred—were crouched as close to the bulwarks as they could get. Fortunately for them, the cursed Roman grenadiers were still concentrating their volleys on the mob.

Balban stared up at the tiers of the Hippodrome. Those tiers were full of men. Thousands and thousands of men—*armed* men—all of whom were milling around uselessly. At least half of them, he estimated, were simply intent on escaping the Hippodrome through the north-east gates. Many of them had already dropped their weapons.

"We can't win an artillery duel," he announced. "Our only hope is to charge across the Hippodrome and overwhelm them with numbers."

All three of the kshatriya officers immediately nodded. One of them said:

"Most of that Roman force are grenadiers. We'll lose men crossing the track, but once we get within hand-fighting range, we'll massacre them."

"Some of them are *cataphracts*!" protested one of the Blue leaders.

"A few hundred—*at most*," snapped Balban. The Malwa pointed a rigid finger at the mob in the tiers above them.

"You've still got at least ten thousand men!" he shouted. "Would you rather use them—or simply die here like sheep in a *slaughterhouse*?"

"He's right," said another of the Blue leaders. Two of the Green chieftains nodded. Balban's hot eyes swept the other faction heads. After a moment, they too indicated their assent.

"All right. At my command, we'll charge out of here and round up as many men as we can. Then—it's simple. Charge to the southwest. As fast as we can."

He looked at the kshatriya. "Make sure our grenadiers are scattered through the crowd. When we get close enough, we can start tossing our own grenades."

One of the faction leaders pointed to a figure huddled in the corner.

"What about the emperor? It'd help if he led the charge. Inspire the men."

Balban did not bother to look at Hypatius.

"If your men need inspiration," he growled, "tell them it's victory or death. That should be simple enough."

He lifted his head and bellowed at his kshatriya. It took not more than twenty seconds to explain the plan. It was simple enough.

"*Nika!*" shouted one of the faction leaders. He pushed his way out of the shelter and sprang upon the lowest tier of the Hippodrome.

He waved his sword, shouting at the mob above him: "*Nika! Nika!*"

The other faction leaders joined him.. They also began shouting, and pointing with their swords to the south-west.

Balban and his kshatriya poured out of the bulwarks. Quickly, they formed a line across the dirt floor of the Hippodrome. At Balban's command, they began marching forward.

Marching *slowly*. Every instinct in Balban—and his kshatriya—cried out for haste. But Balban knew that he had to give the faction leaders time to rally the mob. The Malwa by themselves could not overcome the Romans at the other end of the Hippodrome. They *needed* those thousands of thugs.

So, the kshatriya marched slowly. And began to die, as the grenade volleys came their way. But they were soldiers, and maintained their ranks.

From the mob in the tiers, dozens of men began leaping into the arena. Then hundreds. Then thousands.

Thugs, all of them. But not all thugs are cowards, by any means. And not all of them are stupid, either. Given a choice between battle and the horror of the stampeding crowd—which had already trampled hundreds of men to death—many of them chose to fight.

By the time Balban and the kshatriya were halfway across the Hippodrome, they had been joined by almost six thousand faction members.

Now, Balban ordered the charge.

"Pull them back, Antonina," said Maurice.

Pale-faced, Antonina glanced at him.

"You've only got three hundred cataphracts," she protested.

"*Pull the grenadiers back,*" he repeated. "They're

lightly armored and they've got no experience in hand
combat."

The hecatontarch gestured at the huge mob marching toward them.

"They'll just get in my cataphracts' way," he growled.
"Pull them back and keep tossing grenades. I'll try to
hold as long as I can."

Maurice stalked forward, roaring commands. Antonina
added her voice to his. The grenadiers and their wives
scampered back up the tiers. The Thracian cataphracts
moved in from the flanks, forming a solid line in front
of the grenadiers. The bucellarii didn't wait for Maurice's
order before firing a volley of arrows.

"Aim for the Malwa!" ordered Maurice.

The enemy broke into a charge. There was no discipline to that charge. No formation of any kind. Simply—six thousand men racing toward three hundred.

By the time the traitor army reached the lowest tier
on the southwest curve of the Hippodrome, a thousand
of them had been slain or wounded by grenades and
arrows. The kshatriya, especially, had suffered terrible
casualties—including Balban, who was bleeding to death
in the arena. A cataphract's arrow had ripped through
the great artery in his thigh.

But the traitors sensed victory. Their own grenades
were beginning to wreak havoc. And they were now too
close for that horrifying cataphract archery. True, the
armored Thracians loomed above them like iron stat-
ues—fierce, fearsome. But—there were only a few of
them.

The mob poured up the tiers.

"NIKA! NIKA!"

The cataphracts raised their swords, and their maces.
Soon, now. The first line of the mob was but twenty
yards away.

Thousands of them.

Ten yards away.

The line of thugs suddenly disintegrated. Shredded,
like meat. Stopped, in its tracks, by a thousand plumbata.

The lead-weighted darts sailed over the heads of the cataphracts and struck the charging mob like a hammer. The entire front line collapsed—backward, driving the thugs who followed into a heap.

The cataphracts stared. Lowered their swords. Turned their heads.

Behind them, marching down the tiers in ordered formation, came a thousand Roman infantrymen. Above those infantrymen, atop the uppermost tier of the Hippodrome, was their commander. Standing next to the commander of the Theodoran Cohort.

It did not seem strange, to the cataphracts, to see two generals kissing each other fiercely in the middle of a battle. Not at the time. Later, of course, the episode would be the subject of many ribald jokes and rhymes.

But not at the time. No, not at all.

The cataphracts did not wait for the infantry to reach them. As one man, three hundred Thracians simply charged forward, shouting their battle cries.

Some of them: *"Nothing! Nothing!"*

Most of them: *"Belisarius! Belisarius!"*

And, one enthusiast: "Oh, you sorry bastards are *fucked!"*

An hour later, after clambering over the trampled corpses packed in the northern gates, Sittas and Hermogenes slogged across the Hippodrome.

Their progress was slow. Partly, because they were forced to avoid the multitude of bodies scattered across the arena. Partly, because Sittas paused when he came upon Balban's body long enough to cut off the Malwa's head. And, partly, because they had found Hypatius cowering in the bulwarks and were dragging him behind them.

Belisarius and Antonina were sitting on the lowest tier by the southwest curve of the racetrack. Valentinian stood a few feet away. Antonina was still wearing her cuirass, but she had removed her helmet. Her head was nestled into her husband's shoulder. Her cheeks were marked by tear-tracks, but she was smiling like a cherub.

Sittas dropped Balban's head at their feet.

"You can add that to our collection," he said, grinning savagely.

Antonina opened her eyes and gazed at the trophy. She made a small grimace of distaste. Then, closed her eyes and sighed contentedly.

"How many?" asked Belisarius.

"A hundred and twenty-eight," replied Sittas. "Irene says we got most of them. Beyond that—"

He waved a thick arm, grimacing himself. Not a small grimace, either.

"The place is a slaughterhouse. Especially underneath, in the horse pens."

Hermogenes shook his head. His face was almost ashen.

"Thousands of them tried to escape through the stables."

Belisarius winced. The only entrances to the stables were small doors, barely wide enough to fit a racing chariot.

"Most of them are dead," muttered Hermogenes. "Trampled, suffocated, crushed. Christ, it'll take days to haul the bodies out. The ones at the bottom aren't much more than meat paste."

Hermogenes reached back and hauled Hypatius to his feet. The "Emperor" collapsed immediately, like a loose sack. The smell of urine and feces was overpowering.

"Theodora'll be happy to see *him*," snarled Sittas.

Antonina's eyes popped open.

"No," she whispered. "She's at Hell's gate already." She turned a pleading gaze up at her husband.

Belisarius squeezed her shoulder. Nodded.

Hypatius spoke. "Have mercy," he croaked. "I beg you—*have mercy*."

"I will," said Belisarius. He turned his head.

"*Valentinian*."

Epilogue

An Empress and Her Soul

To Belisarius, the huge throne room seemed more like a cavern than ever, with so few occupants. But Theodora had insisted on meeting him there, and he had made no objection. If the Empress found some strength and comfort in the sight of that huge chamber, and the feel of her enormous throne, Belisarius was glad for it.

She, now, was the lynchpin for the future.

He advanced across the huge room with a quick step. When he was ten paces from the throne, he prostrated himself. Then, after rising, began to speak. But Theodora stopped him with a gesture.

"One moment, Belisarius." The Empress turned toward the handful of excubitores standing guard a few yards away.

"Tell the servants to bring a chair," she commanded.

As the excubitores hastened to do her bidding, Theodora bestowed a wry smile upon the general standing before her.

"It's scandalous, I know. But we're in for a long session, and I'd much rather have your untired mind than your formal respect."

Inwardly, Belisarius heaved a sigh of relief. Not at the prospect of spending an afternoon in seated comfort—he was no stranger to standing erect—but at the first sign in days that there was something in the Empress' soul beyond fury, hatred and vengeance.

A City and Its Terror

For eight days, since the crushing of the insurrection, Theodora's soul had dwelt in that realm. As Antonina had so aptly put it, at the very gate of hell.

Much of that time, true, the Empress had spent with her husband. Overseeing the doctors who tended to his wounds; often enough, pushing them aside to tend Justinian herself.

But she had not spent all of her time there. By no means.

She had spent hours, with Irene, overseeing her *agentes in rebus*—the "inspectors of the post" who served the throne as a secret police—dispatching squads of them throughout the Empire. Those squads assigned to the capital itself had already reported back. The results of their missions were displayed, for all to see, on the walls of the Hippodrome. Next to the spiked heads of Malwa kshatriya—hundreds of them, with Balban's occupying a central position; faction leaders; Hypatius; John of Cappadocia (and all of his bucellarii who had not managed to flee the city)—now perched the heads of three dozen churchmen, including Glycerius of Chalcedon and George Barsymes; those officers of the Army of Bithynia who had been captured; nineteen high noblemen, including six Senators; eighty-seven officials and functionaries; and the torturer who had blinded Justinian.

The torturer's head was identified by a small placard. His face was quite unrecognizeable. Theodora had spent other hours overseeing his own torture, until she pushed aside her experts and finished the job herself.

There would have been more heads, had it not been for Belisarius and Antonina.

Many more.

Theodora had demanded the heads of every officer, above the rank of tribune, of every military unit in the capital which had stood aside during the insurrection. That demand, however, could not be satisfied by her secret police. As cowed and terrified as they were, those officers were still in command of thousands of troops. Shaky command, true—very shaky—but solid enough to have resisted squads of *agentes in rebus*.

So, Theodora had ordered Belisarius to carry out the purge. He had refused.

Flatly refused. Partly, he told her, because it was excessive. Those men were not guilty of treason, after all, simply dereliction of duty. What was more important, he explained—calmly, coldly—was that such an indiscriminate purge of the entire officer corps in Constantinople would undermine the army itself.

He needed that army. Rome needed that army. The first battle with the Malwa Empire had been fought and won. There were many more to come.

In the end, Theodora had yielded. She had been satisfied—it might be better to say, had accepted—the dismissal of those officers. Belisarius, along with Sittas and Hermogenes, had spent three days enforcing that dismissal.

None of the officers had objected, with the sole exception of Gontharis, the commander of the Army of Rhodope. A scion of one of the empire's noblest families, he apparently felt his aristocratic lineage exempted him from such unceremonious and uncouth treatment.

Belisarius, not wishing to feed further the nobility's resentment against Thracians, had allowed Sittas to handle the problem.

The Greek nobleman's solution had been quick and direct. Sittas felled Gontharis with a blow of his gauntleted fist, dragged him out of his headquarters into the Army of Rhodope's training field, and decapitated him in front of the assembled troops. Another head joined the growing collection on the walls of the Hippodrome.

Immediately thereafter, Sittas and his cataphracts marched to Gontharis' villa on the outskirts of Constantinople. After expelling all the occupants, Sittas seized the immense treasure contained therein and burned the villa to the ground. The confiscated fortune, he turned over to the imperial treasury.

The treasury's coffers were bulging, now. Theodora had executed only nineteen noblemen. But she had confiscated the fortunes of every noble family whose members had even the slightest connection with the plot. The confiscations, true, had been restricted to that portion of such families' fortunes which were located in the capital. Their provincial estates—to which most of them had fled—were untouched. But, since most aristocrats resided in the capital, the plunder was enormous.

The same treatment had been dealt to officials, bureaucrats, churchmen.

None of them objected. Not publicly, at least. They were glad enough to escape with their lives.

A Populace and Its Glee

The great populace of the city had been untouched.

Indeed, after a day, the populace came out of hiding and began applauding the purge. Throngs of commoners could be found, from dawn to dusk, admiring the new decorations on the Hippodrome. The heads of bucellarii meant little to them, and the Malwa heads even less. But the heads of high officials, nobles, churchmen—oh, now, that was a different matter altogether. Often enough, over the years—over the decades and centuries, in the memory of their families—had such men extorted and bullied them.

John of Cappadocia's head, of course, was the most popular attraction. He had often been called the most hated man in the Roman Empire. Few had doubted that claim, in the past. None doubted it now.

But the populace also spent much time admiring the heads of the Hippodrome factions. For the first time in their lives, the common folk could walk the streets of Constantinople without fearing an encounter with faction thugs. The leaders of those thugs—with the exception of a few who had escaped Irene's eye—were all perched on the wall. And, within days, those who had escaped the slaughter joined them—along with two hundred and sixty-three other faction bravos. Such men might have escaped Irene's eye, and the eyes of the *agentes in rebus*. They could not escape the eyes of the populace, who ferreted them out of their hiding places and turned them over to Hermogenes' infantrymen. Or, often enough, simply lynched them on the spot and brought their heads to the Hippodrome.

The more prosperous residents of Constantinople—and there were many of them, in that teeming city: merchants, shopkeepers, craftsmen, artisans—did not share the unadulterated glee of their poorer neighbors. They were not immune to that glee, of course. They, too, had suffered from the exactions of the high and mighty. But— as is usually the case with those who have something to lose—they feared that the purge might widen, and deepen, and grow into a cataclysm of mass terror.

Their fears were exaggerated, perhaps, but by no means groundless. On any number of occasions, Hermogenes' infantrymen had prevented mobs from beating or murdering a man—or an entire family— whose only real crime was unpopularity. On two occasions, the turmoil had become savage enough to require the intervention of Sittas and Belisarius' cataphracts.

Theodora's rage had shaken the entire city. Shaken it almost into pieces.

It was Antonina, more than anyone, who had held the city together. Partly, by the hours she had spent with Theodora, doing what she could to restrain her friend's half-insane fury. But, mostly, Antonina had held the city together by marching through it.

Hour and hour, day after day, marching through Constantinople at the head of her little army of grenadiers, and their wives, and their children.

"Marching" was not the correct word, actually. It would be more accurate to say that she and her Theodoran Cohort *paraded* through the streets. Gaily, cheerfully—and triumphantly. But theirs was not the grim triumph of cataphracts, or regular soldiers. Their was the insouciant triumph of humble Syrian villagers, who were sightseeing as much as they were providing a sight for the city's residents.

Who could fear such folk? With their families parading with them? After the first day, none. By the second day, Antonina's parades had become as popular as the grisly display at the Hippodrome. By the third day, much more popular.

Much more popular.

The vicinity of the Hippodrome, for one thing, was becoming unbearable due to the stench. Gangs of slaves were hauling out the bodies and burying them in mass graves. But there were thousands of those bodies, many of them—as Hermogenes had said—not much more than meat paste smeared across the stone floors and walls. Fortunately, it was winter, but even so the bodies were rotting faster than they could be removed.

For another, the vengeful glee of the common folk was beginning to abate. Second thoughts were creeping in, especially as those people sat in their little apartments in the evening, enjoying the company of their families. Reservations, doubts, hesitations—as fathers began wondering about the future, and mothers worried over their children.

The death of arrogant lordlings was a thing to be treasured, true. But, at bottom, none of Constantinople's commoners thought Death was truly a friend. They were far too familiar with the creature.

No, better to go and enjoy Antonina's parades. There was nothing, there, to frighten a child. Nothing, to worry a mother or bring a frown to a father's face. There was only—

Triumph, in the victory of humble people.

Enjoyment, in the constant and casual conversations with those simple grenadiers, and their wives. And their children, for those of an age—who gazed upon those lads and lasses with an adulation rarely bestowed upon rustics by cosmopolitan street urchins. But *those* were the children of *grenadiers*—a status greatly to be envied.

And, most of all, a feeling of safety. Safety, in the presence of—*her*.

She—the closest friend of the Empress. Whom all knew, or soon learned, was striving to hold back the imperial madness.

She—who smote the treason of the mighty.

She—who was of their own kind.

She—who was the wife of Belisarius. Rome's greatest general, in this time of war. And Rome's sanest voice, in this time of madness.

Belisarius had already been a name of legend, among those people. Now, the legend grew, and grew. His legend, of course. But also, alongside it—swelling it and being swollen by it—the legend of Antonina.

"The whore," she had often been called, by Rome's upper crust.

The populace of Constantinople had heard the name, in times past. Had wondered. Now, knowing, they rejected it completely.

"The wife," they called her; or, more often, "the great wife."

Her legend had begun with the words of a famous holy man, spoken in distant Syria. The grenadiers passed on his words to the people of Constantinople. The legend had expanded in a kitchen, here in the city itself. The grenadiers and the cataphracts told the tale.

Soon enough, that pastry shop became a popular shrine in its own right. The shopkeeper grew rich, from the business, and was able to retire at an early

age; but, an avaricious man, he complained to his
dying day that he had been cheated out of his
cleaver.

The legend grew, and swelled. Then, five days after
the crushing of the insurrection, Michael of Macedonia
arrived in Constantinople. Immediately, he took up
residence in the Forum of Constantine and began
preaching. Preaching and sermonizing, from dawn to
dusk. Instantly, those sermons became the most popular events in the city. The crowds filled the Forum and
spilled along the Mese.

He preached of many things, Michael did.

Some of his words caused the city's high churchmen
to gnash their teeth. But they gnashed them in private,
and never thought to call a council. They were too
terrified to venture out of their hiding places.

But, for the most part, Michael did not denounce and
excoriate. Rather, he praised and exhorted.

The legend of Antonina now erupted through the city.
So did the legend of Belisarius. And so, in its own way,
did the legend of Theodora.

By the end of the week, the overwhelming majority
of Constantinople's simple citizens had drawn their
simple conclusions.

All hope rested in the hands of Belisarius and his
wife. Please, Lord in Heaven, help them restore the
Empress to her sanity.

The great city held its breath.

An Empress and Her Tears

The Empress and her general gazed at each other
in silence, until the servants placed a chair and withdrew.

"Sit, general," she commanded. "We are in a crisis. With Justinian blinded, the succession to the
throne is—"

"We are *not* in a crisis, Your Majesty," stated Belisarius firmly. "We simply have a problem to solve."

Theodora stared at him. At first, with disbelief and suspicion. Then, with a dawning hope.

"I swore an oath," said Belisarius.

Sudden tears came to the Empress' eyes.

Not many, those tears. Not many at all. But, for Belisarius, they were enough.

He watched his Empress turn away from Hell, and close its gate behind her. And, for the first time in days, stopped holding his own breath.

"A problem to solve," he repeated, softly. "No more than that. You are good at solving problems, Empress."

Theodora smiled wanly.

"Yes, I am. And so are you, Belisarius."

The general smiled his crooked smile. "That's true. Now that you mention it."

Theodora's own smile widened. "Pity the poor Malwa," she murmured.

"Better yet," countered Belisarius, "*let us pity them not at all.*"

A Man and His Purpose

In the cabin of a ship, another Empress argued with a slave.

"We will arrive in Muziris tomorrow. You must now decide. I *need* you, Dadaji. Much more than he does."

"That may be true, Your Majesty." The slave shrugged. "The fact remains, he is my legal master."

Shakuntala chopped her hand. "Malwa law. You were bought in Bharakuccha."

Again, Holkar shrugged. "And so? The sale is legally binding anywhere in the world. Certainly in the Roman Empire. Malwa India has not, after all, been declared an outlaw state."

The Empress glared. The slave held up a hand, trying to mollify her.

"I am not quibbling over the fine points of law, Your Majesty. The truth is, even if the Malwa Empire were to be declared outlaw"—he chuckled—"although I'm not sure who would be powerful enough to do so!—I would still feel bound to my obligation."

He took a deep breath. "I owe my life to the general, Empress. I was a dead man, when he found me. Still walking—still even talking, now and then—but dead for all that. He breathed life back into my soul. Purpose."

Shakuntala finally saw her opening.

"*What* purpose?" she demanded. "The destruction of Malwa, isn't it?"

Dadaji leaned back. He and the Empress were seated, facing each other three feet apart, each on cushions, each in the lotus position. He eyed her suspiciously.

"Yes. That. One other."

Shakuntala nodded vigorously, pressing the advantage.

"You can serve that purpose better as my imperial adviser than you can as his slave," she stated. "*Much better.*"

Holkar stroked his beard. The gesture, in its own way, illustrated his quandary.

As a slave, he had been forced to shave his respectable beard. That beard, and the middle-aged dignity which went with it, had been restored by Belisarius. It was a symbol of all that he owed the general.

Yet, at the same time—it *was* a badge of his dignity. Full, now; rich with the gray hairs of experience and wisdom. Foolish, really, to waste the beard and all it signified on the life of a slave. A slave who, as Shakuntala rightly said, was no longer of great use to his master.

Stroke. Stroke.

"How do you know I could serve you properly?" he demanded.

Shakuntala felt the tension ease from her shoulders. Get the argument off the ground of abstract honor and onto to the ground of concrete duty, and she was bound to win.

"You are as shrewd as any man I ever met," she stated forcefully. "Look how you managed this escape—and all the preparations which went into it. Belisarius always relied on you for anything of that nature. He trusted you completely—and he is immensely shrewd himself, in that way as well as others. I need men I can trust. Rely on. Desperately."

Stroking his beard. "What you *need*, girl, is prestige and authority. An imperial adviser should be noble-born. Brahmin. I am merely vaisya. *Low*-caste vaisya." He smiled. "And Maratha, to boot. In most other lands, my caste would be ranked among the sudra, lowest of the twice-born."

"So?" she demanded. "You are as literate and educated as any brahmin. More than most! You know that to be true."

Holkar spread his hands. "What does that matter? The rulers and dignitaries of other lands will be offended, if your adviser does not share their purity. They would have to meet with me, privately and intimately, on many occasions. They would feel polluted by the contact."

The Empress almost snarled. "Damn them, then! If they seek alliance with me, they will have to take it as it comes!"

Holkar barked a laugh.

"Tempestuous girl! Have you already lost your wits—at your age? *They* will not be seeking alliance with you, Empress. *They* are not throneless refugees, hunted like an animal. *You* will be knocking on their doors, beggar's bowl in hand."

With amazing dignity (under the circumstances; she *was*, after all, a throneless refugee): "I shall not."

"You shall."

"*Shall not.*"

Dadaji glowered. "See? Already you scorn my advice!" Shaking his finger: "You must learn to bridle that temper, Empress! You will *indeed* treat with possible allies with

all necessary—I won't say humility; I don't believe in
magic!—*decorum*."

Glower.

"And another thing—"

Shakuntala spent the next hour in uncharacteristic
silence, nodding her head, attending patiently to her new
adviser. It was not difficult. His advice, in truth, was
excellent. And she had no need to rein in her temper.
Even if he had been babbling nonsense, she would have
listened politely.

She had her adviser. In fact, if not yet in name.

At the end of that hour, Dadaji Holkar reined himself in. With a start of surprise.

"You are a treacherous girl," he grumbled. Then,
chuckling: "Quite well done, actually!" He gazed at her
fondly, shaking his head with amusement.

"Very well, Empress," he said. "Let us leave it so: I
will send your request to Belisarius. If he agrees, I will
serve you in whatever capacity you wish."

Shakuntala nodded. "He will agree," she said confi-
dently. "For reasons of state, if no other. But he will
want to know—what do *you* wish? What will you tell
him?"

Holkar stared at her. "I will tell him that it is my wish,
also." Then, still seated, he bowed deeply. "You are my
sovereign, Empress. Such a sovereign as any man worthy
of the name would wish to serve."

When he lifted his head, his face was calm. Shakuntala's
next words destroyed that serenity.

"What is your other purpose?" she asked.

Holkar frowned.

"You said, earlier, that the destruction of Malwa was
one of your purposes. One of two. Name the other."

Holkar's face tightened.

Shakuntala was ruthless.

"Tell me."

He looked away. "You know what it is," he whispered.

That was true. She did. But she would force *him*
to face it squarely. Lest, in the years to come, it

gnawed his soul to destruction. Youth, too, has its bold wisdom.

"Say it."

The tears began to flow.

"*Say it.*"

Finally, as he said the words, the slave vanished. Not into the new, shadow soul of an imperial adviser, but into what he had always been. The man, Dadaji Holkar.

In the quiet, gentle time that followed, as a low-born Maratha sobbed and sobbed, his grey head cradled in the small arms of India's purest, most ancient, most noble line, the soul named Dadaji Holkar finished the healing which a foreign general had begun.

He would help his sovereign restore her broken people.

And he would, someday, find his broken family.

A Family and Its Resolve

Ironically, Dadaji Holkar had already found his family, without knowing it. He had even, without knowing it, helped them through their troubles.

Standing next to the stablekeeper in Kausambi, watching the rockets flaring into the sky, he had been not half a mile from his wife. She, along with the other kitchen slaves, had been watching those same rockets from the back court of her master's mansion. Until the head cook, outraged, had driven them back to their duties.

She had gone to those duties with a lighter heart than usual. She had no idea what that catastrophe represented. But, whatever it was, it was bad news for Malwa. The thought kept her going for hours, that night; and warmed her, a bit, in countless nights that followed.

His son had actually seen him. In Bihar, rearing from his toil in the fields, his son had rested for a moment. Idly watching a nobleman's caravan pass on the road nearby. He had caught but a glimpse of the nobleman himself, riding haughtily in his howdah on the lead elephant. The man's face was indistinguishable, at that distance. But there was no mistaking his identity. A Malwa potentate, trampling the world.

The overseer's angry shout sent him back to work. The shout, combined with the sight of that arrogant lord, burned through his soul. From months and months of hard labor, the boy's body had grown tough enough to survive. But he had feared, sometimes, that he himself was too weak. Now, feeling the hardening flame, he knew otherwise.

Stooping, he cursed that unknown Malwa, and made a solemn vow. Whoever that stinking lord was, Dadaji Holkar's son would outlive him.

Holkar had not come as close to his daughters. As planned, Shakuntala and her companions had taken a side road before reaching Pataliputra. They had no desire to risk the swarming officialdom in that huge city, and so they had bypassed it altogether.

Still, they had passed less than fifteen miles to the south. Thirteen miles, only, from the slave brothel where his daughters were held.

In a way, Dadaji had even touched them. And his touch had been a blessing.

The soldiers at the guardpost where Shakuntala had browbeaten the commanding officer, had contributed to his humiliation later. The bribe had been very large, and their officer was a weakling. An arrogant little snot, whom they had browbeaten themselves into a bigger cut than common soldiers usually received. With their share of the bribe, they had enjoyed a pleasant visit to the nearest brothel, on the southern outskirts of the city. They had had money to burn.

Money to burn, and they spent it all. Gold coin from the hand of Dadaji Holkar had found its way into the hands of his daughters' pimps. The girls were popular with the soldiers, and they had paid handsomely.

It cannot be said that the soldiers were popular with

the girls. None of their customers were. But, in truth, Holkar's daughters had been relieved to spend two days in their exclusive company. The soldiers were not rough with them; and, young men, unjaded, were not given to the bizarre quirks that some of the local merchants and tradesmen preferred.

After the soldiers left, their pimps informed the girls that they had decided to turn down the various offers which had come in for their purchase, from other brothels. Holkar's daughters had known of those offers, and dreaded them, for they would result in separation.

But the pimps had decided to keep them. They were popular with the soldiers. Steady business.

The brothel-keeper even tossed them one of the coins. A bonus, he said, for good work.

That coin, in the endless time which followed, was his daughters' secret treasure. They never spent it. Sometimes, late at night, in the crib they shared, the girls would bring the coin from its hiding place and admire it, holding hands.

It was their lucky coin, they decided. So long as they had it, they would be together. The family of Dadaji Holkar would still survive.

An Empress and Her Decision

As she watched Dadaji's tears soak her royal skin, the Empress Shakuntala made her own decision. And reaffirmed a vow.

She had never thought much about purity and pollution, in her short life. She had resented the caste system, half-consciously, for the many ways it constrained her. Had even hated it, half-consciously, for the inseparable barrier which it placed between her and her most precious desire. But she had never really thought about it, before. It had simply been there. A fact of life, like the three seasons of India.

She began to think about it, now. Her thoughts, unlike her heart, were very unclear. She was young. Rao, in times past, had tried to teach her some aspects of philosophy, and devotion. But the girl she had been had not taken to those lessons kindly. His soft words had met none of the enthusiastic attention which had greeted his training in other, much harder, fields.

Now, she began to think, and learn.

She had learned this much, already. Watching a foreign general, she had seen Rao's forgotten lessons come to life. Hard fists, and harder steel, were like snow at the foot of mountains. Mountains called minds, which produced that snow, and then melted it when they so desired. Only the soul matters, in the end. It towers over creation like the Himalayas.

She made her decision. As she rebuilt Andhra, she would gather what there was of human learning and wisdom around her throne. She would not only rebuild the stupas, the viharas. She would not simply recall the philosophers, and the sadhus, and the monks. She would set them to work—mercilessly—driving them one against the other. Clashing idea against idea like great cymbals, until truth finally emerged.

That doing, of course, required another. And so, watching her purity imperilled by the racking tears of the low-born man in her arms, and drawing strength from that pollution, she reaffirmed her vow.

I will make Malwa howl.

An Empire and Its Howl

Malwa *was* howling. As yet, however, only in the privacy of the Emperor's chambers. And only, as yet, howling with rage. Fear was still to come.

The rage blew inward, centered on Malwa itself. The fate of Lord Venandakatra hung in the balance.

"I always told you he was a fool," snarled Nanda Lal. "He's smart enough, I admit. But no man's intelligence is worth a toad's croak if he cannot restrain his lusts and vanities."

"You can no longer protect him, Skandagupta," stated Sati. "You have coddled him enough. He—not the underlings he blames—is responsible for Belisarius. For Shakuntala. Recall him. Discipline him harshly."

Link, then, was all that saved Venandakatra from disgrace. Or worse.

"NO. YOU MISS THE GREAT FRAMEWORK. VENANDAKATRA WAS JUST APPOINTED GOPTRI OF THE DECCAN. TO RECALL HIM IN DISGRACE WOULD HEARTEN THE MARATHA. SHAKUNTALA IS IMPORTANT, BUT SHE IS NOT AS IMPORTANT AS HER PEOPLE. BREAK THAT PEOPLE, YOU BREAK HER."

The Malwa bowed to their overlord.

"BREAK MAJARASHTRA. TERRORIZE THE MARATHA MONGRELS, TILL THEIR BASTARDS WHISPER FEAR FOR A MILLENIUM. PULVERIZE THAT POLLUTED FOLK."

"FOR THAT, VENANDAKATRA WILL DO. PERFECTLY."

A Husband and His Thoughts.

The day before his departure to join Lord Damodara's army, Rana Sanga spent entirely with his wife. Late that night, exhausted from love-making, he stroked his wife's hair.

"What are you thinking?" she asked, smiling. "All of a sudden, you've got this serious look on your face."

"Hard to explain," he grunted.

His wife reared up in the bed, the coverings falling away from her plump figure.

"Talk," she commanded, wriggling her fingers threateningly. "Or I tickle!"

Sanga laughed. "Not that! Please! I'd rather face Belisarius himself, with an army at his back."

His wife's amusement died away. "That's what you were thinking about? Him?"

Her face tightened. The Persian campaign was about to begin. She knew Sanga would, soon enough, be facing that—*terrible Roman*—on the battlefield. And that, for all her husband's incredible prowess at war, this enemy was one he truly respected. Even, she thought, feared.

Sanga shook his head. "Actually, no. Not directly, at least."

He reached up his hand and gently caressed her face. Plain it was, that face, very plain. Round, like her body.

He had not married her for her beauty. He had never even seen her face, before she lifted the veil in his sleeping chamber, after their wedding. Theirs, in the way of Rajput royalty, had been a marriage of state. Dictated by the stern necessities of dynasty, class, and caste. Of maintaining the true Rajput lineage; protecting purity from pollution.

He had said nothing, on the night he first saw his wife's face, and then her body, to indicate his disappointment. She had been very fearful, she told him years later, of what he would say, or do—or not do—when he saw how plain she was. But he had been pleasant, even kind; had gone about his duty. And, by the end of the night, had found a surprising pleasure in that eager, round body; excitement, in those quick and clever fingers; gaiety and warmth, lurking behind the shyness in her eyes. And, in the morning, had seen the happiness in a still-sleeping, round face. Happiness which he had put there, he knew, from kindness far more than manhood.

Young, then, filled with the vainglory of a Rajput prince already famous for his martial prowess, he had made an unexpected discovery. Pride could be found in kindness, too. Deep pride, in the sight of a wife's face glowing with the morning. Even a plain face. Perhaps *especially* a plain face.

The day had come, years later, when he came upon his wife in the kitchen. She was often to be found there. Despite their many cooks and servants, his wife enjoyed preparing food. Hearing him come, recognizing his footsteps, she had turned from the table where she was cutting onions. Turned, smiled—laughed, wiping the tears from her eyes—brushed the hair (all grey, now—no black left at all) away from her face, knife still in her hand, laughing at her preposterous appearance. Laughing with her mouth, laughing with her eyes.

Twice only, in his life, had the greatest of Rajputana's kings been stunned. Struck down, off his feet, by sudden shock.

Once, sprawling on a famous field of battle, when Raghunath Rao split his helmet with a dervish blow of his sword.

Once, collapsing on a bench in his own kitchen, when he realized that he loved his wife.

"You are my life," he whispered.

"Yes," she replied. And gave him a fresh sweet onion, as if it were another child.

"I was thinking of your face," he said. "And another's. The face of a young woman. Very beautiful, she was."

His wife's lips tightened, slightly, but she never looked away.

"I have always told you I would not object to concubines, husband," she said softly. "I am not—"

"Hush, wife!" he commanded. Then, laughing: "The farthest thing from my mind! Even if the woman in question was not the Emperor's own daughter—hardly a woman for a Rajput's concubine."

His wife giggled. Sanga shook his head.

"I was not matching the two faces that way, dearest one. I was—ah! It is too difficult to explain!"

"The tickle, then!"

She was as good as her word. But, for all the gleeful torment, Sanga never did explain his thoughts to her. Not that night. Not for many nights to come.

They were too hard to explain. Too new. Too bound up with new secrets. Too twisted into the misty coils of the far distant future which he had glimpsed, in the chamber of Great Lady Holi and the *being* for which she was a mere vessel.

Eventually, his wife fell asleep. Sanga did not, for a time. He was kept awake by thoughts of lineage. Of the plain face of his wife; the lines of her face which he could see coiling through the faces of his children, alongside his own. Of the beautiful face of an emperor's daughter, destined to be the vessel for the perfect faces of future gods.

The lineage of his life. Life that was. Life that is. Life that will be.

He contemplated purity; contemplated pollution. Contemplated perfection. Contemplated onions.

Most of all, he pondered on illusion, and truth, and the strange way in which illusion can become truth.

And truth become illusion.

A Creation and Its Understanding

When the general finally left the Empress and walked out of the palace, the day was ending. Drawn by the sunset, Belisarius went to the balustrade overlooking the Bosporus. He leaned on the stone, admiring the view.

An urgent thought came from Aide.

There is more, now. More that I understand of the message from the Great Ones. I think. I am not sure.

Tell me.

They said to us—this also:

Find everything that made us.

*Find passion in the virgin, purity in the
whore;
Faith in the traitor, fate in the priest.
Find doubt in the prophet, decision in the
slave;
Mercy in the killer, murder in the wife.
Look for wisdom in the young, and the
suckling
need of age;
Look for truth in moving water; falsehood
in the stone.
See the enemy in the mirror, the friend
across the field.
Look for everything that made us.
On the ground where we were made.*

Silence. Then:

Do you understand?

Belisarius smiled. Not crookedly, not at all.

Yes. Oh, yes.

I think I understand, too. I am not sure.

"Of course you understand," murmured Belisarius.
"We made you. On that same ground."

Silence. Then:

You promised.

There was no reproach in that thought, now. No
longer. It was the contented sound of a child, nestling
its head into a father's shoulder.

You promised.

DAVID WEBER

Field of Dishonor

Honor goes home to Manticore—and fights for her life on a battlefield she never trained for, in a private war that offers just two choices: death—or a "victory" that can end only in dishonor and the loss of all she loves....

Flag in Exile

Hounded into retirement and disgrace by political enemies, Honor Harrington has retreated to planet Grayson, where powerful men plot to reverse the changes she has brought to their world. And for their plans to suceed, Honor Harrington must die!

Honor Among Enemies

Offered a chance to end her exile and again command a ship, Honor Harrington must use a crew drawn from the dregs of the service to stop pirates who are plundering commerce. Her enemies have chosen the mission carefully, thinking that either she will stop the raiders or they will kill her . . . and either way, her enemies will win....

In Enemy Hands

After being ambushed, Honor finds herself aboard an enemy cruiser, bound for her scheduled execution. But one lesson Honor has never learned is how to give up! One way or another, she and her crew are going home—even if they have to conquer Hell to get there!

continued 📖

PRAISE FOR
LOIS MCMASTER BUJOLD

What the critics say:

The Warrior's Apprentice: "Now here's a fun romp through the spaceways—not so much a space opera as space ballet.... it has all the 'right stuff.' A lot of thought and thoughtfulness stand behind the all-too-human characters. Enjoy this one, and look forward to the next." —Dean Lambe, *SF Reviews*

"The pace is breathless, the characterization thoughtful and emotionally powerful, and the author's narrative technique and command of language compelling. Highly recommended." —*Booklist*

Brothers in Arms: "... she gives it a geniune depth of character, while reveling in the wild turnings of her tale. ... Bujold is as audacious as her favorite hero, and as brilliantly (if sneakily) successful." —*Locus*

"Miles Vorkosigan is such a great character that I'll read anything Lois wants to write about him. ... a book to re-read on cold rainy days." —Robert Coulson, *Comics Buyer's Guide*

Borders of Infinity: "Bujold's series hero Miles Vorkosigan may be a lord by birth and an admiral by rank, but a bone disease that has left him hobbled and in frequent pain has sensitized him to the suffering of outcasts in his very hierarchical era.... Playing off Miles's reserve and cleverness, Bujold draws outrageous and outlandish foils to color her high-minded adventures." —*Publishers Weekly*

Falling Free: "In *Falling Free* Lois McMaster Bujold has written her fourth straight superb novel. ... How to break down a talent like Bujold's into analyzable components? Best not to try. Best to say 'Read, or you will be missing something extraordinary.' " —Roland Green, *Chicago Sun-Times*

The Vor Game: "The chronicles of Miles Vorkosigan are far too witty to be literary junk food, but they rouse the kind of craving that makes popcorn magically vanish during a double feature." —Faren Miller, *Locus*

MORE PRAISE FOR
LOIS MCMASTER BUJOLD

What the readers say:

"My copy of *Shards of Honor* is falling apart I've reread it so often. . . . I'll read whatever you write. You've certainly proved yourself a grand storyteller."
—Liesl Kolbe, Colorado Springs, CO

"I experience the stories of Miles Vorkosigan as almost viscerally uplifting. . . . But certainly, even the weightiest theme would have less impact than a cinder on snow were it not for a rousing good story, and good storytelling with it. This is the second thing I want to thank you for. . . . I suppose if you boiled down all I've said to its simplest expression, it would be that I immensely enjoy and admire your work. I submit that, as literature, your work raises the overall level of the science fiction genre, and spiritually, your work cannot avoid positively influencing all who read it."
—Glen Stonebraker, Gaithersburg, MD

" 'The Mountains of Mourning' [in *Borders of Infinity*] was one of the best-crafted, and simply best, works I'd ever read. When I finished it, I immediately turned back to the beginning and read it again, and I can't remember the last time I did that."   —Betsy Bizot, Lisle, IL

"I can only hope that you will continue to write, so that I can continue to read (and of course buy) your books, for they make me laugh and cry and think . . . rare indeed."   —Steven Knott, Major, USAF

What Do You Say?

<u>*Send me these books!*</u>

Shards of Honor	72087-2 ◆ $5.99	☐
Barrayar	72083-X ◆ $5.99	☐
Cordelia's Honor (trade)	87749-6 ◆ $15.00	☐
The Warrior's Apprentice	72066-X ◆ $5.99	☐
The Vor Game	72014-7 ◆ $5.99	☐
Young Miles (trade)	87782-8 ◆ $15.00	☐
Cetaganda (hardcover)	87701-1 ◆ $21.00	☐
Cetaganda (paperback)	87744-5 ◆ $5.99	☐
Ethan of Athos	65604-X ◆ $5.99	☐
Borders of Infinity	72093-7 ◆ $5.99	☐
Brothers in Arms	69799-4 ◆ $5.99	☐
Mirror Dance (paperback)	87646-5 ◆ $6.99	☐
Memory (paperback)	87845-X ◆ $6.99	☐
Falling Free	65398-9 ◆ $4.99	☐
The Spirit Ring (paperback)	72188-7 ◆ $5.99	☐

LOIS MCMASTER BUJOLD
Only from Baen Books

If not available at your local bookstore, fill out this coupon and send a check or money order for the cover price(s) to Baen Books, Dept. BA, P.O. Box 1403, Riverdale, NY 10471. Delivery can take up to ten weeks.

NAME: _____

ADDRESS: _____

_____

I have enclosed a check or money order in the amount of $ _____